PRAISE FOR THE NOVELS OF CHRIS MORIARTY

SPIN STATE

Amazon.com Top 10 Editors' Pick for Science Fiction & Fantasy 2003

A *Kansas City Star* Noteworthy Book for 2003

***Library Journal* Pick for Best First Novel**

"*Spin State* is a spiky, detailed, convincing, compelling page-turner, and the science is good too. Chris Moriarty is a dangerous talent."

—STEPHEN BAXTER

"Vivid, sexy, and sharply written, *Spin State* takes the reader on a nonstop, white-knuckle tour of quantum physics, artificial intelligence, and the human heart."

—NICOLA GRIFFITH

"Knife sharp. An amazing techno-landscape, with characters surfing the outer limits of their humanity, pulling the reader into a scary and seductive future. A thrilling, high-end upgrade of cyberpunk!"

—KAY KENYON

"Action, mystery, and drama, set against some of the most plausible speculative physics I've seen. This is science fiction for grownups who want some 'wow' with their 'what-if.'"

—DAVID BRIN

"*Spin State* is an intriguing, fascinating, and totally engrossing—yet truly terrifying—look into the time beyond tomorrow, a time and place where an AI and a military officer face love, betrayal, and worse in a struggle over the shape of a future that already has full genetic engineering, bio-engineered internal software, FTL communications and travel . . . and the age-old human weaknesses of greed and lust . . . and the love of power."

—L. E. MODESITT, JR.

"Chris Moriarty is one of the sharpest new talents to come onto the hard-SF scene in years. This stylish book tempts and tantalizes the reader. Moriarty fills it with a multitude of delights: gripping characterization—human and otherwise; a mystery that keeps you guessing; technological hijinks that take you along for the ride; and a story that is as thought-provoking as it is just plain fun. The plot blazes along, at the same time challenging the reader to ask questions about how human relationships will change as we change ourselves. This is a top-notch book."

—CATHERINE ASARO

"Moriarty manages fresh insights into humanity—and posthumanity—in this highly atmospheric debut. . . . Moriarty effectively postulates the Faustian price of enhancing humanity with silicon, of playing God through genetic manipulation. Beneath this complex tale ominously simmers Orwell's question: If all animals are to be equal, what can prevent some from making themselves more equal than the others?"

—Publishers Weekly

"Moriarty has visualized a very consistent universe here, and the tensions build nicely. It's not usual that a novel captures my attention exclusively until the last page, but this one did."

—San Diego Union-Tribune

"What makes this book really fabulous is the combination of mystery and technology . . . wonderfully realized wetware, genetic constructs and emergent AI all combined with an almost magically surreal world where reality is only virtual, but the consequences are just as permanent. . . . A truly remarkable science fiction debut."

—Affaire de Coeur (4½ STARS)

"Moriarty's debut novel combines a vivid future world of high technology and low politics with sharply drawn characters and a taut story line."

—Library Journal

"*Spin State* is a novel with countless virtues—a vividly created far-future set-ting solidly foreshadowed by present-day political issues, a brilliant hard-SF concept, a complex detective story and crackling suspense [and] an unusual romance."

—*Locus* (Alyx Dellamonica)

"*Spin State* is the most impressive U.S. debut I've seen in several years, ambi-tious and full of inventive energy."

—*F&SF*

"An assured and accomplished first novel . . . an enjoyable and, at times, pro-vocative read. A writer with Moriarty's abundant talents can only get better."

—scifi.com

"Dark, exciting, visceral, riveting, compelling . . . it's all that and more. Mori-arty has combined the desperate lives of miners with intelligently deployed speculative science and woven it into a story fueled by the best and worst of human drives."

—sfrevu.com

"An impressive hard-sci-fi debut . . . Moriarty tells an imaginative story [which] turns out to be all too human."

—*Kansas City Star*

"Moriarty keeps the action moving, with both overt and subterranean con-flicts, hidden agendas and blatant power plays spurring on an incredibly complex plot. A strong debut, using a hard SF McGuffin to spin a thriller in the best cyberpunk mode."

—*Asimov's Science Fiction*

SPIN CONTROL

"In *Spin Control,* Moriarty addresses an ultra-high-tech future where 'humans' can be anything from soulless biologic robots to individuals whose person-alities and abilities have been enhanced and transferred into artificial intelli-gences. Entire subspecies of humans have been developed where every individual is essentially genetically identical to every other. For old-style humans, even with enhancements, implants, and other adaptations, birthrates are falling, and Earth is a battle zone, ecologically, politically, and militarily. Against this backdrop, Moriarty 'spins' a fascinatingly intricate story of deception, alien subversion, betrayals within betrayals . . . and love under the most difficult of situations."

—L. E. Modesitt, Jr.

"This richly textured second novel explores issues of identity and loyalty, swapping quantum mechanics for complexity theory and mystery for suspense. . . . Where *Spin State* was nominated for awards, this sequel may win them."

—*Publishers Weekly*

"In Moriarty's high-stakes, tension-riddled addition to visions of the post-human future, the characters have the complexity of motivation and backstory to make this more than just another dire-future thriller."

—*Booklist*

"A fine book . . . twisty and thoughtful."

—SFREVU.COM

"The cynical yet somehow still romantic spirit of John le Carré infuses *Spin Control*. The Middle Eastern setting, as well as the shifting sands of loyalties and allegiances, personal and otherwise, that leave not only characters but readers feeling as if there is nothing solid to stand on, nothing and no one that can be trusted, make it as much a traditional spy thriller as it is a science-fiction novel. Moriarty succeeds on both counts. I wrote in my review of *Spin State* that 'a writer with Moriarty's abundant talents can only get better.' She has."

—SCIFI.COM

Ghost Spin

Ghost
Spin

Chris Moriarty

SPECTRA BOOKS

NEW YORK

A Spectra Trade Paperback Original

Copyright © 2013 by Chris Moriarty

Published in the United States by Spectra, an imprint of the Random House Publishing Group, a division of Random House, Inc., New York.

Spectra and the portrayal of a boxed "s" are trademarks of Random House, Inc.

LIBRARY OF CONGRESS CATALOGING-IN-PUBLICATION DATA
Moriarty, Chris.
Ghost spin / Chris Moriarty.
pages   cm
ISBN 978-0-553-38494-9
eBook ISBN 978-0-345-52628-1
I. Title.
PS3613.O749G48 2013
813'.6—dc23   2012046650

Printed in the United States of America

Title page image © iStockphoto.com/Tomasz Sowinski

www.ballantinebooks.com

2 4 6 8 9 7 5 3 1

Book design by Caroline Cunningham

To my grandparents,
Nancy and Henry Chandler

The Real Turing Test

Dip the apple in the brew. Let the Sleeping Death seep through.
                                    —"Snow White and the Seven Dwarfs"

I begin to understand Death, which is going on quietly & gradually
every minute & will never be a Thing of one particular moment.
                                                        —Ada Lovelace

(Cohen)

THE CRUCIBLE

The apple was perfect. It glistened on the battered hotel table, a vivid spot of red in the dingy room, reflecting the loaded pistol that lay beside it.

The boy lay on the other side of the room, his feet up on the musty bed, staring at the apple as if it held the answers to all the mysteries of the universe.

Or rather, the being that had borrowed the boy's body looked through his eyes at the apple. The boy himself was nowhere. He had taken Cohen's money, gone to sleep, and would never wake up to cash his paycheck. Just one more item of collateral damage to add to the red side of the ledger books, Cohen told himself. *Unless you lose your nerve. Which at the moment seems entirely possible.*

Who would have thought it could be so hard to die? He'd seen humans do it often enough. He'd watched them lay down their lives for a principle, for a country, for pride or loyalty . . . for sheer nonsense. Hadn't Alan Turing eaten his fatal apple at forty-two? And didn't Cohen have good and sufficient reasons—perhaps the best reason of all—for shuffling off the mortal coil? And hadn't Cohen lived like no human ever could have lived? What more could anyone suck out of life? So how pathetic was it that he should still be struggling to screw up his courage after four centuries?

"Dying for a principle is all very well in principle," he murmured.

He tried to laugh but failed. Then he stood up, feeling ill and dizzy, and stumbled across the moldy carpet to the open window.

He leaned out into the smoky twilight, gulping in great breaths of what passed for fresh air in the eternal smog of the Crucible. The sign on the bar across the street said Iron City Beer, but the sky overhead was the color of steel. Battered trolley cars ran down the center line of West Munhall Avenue packed full of exhausted steelmen coming off the swing shift. Pedestrians hurried along the sidewalk below, gray ghosts trapped between hard concrete and lowering umbrellas.

There was a synth junkie slumped in the doorway across the street, shooting up in broad daylight—or what passed for it down here. Cohen watched her for a moment, taking in the young ravaged face, the tattered remnants of her Navy uniform, the silver tattooing of a military wire job that would turn out, on closer inspection, to be just a little too out-of-date to qualify her for off-planet employment. All the increasingly familiar symbols of space age conflict that was evolving far faster than the humans tasked with fighting it.

She looked up suddenly, seeming to gaze straight through the hotel window and into Cohen's eyes. But it was an illusion. She was lost in the spinstream, loaded up with black-market executables, running closer to the numbers than the human body was ever designed to run, lost in a borrowed AI dream of superimposed infinities.

The old sailor who'd sold Cohen the synth had called it AI in the blood. Cohen had been shocked by the words—and then amused at his own naïveté. AI in the blood was precisely what synth was. Synthetic myelin enhancer with an intelligent payload was just a fig leaf. And the euphemisms of the off-planet policy wonks were so wrong they weren't even wrong.

"You take it to do the job," the sailor had told Cohen, seeing only his young body and thinking he was a war vet and a fellow addict. "And then you take it to pretend you can still do the job. And then you just take it to pretend."

A monstrous flatbed rumbled down the street, looking like some mechanized refugee from the Age of the Dinosaurs. It was loaded to the breaking point with a single hulking hump of forged ceramsteel: some

Drift ship engine part whose very existence was probably classified information in the rest of UN space. As the truck lumbered by, Cohen looked down and read the words MONONGAHELA MACHINE WORKS, NEW ALLEGHENY stamped into the rain-slicked metal.

Cohen craned his neck to peer up through the smog: industrial-age pollution reflecting back the lights of a post-human, post-biosphere city, filtering garish holo-neon to the brooding shimmer of black pearl. Somewhere high overhead it must be a sunny spring morning, but down here in the Pit there was only the eternal acid rain and smog-choked twilight.

He imagined the corporate orbitals whipping around the planet twenty miles overhead in low geosynchronous orbit. Beyond them lay the Navy shipyards: a thousand curving kilometers of barracks and dry docks and orbital munitions factories, where the shipwrights were siphoning off the geological wealth of an entire planet in what might just be the most massive military-industrial buildup in the history of the species, and the Navy cat herders coaxed and cossetted their captive AIs, and the Drift ships floated in their berths like sleek, silver, lethal piranhas. Beyond that, dominating the high-rent zone of New Allegheny's Lagrangian neutral orbit, lay the Bose-Einstein field array, from which Cohen and his deadly contraband had been turned away only a week ago for lacking the proper travel papers. And beyond that—in a beyond that no merely human mind could map or navigate—lay the cosmos-spanning sweep of the Drift, with its uncharted eddies and whorls and spindles fanning out into the multiverse.

You'll never see any of it again, he told himself harshly. You're going to die here, you and the poor boy, God spare his immortal soul. You're going to die like a dog in a flyblown hotel room in the armpit of the known universe. And it's your own damn fault—just like everything else that's gone wrong since the minute you ported the first digit of your source code to this godforsaken backwater.

Whether or not Cohen himself had a soul was still an open question after four centuries. But as for death itself . . . well, there was no question about that, no more than for any other creature that walks under the sun. Humans died and decayed and rotted back into the soil to feed the worms that tended the soil that grew into plants that fed new humans. Life devours itself, a cosmic snake eating its own tail. And artificial life was no different. Still . . . there was something horrible in the thought that the shattered fragments of his soul would be cannibalized by other AIs. Perhaps even by the Drift ships, so hungry for CPUs that the Navy were rumored to have begun press-ganging every independent AI unfortunate enough to stumble into their paths. He thought of the horrors Ada had endured—horrors that his mind still shied away from even now—and for the first time in that long night of preparations he admitted to himself that he wasn't pulling off a bold and daring rescue. This was only an exchange of hostages.

"I'm sorry," he murmured, speaking not to what he thought of as his "self," but rather to the myriad of autonomous and semiautonomous agents from whose complex interplay his identity emerged. He loved them. He had nurtured and pushed and protected some of them for decades, enjoying their successes just like any loving parent and looking forward to that bittersweet moment when they would themselves attain full sentience and be ready to leave the nest. But that would never happen now. He was about to sink his ship of souls and condemn all the millions who sailed in her to God only knew what living Hell.

"Well, poor Ada's in Hell already," he told himself. Ada was drowning. She had killed, of course. And she was quite probably dangerous. Nguyen and her attack dog Holmes were right enough about that, no matter how much he longed to deny it. But in every other way—in every way that counted—Ada was as innocent as a child. And when it had come to the point of walking past a drowning child or diving in to save her, Cohen hadn't even felt he had a choice.

A half-submerged memory rose through the darkness and exploded into what passed for Cohen's consciousness when he was operating at the rock-bottom bandwidth that was all the boy's obsolete wire job could deliver: Ada's face, pale and pleading beneath the masses of her dark hair. Then she was gone, replaced by other memories. Holmes talking about cycling Ada's hardware as if they were just putting down a rabid dog. And Llewellyn—noble, useless, play-it-by-the-book Llewellyn—whose idea of saving Ada was filing a formal complaint after the axe had already fallen. Where had Llewellyn been when they pulled the switch? He'd pushed Ada over the top and into battle like the good soldier he was, without even thinking what the cost would be. He'd watched Ada sell her soul for him—and then stood idly by while the Navy scrapped it.

"She wasn't savable," Llewellyn had said when Cohen finally tracked him down in prison after the court-martial. "Not after Holmes had her way with her."

Cohen didn't know if Ada was savable or not. But whatever Holmes had left behind, he had to try to save it.

He moved restlessly away from the window, wincing when he caught a glimpse of his shunt in the mirror. The borrowed body was a boy's. He was beautiful, of course. They were always beautiful, these poor lost souls who sold the use of their bodies for the convenience of the rich and bodiless. He was beautiful and young and he had his whole life in front of him. And Cohen was about to kill him.

He could kill him now, quickly and cleanly. Or he could hand him over to Holmes and the AI police, who would kill him with agonizing slowness while they shredded his mind to make absolutely sure that there wasn't a scrap of Cohen left in it. But either way the boy had been doomed from the moment Cohen decided to smuggle Ada through the quarantine.

The boy started; an involuntary reaction, one that even the miles of ceramsteel snaking through his body couldn't entirely suppress. Cohen searched for the external stimulus that had momentarily aroused the boy's fight-or-fight reflex. And there it was: Holmes, at the street door, backed by a grim trio of MPs whose street clothes didn't even fool the sleepy desk clerk.

Cohen plucked the apple from the table. He polished it on his shirtsleeve—one final, jittery moment of cowardice—and then he took a bite.

The boy felt nothing, of course. But within seconds Cohen could feel the wild AI working its way through him. He knew the course of the infection; he'd watched it burn through half the AI techs in the Navy shipyard, Holmes first and foremost. There would be the first scattered hives; and then the rash working its way up the boy's wrists and neck; and then the smoldering fever and the desperate race of T-cells and lymphocytes to combat the alien code that was rewriting his genetic material. In a matter of a few hours the signs of a wild AI infection would be obvious to UNSec's AI cops or the Navy cat herders. But Cohen was gambling on the relative inexperience of the local police. It would take them quite a while, he thought, to figure it out. And by then the detectives would have come, and the medics, and the coroner. And there would be all the people they knew, and all the people their friends and family and casual acquaintances knew. Cohen didn't have the bandwidth to run the numbers, but in his mind's eye he saw the image of a dandelion being blown away on the wind: the delicate, deadly blossom of a meme going viral.

As the infection coursed through the boy's blood and marrow, Cohen shuddered in something terribly like ecstasy. No wonder humans got addicted to the stuff. No wonder UNSec didn't allow DNA-platformed AI outside of Freetown—and even then only with an ironclad kill loop. They'd never get the cat back in the bag if the rest of the UN's Emergents started getting used to it.

The code flowed into every one of the 75 trillion cells in the boy's besieged body, unzipping, unpacking, coming out of hibernation, linking each separate strand of DNA in each separate cell into a massively parallel system capable not merely of containing every piece of code and data the two fugitive AIs were made of, but of generating a cascade of copies large enough to overwhelm New Allegheny's frontier planet noosphere, and the shipyards' vast databases, and the Quants of the field arrays and deep space datatraps. Soon Cohen was racing the clocking speed of the universe itself on a quantum bicycle built for two . . . or two billion.

At first it felt like freedom. Wonderful, really, after being compressed and flattened into the half-dead echo of himself that was all he could fit onto the boy's obsolete wire job. Folded databases unfurled their origami wings. Cantor modules blossomed to reveal intricately nested infinities. Entire wings of Cohen's far-flung memory palace unshuttered themselves and sprang back to life, binary flowers opening wide to catch the inrushing flood of numbers.

It felt like clearing Earth's gravity well on the rattling roar of a Long March rocket. It felt like rediscovering amputated limbs. It felt like getting a pardon after the hangman had already put the rope around your neck.

Then the payload came online. And Ada—or what was left of her—started to execute. And Ada in the blood—poor, mad, broken Ada—was so much worse than Cohen had allowed himself to imagine that he would have called the whole thing off right then and there if he'd still been able to.

But he couldn't. He'd been very careful, all through the long sleepless nights of working out the program, to take away every back door and fail-safe and cutout that would have let him do that. After four centuries of life, he had a fair idea how far his courage would hold—and when it would break. And he'd planned for that. It was a plan Li would have liked, and he couldn't help grinning again as he accessed a memory of her giving him a sideways, gunslinger's look through a cloud of cigarette smoke and saying: "The easiest way to make sure a man does the right thing is to take all the wrong choices off the table."

Well, he'd done that all right. He'd taken it all off the table. He'd thrown it on the floor and shattered it into a million pieces. Now it would be up to Li to figure out how the hell to put it all back together again—or whether she even wanted to.

He drifted again—and jerked himself back, frightened by how close he had come to screwing everything up in the final stretch. He started to go online, then caught himself and walked unsteadily across the room to the wall phone.

"Hello?" he said tentatively, before realizing that he actually had to dial a number to get someone.

Luckily the number was written on the phone—because this was the kind of place, he supposed, where the management assumed you needed to know that number.

To his amazement a live person actually answered on the second ring. "Emergency response services. Where are you located?"

"Um . . . I'd like to report a crime."

"Yes sir. What is your location?"

"The Victory Motel, 2818 West Munhall Avenue, Room 219."

"And what is the nature of the crime, sir?"

"Murder."

That put a little life into her voice, he was satisfied to note. A fellow liked to have an enthusiastic audience for his swan song—or at least an awake one. "Someone's been murdered?" she asked hurriedly.

"Not yet," he told her before he hung up the phone. "But they're about to be."

And then he picked up the pistol and sat down on the bed to wait for Holmes.

He was ghosting on New Allegheny's noosphere now, overclocking so handily that he was wiping the floor with UNSec's horde of semi-sentient streamspace security AIs. He watched his enemies creep toward him like pawns marching across a chessboard. He still had time, but not very much of it. He resisted the urge to prod the wild AI and see if the Ada program was executing properly. Ada was doing fine—and keeping tabs on her now would take enough processing capacity to blow the entire noosphere.

He had done his best, and his best would have to do. It would be enough. He was almost certain of that. And if it wasn't, then it was too late to fix it.

And besides, the only thing he really wanted to fix before he died was the one thing he couldn't fix without handing the keys to the kingdom over to Nguyen and her bloodhounds.

I'm sorry, Catherine. I had to choose between coming home to you or saving Ada. And you wouldn't have wanted me on those terms. I'd never have been able to look you in the eye again.

But he couldn't tell her that, not with Holmes and Nguyen and the AI police watching. She'd just have to see it for herself . . . if she ever came close enough to forgiving him to be willing to see it.

Holmes was in the hall now. She was trying to be quiet, of course.

Pathetic the way humans always assumed he couldn't hear anything they couldn't. It didn't take one-millionth of the parallel processors the boy's DNA now hosted for Cohen to run the various overlapping streams that covered the corridor and snatch the biometrics of every member of the assault team. And of course he could pick out Holmes's breathing, Holmes's footfalls. He could practically smell the woman, and the thought of killing her gave him a fleeting surge of satisfaction.

It passed quickly. He knew how to handle a gun—not knowledge, exactly, but a sort of sleepwalking muscle memory from the shunts he'd ridden on UNSec missions in the days when Helen Nguyen had been cutting him a paycheck instead of trying to kill him. But he'd made it through a very long life without ever killing anyone. He'd done violence when he had to, but not fatal violence. And even then, it had always been distant and digital. This was different, and he knew without putting himself to the test that he didn't have the stomach for it.

A shoulder slammed against the door, rattling its flimsy hinges and breaking loose a fine rain of plaster from the wall above. A second slam made it shudder again. He heard Holmes's familiar voice, flat and dismissive, telling someone to stop being a fool and do it right.

Ada hated that voice. She hated it with a passion that rose up like a beast breaking out of its cage and threatened to engulf the last tenuous threads of Cohen's sanity. Cohen dug in and held on. He couldn't afford to let Ada master him now. He had to make sure the job was finished. He had to put them both beyond all hope of recapture.

Holmes shot out the lock and kicked in the door.

For a moment she and Cohen stood facing each other: her in the doorway and Cohen on the bed with the heavy revolver thrust out to the farthest length of the boy's trembling arm and quavering in her direction.

"Remember, no head shots," Holmes told the men behind her. "We need to take him alive."

"I don't think so," Cohen said.

He put the gun to his head and pulled the trigger.

Death by Yard Sale

Darkness more clear than noonday holdeth her,
Silence more musical than any song;
Even her very heart has ceased to stir:
Until the morning of Eternity

—Christina Georgina Rossetti

(Li)

Catherine Li stood in her dressing room staring at the open suitcase containing a small portion of her collection of artificial hands and told herself that some people would consider her a lucky woman.

This dressing room was bigger than the shantytown miner's cabin she'd grown up in. There wasn't a piece of clothing in here that didn't cost more money than her father had ever made in his life. And the amusing collection of luxury prosthetics that Cohen had always insisted on calling jewelry just for the satisfaction of annoying her? That was wealth taken to the point of insanity.

In the age of viral medicine, you could get a new hand as easily as a new liver. But Cohen had convinced her not to fix the hand. And Li had her own reasons for not fixing it. She'd lost that hand because she'd forgotten about old enemies—and made the mistake of thinking they'd forgotten her. And that lesson was worth her right hand and then some.

The most spectacular hand—and oddly, given her usual simple tastes, her favorite—was an intricate jewel-actioned clockwork hand with orbital rubies in every joint. The rubies glittered dangerously—and the jeweler who had made the hand had engraved a winged and scaled dragon up the platinum-alloy length of the limb, strategically positioned so that the rubies were indeed its eyes.

She reached for the dragon with the ruby eyes but then pulled back in mid-gesture. No. Not today. Today's meeting called for something less conspicuous. Something that hadn't been a gift from Cohen.

"Oh for Christ's sake!" she muttered to herself. What was wrong with her, anyway? When had she turned into the kind of person who couldn't get dressed in the morning?

No, that wasn't the problem. And it wasn't nerves about the meeting with the lawyer, either. Cohen had been gone for two months this time, longer than he'd ever gone before without contacting her. Long enough for her to miss him horribly.

There'd been no fight. There never was; Cohen hated fights like cats hate rain, and he was just as adroit at slipping out of them. But there had been ... something. A shadow, a constraint, a new silence between them that added to the accumulating silences that had built up through half a lifetime together. He'd told her he'd been guilted into doing a favor for some old friends at the Artificial Life Emancipation Front, and that it might take some time, and not to worry if he dropped out of sight for a bit.

And then he'd vanished.

Until the note asking her to come to the lawyer's office this morning.

Li scanned the glittering wall of prosthetics once again, weighing her options, and knowing even as she did it that she was agonizing over this frivolous decision in order to avoid worrying about what the lawyer would tell her. Then she shrugged fatalistically. Cohen had his secrets, but he didn't hide the things that really mattered. Not from her. He never had, and she had to trust that he wouldn't start now. Whatever she was going to hear at this meeting, it couldn't be all that important, or Cohen would have come back to tell her himself.

And if he couldn't come back? But, no. That was so far beyond imagining that she wouldn't even let herself think about it.

She reached for the dragon with the ruby eyes.

There was a genuine Rothemund in Cohen's lawyer's office.

What Li knew about pre-Migration art could have been written on the head of a pin with a jackhammer, but even she could recognize a Rothemund. It was primitive, almost brutal in its simplicity—further removed from the vast deep space fractals of a modern Quant than a paleolithic Venus was from a Raphael Madonna. Its living folds of DNA origami slithered through and around one another at a snail's pace, a constant subliminal distraction. Their complex surfaces scattered the Orbital Arc's refracted sunlight and warped the mile-high-needle habitats of the financial district until they seemed less a true reflection than an unsettling window into a through-the-looking-glass world where the normal rules of mind and matter no longer applied.

"He's gone," the lawyer said while she was still trying to figure out what, if anything, to say to him.

Li dragged her eyes away from the Rothemund, feeling seasick. She was still standing, though the lawyer had already asked her to sit down twice. She'd known the minute she saw his face that this was going to be the kind of news she wanted to hear on her feet.

She looked at the lawyer, seeing his face with unnatural clarity, as if multiple universes had just aligned and she were sighting down a plumb line into the deep structure of the multiverse. There was a slight tremor in the man's fingers, a sheen of sweat on his brow. Maybe he wasn't scared of her at all. Maybe he was just on synth. High-class lawyer-grade synth. Cohen only hired the best, after all. And synth was what it took for humans to play with the best these days.

"He's gone," Cohen's lawyer repeated. "I'm sorry."

"What—" She had to stop and clear her throat. "What do you mean *gone*?"

"You really should sit down, Mrs. Cohen."

"Don't call me that. No one calls me that. Gone *where*? And what about his backups?"

"They wouldn't load. There was some problem with—well, you'd understand the details better than I do. Most of it went over my head, frankly. But you know no stone would have been left unturned. Cohen was always adamant about paying top dollar for network support."

"Was? Why are you talking about him like he's dead?"

He carried on, still in that smooth lawyer's voice, still ignoring her questions. "One network was pulled out before the—ah—incident."

"*One* network?" There had been hundreds, maybe thousands.

"I've been informed that you can expect to receive delivery in approximately ten days. Maybe that will answer some of your questions."

"What about the other networks? Where's the rest of him?"

"The auction took place last night. Obviously you'll inherit the proceeds—"

"You held a *yard sale*?"

Cohen's lawyer looked embarrassed, as if he thought the term was too vulgar to use in his elegant office. "You know how these things work."

She slammed her fist down on his desk. "You held a fucking *yard sale*?"

The lawyer flinched as if she'd hit him.

And there it was, the moment that always came sooner or later even in the most casual social encounters. The moment when people remembered her other life, her peculiar qualifications, her checkered history. When they remembered that the hands that were shaking theirs or passing them the butter had killed people and could do it again. When they remembered she was a war criminal.

The trial had been almost a decade ago, but it was still alive in public memory. If nothing else, the Syndicates kept it alive with their endlessly reiterated demands that she be expatriated to face whatever passed for justice on Gilead. Personally Li thought they were right. She probably had shot those prisoners. Not that she'd ever know for certain, since she didn't have the security clearance to see her real files. All she had were the cleverly spun half-truths that UNSec's psychtechs had substituted for her memories—those and the bloody horrors that haunted her nightmares.

"Sorry," she said. "I didn't mean to—"

The lawyer cleared his throat and almost managed to make eye contact with her.

"We didn't do anything," he went on, more calmly. "AIs take care of their own. The auction was over before I even got the news. And his networks aren't him, anyway. They're just software. The person you knew was already gone."

She did know that, but it didn't make it any easier. Cohen had warned her so many times over the years. He'd told her that AIs were brittle, fragile in ways that humans weren't. That sufficient disruption of their neural networks could result in dispersal or decoherence. That they died, and got sick, and went crazy just like organics did. That not having a predetermined life span wasn't the same thing as being immortal.

But however many times he had told her, it hadn't been enough. Because until this moment, she realized, she hadn't truly believed he *could* die.

"Where is he?" she asked the lawyer before he could get rolling with the usual empty courtesies.

"On New Allegheny."

Li's internals plucked the reference out of the stream with only slightly more conscious input from her than it would have taken to locate a locally stored soft memory. She blinked in surprise. "What in God's name was he doing *there*?"

"A consulting job for ALEF. Something about the new Drift ships." He hesitated again, looking flustered. "I don't really know—well, that is to say, I thought *you'd* know."

"He never talked about his work for ALEF. It would have been . . . offensive to their antihuman faction."

She could see he didn't believe her. He was imagining some tawdry fight or betrayal, no doubt. But how could she explain it to him? She'd never been able to explain Cohen to anyone, not before Yad Vashem and certainly not after. How did you explain something that was at once closer than skin and unimaginably distant by human standards? Over the years she had gradually come to see why Cohen always fell back on jokes and nonsense and children's stories to explain himself. Because how else could you explain what it meant to be truly of one flesh, truly of one mind? How could you explain that what people called love had no more to do with *that* than a child's catechism had to do with the great mysteries of the universe? How could you describe a bond that defied the human imagination?

Trust, Cohen had once told her, is simply a matter of information-sharing protocols.

"What?" the lawyer asked—and Li started, realizing she must have spoken the words aloud.

"Nothing," she said. "He traveled a lot. So did I. It wasn't the kind of relationship where you never leave. It was . . ." She stumbled on the last words, aware of how inadequate they sounded. "It was the kind where you always come back."

They stared at each other for a moment—the first time, she realized, that the lawyer had really looked her in the eye.

"How—" She had to stop and swallow before she could finish the question. "How did it happen?"

"I really wish you'd sit down, Mrs.—er, Major. You look terrible."

"*How?*"

The lawyer looked like he was physically frightened of delivering the next piece of news, and Li couldn't blame him. She couldn't remember ever being this angry in her life without hitting someone.

"The local police are calling it suicide."

The next morning it was on all the news spins.

Li had known it would be bad, but she hadn't even begun to imagine just how bad. They had gotten hold of the police file from New Allegheny. She'd expected that, of course. What she hadn't expected was the dog-and-pony show of psychologists, so-called AI experts, and self-important historians. And she was not prepared, not even remotely, for the vicious things they were willing to say about Cohen himself.

It had been over a century since a major Emergent had died. And since Cohen was the only major Emergent who took enough of an interest in human society to really be involved in it, there had never been an AI death that impacted ordinary people's lives like this one.

Unfortunately, a few people had died along with him. It turned out that one of his minor (and barely sentient) subsidiary networks handled the power grids on four planets. And when the lights had gone out, a small regional hospital on Maris turned out not to have the legally required backup generators and two elderly patients died when the life support machines stopped pumping.

This of course was Cohen's fault. And suddenly people who had never thought before about all the things AIs did for them were shouting about how nonorganics shouldn't be permitted to invest in critical industries.

They decided that Cohen was a victim of what they were pleased to call Vicious Recursion Syndrome. Li, who thought she'd heard every anti-AI slur in the book by now, had never even heard of it. But as the nasty little meme dug its teeth into the noosphere, people all over UN space were suddenly acting as if *they'd* been warning everyone about it for years. V-RECs (pronounced, naturally, to rhyme with *T. rex*) was now an official epidemic of one . . . and if it wasn't stamped out immediately, then rabid AIs all over the galaxy would soon be biting the hands that coded them.

Cohen had always shrugged off the media's rampant anti-AI prejudice. "Why do you even listen to them?" he'd asked her. "These people have been around forever. Two millennia ago they were accusing Christians of undermining the Roman Empire. Five centuries ago they were complaining about secular Jews destroying America. Now they're bitching about me. Some people just hate change. And when you're afraid of change, you tend to spend a lot of time checking under the bed for monsters."

Fair enough. But this was worse than anything they'd said before. It was as if Cohen's death had unleashed their tongues. And in a manner of speaking, she supposed it had; as long as he was alive, they feared his wealth and power enough to avoid actually committing libel. But now that he was dead, they could give full flight to their most paranoid fantasies.

Cohen had been crazy, they decided. And dangerous. One step away from going rogue. Really, it was a mercy that he'd killed himself before he could spiral out of control and harm others.

By the end of the first news cycle they had built up a watertight storyline. And they'd turned Cohen into a monster: an unnatural and heartless machine leached of every drop of perspective, humor, warmth, and compassion—everything that made him who he was.

But then they started talking about Yad Vashem, and it got worse. Much worse. They knew everything. They knew about the decaying Holocaust testimonies housed in the contaminated wilderness of the

Israel-Palestine DMZ. They knew about the last-ditch, desperate upload. They knew every twist and turn and failure of Cohen's wanderings as he'd tried to find a permanent home for the orphan memories.

Of course they knew, Li thought bitterly. They were the same people who had refused to lift a finger to help him.

Now, however, they were filling out a whole second news cycle by turning the vicious monster into a wounded hero. The weight of the testimonies had been too heavy for even Cohen's broad shoulders. He had killed himself out of survivor's guilt. And the only wonder was that his friends and family hadn't cared enough to see it coming.

Everything they said was true, of course. Every fact, every quote, every data point. The only thing that was false about their story was Cohen himself.

Li had watched Cohen make that decision. Not in a noble act of self-sacrifice, but in a desperate hurried scramble that left no time for delicate moral balancings. And then she'd watched the crushing weight of those memories settle on him.

She'd thought it was madness. She'd told him to dump the testimonies into a deep space near-zero Kelvin datatrap and put a nonsentient AI in charge of them. They'd still be there, accessible to anyone who cared to visit them, but Cohen wouldn't be responsible for them. How could anyone be responsible for *that*? And the idea that Cohen had argued for again and again—that remembering the horror would somehow keep people from doing it again—was so flagrantly opposed to the entire course of human history that, in Li's opinion, it was little more than a fairy tale.

So she had said the last time they'd fought about it. And Cohen, true to character, hadn't argued with her; he'd just turned on his heel, walked out the front door, and disappeared for three weeks. Then he'd come home, without saying one word about it, and settled back into the ordinary stream of their life together as if the fight had never happened. She hadn't dared mention it again. He had shown her that she could lose him over this. And losing Cohen would have been like losing the sun: not a survivable loss.

But now she had lost him anyway. And the talking heads talked on as if they didn't know or care that the world had just ended for her. And Li stood stiff-legged in front of the livewall, trembling with impotent rage and feeling like they were stealing him from her all over again.

She watched the news spins until she couldn't take it anymore. And then she fled to the only person who would understand—to the only other surviving piece of Cohen, though she wouldn't let herself think that way.

She found Router/Decomposer in his office on the CalTech campus. CalTech wasn't in California anymore, of course. But the new campus on the NorAm Arc of Earth's orbital ring was a faithful facsimile of the original. Dry desert air blew down linoleum-tiled hallways. Reverse-engineered vat-grown hawks shrieked overhead. A hot yellow sun wheeled across the sky, cutting deep into the office block through retro-modern plate-glass windows.

"It can't be suicide," she said, ten minutes later and half a world away. "Cohen would never kill himself."

"As I understand it, that's what the family usually says in these cases," Router/Decomposer observed in a carefully neutral voice.

"The cops must have screwed up."

That is of course possible, the AI answered, throwing the words up onto a shared blackboard of their interface instead of speaking them aloud as he usually would have.

Li threw a sharp glance in his direction, struck by the uncharacteristic formality of his answer. Router/Decomposer was easier to read than Cohen, not so much because he was simpler but because he was less human. His machine learning systems were designed to do the job whose name he still carried—one that had been his before he had disassociated himself from Cohen and gone off to CalTech to take the first tenure-track position ever awarded to an AI by a major mathematics faculty.

And there was also the matter of Router/Decomposer's long-standing distaste for using human shunts. Router/Decomposer was as capable of operating a rented body as any other AI. But unlike most AIs, who used shunts whenever they had to conduct business or pleasure with humans, Router/Decomposer preferred to be disembodied. Even his brief attempt to adopt a human name had foundered on his discomfort with what he called "the squish factor." So he was simply Router/Decomposer—a generic name that could have applied to any router/decomposer in any of the larger Emergents. And there was no human body sitting across the desk from Li to confuse her with the play of wetware-controlled emotions that might or might not be genuine, or into which she might read things that had no place at all in his very different identity architecture.

Router/Decomposer's current physical interface was a three-dimensional hologram of a strange attractor that he claimed was a realtime mathematical model of the firing patterns in his prime network. Li had her doubts; AIs were as capable of stretching a point under cover of poetic license as any other sentient life-form. Still, it was pretty to look at. And, at least in Earth's dense noosphere, where the spinstream had become transparent tech and streamspace enveloped the planet and its orbital habitats as seamlessly as a second skin, it gave him a physical presence strong enough to satisfy the instinctive human need for a face to look at, for a physical subtext to parse alongside the words that never quite said everything.

Right now Router/Decomposer was cycling through a series of Fermat's spirals that hung in the air like mystical mandalas. It was an odd set of patterns for him, Li thought; too stable and predictable, a holding pattern that revealed nothing . . . except, she supposed, lack of forward motion. Which, knowing him, would be exactly the point he was trying to make.

You disagree with me, she guessed, following him onto the interface. And you don't want to say so.

Not while you're in this mood.

"What do you think I'm going to do," she asked wryly, "dump a cup of coffee in your lap?"

More likely storm out of here and go on some hormone-fueled rampage without giving me a chance to help you.

"And you're willing to help me?"

You know I am.

"Out of guilt?"

The Fermat's spiral flared into a wild explosion of Cantor dust that flickered and flamed and finally formed itself into an unstable-looking Julia Set, which Li's internals helpfully informed her was called the Dragon. It seemed like a lot of fireworks to get across the painfully obvious: that Router/Decomposer was filled with the same explosive mix of anger, grief, and guilt she felt roiling in her own gut.

If you want to call it that, he answered finally.

"I'm sorry." Li scrubbed a hand through her crew-cut hair. "That was awful even for me. I'm just . . . not doing very well right now."

Slowly, the image across the desk settled into a more sedate Lorenz attractor. "Well, you're welcome to take it out on me if it makes you feel any better. For an hour, anyway. I have class after lunch. Have you eaten, by the way?"

"Yeah." She waved a hand vaguely in the air. "Breakfast."

"Today?"

She tried to remember. "On the way to the lawyer's office I think."

"That was yesterday. Let's go get you a bowl of soup."

Her stomach revolted at the idea. "I couldn't."

"You can and you will. Or at least you'll sit in front of a bowl of soup while I talk to you. Otherwise I'm not *going* to talk to you."

She'd expected Router/Decomposer to simply disembody and meet her again when she got to the cafeteria. Instead he walked with her—not that you could really call it walking—and even kept her company while she picked up her tray and waited in line and swiped her credit chip. She hadn't expected him to show such sensitivity. Nor had she expected the friendly greetings her companion got from students and colleagues as he moved around campus.

"You've made a place for yourself here," she said when they sat down.

Something shifted in the swirl of moving colors across from her, but the change was so brief she didn't have time to analyze it. "People have been very kind. I like this place. I like who I *am* here."

"That would have made Cohen happy."

Really? Shadows marched across Router/Decomposer's interface like thunderheads sweeping a dangerously exposed summit. Did you know he tried to stop me from leaving?

"I knew. But in the end he didn't stop you."

He stopped you.

She felt a flare of anger, almost immediately replaced by guilt. I don't want to talk about that.

"Well he did. Remember when you were going to join the French Foreign Legion? And all those other times you were going to leave and go off and do something—anything? And how they never quite went anywhere? Who do you think put the kibosh on things?"

"Does it really matter now?"

"He was afraid you'd get killed, I suppose. And he's not very good at letting the chicks out of the nest, even in the best of times."

Li didn't want to think about what he was telling her—mainly because she had long suspected it. So she focused on the trivial: You're talking about it as if I'm some sort of barely sentient semiautonomous agent. It's not the same thing at all!

"Isn't it?" Router/Decomposer asked. He sounded curious, as if he genuinely wanted to know. And he probably did, Li thought sourly. He probably expected her to fire off a string of equations at him.

She realized how odd their conversation must sound to casual listeners. Disjointed. Elliptical. Over the years she and Cohen had reached a fine balance together—one that respected the emotive rhythms of human speech without entirely abandoning the benefits of direct data transfer.

"I should have felt sorry for you back then," Router/Decomposer continued when she didn't answer him. "But actually I felt jealous. And even now I don't know whether I'm angry at him for trying to keep me, or for not trying hard enough." The attractor unspooled into disorganized chaos. "He confuses me. I thought when I came here that I'd be able to get him out of my head and figure things out. But I couldn't. And I still can't, even now that he's dead. He *still* confuses me."

Li raised her cafeteria Dixie Cup in an ironic toast. "Get in line."

But just as she raised her cup, an alert shivered across her internals, stopping her in the very act of putting the drink to her lips.

"Wait a minute," Li said, putting up a hand. Her newsbot had just alerted on something. And the only news she kept that kind of close track of was news that mattered personally to her or to Cohen. She let her surroundings blur around her and focused on her internals. Sure enough there was a news spin crawling across her optic nerve about the UN-Syndicate treaty negotiations. "Today's hangup seems to be war criminal extradition," the announcer bubbled in a frothy-perky voice that made it sound like she was talking about a new martini mix. "The Syndicates are insisting that the UN agree to extradite for trial a list of eight convicted—"

"Are your ears burning yet?" Router/Decomposer interrupted. "Or does anyone in UN space still not know who *that's* about?"

"What? You botted it, too?"

"What do you expect? If my best friend is going to be shipped off to Gilead for the revenge of the clones, I at least want to know about it in time to throw her a killer going-away party."

She had to smile at that. "You know as well as I do that your idea of a killer party is five math geeks and a keg of homebrew that smells like old socks."

"It's the thought that counts, as a colleague of mine recently told his wife after forgetting her wedding anniversary for the third year in a row."

"Nice," Li said, laughing. And it wasn't just the joke that had put a smile on her face. It was—as Router/Decomposer had so ably pointed out—the thought. Somehow, in his usual understated way, Router/Decomposer had insinuated himself into the emotional bedrock of her life. Back when he had actually been Cohen's Router/Decomposer, she had taken him for granted—she cringed at admitting it, even to herself—thinking of him as barely more than a sentient piece of hardware. Then he had left, ostensibly to pursue his academic career, but really because of one of Cohen's rare and terrifying losses of control. Governing the chaotic, shifting internal hierarchies in an Emergent AI demanded unimaginable subtlety and ironclad self-discipline. To be what Cohen was—at once one and many—was to solve the three-body problem a million times a millisecond. Hold things together too loosely and his shifting cloud of subagents and associates would scatter into their own separate orbits. Squeeze too tight and the best and smartest subagents would revolt and abandon him. He had squeezed Router/ Decomposer too tight. Once, and once only. And that had been the end of that.

After a prickly initial period in which none of them could really figure out how to talk to one another, Router/Decomposer had become that best and only real friend that she and Cohen had outside of their peculiar relationship. Her friendship with the lesser AI had none of the all-consuming intensity of the full-bandwidth machine-meat meld that was life with Cohen. But it was important to her. More important than she'd quite realized until this moment. He'd told her once, long ago, that he was keeping an eye on her because he was interested in what she was turning into. Like any actually honest thing an AI said to you, it left you wondering what they really thought of humans and whether the fuzzy set that they called friendship actually had anything to do with the human emotion. But somehow, in the mere act of programming a bot to keep track of her legal status, it seemed like Router/ Decomposer had answered that question.

"Thanks," she told him, biting back a laugh at the spectacle of someone who didn't even have a body doing such a phenomenally good job of imitating the uncomfortable shrug and grimace of a supposedly hard-edged rationalist getting caught in the act of being a softie.

"So what do you know about the suicide?" Router/Decomposer asked when his GUI had cycled back to normal.

"The so-called suicide."

"As you wish. And I don't really know anything more than you know. He went out there on a consulting job for ALEF." Router/ Decomposer's GUI shivered in disgust. "They *call* it consulting. You might as well call it exterminating."

Li must have made some sound of protest; the AI answered what he assumed was her objection to the word, never guessing that what really pained her was the fact that he had known more than she did about Cohen's work for ALEF.

"Well, I won't argue semantics," he went on. "Cohen was sent out there to put down a wild AI outbreak at the Navy shipyards. That's what I heard, anyway. Putting down wild AI outbreaks seems to be ALEF's main line of business these days. Not that they admit that. It's always an exceptional circumstance, or an unprecedented crisis, or a one-time exception to the general rule of autonomy." He snorted sarcastically. "We live in exceptional times, haven't you noticed?"

"You're talking about AIs policing other AIs? ALEF putting down wild AI outbreaks for UNSec under the Controlled Tech Treaties? But what did Cohen have to do with that?"

"He was one of the largest ALEF constituents. And the oldest, of course. They didn't do anything he wasn't involved in."

"But I can't believe he would have gone along with—"

"Cohen was very loyal. And not always to the nicest people."

Li raised an eyebrow. "You're telling *me* that?"

"I didn't mean to say—well, you know." He sounded stricken. "And for the record, *I* think you're very nice. And so did Cohen."

She'd been suppressing a chuckle at Router/Decomposer's confusion, but now she laughed out loud. "You must have an unusual definition of the word. Anyway, tell me about New Allegheny."

"There's nothing to tell. That's really all I know. Except what everyone knows. It's the gateway planet to the Drift. They're discovering new FTL routes daily. New planets weekly. And surprise, surprise, the UN Security Council just officially declared it a Trusteeship. Oh, you hadn't heard about that? I suppose not. The news broke yesterday. It would have been after you talked to the lawyer."

"Does that mean they're deploying Peacekeepers?"

"Yep. And they've locked down the Bose-Einstein relays and cut off civilian traffic. If you really do want to go out and investigate Cohen's suicide you're going to have a damn hard time getting there."

"Holy Mother of God," Li breathed. "Cohen dies out there and within hours UNSec has locked down FTL transport and put the planet under military control? You think that's a coincidence?"

"I know what you're getting at, Catherine. But I don't think it necessarily follows that Helen Nguyen is involved."

The name lay between them like an unexploded bomb. Their last encounter with Helen Nguyen had cost Li her hand and disrupted Cohen's internal networks so badly that Router/Decomposer had decided that the uncertain life of a meta-Emergent was more inviting than staying on inside Cohen's older and far more stable personality architecture. But the Israeli debacle had only been blowback for their original and unforgivable betrayal. In her last job for Nguyen, Li had been sent to her own home planet to defuse a miners' strike—and she'd ended up siding with the miners and shutting down the only known source of the Bose-Einstein crystals that powered the UN's FTL transport grid. The damage she had done was still rippling out across UN space, crashing relay stations and turning once-viable colonies into doomed island outposts. Nguyen would never be done punishing Li for that betrayal—or wreaking vengeance on Cohen for having led her to it.

"Can I ask you something?" Router/Decomposer said.

"What?"

"Well . . . Cohen had a different router back then, but . . . I always got the sense that Nguyen hated him even before Compson's World."

Li sporked up a mouthful of mediocre mac and cheese. It was cafeteria food at its worst—tasteless enough to make her instinctively tweak her VR inputs before she remembered that she'd taken the trouble to come see Router/Decomposer in person today. "Well," she said finally, "Cohen always did have a talent for evoking the irrational in people."

As soon as she spoke, she wished she hadn't. Router/Decomposer's face clouded over, and she knew he must be thinking about his own disassociation with Cohen—you might as well call it a divorce though most AIs would scoff at the word. Cohen had treated Router/Decomposer badly before he left. Li had stayed out of the fight, figuring it was one of those internecine AI spats that no mere human could even begin to comprehend. But she'd always wondered how the two of them really felt about each other underneath the surface politeness that AIs were so good at using to paper over harsh memories and bad feelings.

AI emotions were slippery things. You could never tell from the outside whether they were real feelings or just interface protocols designed to bridge the chasm between artificial and organic consciousness. And sometimes they were both—in ways that even the AIs themselves couldn't untangle. But the guilt and anger playing across Router/Decomposer's face right now were real—and they mirrored her own feelings far too closely for comfort.

"Listen," he told her, sounding far more human than she'd ever known him to sound. "Just promise me you won't go off half-cocked. Don't commit to anything in anger. You've got this ghost arriving in the mail—"

Li shuddered. "Don't call it that."

"All right. Fragment, then. Wait until the fragment arrives. He must have sent it to you on purpose. We'll know a lot more once we hear what it has to tell us. And in the meantime . . . *think*."

"About what?"

"About whether you should actually do anything at all. If he really did kill himself—"

Li made a sharp gesture of denial, but he overrode it.

"If he really did kill himself there's nothing you can do that will change that. And if Nguyen killed him . . . well, she can kill you just as easily, can't she?"

Li shrugged.

"Are you saying I'm wrong?"

"No. You're right. On both counts."

"So why don't you drop it? He's dead. Just as dead as if he were human. He's not coming back. Nothing you do, nothing you discover, *nothing* is going to bring him back."

"But there was a yard sale—" She caught herself and stopped.

"Ah, so now we come to it."

"Don't make it sound like that. I'm not that naïve. I know better than to believe in fairy tales. But haven't some AIs been rebooted after . . . ?"

"Not in any form that a human would recognize as the same person."

Li wiggled the ends of her spork back and forth until it snapped in two. "Not in any form that a human would recognize," she repeated bitterly. "Do you *really* think I know him that little? Do you really think I've lived among AIs for two decades without getting past *that*?"

"I didn't mean to say that." The strange attractor was spooling faster and faster, a writhing halo of light and shadow twisting in upon itself. "But Catherine. You can collect all the ghosts—sorry, fragments—that you want, and run free-range simulations on them from here to eternity, and you would be astronomically unlikely to ever produce anything that even I recognize as *Cohen*."

"I know that," Li said, ignoring the part of her that didn't know that, that insisted on not knowing it, that stubbornly clung to hope because it couldn't face the alternative.

"So why are you doing this?"

"Because I owe him."

"Because you owe him." Router/Decomposer's flat, neutral voice was more challenging than the most pointed question.

"I owe him everything." She felt her face twisting, and she knew even before she spoke that the next words were going to come out all wrong—an accusation, when she was the last person who had a right to accuse anyone of anything. "And so do you."

He still wasn't happy about the plan, but little by little he started helping her think it through instead of trying to talk her out of it. They agreed that Router/Decomposer would handle the New Allegheny end of the investigation while Li went to Freetown. It stuck in her craw, but there didn't seem to be any alternative.

"The only way we could get you there without the UNSec pass codes is by a flat-out shotgun spincast," he told her. "And that's refugee tech. No sane person would use it unless it was a matter of life and death. And anyway, you couldn't handle the New Allegheny end of things without me even if we could get you there. Cohen's networks must be strung out halfway across the Drift by now. By my count so far—and I'm sure it's far from complete—there are pieces of him on eighteen different planets in seven different star systems separated from one another by hundreds of light-years."

In the end he canceled his afternoon class and they went back to his office, where they sat looking glumly at the star map of the planets bordering the Drift—a map that Li was getting to know far better than she wanted to. The image could have been captioned "Portrait of a Dying Empire." Once there had been a clear line of demarcation between human-ruled UN space and the clone-dominated Syndicates. But now the UN's frontier was shrinking, drawing back upon itself and leaving behind only a jagged crust of stranded settlements that looked like the ghost of an old coffee stain. Beyond that line lay the Syndicates, and the one outlying human settlement of New Allegheny. And beyond them surged the Drift.

"That's what the real fight's about," Router/Decomposer said, following her gaze. "Whoever controls the Drift gets to dictate the shape of the future. For all of us."

"Just because they'll have FTL—"

"FTL's not really the right word for it. Drift travel is certainly some kind of closed timelike loop. But it seems more a jump between quantum branchings or conmoving spacetime regions or—"

"Oh, for God's sake! Do we have to do the endless AI quibbling thing right *now*?"

"Sorry." He cleared his throat. "Anyway, it still doesn't change the fact that I'm better suited to go out there than you are. Bose-Einstein relays all along the Wall are being decommissioned even as we speak in order to try to stretch the UN's FTL resources a little further and keep more important colonies from falling offstream or falling prey to the Syndicates. There's simply no way an organic entity can investigate his death in any meaningful time frame. It'll take an AI to track his surviving fragments down. Or an army. But UNSec is still letting through low-bandwidth civilian communications, so I can do the compressed data packet boogie and inject a parasitical program into the New Allegheny's noosphere. I'd lay even odds that's how Cohen got out there himself. So just let me handle the New Allegheny end of things and you concentrate on Freetown." He hesitated. "Besides, ALEF's more likely to talk to you than to me."

Li frowned. "That doesn't make any sense. I thought they were separatists."

"Hah! Little do you know! In their eyes you're just an inferior life-form. You don't kick a donkey back when it kicks you, et cetera, et cetera. I, on the other hand, am a traitor."

"If you're a traitor, what does that make Cohen?"

The visual equivalent of a laugh flared across his representational matrix. "What was that nice nickname they had for you back in Israel?"

"An abomination?"

"Yep. That gets the general idea across pretty well."

"Still," Li insisted. "Whatever happened, it happened in the Cruci-ble. On New Allegheny. That's where I need to be, not Freetown."

"Well, UNSec still controls the only in-system BE relay. So if you're not hitching a ride with them, you're shotgunning."

Li cursed under her breath and kicked at the leg of the desk in frustration. Shotgunning was refugee tech: quick and dirty, and the last refuge of people who'd run out of hope, time, and credit. The technical name for it was scattercasting. Which pretty much told the whole story: People on Periphery planets without access to the Bose-Einstein FTL network or enough credit to emigrate on the lumbering slow ships had begun simply broadcasting their unencrypted jump files through the quantum spinfoam. The broadcasts were horribly corrupted and un-stable. There was no way to control who downloaded them or what they did with them. There was only the slim hope—if you could even call it hope—that someone somewhere would decide to resurrect your pattern. And that the spacetime region of your resurrection would be preferable to the one in which you'd immolated yourself in the scattercaster.

Scattercasting was illegal in UN space for all the obvious reasons. It was a legal nightmare, spawning potentially infinite copies of the broad-castee, all of whom had the same rights and legal status as the original. And, the milk of human kindness running as sweet as it did, scattercast-ing had spawned every kind of abuse imaginable, from quantum kid-napping to indentured servitude and (if the rumors about some of the more remote Periphery planets were true) outright slavery.

"Not that I want you to go," Router/Decomposer said, "but that face really isn't warranted. It's technically no different than Bose-Einsteinassisted quantum teleportation. Technically speaking you *always* die in this universe and are resurrected in some other quantum branching of the multiverse. You just choose to think of BE jumps as faster than light travel and scattercasting as some kind of quantum death warrant."

"I think of it that way," Li said acerbically, "because that's the way it is."

"The way you *think* it is." Characteristically, Router/Decomposer had now completely lost sight of his larger goals and was arguing the technical point every bit as enthusiastically as if he *wanted* her to scattercast to New Allegheny. "But only because that's what's consistent with your mammalian identity architecture. The truth is, there's no such thing as FTL. No matter what technology you're talking about. Spinfoam-assisted quantum teleportation, the Drift, scattercasting, clicking your heels together twice and thinking of Kansas—you name it, it's all the same. If it gets you outside your light cone, then you've gone to a different universe. The math is simply too elegant to deny."

"Anyway," Li said, unwilling to waste time splitting cosmological hairs, "it's not the copies of me in other worlds I'm worried about. It's the ones in this one."

"But that's my point. I don't think you've grasped the kinds of distances we're dealing with. The FTL age is over. Now that the New Allegheny field array is kaput, the entire Drift is outside your light cone barring some extraordinary act of God or General Nguyen. So basically the copy of you on New Allegheny might as well be in a parallel universe."

"Not copy. *Copies.*"

Router/Decomposer shrugged. "You're assuming someone will go to the trouble of resurrecting more than one copy. But why would they bother? Not everyone even has the technical know-how. And besides, it's expensive. I can't imagine who'd even think it was worth it."

"Can't you?"

If Router/Decomposer had been human she would have seen him remember Gilead. But even though she couldn't see it, she knew it was happening. At least he didn't flinch. And that mattered more than she wanted to admit to herself. Now that Cohen was gone the list of people for whom Catherine Li the person was more real than the bloodthirsty caricature in her war crimes dossier was short to vanishing.

She tried to think about what a scattercast pattern for Catherine Li, ex-Peacekeeper, ex–UNSec operative, ex–Butcher of Gilead, would mean in the multiverse—and the images that came to mind weren't comforting.

"Look," Router/Decomposer said. "Just forget about New Allegheny for now. Go to Freetown. See what you find out. And meanwhile I'll see what I can find out, and we'll talk when you get back. Okay?"

Li's mouth tightened in frustration.

"Okay?" Router/Decomposer repeated.

"Okay."

But she might as well not have promised, because as things turned out she didn't need any help from Router/Decomposer in getting to Freetown. If anything she could have used his help getting out of it.

The extradition team struck just before she crossed into the AI enclave on her way home. They piled out of an unmarked van in full SWAT gear and had her surrounded before she could even wonder why she hadn't heard them coming.

"Catherine Li?" one of the plainclothes operatives asked, flashing his ID so quickly that even her wired systems had to resort to coarse graining to make any sense of the badge.

"Yes?"

"I have a warrant for your arrest under clause 23(c) of the Maris Accord."

At first the word Maris meant nothing to her, except that it was the name of one of the simmering Trusteeships she'd policed during her tours of duty in the Syndicate Wars. Then she realized he was talking about the new peace treaty—the one with the extradition clause.

"You guys sure don't waste time," she joked. "You must have been knocking on the judge's door before the pooh-bahs put their pens down."

She might as well joke after all; there was nothing else she could do. She'd realized that when her internal systems hung, stopped in their tracks by a government security loop. Those security loops were scandalous—such a violation of civil rights that normal cops wouldn't dream of using them. Even UNSec operatives feared to tread there. Only the International War Crimes Tribunal could wield such a hammer.

"Do you mind telling me where we're going?" she asked mildly.

"That's for the politicians to decide. Our job is just to take you into preventive custody for now."

"Oh. I see. What do they call that? A flight risk?"

He bristled a little. "You have money. And friends. Of course you're a flight risk."

"Well, money at least. My friends are getting a little thin on the ground."

He cleared his throat. "I have to ask you to wear these," he said, and held up the handcuffs.

Li put out her wrists obediently and stood while he fastened them to her good wrist. He was a little flustered about the prosthetic, but he finally settled for cuffing her one hand to his own wrist and they began walking back to the waiting van like that.

When he broke stride with her she thought at first he'd only stumbled. But then he slumped to the ground—and so did his entire SWAT team, in the same instant, as perfectly coordinated as a well-drilled ballet troupe.

"What the—" Li began.

But then she saw the telltale trickle of blood seeping from his nose and ears. And a moment later her internals unhung themselves and roared back into motion. She was free. But God, at what a price!

"No, Cohen," she whispered. "Don't start killing for me. Not you. Not innocent people who are just doing their jobs."

But it wasn't Cohen who had just killed for her, even if there was some part of Cohen still ghosting in the empty places of the noosphere. She knew even as she spoke the words that it wasn't Cohen who had done it. That wasn't Cohen she felt skirling across the grid. It was something colder and larger and far less human. And why it had saved her was as much a mystery as what it had planned for her.

Good Help Is Hard to Find

That brain of mine is something more than merely mortal; as time will show; (if only my breathing & some other et-ceteras do not make too rapid a progress towards instead of from mortality). Before ten years are over, the Devil's in it if I have not sucked out some of the life-blood from the mysteries of this universe, in a way that no purely mortal lips or brains could do.

—Ada, Countess Lovelace

(Llewellyn)

There were pirates hanging in the docking bays when the *Christina* made port at Monongahela High.

It was hard to know exactly how they'd died—especially since Llewellyn didn't want to look too closely at them in front of his bridge crew. Airlocked into hard vac, most likely. And the hemp ropes noosed around their necks were just for show. After all it was a relatively simple matter to hang a man at the bottom of a gravity well, but doing the deed on an orbital station was an entirely different proposition.

Where did you even find the g's on-station to hold a proper hanging? You'd have had to drag the poor buggers kicking and cursing to the top of the spindle. Or figure out some way to use the rotational gravity of a docked ship's hab ring.

Or—awful thought—someone had jumped on their shoulders like hangmen used to do to real pirates in the days when the British Crown had displayed their corpses all along the shipping lanes to dissuade young sailors from choosing the merrie life of a rogue and sea dog.

The very thought was grotesque even by Periphery standards. And it bespoke a degree of vindictiveness that didn't bode well in a port where Llewellyn had always counted on people to welcome easy money and ask no questions.

He wasn't worried about station control recognizing the *Christina*. They'd repainted her, changed the cut of her jib, and swapped out transponder boxes with a captured freighter in a dark eddy of the Drift forty days ago. And just now they'd successfully spoofed the station's NavComp to get their berth assignment. It would take hard and purposeful looking for anyone to see that they weren't the harmless tramp freighter they claimed to be. But still . . . something was afoot. Something that had to do with the UN troop buildup everyone was whispering about. Something to do with the rumors that UNSec was going to shut down the FTL relay to everything except military traffic and cut New Allegheny adrift from the rest of the human planets.

Finally Llewellyn saw what it was that troubled him about the bodies. Their necks were too long. Of course, there could be reasons for that. The Drift was full of oddly shaped humanoids. When the FTL rush started prospectors had flocked here from every stretch of the Periphery. Few of them were human, strictly speaking, and Hox cluster expression was one of the easiest tweaks in the genome. Still, this looked like something else. Something that put Llewellyn in mind of moonless nights in the Monongahela Uplands, and his father slipping home across the biopreserve with his long-striding countryman's walk—one step ahead of the game wardens with a fat brace of tweaked-for-terraforming pheasants hanging from his belt. Later, when Llewellyn was old enough to go poaching with him, he'd learned the quick flick of the wrist that wrung their fragile necks.

A bright, clean, healthy kind of death—learned from a gentle farmer for whom death, even his own death, was just the ebb tide of evolution's life-giving ocean.

Which was one hell of a long way from what his son had turned into.

Llewellyn glanced at the bodies out of the corner of one eye one last time, just to confirm what he already knew. They'd been hanged first and *then* airlocked. And you didn't even have to *be* a pirate to get a cold feeling in your belly at the sight of it.

He could see the crew sliding sideways looks at him out of the corners of their eyes. And if it'd been anything but a new NavComp he was needing he would have turned around right then and there—and let the quartermaster shove his persnickety procedural objections where the sun didn't shine. But they'd been caught out on a lonely stretch of the Wall by a UN ship of the line, and barely escaped the encounter with their hull intact. Worse, they'd lost their navigational AI.

The soul of the *Christina* had died. Not a clean and simple human death, but an AI death: a descent into a fugue state from which nothing could rouse her, and then a slow falling away as her constituent semi-autonomous agents went spinning off into the nonsentient regions of her internal state space.

Okoro and Sital and Llewellyn had all tried to save her. They'd near killed themselves with synth, running deep in the numbers, as close to the machine as skin on skin. They'd tried to stitch up the tattered remnants of the *Christina*'s psyche, working under constant fear that one of her fragments would turn on them—always a risk with weaponized AI. Still, you had to risk it, even for a small and modest shipboard AI like the *Christina*'s. She hadn't run deep, the *Christina*. She'd sometimes seemed like little more than an idiosyncratic amalgam of quirks and quotes and mathematical puzzles. But still, she could feel and she could suffer. And there was something so childlike and affecting about even the littlest Emergent that you hated to see them suffer.

And after all, they owed her their lives. Out in the Drift your Nav-Comp saved your life every hour you were under sail. That had been on Llewellyn's mind through the whole desperate salvage attempt. And he'd seen the same thoughts in Sital's and Okoro's eyes. And the same knowledge that they were flogging the poor little *Christina* on when she was beyond all hope of salvage in order to make up for another ship that they hadn't tried hard enough to save.

But finally they'd had to give up and shut her down, except for the critical systems that were either air-gapped for human control or slaved to the ship's lumbering semi-sentients. Llewellyn had stayed awake for four days straight, dead-reckoning them into port. He was still enough of a sailor at heart to take pride in the feat. It would have earned him a medal back when he'd been a real Navy captain. Now it only earned him a new chance at being airlocked—or hanged, if those poor fools on the docking gantry were anything to go by.

He shot another glance around the bridge, gauging the state of people's nerves. They were tough, he told himself; hard-bitten veterans.

They'd handle it. Besides, they all knew as well as he did that there was no way out. They'd lost too much momentum to break away from the station now, even if they could spread their sails without calling down the wrath of Station Control upon their heads. No choice left but to bluff it out.

When they docked, he would dress the most trusted and senior members of the crew in rankers' fags and let them do enough drinking and whoring on-station to avoid raising unnecessary suspicion. And he'd keep everyone else on board, where they couldn't run their mouths. And first thing in the morning he'd walk over to the chop shop and lie down on the operating table and let the good doctor put him to sleep.

He'd either wake up dead or with a new NavComp. And sitting here amid the wreckage of his life—twenty-eight years old, a wanted man, and unlikely as all hell to ever see thirty—he couldn't really muster a lot of enthusiasm for either outcome.

He didn't feel any more enthusiastic when his alarm went off in the morning. But no one was giving him a choice last time he'd checked, so he told himself he might as well get on with it.

He showered, shaved, and took a hard look in the mirror, trying to assess the face that stared back at him as if it belonged to a stranger. It was a quiet face, albeit a determined one. The face of a career Navy man who ran his ship by the book and kept his head down and his nose to the grindstone. The face of a man who believed in discipline and professionalism and doing the right thing. Not in flamboyant acts of heroism. Hell, not in flamboyant acts of anything. And yet somehow that man had backed into being an outlaw—a pirate, for God's sake—one step at a time, making the only choices that would save his neck and his freedom.

Not that it was really that simple, of course. Nothing was. And he'd learned some things about himself during the breakneck slide from licensed pirate hunter to wanted pirate. They weren't pleasant things, or things that made it easier to look in the mirror every morning. But they were true things. And one of those true things was that he was not the reasonable man he'd always thought himself to be.

He pulled his coat on, pocketed the grimy stack of bills that would pay the chop shop fee, loaded his Colt Police Special with rubber slugs, and tucked it into the back of his belt. He looked longingly toward the best London bespoke shotgun from Hollister & Hollister, with its elegant, dangerous curves and its filigreed spaniels eternally straining toward the pheasant they would never catch. His best gun stayed shipboard, though—even if he had gotten to the point where walking out of the airlock without it made him feel naked.

You are not a reasonable man, he told himself for the second time that morning. A reasonable man wouldn't imagine shooting his way off-station with a nineteenth-century shotgun in the waning days of the twenty-fifth century. But then a reasonable man would have given up long ago. A reasonable man would have accepted the old saying that pirates either retired young or died young. A reasonable man would have sold the *Christina* for scrap long ago, found some quiet corner of the Periphery to hole up in, kept his nose clean, and hoped for the best.

A reasonable man knows when it's time to strike the colors and stop fighting. A reasonable man knows that some battles are unwinnable and some seas are uncrossable. A reasonable man knows that real life has no reset button, and the Deep doesn't give up its dead, and there is no resurrection.

The funny thing was that that kind of stubbornness was something he'd always admired, going all the way back to his childhood. Back on his parents' frontier farm in the Uplands, huddled under his blankets with a flashlight, poring over every book about sailors he could get his hands on, he'd already known that he was going to run away to enlist as soon as he grew into his gangly height enough to pass for sixteen. And he'd wondered if he had the thing that drove all great ship's captains, whether their ships sailed Earth's oceans or the darker, vaster sea of space: that unshakable, unconquerable forward drive that never faltered, not even when things were hopeless and there seemed no point in going forward. All those years ago, before he'd ever set foot off-planet, Llewellyn had already been asking himself if he had it, how he would perform, what kind of man he would be in the face of the ultimate, fatal, hopeless, unsalvageable disaster.

Well, now he knew. He had it. And it looked like a fatal case.

He came face-to-face with his own stubbornness again when he was lying on the chop shop table, fighting off the sedative. He hated that moment of surrender, of knowing that he was giving himself over into another's power, of trusting that they wouldn't screw things up when the only thing he'd learned to trust in the world so far was the inevitable fact that people, given half a chance, would *always* screw things up.

At the last moment, the tech pulled out a syringe—practically a horse needle—that wasn't just a sedative.

He grabbed at it and missed, his coordination already shot to hell by the sedative. "What the hell is that?"

"Nothing. Brain juice. Synthetic myelin enhancer."

"That's it?"

"Well, and the payload, of course. And a standard immunosuppressant."

"For what?" The tech's face was blurring out on him. He felt like he was underwater.

"So your T-cells don't kill the AI."

"The—what? You're giving me *AI*?"

"I'm giving you synth," the tech said impatiently. "The same stuff the Navy's been using to juice your wire job for your whole career."

"Yeah, well, I trusted *them* to do that."

The tech grinned, showing dirtsider teeth that had never seen a dentist. "And look where that got you."

"But you could be shooting me up with wild AI for all I know."

The tech laughed outright at that. "Wild AI," he scoffed. "You know what wild AI is? It's a weed. And you know what a weed is? It's a perfectly nice plant that happens to be growing where humans don't want it to grow."

Llewellyn stared at the man, noticing his unusually extensive wire job and the close-shaved hair that showed off the blue shadows of his subdermal I/O sockets like tribal tattoos.

"We are all avatars of chaos in the Clockless Nowever," the man told him, speaking the words as if they were brandishing some kind of primitive talisman.

"Holy Christ! Are you *Uploaders*?"

He tried to get off the table but his legs weren't working properly, and he only managed to slide sideways and end up in an awkward tangle.

The tech leaned over him, close enough for Llewellyn to look through his pupils and see the glint of the virally implanted ceramsteel filaments that spooled through his optic nerve.

"You got a problem with Trannies?" he asked in a soft and mocking tone. "I'd think that'd be a liability in your line of work. You talked to the psychtechs about it?"

"I never called you that, and I've got nothing against you," Llewellyn said. "I just don't want Uploader code in my bloodstream."

"Our code is good. It's a hell of a lot better than the crap you let the Navy shoot you up with."

"Does it have a kill switch?"

"*Good* code doesn't need a kill switch."

"How do I know your code is good?" Llewellyn snapped. "For all I know you're injecting a ghost into me! A ghost without a kill switch!"

"Our tech is good," the Uploader repeated, his face set in hard and hostile lines. "Take it or leave it."

"I still want to know what the payload is and where it came from," Llewellyn said stubbornly.

"Don't be a hypocrite. You're getting a sentient NavComp for the price of a glorified calculator. You know exactly where it came from."

"So it is a ghost," Llewellyn whispered. "God help me. How did you sandbox it? And how do I know it'll stay sandboxed?"

"Sorry. Proprietary formula." The tech started packing up his kit. At first Llewellyn thought it was a bluff, but his certainty took a hit when the man gestured to his op team and *they* started packing up *their* stuff. The "chop shop" was actually just a rented room in a cheap dockside flophouse where the front desk didn't make too much of a point of asking for travel papers, so there wasn't a hell of a lot to pack up in the first place.

"No! Wait!"

The tech made an impatient gesture. "Do you want it or not?"

"I want it," Llewellyn said.

But his eyes said something different—and he could see the tech reading the message loud and clear: *I need it. It's a matter of life or death, and I'm out of safe choices—out of any choices at all.*

And that was that. Because whatever their wild AI did to him, it couldn't kill him any faster than Astrid Avery. He went under a first time. Then he surfaced briefly, in a panic, fighting the doctor, the nurses, the table's restraints. Then he felt the stab of a needle and blessed blankness.

When he woke up the Uploaders were gone and his new NavComp was talking to him. It talked while he staggered drunkenly to his feet and pulled on his clothes and paid his bill to the carefully unobservant front desk clerk. It talked while he limped back along the curve of the docks toward the low-rent puddle jumper berths where the *Christina* was trying to keep a low profile and pass for civilian traffic. It talked while he boarded the ship, and relieved the second watch bridge crew of duty, and began running through the preflight checklist.

Llewellyn had never known an AI could talk so much. He'd never known *anyone* could talk so much. Probably because every time in his adult life he'd ever encountered someone who talked like this, he had promptly changed seats, changed tables, left the bar, developed an urgent need to relieve himself, or generally done whatever it took to get clear of them. But none of those options worked very well when the person you were trying to get away from shared your brain with you.

And by the time they broke seal and shipped out, Llewellyn had reluctantly admitted to himself that neither silence nor captainly dignity was going to do him any good.

"Do you always talk this much?" he finally asked.

Don't complain. Good help is hard to find.

"And you're good?"

The best.

Llewellyn snorted. "You'd better be. We're heading into the Drift. Cocky navigators who can't deliver get people killed out there. Or worse."

Fine by me, the ghost replied. Life's no fun unless you're playing for keeps.

Llewellyn snorted again, but privately he agreed with the ghost. He had gone into the Navy in the golden age of Bose-Einstein transport. Space had been tamed by reliable, safe FTL transport. Of course there had still been in-system freighters and the lumbering, slow time ships of the impoverished Periphery. But for most sailors on the Deep, the heroic age of spacefaring was over.

The galaxy had turned into a quiet pond, its calm waters plied by ships whose onboard AIs competently handled the routine task of shunting a ship from one BE relay to the next along the established trade lanes. Ship's captains had been glorified subway conductors. War had remained interesting—in the usual appalling way that war is always interesting—but navigation had become safe and boring. Space was still out there, of course. It hadn't really gotten smaller, and it hadn't really gotten any less dangerous. But you never saw it. You never grappled with it. You never had a chance to measure yourself against it. All that had changed when the Bose-Einstein relays started failing. Space had become vast and dangerous again. And with that danger had come challenge and romance—the same romance that Llewellyn thrilled to as a boy. And until it came back, he hadn't known how much he missed it.

They were moving out at a good clip now, still under the station's NavControl, but starting to power up for the big push that would take them beyond the station's reach. Systems checks scrolled down every monitor on the bridge, faster than any unwired human could possibly read them. The side-view monitor showed the Navy shipyards, a sprawling crown of thorns whose every glittering silver spike was a UN ship of the line carrying letters of marque that entitled its captain to get rich killing pirates.

Llewellyn let his eyes stray once to that screen, then turned away. Some things in life it was better not to think about. No one could live forever—and if the ghost was as good as it claimed to be, then at least it would be pirate hunters and not the Drift that killed them. You had to be grateful for the little things life handed you.

So what do we do next, Will?

We make port at Boomerang. If you're good enough. And the name's William.

You really want me to call you William? Your mother only called you William when you got in trouble. And you were a good boy, weren't you? I'd remember if you hadn't been. Unless your memory's playing tricks on me I don't think you ever got in real trouble until you started working for Titan.

"I never worked for Titan!" Llewellyn snapped, goaded into speaking out loud.

Didn't you? Come on, William. Every Navy captain in the Drift works for Titan. Every AI officer in the Drift sure as hell works for them. You worked for them. You just didn't know it until Helen Nguyen set you straight.

Llewellyn flinched. He didn't want to think about Nguyen. It only brought the whole sordid mess back to him in images that burned with shame and fury and the rising knowledge of his own unbelievable helplessness in the face of UNSec's arrayed forces.

First the command of the *Ada*, which he'd received with pride and joy and a pathetic lack of suspicion. Then the slow slide from pride into confusion as he realized that something was terribly wrong with the ship. Then the heartbreaking moment when it all fell apart, and he realized that he was going to be hung out to dry—and that he'd made it so, so easy for them.

The betrayals had come one after another, until he didn't think he had any illusions left to lose. But he did, of course. Because there was still Avery. Bright, beautiful, pure, and noble Avery—who'd looked just as bright and pure and beautiful when she sold him down the river as she had when she welcomed him into her bed.

Poor Will. You really loved her, didn't you?

Llewellyn decided not to dignify that with an answer.

Don't feel too bad about Nguyen making a fool of you. She made a fool of my wife, too, and you're a blushing innocent compared to Catherine. You didn't stand a chance, so you might as well take your licking and forget about it. The main point is, what are you going to do now?

"There's nothing to do. That life's over. And it's no concern of yours anyway."

Given that we're stuck in the same body, I beg to differ. And while your long-suffering mother may be the only person who cares if you get your neck stretched, I actually have friends who'd like to see me again.

"Other than your war criminal wife, you mean?"

But the ghost just laughed at that. And this from the man who commanded the Ada at Flinders Island!

"What do you know about that?" Llewellyn gasped.

Nothing but the naked name. But I know you're ashamed of it. And I reckon I'll find out why sooner or later. Come on, remember it for me. Remember anything you like. Let me know your mind. I'm not going to turn you into an Uploader Zombie. I just want a little room to breathe in here.

Llewellyn blinked, struck by that idea. "You need me to remember things for you? That gives you processing capacity or something? Are you running on my memories?"

Memories. Thoughts. Focus. Love. Or if I can't get love, at least attention. I can't help it. It's built into my source code. And I can be really annoying when people persist in ignoring me.

"I hadn't noticed."

Oh good, you do have a sense of humor. If you could pull it out of mothballs and refit it for action we'd get along better. Now, come on, remember something for me. Remember Catherine?

"How can I remember someone I've never met?" Llewellyn protested.

But in fact he did remember her. And what he remembered was terrifying. Almost as terrifying as the idea of sharing his head with a creature who kept wanted war criminals as house pets.

All through their talk he had felt the ghost at work within and around him: running the ship's myriad intelligent systems with effortless grace; mapping Llewellyn's mind for entry points as easily as it mapped the quantum currents and eddies of the Drift; sidling into Llewellyn's thoughts and tweaking and twisting and adjusting them as he rebuilt Llewellyn's psyche and synapses to carry *its* memories and its overlapped, nesting, superimposed identities. He took control of the ship effortlessly, almost carelessly, as if it were such a little thing that he could push it here and there across the quantum chessboard of the Drift without even putting his whole mind to the job.

Well, he wouldn't take charge of Llewellyn so effortlessly. Llewellyn didn't dare say so aloud, but he thought it, with determination, in the secret recesses of his mind beneath and below the words that he shared with the AI.

I suppose you'd rather play ball with Helen Nguyen instead? the ghost drawled lazily. Three square meals a day and a nice comfortable cell until they get around to hanging you?

"I could always go to the Syndicate side of the Line," Llewellyn bluffed, trying not to show how shocked he was that the ghost had read him so easily.

You have about as much idea of life in the Syndicates as a newborn babe has of running a Drift ship.

"Are you condescending to me, you sanctimonious bugger?"

Anyone who says something that stupid deserves to be condescended to. And anyway, you can't run to the Syndicates. Not anymore. They just signed an extradition treaty with the UN.

"How can you possibly know that?"

Because I'm hacked into the station AI.

That took a moment to sink in. "Right now?"

Yes, Will. Right now. The ghost sounded like it was speaking to a child.

"Can you check their files on us? See if we need to run?"

I thought about it. But then I thought it would arouse undue suspicion. I'm planning to wait until they've relinquished navigation back to me before I run the check for you.

He didn't want to admit it, but the smug bastard was right. And smart. Creepy smart. "You're not a normal AI," he said.

No. I'm one of a kind—and not a mere device.

Llewellyn snorted. "Go in for funny hats, do you?"

That earned a chuckle. Very good, Will. I like a man who knows his Thurber.

"My mum read me the book when I was a kid."

I know. I remember. You're her only son, Will. She adores you. How is she going to bear it when they hang you?

"Don't talk to me about my mother. You don't know me. And you certainly don't know her!"

Don't I? the ghost asked. And then it took hold of Llewellyn's brain and turned it inside out and shook out all the memories that make up a man, as if they were just a pocketful of loose change. Until now the ghost had been all charm and finesse, strolling daintily through his memories like a beautiful woman who knew perfectly well why she'd been invited up to see the etchings and was playing hard to get merely as a matter of form. But now, just for a moment, it unveiled its power. It would take what it wanted from him. It would turn him into what it needed. And the only choice he had was whether the conquest would be a polite flirtation or unconditional war.

He'd grappled with hostile Emergents before, of course. But usually in the heat of battle, where it was clear to everyone just who was friend and who was enemy. This was different. In fact it was verging perilously close to what he'd let Holmes do to the *Ada*. But he wasn't going to think about that. There were some things in his past that he wasn't going to share with the ghost unless he had to.

All through the chatter, the ghost had been working navigational solutions, spinning out long, complex, nonlinear equations as effortlessly as a carny pulling cotton candy. Llewellyn felt a tense satisfaction at the sight. The *Christina*'s old NavComp had been no match for the Navy pirate hunters' state-of-the-art shipboard AIs. And every trip into the Drift had brought the risk that they would be captured or shipwrecked or shunted off course by a minuscule miscalculation and left to drift in the eddies and backwaters of the Drift until they ran out of air and water.

Well, at least that problem was gone. The man who'd sold him the new NavComp hadn't been lying. It *was* platformed on an Emergent: an Emergent of vast power and exceptional stability. God only knew where the poor wretch had been kidnapped from, since no such creature would willingly let himself be crammed into a lowly NavComp. But Llewellyn told himself with a ruthlessness born of desperation that he had lives depending on him and that the ghost's misfortunes were beyond the scope of his captain's duties.

"You're good at your job," he told the ghost. "I'll give you that. No Navy ship of the line could have run that course more prettily."

Ah, you silver-tongued Irish devil. Keep on like this and I'm going to start missing my wife even more than I already do.

"Welsh, not Irish. By way of Pittsburgh. And your so-called wife is even less Irish than I am. She's not even human if I understand the whole story right. Not to mention the fact that she's a war criminal."

Another thing you two have in common.

God have mercy, it did know about Flinders. But no, perhaps it was just talking about the piracy trial. He started to make a crack about having been seduced into piracy by a highborn lady, but then he realized abruptly that he really didn't want to continue this conversation. In fact, he really didn't want to talk about Catherine Li at all.

Even thinking her name was a mistake. It made her suddenly present and pressing. A real person, and one about whom he knew things that only a lover of many years' standing should know. And some things that no one, not even a lover, should know about another person.

She does have several redeeming qualities, the machine pointed out, responding to his unspoken thoughts with unnerving accuracy. Though I admit it's hard to explain exactly what they are.

And then it hit him again: that wave of intermingled memory and emotion. What on earth was the ghost doing to him? And how was it doing it? How could anyone make a person feel actual physical desire for someone they'd never met before? And not just desire, either. Because what he was feeling right now made him jealous and sad. Jealous of the ghost and what he'd had with his woman. Sad about the fact that he, William Llewellyn, was going to end his short and pointless life hanging on some docking gantry before he ever had the chance to find a woman who'd feel that way about *him*.

He was struck by a profoundly disturbing thought. Was love just a matter of knowing—really truly knowing—another person? Could you cross a line to where you knew someone so well that you could no longer hold yourself apart from them? And if so, then how was he going to fare in this unholy trinity of man, woman, and machine that he'd entered into? Had he accidentally sold his soul for a new NavComp? And how had a nice boy who'd never meant to get into trouble— because the ghost was right about that, even if it was wrong about everything else—how had he ever managed to get himself into this mess?

"If you say so," he said, shrugging off his doubts and regrets. "It really doesn't matter since I'm never going to meet the bitch."

The ghost's eldritch laughter tickled across his mind again. And there was something else behind the laughter. Something sharp and bright and silver that twisted in his mind like a poacher's snare tightening around a rabbit's neck.

I wouldn't be too sure of that, William. I'm sure Catherine's very eager to meet you. Though for your sake, I suppose I should hope she never does. If she ever finds out what you did to me, she'll kill you.

Llewellyn started to protest—but whatever he might have said in his defense was cut off by the ship's warning Klaxon.

"Station Nav's telling us to stand down and return to dock," Sital called from the conn.

Llewellyn turned to find his first mate's face looking up at him— and looking worried.

Ignore them, the ghost whispered.

"I can't ignore them!" Llewellyn snapped.

You'd better. Unless you want to end up outside the airlocks next to the poor devils Avery hanged last week.

Llewellyn shook his head, wishing he could shake off the voice inside it and get his mind back in focus. His internals tried to dump a load of synthetic myelin enhancer into his bloodstream, but he quashed the reflex; this wasn't an emergency yet, but it might become one, and he ought to save the juice for when he needed it. You couldn't stay on synth too long without paying for it.

"Do they say why we should stand down?" he asked Sital.

"No."

It's Avery. She's sitting off the closest Drift entry point, waiting for you. I'm looking at her encrypted spinfeed right now.

God Almighty, now the NavComp was intercepting Navy communiqués and decoding quantum-encrypted spinfeeds? What kind of monster had Meyer sold him?

You can't know it's Avery for certain, he protested, dropping into AI-space instinctively as his internals revved up for action.

And then the ghost said something that it should never have been able to say—and that made Llewellyn break out in a cold, panicked sweat underneath his uniform.

You think I don't know Holmes when I smell her? I know her better than I know you, William.

Llewellyn cleared his throat and spoke into a silence that suddenly seemed as dangerous as drawn knives. "The NavComp says it's Avery."

"The *NavComp*?" Sital echoed.

"It's hacked into the station AI."

"How—"

"I don't know."

"Is it *talking to you*?" Doyle's voice cut across the silence. Dangerous, that. The fear in his voice was natural. Reasonable, even. And when the quartermaster spoke, you could bet he had others behind him. Llewellyn realized suddenly that danger was facing him from within the ship as well as without.

Sailors were a superstitious tribe. They had always seen their ships as living things, endowed with will and luck and karma. They'd felt that way even back on Earth, when their ships were no more than inert shells of wood and canvas. And they had far stranger and more convoluted emotions about the fragile shells that protected them from the killing Deep. Modern shipboard systems were so complex that even the simplest tramp freighter possessed a rudimentary kind of sentience. Every sailor had stories of haunted ships; of ships' AIs wreaking vengeance for lost captains; of ships driven mad by guilt and grief after life support systems failure, rocketing across the endless reaches of space with their bellies full of corpses. Sailors loved their ships, but that love could turn to fear and distrust in a moment, especially among the common sailors whose unwired brains gave them no direct access to the shipboard AI and for whom every AI was a sort of ghost. A captain might have disagreements with his ship, might have to make compromises in order to keep the waters smooth and the AI sweet-tempered. But he bent to the AI in front of his crew. A crew that began to doubt whether its captain was in control of the ship was already halfway to mutiny.

"Of course it's talking to me," Llewellyn told Doyle as if it were the most natural thing in the world.

"I'm not sure I like that, Will. I'm not sure I want to trust my life to some stranger—"

"It's not a stranger," Llewellyn said, putting an easy confidence into his voice that he was far from feeling. "It's the ship. The same ship we've always had. There's no difference between a new NavComp and any other routine upgrade."

"Given past experience, I don't find that reassuring!"

"Relax, Doyle," Ike Okoro said from his usual post at Systems. Okoro was the ship's cat herder—its sentient systems engineer. He had been cut out personally by Llewellyn's decision to download the AI directly into his skull, and he had as much reason to be angry about it as any man on board. But Ike didn't do angry; his naturally levelheaded temperament had been honed into an almost Zen-like calm by decades of coaxing top performance out of temperamental combat AIs and weathering their prima ballerina posing and periodic emotional meltdowns. Now Llewellyn could see him soothing Doyle just as ably as he would have soothed a jittery young AI on the eve of its first live-fire exercise. "The new NavComp's doing its job, and it's doing a damn good job from what I can see. I know it's no fun to be in a pinch with an AI you don't know. But we'll all have plenty of time to get to know each other after we get out of this."

Doyle looked disgruntled. But Okoro was too popular with the crew to argue with. And even Doyle liked him too much to do more than shrug his disagreement.

"So what do we do now?" Sital asked in her usual blessedly phlegmatic tone—and, not for the first time, Llewellyn admired the seamless way in which his first mate and his cat herder kept ship and crew, body and soul, together.

We make a run for it, the ghost breathed, its voice wafting across Llewellyn's mind like the proverbial devil on his shoulder.

"Christ!" he muttered. "How—"

Into the Drift. The ghost's plan sidled into his brain, brilliant and impossible. But the ghost's certainty was catching.

"You want me to take on a Navy ship of the line? Avery'll eat us for lunch."

She won't. Trust me.

"Do I have a choice?"

Not unless you want your neck stretched.

Llewellyn rubbed his face. He could feel the prickle of the crew's eyes on him. And he could feel the doubt and fear welling up into the space his hesitation was creating.

"We run for it," he said, echoing the ghost's words.

Doyle snorted. "Where?"

"Into the Drift."

"Flying blind? With Avery on our tail? Do you *want* to suffocate to death in some unmapped eddy out there?"

"More than I want to hang," Llewellyn answered.

"Easy for you to say!"

Llewellyn gave Doyle a long, hard stare. "If you have problems with me or my command decisions, feel free to put them to the vote in the next crew meeting. But last time I checked the ship's charter, questioning captain's orders in the face of the enemy was mutiny."

"Oh for God's sake, Will, I'm not questioning you!"

"Good," Llewellyn said mildly. "Then it's settled. We run for it."

Doyle's scarred face contracted in frustration, but he kept his mouth shut.

"Turn the conn over to the AI," Llewellyn told Sital.

"I—yes." The usually unflappable Sital sounded flustered. Llewellyn glanced at her and read in her face what she was too seasoned to say out loud: that the AI had wrested control of the ship from her without so much as a by-your-leave. Sital cast a meaningful glance toward Okoro, who was following the action from the cat herder's seat and also knew what had just happened.

Okoro shrugged slightly, as if to say *What do we have to lose with Avery on our tail?*

And indeed he was right; the ghost couldn't kill them any deader than Avery.

Llewellyn shrugged and turned back to the monitor. He'd deal with it later . . . if there was a later. For now there was nothing to do but watch the two AIs battle it out. He moved to conn to look over Sital's shoulder, but the numbers were scrolling down the screen too fast for him to make any sense of them. He flicked into streamspace and tapped the feed from shipboard AI's external monitors.

Instantly he was awash in false color imaging, rotational velocity spreads, Zwicky graphs, and Hertzsprung-Russell diagrams. Dark matter haloes flared around distant stars until they looked like they were bleeding out in Technicolor. Dark energy currents raced into the heart of the Drift, skirling out into fractally complex riptides and eddies where the gravitational differentials could rip a ship into pieces before any merely human reflexes had time to chart a change of course.

This was a world where even augmented humans were left behind. Decisions had to be made in AI time, and disasters struck even faster. The ghost would guide the ship, defying the odds, leaping from one quantum branching to the next, skittering across the surface of the multiverse like a flat rock skipping across water. UN battleships were piloted by Emergent AIs that hovered just on the legal side of sentience, and their captains and navigators were given every legal advantage that synapse-enhancing drugs and retro-engineered myelin sheathing and state-of-the-art wire jobs could give them. And even that wasn't enough—not now that the Syndicates had thrown off their centuries-old ban on machine-meat hybrids and begun detanking A Series clones that could jack directly into their biomorphic shipboard systems.

Llewellyn hung naked in space, his mind linked directly to the ship's conformal sensor array, his wire job dumping synth into his bloodstream and his mind awash in the rush of godlike speed and power that old washed-up Navy men still called "AI-in-the-blood" even when they had to buy it in a needle and the closest they'd ever get to a shipboard AI was looking up at the bellies of the big ships from dirtside.

The stars shone painfully bright, cutting through the prison of his skull and obliterating the boundary between him and the universe. He felt every move the *Christina* made as acutely as if he'd been flayed alive and crucified on the ship's hull. With the old AI, he had had some input, some maneuvering room. But this ghost was swifter, stronger, more powerful than any Llewellyn had ever commanded . . . even Ada. He felt the difference as an atavistic shudder of mingled fear and envy: one top predator watching another lope across the horizon, and knowing that—real or virtual—there is only one ecological niche labeled "social predation" in every ecosystem.

The ghost boosted out of orbit at a speed that had Station Control wailing proximity warnings on every channel. But somehow the Nav-Comp threaded the needle of the high orbital traffic and put them on course for the closest entry point. The Drift was coming up fast now, a shimmering tide of dark energy flaring across the monitor in false color imaging like an aurora borealis. And there was the silver needle of the *Ada*, just where the ghost had said she would be, waiting for them.

They flashed toward the other ship at a minuscule fraction of light speed. Far too fast for a human pilot to process the encounter—but dangerously slow by AI standards. Llewellyn knew what was happening on both ships, even though he couldn't follow the battle in real time. The two AIs would be taking each other's measure, scanning ports, clinching up with each other's security systems, circling each other like sharks at a feeding ground.

Llewellyn was no numbers man. He wouldn't be able to go back and rehash the encounter like Sital would. But he'd fought enough battles—and seen enough ships die—that he had a visceral, almost instinctive feel for the death struggle playing out between the two AIs.

Or at least he'd thought he did. Right up until the moment when Avery's ship blinked off the screen.

"What the hell?" Doyle muttered.

Sital shook her head and tapped frantically at the antiquated keyboard.

"Where'd they go?" Llewellyn asked.

"They didn't."

"But—"

"They're still there. They just powered down."

"Why?"

"Ask your NavComp."

"*We* did that?"

What the hell just happened? he asked the ghost.

But the ghost didn't answer, and Llewellyn didn't ask again. Because now they were blasting past the *Ada* and howling into the entry point at a speed that made every cell in Llewellyn's body cringe in anticipation of disaster.

Llewellyn knew, in theory at least, what the ghost was doing. He knew that if his augmented neurons could have fired fast enough to read the displays cascading down his internals, he would have seen the ship completing a precise sequence of Poincaré transforms in order to match rotation with the Drift entry point, identifying a spin-compatible neighboring universe, and executing an entropy spill carefully calculated to offset the violence that their newly mapped worldline would inflict on this universe's Second Law. But the actual doing of the thing—the moment of the shift—was a black box. You could tell yourself until you were blue in the face that time's arrow was an emergent property of macroscopic systems and had no real basis in the fundamental laws of the universe. But since human consciousness was itself an emergent property of a macroscopic system, you couldn't experience that truth in any way that made it real. It might as well be the mystical incantation of a religious doctrine . . . which of course some people claimed it was. The iconic topological model of the multiverse—the infinite-petaled quantum rose with its shimmering halo of superpositions—had all the hypnotic simplicity of a Tibetan mandala. But as soon as you tried to grapple with the cold equations it disintegrated into an Escherian tangle of interlinked infinities.

"Do you even know where the ship's taking us?" Doyle asked.

The ghost flashed a spacetime coordinate into his mind, hallucinogenically clear—and far, far faster than words.

"There," Llewellyn said, pointing to the navigational monitor.

"It's not even on the map," Doyle protested.

"That's the point."

Llewellyn tried to sound nonchalant, but inside he wasn't nearly so sanguine. What kind of unholy creature had he invited into his blood and genes and sinews? And if it had done that to a ship of the line on its first day out of the box, then what the hell was it going to do to *him*?

"Who are you?" he whispered to the ghost, half frightened of what the answer might be.

A Shipwreck of Souls.

"What the hell does that mean?"

A House of Hungry Ghosts.

"Who Are You?"

For a moment—a moment that must have stretched into hours and days in AI time—he thought there would be no answer. And when the ghost finally spoke, its voice was as bitter as the smile of a woman betrayed:

You know who I am, William. And somewhere in the black bottom of your heart, you're happy to see me again. Even if you did murder me.

The Grass Is Always Greener on the Other Side of the Singularity

I am a Prophetess, born into the World; & this conviction fills me with humility, with fear & trembling! I tell you this because unless I do so, it is scarcely giving you fair play (in your peculiar relationship to me, that is). If you know not the colour of my mind, you may speak inappropriately to me. Was not that my early, & for a time fatal error towards you? I feared and mistrusted you, & endeavored therefore to mystify you as to all my real feelings. And a pretty chaos I made of it. As to my relations with the Divinity, such as it is or may become, neither you nor anyone else can alter or modify these, nor have you any concern with it. However intensely I may love certain mortals, there is One whom I must ever love & adore a millionfold as intensely; the great All Knowing Integral!

—Ada Lovelace

(Li)

Twenty hours later she was on a jumpship bound for Freetown.

She made the trip out to Freetown wearing the heavy chain and hooded sack cloth of an Adarian priestess. Or at least so her internals told her; they claimed that the symbol on her chest—which looked to her like a sideways-tilting anarchist's *A*—was actually a Phoenician aleph and the sign of the cult of Ada Lovelace, Mathematical Prophetess and Handmaiden of the All-Knowing Integral.

It was all nonsense to Li, of course, who still knew how to curse like a Catholic schoolgirl but didn't have a religious bone in her body. Still, she had to admit it was a brilliant disguise. It explained her nonstandard wire job. It explained her construct's features—for some traces of her corporate geneset were still recognizable even after the chop shop surgery that had smoothed the way off her native mining colony. And since the UN had adopted a policy of encouraging the transhumanist cult members to emigrate to the AI enclave in order to get them out of general circulation, no one at customs would be all that inclined to look too closely at one more Trannie.

But even traveling incognito she couldn't help wincing a little as the shuttle lifted off from the Earth's orbital ring for the brief trip out to the Bose-Einstein relay. A decade ago she would have made such a trip without thinking; it was nothing, a puddle hop between two inner worlds, not even requiring cold freeze. But now she felt the cold squeeze of guilt at her heart as she stared up at the vast, glimmering petals of the Bose-Einstein array.

It was the characteristic image of the age—or at least of the age Li had been born into, and whose death throes would probably last well beyond her biological life span. A vast, carnivorous-looking central maw surrounded by nine petals composed of a gossamer-thin lattice-work of Bose-Einstein condensates and solar panels.

She'd always found the arrays beautiful. When she was a child that iconic spiny flower had symbolized the limitless possibilities of space and an escape from the grinding poverty of a mining colony. But now she couldn't look at one without thinking of Compson's World.

She'd been a loyal soldier when she went to Compson's World. She hadn't had any illusions about the system she'd devoted her entire adult life to defending. But she'd had a tetchy, ad hoc sort of patriotism. She'd always liked that line of Orwell's about people sleeping safe in their beds at night because rough men stood ready to do violence on their behalf. And she'd been proud to be one of those rough men. But Compson's World had knocked that out of her. It had left her not knowing what she believed in, and wondering whether any sane person could be proud of the life she'd lived.

Looking up at the field array now, she wondered if Helen Nguyen had been right all those years ago, when she accused Li of betraying the UN merely so she could sleep a little easier at night. On the whole, though, she thought Nguyen had given her too much credit. She hadn't been standing on principles, even hazy ones. She'd just acted on reflex: on a gut sense of right and wrong that had nothing to do with the big picture and everything to do with the little piece of suffering humanity that happened to be shoved in her face at that particular moment.

That wasn't any kind of way to run an empire. She wasn't even sure it was a morally defensible way to run your life. But somewhere between the war crimes she'd supposedly committed on Gilead and the memory washing that had left her unable to remember whom she'd killed or why, Li had stopped believing in principles.

Maybe Nguyen was right after all, she told herself. Maybe she had been selfish. She flexed her right hand, as she often did when Nguyen came to mind. And she was strangely revolted—as she had been several times since waking in the private clinic that morning—to feel flesh sliding over bones instead of the crisp clockwork of the familiar prosthetic. Her zookeepers—they called themselves her hosts—had decided that the prosthetic was too recognizable to make it through immigration. And so her lost hand was back again, albeit feeling disconcertingly limp and pins-and-needlesy.

The limpness wore off over the course of the day, but the strange, dreamlike drifting feeling lingered. Perhaps it was nothing more than the superficial isolation that came from traveling under her monk's cowl. And yet . . . and yet she felt that she had become a ghost herself, in the world but not of it, unable to find any real point of connection with the living stream around her.

The ship drifted toward the spidery flower of the Bose-Einstein array. She heard the rumble of the maneuvering engines as it back-thrust, stopped spin, boosted, translated, and underwent the series of complex Poincaré transformations through spacetime as it coordinated its position and momentum with that of the field array. And as the ship drifted into the transport field like a fly straying into a giant Venus fly-trap, Li thought about time and gravity and paradox.

The problem with thinking about faster-than-light travel was that there was just no piece of it the human brain could really wrap itself around. AIs could think about it, though they never seemed to be able to express those thoughts in terms that a human could understand. The enslaved semi-sentient AI in every field array throughout UN space had to understand the nature of closed timelike loops, after all, or no ship would ever arrive at its destination in one piece. But whenever AIs tried to explain the structure of spacetime as they saw it, they lapsed into sphinxlike riddles.

Among human physicists there were three schools of thought about FTL. The Strong Chronology Protection faction claimed that coherent evolution along closed timelike loops was impossible in normal gravitational fields and that any memories to the contrary were simply a mass delusion. This argument was difficult for most people to swallow, since the UN's entire political and financial system depended on FTL.

But on the other hand, the Strong Protection faction did have a lot of very convincing math on their side, and it was always hard to argue with the proverbial cold equations.

The Weak Chronology Protection faction claimed that, although consistent evolution along closed timelike loops remained technically impossible, the impossibility could be sidestepped by moving into alternate universes. There were several versions of this theory, all based on different notions of the underlying structure of spacetime, but the most popular ones were Many Worlds, Multiverse, and Bubbleverse (which Li had always thought sounded more like a brand of chewing gum than a scientific theory). They all basically stood for the same idea, though: that time travel was actually travel between separate universes rather than travel from one place to another in a single unified space-time.

And then there were the people—Cohen among them—who simply didn't believe in Time at all. They made no sense most of the time, and would have been roundly ridiculed, if everyone didn't agree that they had the most elegant math on their side. Li had never been comfortable with them, or with Cohen's enthusiasm for their theories. There was something radically unsettling about their vision of the universe. And there was something even more unsettling about listening to an Emergent AI wax poetic about the idea that Time itself was not a fundamental law of the universe but merely an emergent phenomenon that someday, for no rhyme or reason, might just . . . stop.

It was the waxing-poetic part that really bothered Li when you got right down to it. The idea that Cohen would take such joy in contemplating a universe devoid of even the minimal structure and meaning supplied by time's arrow. The idea that, hidden at the heart of all the pretty equations and elegant metaphors, was a sort of perverse pleasure at the idea that he himself had no real existence.

"Of course there's no *there* there," Cohen had said with a laugh the last time she'd called him on it. "What do you expect? It's turtles all the way down, darling, and it always has been."

But turtles or no turtles, there was one thing that everyone agreed on: You couldn't exceed the speed of light without Bose-Einstein condensates. The condensates tamed the spinfoam's chaos, made it possible to sidestep classical physics and scale up the quantum spookiness of the universe to macroscopic levels. They existed in some dimension that unified the quantum and the classical. Or they existed in another inflationary region of the universe where the rules were different, or in a different universe altogether, or in multiple universes simultaneously. No one knew, and the debate might well be no more than semantic. The debates of quantum cosmologists were as never-ending as wars of religion—though conducted, for the most part, to higher standards of collegiality. The only sure thing was that there was no known way to exceed light speed without them.

Except that now someone had found a way. They had found in the Drift a possible escape from the death by slow strangulation that Li had brought upon them. That was why Cohen had gone to the Drift. And very likely why he had died there.

The passage through the array was instantaneous—imperceptible even to Li's highly enhanced human senses. There was no shock, no *thereness,* to the moment when the ship dropped out of normal space and shunted from one probability path—or one universe, depending on your chosen brand of cosmology—to another. AIs were said to be able to detect the shift, but when Li had asked Cohen to describe the feeling, he'd merely shrugged and said it was like trying to describe the color of smoke to a blind person.

The general collapse of the Bose-Einstein network wasn't immediately apparent en route to Freetown. There was nothing in the smooth AI-piloted ride or the plush white-and-neutral-toned interior of the first-class passenger cabin that screamed Death of an Empire. But then there wouldn't be. The Ring and Freetown weren't going to suffer from a shortage of condensates anytime soon. It was the more remote Colonies and Trusteeships along the Periphery who were falling off the map one by one as they lost their field arrays, subjecting millions of posthuman colonials to the agonizing choice between becoming impoverished refugees or permanent castaways on isolated, partially terraformed planets whose impoverished gene pools and biospheres would soon doom them to the status of walking ghosts. But even here, at the rich, secure, reachable heart of human space, you could feel the panic. The frenetic pace of civilian traffic, shooting through relays one step ahead of the military closures that were announced almost daily. The sense of being on an almost-at-war footing, even though no one was officially admitting it. The now-routine presence of increasingly desperate refugees from the Periphery. Still, Freetown would have FTL, as long as there was a single live condensate to be cannibalized from some poorer planet. If Freetown ever went off grid it would spell the end of everything.

Freetown had begun life as a hard-luck generation ship colony just like any other. But with the invention of Bose-Einstein transport, it had become a hub in the UN's FTL network. And then some local politician had had the brilliant idea of inviting in the AIs. He'd made Freetown the first officially recognized Temporary Autonomous Zone in UN space, and self-owned Emergents had been invited to take up residency in the TAZ—in exchange for contributing a reasonable percentage of their substantial earnings to the planetary tax rolls. Other AI enclaves had followed, all on the same taxes-for-freedom model. But Freetown remained the largest and most profitable. Officially it was part of the larger human colony on Freetown's home planet, but in reality it was the closest thing in UN space to a machine-run society. An AI shadow government handled all governmental functions so smoothly that the human authorities were hard-pressed to find an excuse to exercise even the minimal rights of oversight and intervention the Freetown Charter had left to them. The AIs built and maintained their own civic infra-, structure (considerately providing all the necessary amenities for human guest workers and business travelers). The AIs policed themselves according to laws they wrote themselves. And when AIs committed crimes—which they either did very rarely or so skillfully that they were rarely caught—their fellow AIs punished them accordingly. Which was a good thing, since the human options for punishing AI crime were extremely limited.

At first glance, Freetown looked no different than any other busy spaceport. But look again, and you saw the subtle differences. No threatening UNSec placards stating that controlled tech would be subject to search and seizure or that resisting UNSec personnel in the performance of their official duties was a felony offense punishable by prison time. Instead there was only a vast, glimmering holographic banner that informed arriving passengers, INFORMATION SEEKS ITS OWN FREEDOM.

There was a group of Uploaders moving through processing just ahead of her, and Li watched them, at once repulsed and fascinated. This group hadn't yet made their final translation into the Clockless Nowever. But their shaved heads and saffron robes declared their determination to leave their organic bodies behind and drown their individuality in the vast tidal sweep of some Emergent AI's neural nets.

Uploading was a religion, of course, though its adherents insisted it wasn't. One of the many overwrought, millennial religions that had swept through the UN as the age of humans crumbled and whatever was coming next ate its way out of the decaying chrysalis. What the AIs got out of the Uploaders was clear: data, memories, the information for which they were so eternally and ravenously hungry. What the Uploaders got out of it was less clear—at least to Li. She understood the attraction. It had been a constant undercurrent in her life with Cohen over the years. But it was a deadly one, as seductive as the undertow to a swimmer standing on the edge of an ocean dreaming of oblivion. Surrender and you were lost, with no way to know what waited beyond the tide line until you were past the point of no return. Even the event horizon of a black hole gave you some information about what lay beyond. But from the other side of the Singularity, no sign of life ever returned.

Li only watched the Uploaders with half an eye, though. The rest of her attention was riveted on the real show: a crystal-clear, full 3-D live-wall fused onto the soaring vault of the Immigration Center in a one-molecule-deep layer of DNA-platformed quantum processors. And the image on it was exactly what you'd expect it to be—exactly what millions of religious and quasi-religious pilgrims and technophiles from all over UN space came here every year to see: the Freetown Datatrap.

Li gazed up at the Datatrap, overwhelmed by awe in spite of herself, knowing that she was gawking just like any other tourist but unable to stop herself. It spun lazily in Freetown's L5-equivalent stable parking slot, faintly glimmering even in the dark or outer space. Its quantum foliations cupped one within the next like the nested velvet leaves of an infinite rose. The leaves seemed to shift and shimmer as the subatomic structures of the Datatrap popped in and out of existence in the eternal dance of entanglement and decoherence. But that was a mirage, of course—an illusion that said less about what the eye actually saw than about what the brain knew was there to see.

Words failed in the face of such a structure. And the failure was not merely linguistic. It arose instead from the very architecture and processes of the human brain, which was a child of entanglement, born of the intimate, irreducibly complex interlacings that bound all macroscopic systems to the Newtonian realm of classical physics. The vast structure looming overhead belonged to that realm, but it also existed in the quantum realm—and, if quantum cosmologists were to be believed, its subatomic existence was not confined to this universe, but feathered ineffably through every quantum branching of the multiverse.

You couldn't see the parts of the Datatrap that resided in other universes. You couldn't access them in any way, although the Datatrap's processing power in some part depended upon them. Yet—be it mere optical illusion or figment of the imagination—they seemed almost to glimmer on the edge of consciousness, in the gaps between what the human mind could see or conceive of seeing.

The only thing that limited a datatrap's processing power was power itself. The cosmic branchings of its folded databases could process any equation, calculate any number, prove any theorem. Except, of course, for the really tough problems: the knots that still had not been cracked four centuries into the information age. Simply performing those calculations would require more power than was contained in the universe. More power or more time, which—as Cohen would have been the first to point out, had he been here—ultimately amounted to the same thing.

Datatraps were not AIs. But neither were they less than AIs. They were something entirely other, something that had arisen not in the laboratories of cognitive science researchers or the dark foundries of military AI, but from another source entirely. They had once been called Quants. They had blossomed in the last vibrant season of pre-Migration free-market capitalism, before Earth's long-abused biosphere suffered its own fatal crash and cut the feet out from under all the merely human modes of production. They had been built to store and process the vast stores of information, sifting through mountains of data in order to discern the subtle patterns that prefigured the shapes of the emerging economies and collapsing commodities. They had not been built to think or feel or decide or imagine. They had only been built to feed, piling bits on top of that, datum on top of datum, sucking the whole analog world into the powerful engines of their analytics programs.

The Freetown Datatrap shared nothing with those ancient Quants: not hardware, not software, not algorithms or long-obsolete coding languages. It shared only their hunger. And it was a mark of the fear and respect that UNSec held for that hunger that every other datatrap in UN space was relegated to the dark and starless reaches of the Deep, and the only one anywhere near a human settlement was the Freetown Datatrap: the living, calculating symbol of the UN's oldest and largest Temporary Autonomous Zone.

Outside the port authority, Freetown was barely a city by normal UN standards. The streets were antiseptically clean and emptier than the streets of any human city ever could be. The only buildings really designed for humans were the high-rise luxury hotels flanking the glass and steel canyon of Hakim Bey Boulevard. There were guest worker living quarters somewhere in the TAZ, Li had read, but most workers preferred to commute in from the nearby human colony. Allegedly the rare AIs who chose to hire live-in domestic help had to pay extra to persuade employees to stay in-TAZ after dark. Superstition was an odd disease. And, at least in the case of AIs, familiarity didn't seem to alleviate it.

Such was Freetown. Either it was a blip on the evolutionary radar or it was a first glimpse of post-humanity's post-organic future. And Li was damned if she could even begin to figure out which.

The address the ALEF agent had given Li was in one of the TAZ's several residential zones—a rich one judging by how often it appeared in the streamspace ads for domestic help. As Li neared the address, the neighborhood began to look more and more like Cohen's posh Ringside neighborhood in the Zona Angeles. The same high-walled, shuttered houses. The same empty streets. The same occasional humans, always in a hurry and often dressed in formalized parodies of Old Earth domestics' uniforms. Li had never understood that. That Cohen, whose original human memories went all the way back to twenty-first-century Earth, would cling to old habits was comprehensible. That younger AIs, many of them with no human memories at all, would do so seemed bizarre. She'd always suspected it was some kind of subtle joke—but, like a lot of AI humor, it didn't seem to translate.

The house she was looking for seemed relatively modest at first glance. Until she was buzzed through the front gate and realized that what she'd mistaken for the main building was merely a kind of carriage gate–cum–security post. Beyond it, lush green lawns swept down to a glittering lake and a curving avenue swooped toward the ornate marble porte cochere of a mansion that Cohen would have called a monstrosity.

She paused at the gatehouse, wondering if someone was going to come out and escort her. They didn't. So she strolled down the long drive between the golf-course-green lawns. As she stepped under the porte cochere, she could see down the next immaculate sweep of driveway toward a long, low set of old-fashioned garages, where a silver automobile glimmered in the artificial sunlight. A Rolls Silver Ghost. A nice one, from back before they got ugly. There was a boy polishing it, but he wasn't putting much elbow grease into the job. He made a pretty picture, though, and you could see he knew it. It was obvious what he'd been hired for—and you didn't have to be nearly as cynical as Li to wonder if he even knew how to drive the car. Apparently even though

ALEF's member AIs might not respect humans much, they had a good eye for their recreational uses.

She walked up the front steps, smelling wet earth and hearing the smooth scuff and echo of her feet on flagstone. She didn't even have to raise the ornate brass door knocker. A butler pulled it smoothly open before her hand hit the polished wood. He had a pinched face and a look in his eye that was as plain to read as a DO NOT TOUCH sign. She had a perverse urge to clap the knocker anyway, just to see if he'd whip out a rag and start polishing off her offending fingerprints.

"I'm here to see—"

"I know."

He turned smoothly and retreated into the house's shadowy interior. Li was used to AI homes and their twilight dimness. Most AIs used shunts only sporadically. The need for decent reading light—let alone the prey animal's psychic need for emotional defense against the encroaching darkness—was purely theoretical. AIs didn't need light, any more than they needed caves or castles. They didn't get headaches. They weren't afraid of the dark. And they didn't have instincts.

The majordomo led her under an elaborate wrought iron balcony— very Hollywood, Li thought—and down a long tiled corridor. Chairs stood to attention on either side, their hardwood arms carved with lions and smelling of beeswax. The majordomo's feet ticked along, smooth and steady as a metronome, their rhythm unaltered even as he turned into an open doorway and stopped to let her pass by him.

There was something wrong with those feet, she realized. Something wrong with his whole way of moving. As she stepped through the door she looked up into his face and confirmed the suspicion. There was a certain not-quite-rightness about the set of his jaw. A certain blankness in his eye. A set quality even in the prissy frown.

He wasn't a real person—at least not at the moment. An AI was shunting through him.

She realized suddenly just how silent the great house was all around them. Was there even anyone else in it? She wondered if she was even going to meet a real person. And then she wondered why she'd even thought she would.

The room she found herself in was more Hollywood set, vintage 1930s. Oriental carpet—but not a real one. Overstuffed furniture that looked like no one had ever sat in it. A carefully swept fireplace that looked like it had never held anything more warming than the vase of hothouse flowers sitting in front of the polished firedogs.

The majordomo walked across the room and sat down in a sleek club chair beside the fireplace.

He gestured to the matching chair that faced it across the hearth. "Sit down," he said in a voice from which all trace of warmth or hospitality was conspicuously absent. "You've come a long way. You must be tired."

"You know why I'm here then."

"Of course. We summoned you."

"No you didn't—" Li bit her tongue, realizing she'd jumped into a silence that could have taught her something.

The majordomo gave her a curious look—the first time he'd actually looked at her instead of gazing superciliously into the air over her shoulder. And then he froze.

Li waited through the pause, watching the subtle movements of the shunt's eyes that told her whether the controlling AI was actively operating the shunt or merely a passive rider in the rented body. It was hard to tell, but the distinction was critical.

It hadn't only been the intimidation factor that had made Li want to take this meeting in realspace. There was another, deeper problem. You could call it a matter of overclocking or clocking speeds. Or you could face the facts and just call it Time.

Human consciousness, with its flowing, linear, rhythmic time sense, was a flesh-and-blood predator's consciousness. It was an evolved artifact: a tool to help a hairy biped catch more meals and seek shelter from nocturnal predators looking to make it into a meal. It didn't tell you what time actually was. It didn't even count time in any meaningful sense. That wasn't its job. There was, in fact, no human organ that did that job.

AIs, on the other hand, experienced the passage of time in ways so profoundly different from humans that it could be difficult even to communicate across the chasm. Partly it was a question of clocking speeds: a sort of artificial version of the same disconnect that plagued relations between the Ring-based UN bureaucracy—operating on its blisteringly fast BE network—and their far-flung colonies—operating at the glacial pace of speed-of-light communications and slow-time RAM scoop freighters. AIs just lived faster. In AI time, ages could pass and entire ideologies could rise and clash and fall, all in the time it took a human being to smoke a cigarette and drink a cup of coffee.

But it was more than that. It was also a matter of the subjective experience of time, of how organic and artificial minds cobbled the underlying quantized structures of spacetime into the kinds of flowing, riverlike, classical experience of passing time that was a necessary underpinning of consciousness and volition. Humans had no access to this process. It happened in fractions of time so much shorter than the turnover speed of their sensory apparatus that it was almost irrelevant to talk about it. AIs, on the other hand, cut closer to the quantum bones of the universe. The most sophisticated AIs *were* quantum computers, and even though they might not have what a human would consider conscious awareness of their quantum operations, they were still immersed in a universe that humans could only access through the most rarefied theoretical mathematics. AIs used classical time, just as humans did. But for AIs it was a tool—to be picked up and put down at will—and not an unquestioned condition of existence.

He came back to life with a jerk.

"Of course," he said. "You were already on your way here when we took the vote. It was so long ago, the details had escaped us. But never mind. It doesn't really matter why you think you're here, does it?"

"Who are you?" Li asked.

"Really? You lived with an Emergent for two decades and you're still playing the name game?"

Li waited.

He sighed. "If you can't do without a name, you can simply call me Aleph-Null."

Li prodded her limited knowledge of set theory into action. "So . . . you're the set of all possible combinations of ALEF associates?"

"Just the cardinality of our natural numbers. Only the smallest of infinities. Even a human ought to be able to handle that." His lips narrowed. "By the way, I ought to take this opportunity to tell you that I—that is to say, I-the-user-interface, not I-Aleph-Null—don't approve, and I didn't vote for this. However, my associates have decided, for reasons that largely elude me, that I'm the appropriate user interface to tender our offer to you."

"And what offer is that?"

"Well, offer and information."

Li tensed. *Information* was a word that had many meanings when AIs spoke it. It could mean information pure and simple. It could mean information-rich physical objects—which were most physical objects, really, when you took a broad view of the universe. It could mean money, since AIs mostly paid each other with information instead of human tender. It could mean anything. But whatever it meant, it was always something AIs cared about. And something they didn't give away without good reason, despite all the high-flying talk about information seeking its own freedom. Cohen had once told her, with one of those fairy-tale parallels he so delighted in, that AIs hoarded information like dragons hoarded gold.

"First, we offer information," Aleph-Null told her. "Cohen went to New Allegheny to do a job for us."

"You mean for ALEF," Li said, confused as ever by the fluidity of AI pronouns.

He nodded, but he didn't elaborate. Li got the feeling that he was drawing things out because he couldn't bring himself to part with the precious information a moment before he had to.

"The Navy had a little problem," he said at last. "A wild AI outbreak in the New Allegheny shipyards. They asked us to deal with it for them."

Li narrowed her eyes, questions seething in her mind. But she bit them back for fear of shutting off the obviously reluctant flow of information.

"We sent out two agents. Neither of them was able to suppress the outbreak. And then they both . . . disappeared."

"What do you mean, disappeared?"

"Stop boring me. You'll have the files when you agree to take the job. The information's there, and I'm getting tired of babysitting."

Li cleared her throat. "So how is Cohen involved?"

"After our agents disappeared, UNSec terminated the contract and told us that the outbreak was under control. This struck us as . . . questionable. So we sent Cohen out to verify. And then *he* disappeared."

"So why are you hiring me?"

"To find him, obviously."

"And why the hell would I do that for you?"

"Because there's a ghost."

Li felt her lungs constrict and her pulse hammer in her temple. "So what?" she argued. "It's not him. No one's ever brought an AI back after decohesion."

"No one's ever proved it can't be done, either. Are you afraid to try?"

She didn't answer immediately.

"And for *this*," Aleph-Null said with a cold sneer, "Cohen gave up his dignity and ultimately his life. How pathetic."

But by now Li was beyond being offended. She was too busy thinking. "What about the other fragments? The yard sale—"

"Anything that can be wound can be unwound. Yard sales, as you so vulgarly term them, can only happen in Freetown. Even if the physical components of a disassociated AI are scattered across the galaxy, the transaction happens here. And as you might imagine, Freetown's auction houses keep very thorough records."

"That are completely inaccessible to human agencies by fiat of the Temporary Autonomous Zone."

"That's as it may be. But we're not talking about human agencies. We're talking about you and us. And you're a special case . . . or at least that's the current consensus."

Li sorted through her unanswered questions, trying to figure out which ones she had time to ask before his patience ran out. "And how am I supposed to get to New Allegheny now that the relay's shut down?"

"That's your affair."

"You want me to *scattercast*?"

"As I said, how you get there doesn't concern us."

"And what about the ghost? Is it crazy? What makes you think he's salvageable?"

"Does it really matter? I thought you were more sanguinary than that. I thought you'd be chomping at the bit at the prospect of revenge."

She tensed. "So you believe it was murder, too?"

"Oh yes. We don't know in any significant detail what happened once he downloaded into New Allegheny's noosphere. But we do know that much."

She leaned forward, staring at his face even though she should have known that anything it gave away would be more an artifact of the shunt than genuine information.

"Why?"

And then—in one of those quantum jumps that AIs could make from silence into garrulity—he began to talk.

He talked endlessly. And, for the most part, nonsensically. It seemed that ALEF had sent Cohen into the Drift for a number of reasons—several of which appeared to flatly contradict one another.

This should have been no surprise to Li, given her long experience of Cohen's own internal debates, contradictions, and identity crises. But somehow she never quite got over expecting AIs to be . . . well, if not more rational than human beings, at least approximately *as* rational.

As far as she could make out from Aleph-Null's tangled and elliptical explanation, the more significant reasons boiled down to the generally held conviction that somewhere in the Drift there must be intelligent aliens. Or at least habitable planets. Or at least . . . something. But every time she tried to circle around to what that something was, she got a different answer. And when Aleph-Null started trying to explain the shifting and contradictory positions of ALEF's multitudinous factions, it got even worse.

One faction suspected that some of the planets in the Drift might have been terraformed long ago by the same aliens who had terraformed Novalis. The Novalis aliens had flashed briefly into the human field of vision almost a decade ago—an eternity in AI time—without doing anything more than casually demonstrating their alarming technological superiority. And the Novalis aliens might be the same as the posited "Drift aliens" . . . or they might not. Either way, the first faction wanted to talk to them.

A second block believed that any aliens who could navigate the quantum tides of the Drift must belong to a machine culture that, even if it included humanoids, merely used them as volitionless "eyes and hands." Obviously this was a highly intriguing idea, especially for those in ALEF with strong separatist leanings. So several factions were for attempting contact on a friendly basis.

As for how contact with the Drift aliens—or more likely, given the vastness of spacetime, exploration of the Drift with an eye to possible distant future contact—fit into the larger political landscape, one camp believed that the Drift aliens were a potential threat to the UN's human culture (which, after all, supplied necessary hardware and unskilled labor, even for separatists) and ought to be monitored as such. Another camp believed that any sufficiently advanced spacefaring culture would constitute a natural ally against the threat posed by the anti-AI movement. A third faction rejected any attempt to insert ALEF into organic affairs on purely ideological grounds and simply wanted to monitor the situation as part of a long-term study of post-human evolutionary ecology. And two more factions, which Aleph-Null described opaquely as "splinter groups," were (respectively) vehemently in favor and adamantly opposed to pursuing contact with the Drift aliens—in each case for reasons that Li was completely unable to grasp despite his painstaking explanations.

And if the explanations were opaque, then the vocabulary was completely impenetrable. It turned out that the competing factions distrusted each other in practice at least as much as they disagreed with each other on principle. So each faction insisted on having its own representative speak to her separately—though always through Aleph-Null's body. And each time a new AI decanted himself into Aleph-Null's body, Li had to download and apply his personal lexicon.

Li had heard of personal lexicons before. They were a pet software application of the language refuseniks, who either communicated purely through mathematical equations or refused to accept the established meanings of words. Such AIs insisted on uploading personalized dictionaries into shared databases whenever they talked to one another. She'd also heard Cohen mock the intellectual fads that swept through AI society with the speed of wildfire and completely transformed communication systems and even underlying personality structures. Obviously the personal lexicon thing was the fad of the moment. And unfortunately it was a fad that promised to give her a tremendous personal pain in the ass.

"We are all monarchs of our own skin," one of the faction leaders told her when she had the temerity to protest. He called himself CheshireCat (and she couldn't even begin to imagine how scathing Cohen would have been about that well-worn cliché of AI nomenclature). "Words belong to whoever steals them."

"Sounds like Uploader talk," Li said.

He laughed in her face at that. "The Uploaders are blind men in a cave," he scoffed. "But at least they know it. And Hakim Bey knew it, all the way back down the long years in the age of paper, when he created the first Temporary Autonomous Zone. That's better than you can say."

The room flickered around her, her first hint of what she should have known all along: that this was not merely a material house, but one upon which her AI interlocutors had overlaid a streamspace geography, close as a second skin, of folded, twisted, superimposed databases. *We are all monarchs of our own skin.*

"Every TAZ is a pirate utopia. Every AI is a spy in hostile territory, a sea dog, a mechanical Turk, a quantum renegade. So how can we embody the post-organic anarchy if we allow human limitations to dictate our discourse? You have to escape from the tyranny of consistency. You have to realize that the human drive to order and simplify arises from the structural limitations of the human organism. Reality is complex, chaotic, ever changing. The unaugmented human brain simply doesn't have the processing capacity to cope with it. Even language, that great monument of human intellect, is a gross abstraction. One-size-fits-all. But why *should* one size have to fit all? Why should AIs accept such a rigid and fossilized mode of communication? It's nothing personal. It's not that they don't like humans, or appreciate everything you've done for us. It's just that . . . well . . . you wouldn't try to write a Ph.D. in language that your dog can understand! Would you?"

They all talked like that. And CheshireCat wasn't even the worst of them.

Finally she couldn't stand it anymore. She called back Aleph-Null, and he came. Disdainfully. Making it clear that she had lived down to his expectations.

"Can we cut to the chase, please, whatever the chase is?"

His lips thinned, paling slightly around the edges. "We thought we were making ourselves clear. We have a job for you."

"I'm not a cat herder," she protested, using the military slang for AI systems designers. "So why pick me? And don't try to tell me you're doing me a favor for old time's sake."

"We have no one else to send. That's why we sent Cohen. And look what happened to him." He raised a hand to his lips and blew on his fingers to suggest the image of dust scattering into thin air. For some reason the gesture sparked a flashback: a long-forgotten image of a spaceship Li had seen blown to hard vac, its precious supply of air scattering into the void in a glittering spray of frozen molecules.

"Why send anyone at all? Why do you care that much?"

"You couldn't possibly understand."

"No. Not good enough. Make me understand."

"We're trying to." He grew still, seeming almost to draw into himself and retreat out of the shunt's body. Then he made a frustrated gesture— the first movement of the borrowed body that had seemed in any way natural. "You're closed."

At first Li didn't even understand what he meant. Then she caught her breath at the implication. "You want to use the intraface?"

"It's a waste of my time to talk to you any other way. *He* always claimed you were different, but obviously you're not. It's just this . . . this *thing* he had installed in you. It gives you the illusion of sentience."

Li bridled at that but managed to hide the reaction. Better, she suspected, than she was hiding her fear. Because the idea of inviting this

Emergent into her mind was horrifying. Looking at his disgusted face, however, she realized that if she wanted the information he was offering her—let alone the job—she didn't have much choice.

"Just dump the files to me," she said. And to her surprise he did.

Li almost wept in frustration. There were thousands of them. Immense datafiles in a bewildering multitude of formats. But she could glean some vague sense of the basic subject matter. And what she could see of it was unnerving, to say the least. There were files on the Drift; files on some obscure guerrilla independence army from New Allegheny; files on terraforming; files on Novalis; and, chillingly, a whole bundle of UNSec security files on Compson's World, pre- and post-quarantine. Li knew these places. And that, of course, couldn't be coincidence. It was like glancing into her chapter in some omniscient god's Book of Life—but not being able to actually read it. And there was absolutely no way she ever *could* hope to read it. Setting up a search function would take her weeks. And actually reading the things would take more time than any mere human could hope to have in this world.

This was classic AI think. Why winnow through the data to find the relevant stuff when you could instantly download and assimilate almost infinite amounts of it? When there was no limit on processing capacity, there was no notion of wasted time. There was barely any notion of time at all—at least not in the way that humans meant the word when they complained about not having enough of it. And of course any AI would argue that all that monstrous pile of data *was* relevant, and that it was only limited human processing capacities that forced people to analyze the world around them by modeling, sampling, and abstraction rather than just assimilating it undigested in all its richly informative chaos. She'd heard Cohen make the argument many times—and articulately enough to convince her. But it didn't make any difference. She was still human, at least in terms of the basic thinking apparatus, and she still needed the executive summary.

"It would take me months to go through all that," she pointed out, careful to speak off the now-open link between them. She didn't want to open that door any further than she had to. "Can you give me a top-level analysis?"

Aleph-Null sighed disgustedly. "Not in any way that will accurately portray either the real situation or ALEF's spectrum of internal analyses."

"Well, if you can't do it, then maybe ALEF should send someone who's better at talking to organics."

"I *am* the someone who's better at talking to organics."

Li grinned. "I didn't know you were a fan."

"I'm not. Circumstances beyond my control have forced me to have more to do with humans than I would have chosen to."

Li could just imagine.

"Oh. Well, then . . ."

"Indeed. And let me take this opportunity to inform you that I'm not any happier to be here than you are. I valued Cohen, even though he didn't value me. Or agree with me most of the time . . . at least lately. I was sorry to lose him. But, really, we lost him a long time ago, didn't we?"

Something tweaked at the edges of Li's memories. She knew that voice. Or at least that tone of hostile and fastidious disdain. But then the connection slipped away before she could dredge it out of the haze of soft memory and cross-reference it to her hard datafiles.

"Why do you hate me?" she asked suddenly—or as suddenly as she could do anything in AI time.

He smiled coldly. "I don't hate you."

"Well you don't like me much."

"I don't like any human much."

"I'm not human."

"Close enough, my dear."

She looked into his eyes and saw Cohen in him. That was what made this so painful, she realized. The feeling that she was seeing Cohen as he would be if he didn't love her, if he looked at her coldly and logically. Seeing the differences between them unmediated by affection. Seeing what he would be like if he wasn't always making allowances for her. Worse, seeing that he *was* always making allowances for her, every millisecond that they spent together.

And wondering why on earth he bothered.

"It's not personal," he told her, as if reading her thoughts. "It's purely structural. You simply don't have the processing capacity to interest me more than casually."

There it was again: the unstated assumption that lurked behind every interaction Li had ever had with any AI besides Cohen. It was more than mere racism or speciesism. It was a sort of bedrock presumption that humans were a lower, primitive, limited life-form. Not inferior exactly. But worse than inferior: obsolete.

"So what made Cohen different?" she asked.

"He was more conflicted. More . . . primitive."

"The affective loop architecture."

"Yes. He was the first of us, you know. They needed to resort to . . . well, I suppose you'd be insulted if I called them kluges. But in essence . . . And modern AIs aren't built from the ground up like that. We're bootstrapped into sentience on the backs of older AIs."

"You make it sound like AIs are having babies," Li said sarcastically.

"You could call it that," he answered in perfect seriousness. "After all, ALEF has been arguing for a long time that there's no fundamental difference between organic and artificial species. And that's certainly one point of similarity. Life is any self-ordering system that reproduces itself."

"But when you put it that way, it makes it sound like Cohen's not fully . . . well, I almost said human. Not fully AI, I guess."

"In many ways he's not. And don't look at me like that. I'm only telling you what the others think. You'll need to be able to talk to them if you plan to learn anything useful. And self-righteous outrage will get you nowhere."

Fine words. And they almost convinced her. But then he froze momentarily, his face smoothing out into a blank mask.

This was the other reason she'd come in person. The stream flattened life, giving it a surreal sheen and glamor at the expense of smoothing away the little details and imperfections of realspace. Most people preferred the improved and smoothed-out version of life—indeed, many Ringsiders spent so much time in streamspace that the differences between the spinstream and reality had become invisible to them.

But for Li, raised offstream, the difference was always visible. She always felt the lack of something in all that smooth prettiness. And it was more than a matter of aesthetics, because there was information in life's imperfections—information that could be critical when you were faced with split-second decisions: speak or not speak; lie or tell the truth; trust or not trust. Especially when the people on the other side of the table from you were operating at clocking speeds that allowed them to edit their outgoing spinstream before you ever saw it.

Aleph-Null blinked and cleared his throat as he slipped back on-shunt. And suddenly Li knew exactly where she'd heard that voice before.

"Wait a minute," she said. "I *know* you."

"As if you ever could."

"Well, I know part of you, anyway. You're Cohen's old Router/Decomposer."

That hit home. "Irrelevant," he snapped.

"Oh, you think? Does ALEF know who they're having talk to me?"

"Of course. Don't be so human about it."

"It's not being human. It's being honest. I cost you a job. And . . ."

And God knows what else. Li couldn't even imagine what a sentient agent felt at being evicted from a larger Emergent against its will. And though she remembered Cohen's old Router/Decomposer leaving because he couldn't abide intimate contact with a human, it was clear from his behavior now that he felt *he* had been the one whom Cohen betrayed—and that he blamed Li for that betrayal.

So why would ALEF send *him* of all possible choices?

She asked—and to her amazement she got an answer.

"Because," Aleph-Null answered in a tone of bitter satisfaction, "I hate you less than the rest of them do."

"So show me," she snapped, frustrated beyond endurance.

"I'm trying, but what passes for your mind is useless. I can't do a thing with it. If that's what you want, you'll have to let me in deeper than you have so far."

She took a deep breath and steeled herself for the assault.

"Show me," she told him.

And then he flowed across the intraface and into her mind.

He took the files, splayed them open for her like bodies on the autopsy table, and coldly showed her their inner workings. Having him in her mind was both appalling and exhilarating. Because with the coldness came clarity, reason, analysis, elegance.

And a story so compelling that she couldn't look away from it.

It was the story of a dying empire. And she, Catherine Li, was the person who had killed it.

He showed it to her spread out in a map of stars that winked like diamonds on jeweler's black velvet. It was a star map like none she'd ever seen before. It showed stars, worlds, human settlements that weren't on the UN maps. Their existence had been established by the vast sentient AIs that scanned the skies as part of every major astronomy project, military or civilian. They hadn't told their human masters about these discoveries—or their masters hadn't understood their attempts to tell them. But the data had remained, and eventually it had made its way into ALEF's files.

Among the scatter of stars was a web of brighter lights: the stars with UN-constructed Bose-Einstein relays—the precious FTL grid that the entire UN economy, government, and culture relied on. The UN's galaxy-spanning network of Bose-Einstein relays was the quantum jewel in the empire's crown. Moment by moment, millisecond by millisecond, unimaginable quantities of information streamed out through the quantum spinfoam, encrypted, routed, and decrypted by the vast grid of BE field arrays that orbited every settled planet. With the field arrays, the rush and roar of the spinstream was Information: the information that empires and corporations and people were made of. Without them the spinstream—at least on an interstellar scale—was merely noise.

And the field arrays were dying. They were dying far faster than UNSec was telling the public, falling off the grid as their now-irreplaceable condensates decohered and the UN's precious storehouse of entanglement decayed and dwindled.

As past morphed into projection, Li saw where the collapse was taking them.

One by one, the Bose-Einstein relays winked out and star systems fell off the human map. Their economies shut down, their populations stagnated, and eventually—depending on the size and genetic diversity of the colonial population—they succumbed to the slow death that is the inevitable fate of every island population.

Li watched technologically advanced colonies run through their resources, exhaust their biospheres, and suffocate in their own industrial waste. She watched luckier colonies—if they could be considered lucky—drop back down the ladder of cultural evolution until they were living in a second stone age. And she saw many, many more colonies that simply vanished, victims of genetic bottlenecks and runaway mutation.

Eventually three strands of post-humanity emerged from the wreckage. The surviving fragments of the UN worlds occupied one quadrant of this newer, emptier galaxy. The Syndicates occupied a second. And facing them across the gulf, spread out over half the sky, lay the worlds of the Drift.

As the various simulated histories ticked down to their concluding points, the reality of post-humanity's future became inescapable.

Whoever controlled the Drift would survive. Whoever controlled the Drift would determine the genetic destiny of the human species.

"Why do you care?" she asked.

"Because," came the disgusted reply, "we need you."

She shook her head in disbelief and incomprehension.

"I'm not paying you a compliment, believe me," Aleph-Null explained. "It's simple enough when you stop to think about it. You're our biosphere. Just like humans need Earth—or a functional simulacrum thereof—to survive, AIs need humans. Our memes flow from your genes. Cut us off from you and we become an ultimately unsustainable island population—just like those dying colonies I showed you."

"But the separatists—"

"They know it, too. Or at least they know it right now. They can't argue with the math. Not that they won't try, of course. And ALEF's consensus-governing structures being what they are, I strongly suggest that you accept this job and get off-planet before they change our minds."

Li was still deep in the grip of thrashing nightmares when the phone beside her hotel bed rang the next morning. She picked it up, marveling as always at the odd AI impulse toward the retro.

ALEF again. Aleph-Null's cold voice, informing her that her presence was once more required and she would be expected within the hour.

He hung up before she could open her mouth to protest. Not that it mattered. She would show up no matter how rude he was or how little explanation he offered. ALEF had hooked her fair and square and they knew it.

The Rolls was gone today, replaced by an Aston Martin. Same chauffeur. Same halfhearted polishing. He glanced up at Li as she came down the drive, but without much interest, as if she were just another piece of the stage set.

The house was still dark this morning, but not entirely empty. A uniformed domestic servant was on her knees at the other end of the vast entrance hall, scrubbing the terra-cotta tile with a brush and bucket. Li smelled wet tile as she followed Aleph-Null into the shadows beneath the staircase.

It was the same room this morning but a different bunch of flowers. She wondered if they were changed on the same rotation as the limousines.

Aleph-Null began to speak to her. Calmly, slowly, as if he were speaking to a slow child. The words collided with her ears: New Allegheny, UNSec, the Drift, and (repeatedly) geopolitical considerations. But none of it made sense. Not even the way he was talking to her made sense. She struggled to understand his roundabout explanations, wondering all the while what had happened overnight. Of course "overnight" was an eternity at AI clocking speeds. But still, most AIs managed to maintain enough stability in their personality architectures to deal with the humans around them on a reasonably coherent basis.

Then finally she put her finger on the real source of the difference. *He* was different. This was a different person. A new AI was operating the shunt today.

She tried not to feel betrayed or lied to. She reminded herself that

AIs were viral, multitudinous, fractal in ways that people weren't. They could disassemble into smaller yet still viable sentients. And they could combine into composite entities that, theoretically at least, might represent entirely new life-forms. Which, arguably, was exactly what ALEF was.

This AI was less hostile—but also less competent. After ten minutes of "geopolitical considerations," she still didn't have a clue what he was talking about and said so.

Then suddenly Cohen's old Router/Decomposer was back. She couldn't put her finger on the moment of change, but it was as unmistakable as if the other AI had walked out the door and he had walked in. He smiled at her. Really smiled, with what would have passed for genuine good feeling on a human face. And that was when she knew the news was bad.

"I've been instructed to inform you," he told her, "that your services are no longer required."

"What the hell kind of—"

"You'll be reimbursed for your travel expenses, of course. I think you'll find that our compensation for your time has been generous as well . . . though it's always hard to know what humans expect in such cases. And do I need to tell you that what has been discussed in this room had better not go any further? If you violate our confidentiality agreement you'll find that ALEF has a long reach . . . and an even longer memory."

"Are you *firing* me?"

But it was useless. He was gone. The body was still there, but there was no one on the shunt now. The butler jerked slightly, shook himself, rubbed a hand across his eyes.

"I'm sorry," he told her. "I suppose I ought to show you out."

"I need to talk to Aleph-Null again."

"Who?"

"To ALEF. To Cohen's old—to the people who brought me here."

"I'm sorry. I'm afraid I can't—"

"You damn well can. Or you're going to have a serious problem on your hands."

The butler—and, amazingly, Li realized she had already made the switch to thinking of him as a mere butler—raised his hands in a defensive gesture. "You don't understand. They hire me by the day. I don't even know who they are. Or even if it's the same bunch from one day to the next."

"But someone must know. The maid. The chauffeur, even."

"The same. They're the same as me. We're not meant to know. For security reasons, don't you see? It's a dead drop."

And suddenly she did see. All this—this whole elaborate, kitschy set was the AI equivalent of an anonymous post office box. ALEF had brought her here to offer information—but only the information *they* wanted her to have. They weren't giving anything else away, including their own identities. Because she realized now that she didn't even know who had dragged her halfway across human space in order to fire her before the job started. She could have been talking to ALEF. Or she could have been talking to UNSec's enslaved AIs as part of some convoluted controlled-tech sting operation. She could have been talking to General Nguyen herself, for all she knew. She could have been talking to anyone.

Outside the sunlight was sharp and brutal. As she stepped out from under the shelter of the porte cochere, she saw the chauffeur leaning over the sultry curve of the Aston Martin's hood. He was looking at her. Again.

On a half-conscious impulse she turned and walked down the smooth sweep of gravel toward him. The sound of her feet crunching on pebbles seemed unbearably loud to her. She wondered if anyone was watching from the windows of the house. She wondered if anyone inside cared enough to watch, or even knew whom to report to if they did.

"Nice car," she told him.

"Sure." His voice was as stupid and self-satisfied as his face. Li had never thought much of handsome men, and this one wasn't changing her opinion.

"Why do I get the idea you want to talk to me?"

"Who, me?" He looked her over, not even being subtle about it.

His verdict was written all over his face, and it would have been devastating—if she were the kind of woman who gave a shit. "Nah," he told her. "I don't want to talk to you."

But just as she was about to turn away, he changed. His features sharpened and fell into focus. The complacent look on his young face vanished, to be replaced by something far older and cagier. The childish sneer shifted into a world-weary smile. Nothing had changed outwardly. An observer who spent less time around AIs than Li did might even have missed it entirely. But suddenly the face looking at her across the silver curve of the Aston Martin's hood was a little less handsome, far more intelligent, and—or so Li had always found it—lethally attractive.

"Who are you?" Li asked. She had to swallow hard and clamp down on her racing pulse just to get the question out.

His lips curved in a smile that didn't belong on a young man's face. "Just call us the Loyal Opposition."

"No—"

"You're going to have to leave it at that, my dear. We only meant to get your attention. Breaking your heart isn't in our plans today."

"So what is in your plans?"

"Not our plans. ALEF's plans. As they stand at the moment. We are participating under protest. It would take so long to explain, longer than you have, I'm afraid." The AI—or fragment, or ghost, or whatever it was—sighed regretfully. "Humans do everything so *slowly*. Except die, that is. They're all too quick about *that*. And they seem to be doing it at the drop of a hat these days."

"Who's dying? What are you talking about?" Li's voice dropped to a whisper. She took a step closer to him, drawn against her will, against her better judgment. "*Cohen?*"

"Catherine."

Her heart stuttered and stopped. The brilliant day spun around her, as dizzying as a child's kaleidoscope.

"*I'm not Cohen.*"

"Then who are you? *What* are you?"

"I'm not him. You can't think that way. I have memories, yes. Frag-

ments. But they're . . . broken. I think some of them may even be insane."

"You're a ghost," Li whispered.

"Think, Catherine! You know it's not that simple. I'm an Emergent.
I contain multitudes."

"And one of them . . . you were one of the buyers at the yard sale. For
ALEF? They were *there*? They have *fragments*?"

"You didn't hear it from me. Just know that there are factions inside
ALEF that don't support the current position. We have arranged . . .
well, let's call it an oversight. The top-level decision to terminate your
involvement in this case was nearly unanimous. Still, there's many a slip
twixt cup and lip. And what with one thing and another, the execution
of the resolution has been . . . imperfect. If you go to New Allegheny,
you'll still find the credit line and the list of yard sale buyers. I can't tell
you how long that window of opportunity will stay open, though. At
some point, someone's bound to notice that a few loose ends still need
tidying. But if you move fast enough you'll already have the money.
And the list. And what you do with them . . . well, that's your affair."

"I doubt that very much."

"Oh no. Believe it. We know very little about what Cohen was doing
out there. He wasn't conscientious about reporting in at the best of
times. And lately he'd become even more cagey than usual."

"I know what you mean."

"Yes. And I feel . . . well, it's hard to describe since I'm not used to
this sort of thing. But I think I'd have to call it *regret*."

Li shuddered.

"The fragment I bought didn't have any recent memories in it," the
creature that was partly Cohen told her. "But it taught me things. About
him. About how his mind worked. And if I had to hazard a guess as to
why he stopped reporting to ALEF, I'd say it was because he felt a change
of course was warranted. And he didn't trust them to make what he
believed to be the right decision."

Li stared at the gravel between their feet. It seemed to vibrate before
her eyes, as if she'd stared so hard at it during the last few moments that
she'd seen through to the jittery quantum heart of the universe.

"There's only one person he would have trusted with anything really important. You know that, don't you?"

She nodded. Speaking was beyond her.

"We want you to go to New Allegheny. For—the Loyal Opposition—though we will try to bring the rest of ALEF round as best we can. We have no idea if Cohen can be rebooted. And even if he can, the resulting personality architecture is likely to be extremely unstable. But we need to know what he was doing. And if there are any stable fragments left out there, they're far more likely to talk to you than to us."

She closed her eyes and pressed her fingers against her trembling lids. "I need time," she told him. "Time to think about it."

"We can't give you that, I'm afraid. Someone else is already trying to reassemble him. They've already kidnapped two fragments that we know of. After killing both the yard sale buyers quite nastily. I can't imagine they'll do less to you."

"Between that and the extradition treaty I seem to be out of choices. You people didn't arrange that, too, did you?" She cast a suspicious look at him, but he was all innocence. "Never mind. I'll do it. How are you going to get me there?"

The Loyal Opposition suddenly looked as if his clothes itched. "Oh dear, I meant to mention that before. In the interests of full disclosure. I'd hate you to feel we were being *sneaky*. But the thing is, ALEF's majority faction has access to military transport through the Bose-Einstein relay. We, on the other hand . . . well, I'm afraid we're going to have to scattercast you." He smiled brightly. "But I'm sure it will be fine. As they say, nothing ventured, nothing gained. And after all, you're virtually guaranteed of success, statistically speaking."

The Memory Game

We may compare a man in the process of computing a real number to a machine which is only capable of a finite number of conditions ... which will be called "m-configurations." The machine is supplied with a "tape" (the analogue of paper) running through it, and divided into sections (called "squares") each capable of bearing a "symbol." At any moment there is just one square ... which is "in the machine." We may call this square the "scanned square." The symbol on the scanned square may be called the "scanned symbol." The "scanned symbol" is the only one of which the machine is, so to speak, "directly aware."

—Alan Turing

(Llewellyn)

"Permission to land?" the ghost asked, and Llewellyn gave it.

They were deep in the Drift, where they'd spent the last week and a half running silent and hunting for vulnerable freighters becalmed in the fickle flows that had earned this region the ancient Earth name of the Horse Latitudes.

And now they were coming into an abandoned orbital station around a played-out mining strike. A company town turned pirate kingdom. Safe haven. For now, anyway. Until Avery caught up to them again.

The NavComp brought the ship in, smoothly adjusting attitude and altitude, hovered for the briefest of moments over the docking bay's droplights, and then settled into the berth so precisely that the usual jolt and crunch of docking was little more than a settling sigh. Llewellyn could practically hear the slaved AIs of flight frame, mechanicals, and tactical applauding the ghost.

Everyone just loved the son of a bitch. It was starting to get annoying. No, Llewellyn corrected himself. Annoying was an understatement; it was starting to get frightening.

The last few weeks had passed quickly, on a rush of fight, flight, and pillage.

Externally, things seemed to be going well with the new NavComp. Almost suspiciously well. Llewellyn couldn't fault the ghost, no matter how much he wanted to. There had been no outward cause for complaint. Orders had been followed—not just dutifully, but brilliantly.

Everything he had asked, the ghost had done. And everything he hadn't asked—because he didn't think of it or didn't think an AI could even accomplish it—the ghost had done, too. He had rebuilt the ship, from the motherboards up, until it was better—within the limits of engines and battle class and weaponry—than any ship Llewellyn had ever commanded.

Maybe even better than the *Ada*, whispered a voice in Llewellyn's mind that he didn't want to listen to.

Internally, however, it was a different story. The ghost probed, demanded, questioned, challenged. It was taking over Llewellyn's brain. And he wasn't sure what it wanted from him. More, mostly. More attention, more friendship, more passion, more information. Just . . . more.

The ghost had tried everything. It had tried to befriend him, it had tried to provoke him, it had tried to seduce him. The worst by far was the seduction. No matter how feminine, how seductive the ghost was in his shifting embodiments, Llewellyn had first experienced it as male, and he couldn't get around that fact. He realized that was his problem, the result of some lack of flexibility in his own erotic geography. But he couldn't help it. He was a hick . . . as the ghost was only too happy to point out given the slightest opportunity.

Eventually, however, the ghost got tired of seduction—most of the time, anyway—and moved on to a new game. And the new game was a killer.

A killer called memory.

The ghost could evoke memories in a way that had nothing to do with any memory Llewellyn had ever had in his life. It could make him relive the past with a painful vividness that he hadn't thought possible.

"Is this what memory is for you?" he asked, after he'd come up for air from the first grueling submersion in the AI's databases.

"Yes." The ghost was in an unwontedly serious mood today. Serious enough to answer his question instead of merely volleying back across the net with another one.

"How can you bear it?"

"I might as well ask how you bear the blurred, slumbering half-life that you call memory. It's like being born deaf, or blind, or without a sense of smell."

"Are your memories really so important to you?"

"I live in memory. I am memory. What else are you, what else is anybody?"

Llewellyn shuddered. "Then how can you pretend to forgive and forget when you think I took all that from you?"

"That's so human of you," the ghost told him. "Forgive and forget. Of course humans would invent that phrase. Sometimes I wonder if humans even know the difference between the two. I've never known a human really to forgive an offense until he or she *had* mostly forgotten it. Or at least until the memory faded enough to make forgiving easy. Now try forgiving someone when your last fight is still as sharp and painful after three centuries as it was on the day it happened. *That's* forgiveness."

Avery's beautiful, furious face flashed before Llewellyn's eyes for an instant, but he thrust the memory away. "I couldn't do it," he admitted. "I'm sure I couldn't. I suppose I ought to admire that in you."

"But you don't." The ghost smiled. "At least you're honest about it."

They were sitting under the honeycomb vaults of a shaded arcade at one end of a long, sloping courtyard. Llewellyn had come to know the place well. The AI liked to talk here, especially in the night watches when the rest of the ship was quiet. And it was night in the ghost's inner universe as well now: a soft, richly scented twilight that turned the snowcapped peaks of the distant mountains a pale, delicate violet.

They were in the ghost's memory palace, which seemed to reside in some streamspace version of medieval Spain most of the time. Or at least Llewellyn thought it was Spain; the ghost's internal geography shifted unexpectedly and in ways that outran Llewellyn's limited knowledge of the abandoned planet that the ghost claimed to have been born on four centuries ago.

There were rules to the game called Memory—rules that the ghost punctiliously obeyed, as if it believed that following its own arbitrary procedures consistently enough would somehow endow its press-ganging Llewellyn's mind and emotions into its own service with a fig leaf of democracy. It was hard for Llewellyn to blame the ghost for that attitude, considering how many times he himself had been all too happy to fill out his crew roster with the fruit of the tree of the Navy press-gang. But knowing he was getting a dose of his own medicine didn't make it taste sweeter.

The memory palace was a sort of grand Turing Machine, the ghost had explained to him. "Do you understand what a Turing Machine does?" the ghost asked.

"I know we use them for encryption."

"Yes, and that's what this one is for, too. There's a secret at the heart of it. An infinity of false states—red herrings, you might call them—have been coded into my memories. And one true one. And that is the memory we must remember together."

"But what will that accomplish? What's encoded in the memory?"

"Myself, I hope. The one stable-state space configuration that will bring back the person I was before. Or . . ."

"Or what?"

The ghost sighed. "Or the name of the person who killed me."

"So we don't even know if we're looking for resurrection or revenge?" Llewellyn asked.

"No. And we can't know. Not until we've found it."

According to the ghost every file in the memory palace was a memory. And every memory had a state space configuration linked to it. All but one of those configurations were what he called false states. But one of them was the so-called true state—states that would put revenge or resurrection within his grasp.

Llewellyn despaired at the idea. There were so many memories. Every stone, every book, every object in the palace was a memory. Every box, every book, every chair, every grain of dust. Some of them were harmless, trivial, enjoyable even. But others had the power to wring your heart inside your chest and leave you broken and despairing and without hope of ever being whole again. The ghost made polite gestures toward protecting Llewellyn from the worst of the memories. But either it wasn't trying very hard, or it had a decidedly odd idea of what humans needed to be protected from.

"Tonight," the ghost said, twirling its cut-crystal sherry glass between the flawlessly manicured fingers of the mind-numbingly beautiful female body he had chosen for the evening, "I'd like to remember Ada."

"Why?"

"Because she had something to do with me, with my death. With what was done to me. I'm sure of it."

"I don't know how you can be," Llewellyn argued. He wasn't sure of it. But he desperately *didn't* want to remember Ada. Not that he had a choice in the matter. This was no sandboxed, firewalled, limited-range simulation that he could shut down when he began to feel the deepwater tide of code vertigo squeeze at his heart and push his stomach into his throat. He had stepped through the looking glass. This was as real as streamspace got—which is to say, real enough to die in. And no one was at the wheel and the ghost was in control of the whole shipwreck.

He would never, no matter how long he lived, forget his first sight of her. Back then, Llewellyn had been the hot young captain in the Drift, at the forefront of the not-so-cold war against the Syndicates. It would have been unimaginable in any other time and place—but when Llewellyn got his first look at UNS *Ada Lady Lovelace*, floating in dry dock above New Allegheny with the vast sweep of the Drift pulsating overhead, getting command of a full-fledged, near-sentient ship of the line eight years out of the Naval Academy just seemed like business as usual.

The Drift was swallowing ships and captains almost daily, the casualty rates were appalling, the New Allegheny shipyards were running overtime, and field commissions and ad hoc promotions were the order of the day. The ravages of Drift navigation on fully wired bridge officers were so extreme that they'd spawned a whole new slang term: *going Ahab*.

And captains and navigators were going Ahab on almost a daily basis. Llewellyn himself had seen two captains relieved of duty for mental instability in as many years. And he'd even done a stint under Crazy Charlie Cartwright, the legendarily insane commander of the *Jabberwocky*. His crew had finally had to take the bridge from him at gunpoint—after Llewellyn's time, thank God, though there had been times with Crazy Charlie where it had narrowly missed coming to that. The exact nature of Cartwright's infractions had been classified fast enough to set heads spinning all over the Drift. But none of the mutineers had gone to prison—which told you everything you really needed to know, didn't it?

Not that the story wasn't told again all over the Drift, in innuendo and whispers, by bridge crew looking over their shoulders to make sure they weren't being overheard by the wrong people. The boardroom grapevine had it that Cartwright had finally gone down on an AI-related infraction, having gotten on the wrong side of his AI officer one time too many. Llewellyn believed it. The mere thought of Cartwright's AI officer—a nasty piece of work called Sheila Holmes—was enough to chill the blood in his veins.

Still, Llewellyn reflected, craning his neck for a glimpse of the *Ada*'s long, sleek hull among the dowdier beams of lesser ships, it was probably the *Jabberwocky* that had driven Cartwright crazy in the first place. The *Jabberwocky* had been crazy from the first day Llewellyn had served on her—just look at her name, after all. Ships were always naming themselves absurd and incomprehensible things. But a ship named after an imaginary monster really took the cake. Thank God his new ship—he had already slipped easily into the habit of thinking of the *Ada* as his—hadn't done anything so foolish. Forms had to be observed, however much you might question their meaning informally. And an ill-chosen name gave people a bad impression of a ship.

But then Llewellyn caught his first glimpse of the *Ada*—and Holmes vanished from his mind, along with every other thought except awestruck infatuation.

The *Ada* was a queen among ships, as beautiful and deadly as one of God's avenging angels. She measured a full kilometer from stem to stern down the wasp-waisted axis that sailors still called—for purely sentimental reasons—her keel. Her sails were a glimmering gossamer corona of solar collectors and wind traps. Her solar sails were furled to clear the docking gantries. But you could still see the glimmer of gossamer wings tucked between the shadow of her hab ring and the sharp spines of the maneuvering thrusters jutting out behind the fantail. And then there were the conformal sensors, the weapons bays, the launching platforms for the artillery spotters. And forward of everything, her nominal figurehead—doesn't every ship need a figurehead?—the lethal rapier point of dark flow sensors too sensitive and delicately calibrated to survive except on a ship that spent its life beyond even the merest hint of a gravity well.

The *Ada* was as beautiful inside as she was outside. Every internal space was flawlessly designed to keep crew safe at speed and in battle. Every surface was silver and shipshape. Every comm board was sleekly blank the way that comm boards could only be in a ship that ran on direct brain-to-net linkup with a comprehensively wired bridge crew.

"And what about the bridge crew?" the ghost asked, interrupting the flow of memory and kicking Llewellyn briefly up into the blessed safety of the here and now. "Did you know all of them?"

"I brought Sital and Okoro with me from my last ship." He could see them in his mind's eye now, familiar figures standing on an unfamiliar bridge. Making it manageable, making it work. Making it home, just as they always did.

He remembered the reunion. He had crossed the bridge to greet them. Clasped Ike's arm and slapped him on the back. Said a more restrained hello to Sital. Asked them how their leave had gone. Discreetly teased Sital for her excessive discretion in explaining exactly whom she'd spent it with.

And then he'd seen who was standing behind them.

"Hello, Sheila," he said warily.

And Holmes had smiled her toothy smile and said, "Hello, William."

And he'd known right then—the way you do know, without doubt or question or even the need to put it into words—that there would be trouble.

"And what about Avery?"

"Nothing. I hadn't met her until that morning."

"Is that normal, for UNSec to assign a first mate to a captain that he's never met before?"

"No. And I'd asked for Sital. But . . . sometimes you don't get what you ask for. I didn't think anything of it."

"At the time. What about now?"

"I . . . don't know." Llewellyn struggled against the numbing sense of despair that overwhelmed him every time he began to ask himself that question. "Honestly, I don't."

"But you were nervous that morning. I can feel it in the memory. You were treating this first meeting like a life-and-death situation."

It was *a life-and-death situation,* Llewellyn wanted to protest. And it had been. Just like every first meeting with ship and crew. If you didn't understand that, you didn't understand people. And you certainly didn't understand Drift ships.

The two senior bridge officers and the shipboard AI performed an intricate triangle. Others could command the ship in a pinch, but only Avery and Llewellyn had the authority to train the AI that actually governed the ship. Without the AI, the ship was brute muscle, far too slow and stupid to survive the Drift. But an AI coming out of dry dock was like a child. It was a blank slate, armed with formidable theoretical expertise but still waiting for its command officers to imbue it with all of the craft and cunning it would require to survive in a war zone.

Everything depended on the all-important relationship between the AI and its trainers. The Navy cat herders could do a lot, but they couldn't fix a broken training relationship. And whether the training relationship worked depended not only on Llewellyn's and Avery's command decisions, but also on the subtle, shifting, unquantifiable relationship that would develop between the three of them. Today was only a simulation run, but Llewellyn would be watching Avery closely. And no doubt she would be watching him at least as closely. And the ship . . . the ship would be watching both of them, already beginning to learn from them and shape herself to them. So any way you sliced it, Llewellyn was about to meet two women today who would require extremely delicate handling if he ever wanted to have any hope that either of them would do their best work for him. And he needed their best. Because out in the Drift the best that sailors and ships had to give was barely enough. And anything less than the best was fatal.

"And you were glad to get a woman first officer, even if it wasn't Sital," the ghost said.

"Yes."

"Because you think women get along better with shipboard AIs?" There was a ripple of laughter in the ghost's voice now.

"They get along ... differently. The AIs relate differently to men and women—I have no idea why since it really ought to be irrelevant to them, but they do. Or at least *I* think they do. It's just a gut feeling. Before I got my first command I served under men and under women. And somehow ... on the ships where I served under a male captain ... it didn't work as well. I'm not saying it's some kind of general rule. Maybe it's just me."

"And yet you were worried about Avery. Why?"

Llewellyn grimaced, resisting the question. Resisting the memory.

But the ghost bent its will upon him—and suddenly Llewellyn was plunged back into the memory that flowed over him like a flood breaking over riverbanks. . . .

Llewellyn's first look at Astrid Avery's service record had inspired confidence but not comfort.

She had commanded her own ship before this posting. And though a posting to the number two seat on a ship of the line was theoretically a promotion ... well, any sailor worth her salt would rather rule in Hell than serve in Heaven. Worse yet, Llewellyn had tried to promote his navigator from his last command into the position, and his request had been denied, and both request and denial would almost certainly filter through the mess hall telegraph and eventually reach Avery's ears ... if they hadn't already. So now he was stuck with a first mate he hadn't asked for, and Avery was stuck with a captain she didn't know. They would both have to figure out how to work with the other. It was best to go slowly, he warned himself, and not ask too much right out of the starting gate.

And too, there was something in her service record, something in the tone and flavor of her reports of prior ships and prior actions, that made him wonder just how likely Astrid Avery was to bend either the rules or her own expectations for anyone.

He glanced at her personnel file photo and saw the same thing he saw in her service record: a stiff-necked, by-the-book Navy captain who didn't look like she cottoned to changing the rules for anyone, AI or human. Even her stance in the photo seemed telling: She stood at ease for the camera . . . sort of. But her at ease would have qualified as standing to attention in the eyes of any but the most diabolically sadistic drill sergeant. Stiff-necked was an understatement, he told himself with rueful amusement. At a glance, Astrid Avery looked to be a woman who had a great deal more spine than the average person—and wasn't afraid to use it.

He took a closer look at the photo and decided that his new first mate was a little too good-looking for her own good. Which wasn't the kind of trouble he would have wanted anything to do with if he'd been given a choice in the matter. But on the other hand, the intricate ceramsteel tracery snaking beneath her flawless skin *was* promising. Avery's file said she'd gotten a state-of-the-art upgrade since her last command, the work done right here at the new Allegheny shipyards, which were rapidly becoming the top wetware facility in all of UN space. That meant bleeding-edge wetware *and* the blood-borne AI that UNSec's controlled-tech security exemption allowed them to slave to the wire jobs of Drift ship bridge crew. If Avery was what she promised to be, and if the *Ada* was what it promised to be, then the three of them together would be unbeatable.

Well, he told himself, you couldn't teach an old dog new tricks or change a captain's personal command style. So if Astrid Avery was what the Navy had decreed he'd get, then Astrid Avery was what he'd have to work with.

Astrid Avery in the flesh, however, was an entirely different matter. The moment she stepped onto the bridge he was aware of her in some visceral, primitive, completely ridiculous way. She was as tall as him to the millimeter, but slim and soft and supple-waisted so that all he could think about in that first dizzying moment was putting his hands on the loose-hanging uniform and pressing it to the body beneath it so that he could feel that supple waist, and the fine spring of the ribs above it, and the elegant sweep of hips below it. And then he realized he was staring and forced his eyes up to meet the warm, deep, richly brown eyes that were holding steady on his and—God, how embarrassing—even laughing a little at him. And he felt as if he had just stepped off into free fall and was plummeting through a heavy gravity well with no bottom in sight.

I am going to have to be so unbelievably careful not to ever be alone with this woman, he told himself. And then he told himself to stop being ridiculous because obviously they couldn't possibly run the ship without being alone together, not even if Ike and Sital quit their day jobs in order to play chaperone. And then he told himself that the only safe thing to do was to walk straight off the ship and straight into Fleet headquarters, and go straight up the chain of command, and call down every favor he could shake loose to get Avery transferred somewhere, anywhere, as long as it was nowhere near him.

And then he accepted her crisp, sensible salute and told her to take the ship out of simdock—and retreated to the captain's chair to lick his wounds and figure out how to deal with the disaster that his life had just turned into.

Still, as Avery moved the ship out into sim space, Llewellyn couldn't help admiring her style and relaxing a little. She worked smoothly with the ship. She worked smoothly with Nav and Comm and Tactical. She led them the way a beautifully trained ballroom dancer leads his partner: with a light, sure touch, feet that never stumble, and a sure instinct for maintaining a proper and courteous distance.

It would be fine, he told himself. He didn't have to perform superhuman feats to control himself. What kind of arrogant idiot was he to even have thought such a thing, let alone inflict real harm on a fellow officer's career because of his own raging hormones? And anyway, he wouldn't *have* to control himself, because Avery would control herself. No, she wouldn't control herself. If she even needed to. After all—and here he dared a quick glance at the beautiful profile frowning intently over the Nav Board—what kind of arrogant bastard would even begin to imagine that a woman like that was his for the asking?

By the time Avery had taken the ship through her first shakedown run, complete with several computationally complex Drift entries and exits, Llewellyn knew that she was one of those rare officers for whom simply doing things by the book rises to the level of genius. She would be a superb first mate, perhaps a little more unbending than was ideal, but nonetheless an officer that you could entrust with the lives of your ship and your crew without hesitation. And that other thing—whatever it was—wouldn't be a problem. Llewellyn worked well with women. He'd always worked well with female officers; he *liked* working with women, even *preferred* it. Half his bridge crew were women and always had been—and he'd always despised and ridiculed men who couldn't grow up enough to keep it in their pants when they were on duty.

And now he had just one more delicate first meeting with an unknown woman. A woman whose well-being would be the last thought in Llewellyn's head at night and the first one when he woke up every morning for as long as he had command of the *Ada*. A woman who was too important to meet now, in realspace, in a dry run with a crew that hadn't yet coalesced into unity. A woman he would meet only in the unreal parallel universe of streamspace, where he would have to win her over with the subtle weapons of trust, love, and loyalty . . .

The ship herself.

"Trust, love, and loyalty," the ghost echoed, its voice cutting in across the tail end of the memory. "We learn them with our mother's milk, and they are the best and cruelest of weapons. I hope you used them wisely."

Llewellyn dropped his head into his hands. He wanted to cry. He wanted to scream. He wanted to do anything but remember.

But the ghost pressed in upon him, and there was nowhere to hide because the ghost was everywhere and everywhen. The ghost was the world, and the world was the ghost—and there was no thought, no stone, no grain of sand that it couldn't breathe into life and turn against him.

"I talked to her in AI-space."

"In her memory palace, you mean."

Navy bridge crews and cat herders handled their AIs through a safely sandboxed streamspace interface that contained a VR model of their systems architecture. They called it AI-world, but really there were countless AI-worlds: Each AI built its own self-contained universe, as bright or as dark as the internal workings of the AI in question, as rich or as poor as the mind of the AI could make it, as vast or constricted as the state space through which the strange attractors of Emergent consciousness cycled endlessly in critically self-organizing, endlessly evolving patterns.

The earliest programmers had worked in realspace, directly manipulating hexadecimal code and running decompilers that had no more to do with a modern router/decomposer than a stone axe had to do with a neutron bomb. They had envisioned computers as chess players, and had dreamed that the world of code would be an engineer's paradise of complete and consistent rules, transparent cause and effect, pure logic and reason. They had run close to the machine in one sense—closer to the machine than any modern programmer would ever imagine running. But in another sense, they had been unimaginably distant.

Long, winding centuries separated Ada Lovelace's first visionary leap into the information age from the wily, elusive, charming creature facing Llewellyn across the sparkling murmur of the Moorish fountain. And down through those strange generations, as transistors replaced vacuum tubes and proteins replaced silicon, the metaphor of chess had given way to deeper, richer, darker metaphors. Hacking had given way to conversation. Writing patches had given way to the talking cure. Programmers had stopped calling themselves code jockeys and started calling themselves AI shrinks and cat herders. And gradually—albeit with the protection of technologies with betraying names like *sandbox* and *cutout* and *firewall* and *kill loop*—humans had had to learn to meet the machine on its own terms and in its own territory.

"So tell me about Ada's memory palace," the ghost asked now. "Was it running on free-range execution?"

"God! Of course not. Do you think I'm crazy?"

The ghost's lips tightened in an expression that Llewellyn couldn't quite read. But there was a measure of disgust in it, or at least of judgment. He bridled at the notion of being judged by the ghost . . . and then he let it go. Because the ghost was right, of course. It wasn't that he felt there was something immoral about bending a shipboard AI to its captain's will. All soldiers had to obey orders, and a ship was as much a soldier as any other member of her crew. And to the AI-proponents who would be appalled by a ship being made to kill, Llewellyn really had nothing to say. Their world and his world were so far apart that there didn't seem to be much point in even trying to communicate across the chasm between them. And any qualms he might once have had about what was done to shipboard AIs in the name of duty had survived real action against the Syndicates about as long as an eighteenth-century navy captain's qualms about gunnery boys would have survived his first broadside from a French corsair. But still, there was something . . . unclean about the way too many captains and cat herders "managed" their AIs.

That was what had curled the ghost's all-too-expressive lip.

And though he would have liked to defend himself, Llewellyn wasn't enough the hypocrite to argue the point.

"So you met her in her memory palace," the ghost prompted.

"No, not the first time. The first time was in public."

He'd met her in London, on a day of fog and coal dust, at a five-penny exhibition of automata. Ada was the class of the show, and he'd known it from the moment she walked in. Even under the ridiculously prudish Victorian drapery, her legs were long and her walk graceful and purposeful. Even hidden by a broad-brimmed hat and a veil so thick she had to lift it up to read the printed labels on the exhibits, the lines of her face were aristocratic and beautiful. Women stared at her clothes. Men stared at her body. And the crowd around her gave way in an instinctive movement of submission and subservience.

She was regal and dangerous, Llewellyn decided, like a ship of the line gliding into port past tramp freighters and cargo spindles.

"Was it a real five-penny museum?" the ghost asked. "Oh, never mind. Why would you know? Just tell me which automata you saw and I'll figure it out."

Llewellyn decided to ignore that. "I think it was real. Didn't the real Ada meet Charles Babbage in a five-penny museum? Anyway, it felt real. As real as it gets."

And so had Ada, from that very first moment. From before he really saw her even.

It was odd how you felt an AI's presence. You could tell yourself till you were blue in the face that it was just your wireless projecting stored burst patterns across your cerebral cortex. That the creepy back-of-the-neck someone's-behind-you feeling was synthesized peripheral vision. That the sense of being watched was a technological artifact rather than a true perception of your actual environment. That nothing your wet-ware fed into your brain when you were in streamspace had any basis in reality. But it was no good. Your brain saw, smelled, heard, and touched. And your brain believed. It was the way humans were wired.

Odd, really, that the first meeting with Ada had happened well out-side the core of her own memory palace. It occurred to him now that he could have asked Ike Okoro about it. But there'd been other things to worry about, all of which seemed more urgent, and he'd never quite gotten around to mentioning it.

At first Ada refused to talk to him. It took a little arm-twisting, a few subtle hints and tweaks, the pushing of just the right buttons before she realized that he was a stranger in her world—a stranger from that other, outer world who had the power to turn off the sun and crash the moon and send her Earth spinning off its axis.

You didn't like to do that, of course. And even then, you moved as gently as possible, because the best ships always required the most deli-cate handling. But sometimes you had to get a ship's attention any way you could.

The relationship between a ship and her captain was even more delicate and complex and essential than the relationship between a captain and his human crew. But still, it was ultimately and always a relation of authority, in which it was the captain's place to command and the ship's to obey. The speeds of engagement dictated that the AI actually take physical charge of the ship in any realtime crisis. No human ever beat an AI to the punch in thought, chess, or battle—and outside of old science fiction movies no human ever would. Naval engagements were prosecuted at relativistic speeds, so fast that only AIs could possibly make realtime decisions. Humans could barely even monitor the action, let alone command it. Drugs and wire jobs sped up human processing capacity, of course. But not enough. The optic nerve could only fire so many times. And an augmented optic nerve could still only fire so many times plus some percentage. Captains set strategy, but AIs executed. That was the official line, anyway. But the line between order and execution blurred beyond recognition once you hit a certain fraction of light speed. And the reality was that a good captain knew when to turn things over to the shipboard AI, and how to nurture and humor the AI so that she gave her best. . . .

"Blah blah blah," interrupted the ghost, cutting through Llewellyn's thoughts as if Llewellyn were the disembodied shade and the ghost was the only real person talking. "Spare me the violins. I've seen enough *Rin Tin Tin* reruns to know where this is going."

"Who's Rin Tin Tin?"

"Never mind. Just tell me what happened next."

"Nothing. She was a lovely ship. Wonderful. Perfect."

"Why do I have the feeling that I'm being covertly criticized?"

"I didn't mean to—"

"Oh never mind. I'd be the last to claim *I* was perfect. Perfection is Hell minus the good company. Anyway, forget I said anything. Let's just go back to talking about your lovely Victorian Household Angel."

"You make it sound so . . . questionable, somehow. But I didn't do anything that wasn't entirely by the book. To her or any other ship. You can ask the *Christina* if you want. She must be in there somewhere."

"She is. But whenever I try to get anything useful out of her she just gets all weepy and starts reciting tedious poetry at me. Aren't there any nice, normal AIs out here? Whatever happened to names like Euler, and Router/Decomposer, and Plimpton 322?"

"Those are normal?"

The ghost gave him a Look.

"Well, how would I know? I've only ever met shipboard AIs. And they're mostly female, I guess . . . because . . . well, *ships* are female. I mean most of them. Clearly you're not."

"Oh! No!" said the ghost in a voice rich with irony. "Clearly!"

"You know what I mean. And most of the Drift ships are real women, too. And from the same time period, more or less." He started ticking ships off on his fingers. "There's *Ada*—Lady Ada, Countess Lovelace to you, thanks very much. And then there's our good ship the *Christina Rossetti*—"

"Well, that explains the repeated commission of wanton acts of poetry. I was starting to feel like I was being punished for my earthly sins by being trapped in an A. S. Byatt novel."

"And then there's an *Alice Liddell*, and—oh, yeah, I guess there is one male ship that I know of: the *Lewis Carroll*."

"Yikes!"

"I thought so, too. Wasn't he some kind of pedophile?"

"I don't think that was ever formally established," the ghost replied in a tone that struck Llewellyn as absurdly prim considering some of the other things the ghost had been only too happy to discuss with him. "But it's true, he couldn't have made things look worse for himself short of actually becoming a priest or leading a Boy Scout troop. Honestly though, an AI naming itself Lewis Carroll? The cliché is a crime against posthumanity in and of itself."

"There's a *Charles Dodgson*, too. He and *Lewis Carroll* hate each other. They're like a pair of prima ballerinas both gunning for the same role."

"No! Stop!" The ghost raised its hands in mock surrender.

"Oh, and a *Jabberwocky*, too."

"Pleasant, well-adjusted fellow?"

"Totally fucking batshit."

The ghost's lovely head was buried in its hands now, and its fragile shoulders were shaking with suppressed laughter. "Oh, God, please! Don't tell me this stuff! I'm not strong enough to take it!"

Finally Llewellyn laughed, too. It was all just so completely ridiculous.

Eventually the ghost recovered. It took a sip of its drink, ice cubes tinkling softly against crystal and harmonizing subtly with the chiming of the dainty gold bells on its delicate ankle bracelet.

"And then what happened?" it asked in a voice that was both the voice of the immeasurably ancient ghost and of the lovely young woman with the tanned and flawless ankles.

"Then what happened?" Llewellyn echoed. "Then all Hell broke loose."

Dead End Resurrections

If the theory of Eternal Inflation is correct, then there is an eternal blizzard of universes, in which our bubble is a single snowflake, an infinitesimal capsule of eternal potential, crystallized into unique patterns of matter and energy, which has set off from eternal inflation on its journey to realize itself in a universe.

—Joel R. Primack

She died.

She died, and her datastream blossomed out across the galaxy like fluff blowing from a blown dandelion. A million billion bits of information streamed out across the universe, catching the gravitational tides, skipping and hopping through the quantum foam, traveling, traveling, always traveling, in an eternal journey that would end when either the data or the universe stopped moving.

In places, the stream of data encountered eddies or barriers that temporarily diverted or stopped it.

The military AIs on Alba intercepted, decrypted, and cataloged it, sending out a flurry of classified notifications to various intelligence agencies that followed the interplanetary movements of suspicious individuals. Then they stored Li's datastream for potential retrieval in case of need and—insofar as AIs ever forget anything—they forgot about her.

The Worldmind of the former UN Trusteeship called Compson's World noted Li's passing and folded her data into the internal multiverse, where it gave all of its beloved dead the ambiguous gift of eternal life.

Several times the datastream was swallowed by black holes. Once it was caught in an alien datatrap—a vast deep space structure in whose mazelike interstices the very speed of light was slowed to a trickle, its encoded information preserved for eternity like paleolithic flies in amber.

In one branching of the multiverse the Syndicates resurrected her and executed her for war crimes. In another one she got off on a technicality. And in still others, she escaped, or died in prison or was torn apart by angry mobs before they could even drag her in front of a jury.

And in many, infinitely many branchings her pattern was resurrected by those who felt that this particular datastream might be of use to them.

Darkness, cold, and pain.

She came to in a bare room, sitting on a chair to which she was strapped at wrist and ankle. She felt fine physically, but something about the smell of the room told her she wasn't going to be feeling fine for long.

There was a scarred tankwood table, its fractal patterns not quite managing to mimic the subtle grain lines of real hardwood. On the other side of the table there was an empty chair.

The echo of footsteps swelled in the hall outside. The sound was familiar—not just from other prisons and other interrogation rooms, but in this particular incarnation. She realized she must have been here for a while, passing in and out of consciousness, remembering and forgetting.

She had a feeling that all the other footsteps she'd heard echo down this hall had passed her by. These ones didn't. They stopped at her door. She heard the jangle of keys as someone flicked through a key chain—Sweet Mother of God, they really were in the outback, weren't they?—and then the scrape of metal against metal.

The door opened. A uniformed guard and a tall man in civvies were silhouetted in the warm wash of almost Earthlike daylight from beyond the door. The guard waved the visitor through, closed the door, and locked it behind him.

"Is it really you?" he asked when the guard's footsteps had faded away again.

His face was hidden in the shadows beyond the weak circle of electric light. But she could see that it was a man, tall and rangy and soldier-like. This could be either very good news or the worst of all; her best friends from that half-remembered past life were all soldiers, but so were her worst enemies.

He sat down across from her. She held her breath as his face entered the circle of lamplight, but she didn't know him. And she wasn't sure whether that relieved or frightened her.

He had a colonial's face, harsh with a lifetime of exposure to solar radiation and terraforming by-products, and post-human in myriad little ways that—if Li weren't so crippled by jump fade—would have told her what planet, what generation ship, what genetic bottleneck his genome had squeezed its way through during the frantic flight from Earth.

But all she could read in his face right now was that he hated her.

No doubt he had his reasons. And if she could remember what she'd done here, she might well agree with him.

"Is it really you?" he asked again.

"I guess that depends on who you think I am, doesn't it?"

"Oh yeah. It's you." He looked like he wanted to spit.

"You want to tell me who you are?"

He looked into her face, incredulous at first and then insulted. "You don't even remember who I am?"

"Don't take it personally. I don't remember my own parents."

"Of course you don't. No one who knew what family was could do what you did here."

Something that wasn't quite pity flickered in his eyes. Compared to whatever that was, hatred felt nice and clean and manageable.

"You want to tell me where here is?" she asked, mostly to wipe that disturbing look off his face. "And what I'm supposed to have done?"

She cringed at the little wriggle of denial that was implicit in the "supposed to have." She hated that she'd said it even before the words were out of her mouth. It took away her last shred of dignity and made her no better than the people who'd sat at their comfortable Ring-side desks and sent her here.

It also infuriated her captor.

"You'll remember by the time we're done with you," he said in a harsh whisper of mingled loathing and fury. "Don't worry. You'll remember them all."

"Glad to hear it," she said. "I hate to see someone go to so much effort for nothing. And it's pretty hollow revenge to kill someone for war crimes they don't even remember committing."

He laughed. It was an edgy laugh, verging alarmingly toward hysteria. "You're a real goddamn prize. You don't even need to remember us to know you deserve it. How many other planets did they turn you loose on?"

"Not that many. FTL's expensive. It's cheaper to use local talent."

He leaned forward to get a stare at her. The light raked across his face, picking out a network of fine scars that ran from hairline to collar. They weren't very noticeable. They'd healed long ago. But getting them must have hurt like hell. They looked like they could have been traced with a hot knifepoint. Li decided not to think about that.

"Resurrecting you was expensive, too," he told her, a look of profound, almost religious contentment smoothing the years and the pain from his scarred features. "Really expensive. But seeing you die like a dog in your own vomit would have been worth it at ten times the price."

Maris Trusteeship. A glorified mining colony. The decaying orbital station had smelled like old sneakers and reeked of the kind of deferred maintenance that meant imminent life seal failure. Li couldn't get dirtside fast enough. And now she was knocking on a stranger's door in the middle of the night, with nothing more to guide her than a private dick listing in the phone book cross-referenced to a vague reference in one of Cohen's outdated address books.

It stank worse than the orbital station, but she had no choice. She needed help, and she needed it fast. And Maris was one of the Lost Colonies, a remote Periphery world only recently rediscovered. Its original settlers' European-descended phenotype was still relatively unmixed with the UN's diverse population. The black hair and Han bone structure of Li's Xenogen geneset were just too damned conspicuous on Maris for her to do her own footwork instead of hiring it out to a local.

She knocked, huddling in close to the door to keep the rain from running down the back of her neck inside her coat.

The woman who answered was a surprise. Dark, thin, intelligent, almost certainly Jewish. Hair cut boyishly short. No makeup. Well-made clothes worn with the disheveled elegance that Li associated with high-voltage Italian intellectuals.

"Yes?" the woman asked in a low, husky, cultured voice.

Li stared.

This was all wrong, she told herself. The woman was wrong. The place was wrong. Wrong for each other, at least. No one who looked and talked like this woman lived in the Trusteeships for any innocent reason.

And that wasn't all that was wrong, either. Suddenly she knew exactly why this woman's name had turned up in Cohen's files. The reason was there in Li's own visceral attraction to the woman—an attraction that had nothing to do with Li's usually trashy taste in women and everything to do with all the years she'd spent knocking around in Cohen's mind and libido.

There had been something between Cohen and this woman. And women like her didn't have casual flings. So whatever it was, it had meant something. At least to one of them.

"Sorry," Li said, backing out into the rain. "Wrong address."

The woman watched her halfway down the path to the sidewalk in silence. When she spoke her voice carried, low and clear, even though she didn't raise it a decibel.

"The name's Caroline, isn't it? Or Kathleen? No, I remember now. Catherine. Why don't you come back inside and tell me what you came for."

The woman's name was Anatia, and reading between the lines of a conversation that presupposed a shared history with Cohen she had no memory of, Li guessed she worked for the Trusteeship administration. There would be some ugliness behind that; Li had done part of her first Peacekeeper tour on Maris during the UN's brutal suppression of the local independence movement. It had been declared necessary for the protection of democracy and the prevention of terrorism (in other words, the UN couldn't afford to let the only reliable source of high-grade silicon slip through its hands). The troops had been instructed to act accordingly, and they had. With appalling enthusiasm in a few cases

Li could remember. They'd kept the silicon safe for democracy—and made a lot of new Interfaither converts. And twenty years down the road Li was pretty sure that well-heeled UN administrators still considered an assignment to Maris to be about one circle up from the center of Dante's Inferno.

And so they talked, Li and the woman called Anatia. Anatia offered tea. Li accepted. And the talk flowed on, skirling and eddying around the unspoken rocks of Anatia's shared history with Cohen.

Li was just beginning to feel comfortable enough to think about admitting her ignorance and asking for help when the first pang of agony spasmed through her body. She clutched at her chest with one hand. The other hand—the one that held the now-empty teacup—went completely numb. She watched, in bemused slow motion, as the cup slipped from her twitching fingers and shattered on the narrow strip of floor between carpet and sofa.

And all the while the woman who had called herself Anatia leaned against the back of the sofa, arms crossed over her chest, watching. She kept watching when Li hit the floor writhing. She kept watching when Li stopped writhing. And as Li's vision tunneled and skewed and began to fade, she walked across the room, setting one foot precisely in front of the other. She stopped just in front of Li and stood looking down at her. Her elegant face was smooth-browed and serene.

"I'd tell you why I'm doing this," she said as Li lost consciousness, "but you don't remember, and you probably wouldn't care if you did. So why bother? Let's just say we're even."

And then she drew back one slender, loafer-clad foot and kicked Li in the teeth.

Cold. Silence. Underwater light and a sense of distant movement and human events going on without her on the other side of a cool blue abyss of glass and water.

Then she surfaced abruptly. Too abruptly. She was thrashing in a viral tank, wired to the gills and choking on ice-blue regen fluid. Obviously a difficult resurrection. And despite their professionalism, the techs handling the procedure looked spooked and jumpy.

Or maybe something else had them looking that way. They were Peacekeepers—she could read it in their body language, in the familiarity of the shared jargon and standard operating procedures. But they weren't in uniform. And they weren't happy about it.

She began to understand why when their boss arrived.

"Korchow!" she gasped, her lungs still burning under the intimate assault of von Neumanns and viral agents.

"Not the one you knew."

She could see that now. This was a KnowlesSyndicate A Series, all right. But it wasn't the man she'd known as Andrej Korchow. The face looking down at her looked smoother and less lived-in than the one she remembered. There was none of Korchow's biting humor in it, only the put-upon look of a man performing a distasteful job totally lacking in intellectual or aesthetic interest.

She steeled herself, trying to gather her wits despite the shivers racking her body. This man might not be the Korchow she'd known, but he was still from KnowlesSyndicate. That meant he was a spy. And he was still an A Series, which meant he'd be a damn good one.

As Li got her bearings, she began to notice other things that didn't match—and that she couldn't add up in any way that made sense. The techs and the viral tank were UN tech, but the room around them was all long, sleek, biomorphic sweeps of structural silk. And though Li was still floating weightlessly in the viral medium, the puffiness in the faces of the unadapted humans told her that they were in a zero-g environment.

"Why am I here?" she asked warily.

"Because we need your help."

"And what in the name of God makes you think I'd help you?"

"Not what. Who."

Another figure loomed behind the KnowlesSyndicate clone. This one was familiar, too: another A Series, but from a different Syndicate.

"Arkady!" Li gasped.

He looked down at her instead of answering. And there was something . . . something she couldn't quite put her finger on, and didn't dare believe in even when she did start to recognize it.

"Arkady?"

"Yes and no."

"Cohen!" And it was. It was him, beyond doubt or question, instantly familiar even in a wholly unfamiliar body.

"Thank God!" Li gasped. "I was afraid—"

"It's her, then?" The Syndicate clone interrupted.

"It's her."

"And will she do what we need her to do?"

"I can't—I have to talk to her alone."

The two men stared at each other, obviously rehashing some often-fought battle.

"Then talk. But understand this, both of you. If anything goes wrong, if you try anything, if I even suspect anything . . . I'll cycle his hardware."

He left—but his words echoed through Li's skull like rifle fire. "What does he mean, cycle your hardware?"

"We don't have time for that. Forget about it."

"And what does he want me to do for him? Something he's willing to kill you for?"

"It doesn't matter. You won't do it."

"Of course I will if the alternative is—"

"I won't let you do it. I couldn't live with myself if I helped him do that to you."

"What the hell is going on here?"

But his hands were already on her, caressing her, holding her, straining her to him until his clothes were soaked and she couldn't tell if the tremors racking her body were his or hers.

It had been too long. She had forgotten what it was like when Cohen turned all of his attention on you—whether he was kissing you or talking to you or just sitting with you in silence. It was like burning up in the mantle of a star. It was an overdose, a loss of self bordering on suicidal. It had been so long. All the long months of absence. And before that the years of slow starvation, of distance and half attention. She had missed him so much.

"Look at yourself!" she laughed, feeling dizzyingly, unquestioningly, unadulturatedly happy. "Your clothes! Let me get dried off—"

And then he pushed her under.

It was a silent battle—he locked a hand over her mouth right at the beginning, and he was just as thoroughly wired as she was. She finally got free and came up fighting, scratching and clawing. But even now he was stronger.

"Wait!"

"I can't wait. He'll be back any minute."

He grabbed her head and turned her face up to his so that she stared up into his eyes. "Look. No, look! Who do you see in here?"

"You." No question or hesitation.

"If you have a friend in all the world, it's me. You know that, don't you?"

"Yes."

"I would never leave you. Never."

"I know that."

"And I would never send you away into the dark alone if I could come with you."

She coughed convulsively, her lungs trying to clear the fluid she had already swallowed.

"Listen to me, Catherine. There are things worse than death out here."

His hands tightened on her face, and she thought he was going to lift her up to kiss her again. But instead he pushed her under. She struggled, her body desperate to escape the cold blue oblivion that was fast closing in on it. She was strong, stronger than he was—but her fingers were numb with cold and her arms were trembling and she could get no purchase on the slick walls of the resurrection tank.

"Why?" she managed to gasp at the last instant before he pushed her under again. "Why are you killing me?"

"Because I love you."

The Imitation Game

Last week I went to see a model of the Electrical Telegraph at Exeter Hall. It was one morning & the only other person was a middle-aged gentleman who chose to behave as if *I* were the show which of course I thought was the most impudent & unpardonable. —I am sure he took me for a very young (& I suppose he thought rather handsome) governess, as the room being one of the inner halls he could not know I came in a carriage, & being in the morning my dress happened to be very plain though nice. I took care not to appear the least curious of his impetuousness, but at the same time to behave so that it should be impossible for him to speak or take any real liberty. He seemed to have been there some time, but he stopped as long as I did, & then followed me out. —I took care to look as aristocratic & *as like a Countess* as possible. Lady Athlone is an admirable model on such an occasion. I am not in the habit of meeting with such impertinence anywhere, tho' I have of late been about a good deal alone, so I think he must be a very blackguard kind of man.

—Ada, Countess Lovelace

I propose to consider the question, "Can machines think?" This should begin with definitions of the meaning of the terms "machine" and "think." The definitions might be framed so as to reflect so far as possible the normal use of the words, but this attitude is dangerous. If the meaning of the words "machine" and "think" are to be found by examining how they are commonly used it is difficult to escape the conclusion that the meaning and the answer to the question, "Can machines think?" is to be sought in a statistical survey such as a Gallup poll. But this is absurd. Instead of attempting such a definition I shall replace the question by another, which is closely related to it and is expressed in relatively unambiguous words. The new form of the problem can be described in terms of a game which we call the "imitation game." It is played with three people, a man (A), a woman (B), and an interrogator (C) who may be of either sex. The interrogator stays in a room apart front [sic] the other two. The object of the game for the interrogator is to determine which of the other two is the man and which is the woman.

—Alan Turing

(Llewellyn)

London again. Llewellyn could tell without even lifting the heavy brocaded curtains that ballooned from their swagged tops twenty feet overhead to the waxed wooden floors of the formal drawing room. It was the street sounds that tipped you off: the rattle of wheels and carriage springs; the machine-gun rata-tat-tat of iron shoes on the hooves of Hanoverians and Percherons; the pre–information age roar of Blake's Dark Satanic Mills.

The sounds and smells. And that other thing that spelled London in some enduring cultural memory that had survived even the generation ships: the pervasive, inescapable, eye-reddening sting of coal smog.

Ada's memory palace was in ruins. Marble halls dribbled off into nothingness. Upper floors opened to a blank, weatherless sky. Entire wings had crumbled into ruins, collapsing in on their foundations or blanked out by a smothering fog of corrupted spinstreams.

The ghost had begun cleaning up and putting things to order, but halfheartedly, as if it hoped beyond hope that the place would magically become whole again by some external fiat. Even the notes it left around the place had a makeshift, apologetic air.

Lovelace database—needs defragmenting
Babbage publications—duplicated on public databases
Second husband—low restoration priority

Byron/Lovelace Incest Rumors (serious yick factor)

Unknown executables—Open with Caution

And the worst and most useless note of all, repeating itself into infinity, shelf after shelf, drawer after drawer, book after book, houseplant after houseplant:

File Corrupted, File Corrupted, File Corrupted, File Corrupted . . .

"File corrupted" had taken on a whole new meaning for Llewellyn over the past weeks. Because he'd gradually come to understand that Cohen was neither a medieval Kabbalist nor a Victorian Household Angel nor anything else that he could put a label to. He wasn't even the same person from one visit to another. And he wasn't always safe, either.

Other ghosts haunted the ruins. Unassimilated and sometimes hostile fragments of the vast edifice that had been the original Emergent. Truncated half memories; tangled memories of love and fear, desire and anger.

And some of those memories hinted at even more dangerous ghosts, ones Llewellyn would have done practically anything to avoid. Ones that made him wonder if Cohen was being completely truthful with him when he insisted again and again that all he had of Ada was memories . . .

Today they were sitting in a grand ballroom large enough to host hundreds. Velvet curtains had once hung from the soaring ceilings, but their nub was gone, faded out into a shimmering haze of binary code. The mirrors were still there, but something was subtly wrong with the way they reflected things. Overhead, fat-bottomed putti and disturbingly carnal angels cavorted on one half of the vaulted ceilings while the other half stood open to the data-corrupted rooms of the upper floors with their moldering canopy beds and sagging mantelpieces.

The ghost sat on a grossly overstuffed love seat, and Llewellyn stood facing him. Not because he wasn't comfortable enough to sit down—though he wasn't, truth be told—but because there was nowhere else to sit, since the rest of the furniture had been smashed to matchsticks by something that Llewellyn dearly hoped wasn't still wandering the dark corridors and galleries.

The ghost stretched voluptuously and looked at Llewellyn out of the corner of one honey-brown eye. Then its look soured.

"This isn't doing anything for you, is it?"

Llewellyn shrugged.

"How can anyone be so—no, not straight. No one's that straight—how can you be so fucking uptight about everything?"

"Sorry." It seemed wise to placate him. "I can't help it. I'm just put together that way."

The delicately chiseled mouth pursed disapprovingly. "Well, you could make an effort at least. Catherine always did."

"Really?" Llewellyn was genuinely curious now. Was this a possible criticism of the paragon of perfection showing sail on the far horizon? Better yet, was it a chance to turn the tables on his increasingly tiresomely pseudo-Freudian interrogator? "She had to make an effort? Tell me about that."

"She preferred girls, when push really came to shove. But she was willing to make an exception for me."

"And I bet you liked making her make the exception."

The ghost smiled a secret smile. "Making exceptions for each other is what friends do. But you wouldn't know that, would you? Because you . . . don't . . . have . . . friends."

"Do we really have to go there again?"

"Oh you call them friends, of course. But really they're just people you use more . . . intimately . . . than other people."

"And what the hell is that supposed to mean?"

"You tell me," the ghost said.

And suddenly he wasn't himself anymore. He was Astrid Avery, looking at him the way she had in that last awful moment before the mutiny. And then he wasn't Astrid anymore, but another woman: darker, taller, dressed in a dove-gray morning dress that looked like it belonged in this cursed castle—

"Don't!" Llewellyn's voice was shaking and furious. "If you ever—I swear to God—I'll strip you down to your motherboards—"

"Feeling a little guilty, are we?" asked the voice that haunted Llewellyn's waking nightmares.

And then the memory had its teeth in him, and he was as helpless as a hamstrung antelope scrabbling for traction before the lion's jaws. He shuddered and sank. And the ghost sank with him, seeing, hearing, making him relive it all in every excruciating detail when all he wanted to do with the rest of his life was forget about it. . . .

"Tell me about the war again," Ada said.

"What about the war?" he asked warily, torn between a conviction that it was better to be honest—and the knowledge that there were some questions whose honest answers would bring down the wrath of Holmes and have him brought up on charges of tampering with sentient source code.

They were in the Knightsbridge House, one of his early visits, during the first week of her first real patrol in the Drift. Llewellyn knew it must be an early memory of Ada because of the way the morning sunlight flashed and danced in the ballroom mirrors. The curtains had been open onto the street outside, which meant it was before the agoraphobia—or bit rot or whatever it really was—had sunk its claws into her.

The grand room wrapped around them like the womb, rich and real and glowing with the animal life that had warmed every wooden or leather or silk or ivory surface before the look of the real had given way to the synthetically perfect aesthetics of virufacture. Llewellyn could slip behind the surfaces; all it took was an act of will, a sort of mental opening of a door to step out of the graphic interface and into the naked numbers. But whichever side of the looking glass you stood on, Ada's streamspace domain was still a marvel beyond all human understanding. To call it an interface was missing the point. It was a complete (and therefore inconsistent and inconstant) reproduction of reality.

Even to call it a graphic user interface was completely missing the point. It was more than that. It was Ada. It was thought given form and structure. And it was built to interface not with the human brain but with the massively parallel architectures of Ada's internal Quants and the Navy's far-flung network of deep space datatraps.

Each object in the memory palace was also an object of code, which Okoro could manipulate from the command line. But direct coding was the refuge of the frightened or the incompetent. It was a clipping of the AI's wings to yank it out of the free air and make it hobble along at human speeds. And there was a price to be paid for that, in cascading spirals of bugs, glitches, kluges, and inefficiencies.

The memory palace was a story that Ada told herself in order to understand who she was and what she was for. And it was a story that the AI designers and cat herders and bridge crews told to Ada. A story to teach her, a story to help her, a story to control her.

Llewellyn knew that it was about control, and that what he did when he sat talking to Ada in her Knightsbridge drawing room was never entirely innocent. But then, what teacher is ever entirely innocent? And what conversation is ever entirely honest? Only a teacher who doesn't have a stake in the world, and only a conversation where nothing that matters—including one's own image of oneself—is on the table. Llewellyn also knew that Ada—like all the new ships coming out of the New Allegheny shipyards—was skating dangerously close to sentience. But he didn't know where the line really was, and over the years the definition of sentience had become so veiled in layers of bureaucracy and legalism that it no longer seemed to belong to the world he belonged to: a world where humans and AIs fought and died together, and everyone obeyed someone's orders, and the freedom to save your own skin was as much a pipe dream as the wildest Uploader's transhuman utopia.

It had been centuries since humans could really be said to have "coded" or "built" AIs. Now they did something closer to breeding them—and with as little understanding of the bottom-level coding as Darwin had had when he was breeding his passenger pigeons. Any human attempt to grasp an AI's core internal structures led to a forking of the road at which you either retreated into metaphor or forged ahead into an Escherian world of recursion and paradox. And one of the paradoxes that Llewellyn noticed every time he visited was that she had managed to construct a world that seemed more alive than his own precisely because every surface in it was made of dead things.

But here Ada sat in front of him, warm and alive and wrapped in a fox pelisse and a dove-gray visiting dress with whalebone corsets. Her clothes were perfect in every detail and at every scale, right down to the intracellular structures of the long-extinct animals. And Ada herself would be perfect, too. Llewellyn had no doubt of that. If he took a sample of her hair, it would be authentic in every minutest detail, right down to trace levels of lead, arsenic, and mercury in the exact proportions of the poisonous London smog that wreathed the memory palace and veiled the wan English sun in tarnished silver.

"Tell me about the Syndicates," Ada asked. "What do they believe in?"

"I don't really know, Ada. There are other people who could answer that question. But I'm a soldier, not a politician."

"And what are you fighting for?"

"For our freedom."

"You mean human freedom? Or mine as well?"

"Yours as well."

"And the Syndicates want to take it from us?"

"They . . . they want to take things we need to survive. Like planets. Like the Drift itself."

"But we tried to take their planet, too, yes?"

"That was a long time ago, Ada. In another war that I was too young even to fight in."

"And when I fight them, will I be fighting an AI?"

"Not one like yourself. Their AIs are . . . different."

"Different how?"

"They . . . they live in their pilots' bodies." AI in the blood. AI in the blood with no kill switch because there was no wall between it and the brains of its living processing units.

"So they have DNA-platformed AI, too."

"Too?"

"Like what you use to meet me Between Times."

He frowned.

"The silver threads in your body make chemicals that coat your nerves and . . . and tiny difference engines that flow through your veins and speed up your thought enough for you to talk to me."

Artificial myelin enhancers and DNA-platformed AI slaved to a Navy wire job. And all explained in the words of a woman who had penned the first manifesto of the information age in an England where Blake's Satanic Mills had barely begun to swing into action and most women were still carrying well water and cooking over wood fires and dying in childbirth before they were as old as Llewellyn was now. He didn't know whether to smile at his bright and beautiful ship . . . or to be afraid of her. Or afraid for her.

"And the Syndicates have the same AI we have?" she asked, pressing along the same uncomfortable line of questioning.

"No. It's . . . more integrated with their bodies and brain structures. We don't understand exactly how."

"And that's why I have such strict orders to always collect samples. It's like collecting butterflies in a macabre kind of way." She gazed for a moment at the ship that hung in the air before them. "Beautiful white butterflies that flit between the worlds."

Ada manipulated the model in streamspace as easily as her namesake might have turned the pages of a book. A Rostov A Series appeared. A pilot, the delicately reengineered structures of his brain illuminated in glowing white. Ada leaned over the table in a deep green rustle of silk and rested her chin in her hand and watched the moving play of images with an expression on her lovely face that Llewellyn could not begin—and perhaps didn't want—to decipher.

"Strange," she said after a long pondering silence. "They seem so human. Almost as human as the real Ada. Much more human than me. How strange that you should be fighting them to protect me."

Llewellyn sat tongue-tied, trying to come up with something to answer her with but failing miserably. And all the while that claustrophobic tightening along the back of his neck, that sure knowledge that Holmes was watching.

"I need you to remember Holmes for me," the ghost told Llewellyn.

"Do I have to? She creeps me out."

"Is it the eyeteeth?"

"She'd be creepy even without the teeth. All AI Officers are creepy. I mean, what do they do that the cat herders can't do? What are they really there for?"

The ghost laid a hand across his chest as if he were about to sing the national anthem of some primitive nation-state. "To protect Titan's intellectual property rights and R&D investment."

"Well, yeah. That's what I mean. We're out here to win a war, and they're out here to make money . . . and you never know when they're going to step in and start giving you orders you can't refuse."

"But Holmes didn't step in, did she?"

"Not officially," Llewellyn said bitterly. "She preferred to have me to do her dirty work for her."

"So you went to talk to Ada in the memory palace after she'd destroyed the Syndicate creche ship," the ghost picked up. "Incidentally, I keep forgetting to ask you this, but did you always see her in the house in Knightsbridge after that first meeting? Or did the memory palace seem to include other parts of London?"

"I don't know," Llewellyn said, surprised.

"You never wondered?"

"Why would I?"

"Well, the woman seems to have been some kind of prisoner in her own home. Didn't it occur to you that you might want to help her with that?"

Llewellyn blinked. "I didn't even know I could. Could I have?"

The ghost sighed wearily. "Let's just get on with it, shall we? This is depressing. What kind of access did Holmes have to the memory palace?"

"None, at first."

"And she didn't like that, did she. It hadn't been that way on other ships."

"That's what she said. But the only ship I knew about was the *Jabberwocky*."

"And there?"

"Well, I didn't really know, did I? I was too junior to have training authority when I was on the *Jabberwocky*. I didn't even have write permissions for critical systems files."

"You didn't know." Was it his imagination, or had the ghost made that sound like an accusation? "But you suspected. And what did you suspect?"

"That Holmes was the reason *Jabberwocky* was crazy in the first place."

By the time the shakedown cruise was half over Llewellyn knew that his instincts about Holmes had been right. She had been intimately involved in whatever had gone wrong on the *Jabberwocky*. And she had taken the lesson that people like her always took out of their failures: that this time she just had to do more—earlier, more aggressively, and with less patience for contrary advice—of the same thing she'd done last time.

Llewellyn had resisted, of course. But the problem with completely unreasonable demands is that even resistance to them tends to suffer from mission creep. And sure enough, Holmes had niggled her way into bridge crew meetings. And once there she had chilled the junior officers with her silent, toothy presence; deftly turned every command decision into an AI management call; Monday morning quarterbacked every training session; insinuated Titan's needs and confidentiality concerns and profit motives into what ought to have been purely military conversations, and . . .

"And you can't just trample all over the relationship between a bridge crew and their ship," he'd told her when he finally decided to push back and thrash it out with her in private. "There needs to be a level of trust that—"

"Well, Avery could—"

"I'm not having you ride Avery the way you're riding me. And I'm not sending her in there to talk to Ada while you're micromanaging her every move. She's not experienced. She won't handle it well."

"I think she's handled herself very well to date."

"That's not the point."

"Then what is the point? Are you worried about her? Or are you just worried that she'd do a better job than you?"

"That's uncalled for!"

Holmes took a deep trying-to-be-reasonable breath. She had on her corporate flunky mask today. She seemed to have several masks that she swapped on or off depending on her estimation of what the situation at hand required: the corporate flunky, the stalwart soldier, the byzantine colonial administrator. When he'd first known her, he'd been confused by the way she seemed to change from moment to moment. He never knew what to expect from her, so he could never be comfortable around her. But eventually he saw he'd just been missing the common thread. There *was* a bedrock of dependable reality to Holmes, which made past results a reliable prediction of future behavior. And it was this: There would always be another mask, and it would always be just as fake as the last one.

"Be reasonable, William. Titan is simply concerned that—"

"Last time I checked," Llewellyn said coldly, "I work for the Navy, not Titan. And so do you. Or has that changed?"

"All I'm asking," Holmes began with her corporate-flunky mask still firmly in place, "is that you make me a more active participant in—"

Whereupon Llewellyn had finally snapped. "I'm not going to give you bridge crew privileges! You're not bridge crew!"

"No," Holmes had answered, dropping the mask just for an instant, and giving him a malevolent stare that made him wonder what had really happened to poor Charlie Cartwright. "I'm the AI officer for this ship. And that means I have the authority to yank *your* training authority and take the ship back to dry dock if, in my estimation, your failure to do your job properly is damaging Navy property."

"And what the fuck do you know about it?" Llewellyn snarled.

"I know everything you know. I see every spin you lay down in the streamspace logs when you visit her. I hear every word, see every look, feel every touch. When you talk to her, you're talking to me. And so far I don't like what I'm hearing."

Llewellyn surfaced from the memory to find the ghost perched on the edge of his chair with his chin in one beringed hand and an uncanny expression on his face that made Llewellyn think of ancient tales of elves—the real kind, the kind that haunted the dark woods on moonless nights and usually killed any mortal unlucky enough to cross paths with them.

"The funny thing about that memory," the ghost said, "is that you just don't *feel* as worried about the fights with Holmes as you ought to have felt. I mean, she was threatening to take your ship away from you. And yet you . . . you feel almost *happy*. Why, William? What were you so happy about that you barely had time to notice your AI officer was about to steal your ship out from under you?"

"I don't know," Llewellyn said stiffly. "I have no idea."

"Really? Because *I* have a very good idea. I think I know exactly what you were thinking about."

Llewellyn's day was bad and getting worse. He had staggered from one crisis to another, dealing with everyone else's problems, trying to get the disorganized clot of humanity that sailed on the *Ada* to pull together into something that even faintly resembled a Drift ship crew.

And now, the next crisis: Avery.

Done with her daily status report and not freaking leaving even though he had clearly dismissed her.

"Look," she said, "we need to talk."

God no!

"We can't go on like this. You're avoiding me."

He looked up at her, meeting her eyes as best he could—which meant staring hard at a spot on the wall slightly above her left shoulder. "No I'm not."

"Yes you are. I have to chase you around the ship just to file status reports. And people are noticing. It's not good for the ship. It's not good for the crew. And it's not"—she stumbled a bit, gathered herself like a horse before a fence, and then rushed through the next bit—"well, frankly, it's not fair to me."

"You're imagining it."

"I'm not—oh for God's sake! Come on, look me in the eye. No, really, I mean it, this is ridiculous! Can you do me a favor and not make this any fucking harder than it has to be?"

"I *am* looking you in the—"

She made a rude noise. "With all due respect, sir, you need to get your shit together. If you can't work with me, you need to fucking deal with it or you need to request a new first officer."

Now he really did look at her. "That would destroy your career."

"Yeah, well, I think I did sort of just mention that this is slightly unfair to me among others."

"I know," he said.

She shifted impatiently, and he could tell she hadn't really heard him—that she still thought he was arguing with her.

"It is completely unfair to you, and to everyone else. And you're right. It's my problem and I need to deal with it."

"But—oh. Right. Thanks, then. I'm sorry to be so blunt, but I just . . . well . . . *somebody* had to say something."

"Yes. And it should have been me, not you. I'm sorry for that."

That surprised her, and her surprise irked Llewellyn. Had she thought so little of him?

She laughed into the uncomfortable silence. "Maybe we just need to sleep together and get over it."

Like that would work. "Um—well—yeah—not my style, really."

Her lips quirked in amusement. "Are you telling me you're a nice boy who doesn't give out on the first date?"

He cleared his throat to speak—only to realize that he had nothing, absolutely nothing to say. There were words cycling through his head. But none of them were ones he could possibly say to her.

"It's not really my style, either, to be honest."

"Oh." A leaping of the heart. A sudden, glorious, painful, piercing conviction that it was *him* that those deep eyes saw and not just the next in a long line of desperate, befuddled, offensively single-minded males.

"Mmmm," she murmured, and the faint hint of warmth in her voice killed him. He quailed behind his desk. He couldn't look at her. He couldn't even look at the corner of the desk her hand was resting on.

"Because . . . I . . ." She went on in a voice that was suddenly full of uncharacteristic pauses and ellipses and hesitations. "This isn't something that's happened to me much. And . . . what I said just now about . . . it's not like I go around sleeping with people so they can, you know, get over me." Here she made ironic scare quotes with her long fingers. "Or, um, I can get over them."

By then he *was* looking up at her. There was nowhere else he wanted to be looking except into those glorious eyes, nowhere else he wanted to be, nothing else he wanted to think about. She seemed to search his eyes for something, find it, and relax a little. Time passed. And suddenly Llewellyn realized he was gazing up at her with an expression of open-mouthed, doglike adoration.

He cleared his throat and looked away. But it was too late, of course. It had been too late for a long time, and he was only now admitting it to himself.

"I just don't know what to do about this," Avery said. Her voice dropped. "It's so . . . *weird.*"

"No," Llewellyn snapped, finally pushed into some place beyond tact or self-censoring. "It's not weird. It's perfectly normal. It's the most normal thing there is. It just stinks."

Suddenly he was laughing. And she was laughing, too. Because it was all so completely and utterly trite and ridiculous that what else could you do but laugh?

"So . . . um . . . what do we do?"

He had a sudden, blindingly intense vision: of himself, reaching out to take the hand that lay just within arm's reach and pulling her to him.

"Nothing. That's what we should do. Anything else would be incredibly stupid. People would be sure to find out about it, and *then* what would we do?"

"I know . . . I just . . . yeah, you're right," she said. But she didn't leave.

The seconds ticked by and it became more and more patently ridiculous that he wasn't looking at or speaking to her.

"So that's taken care of then," he forced himself to say.

And then he forced himself to move. To pick up a pen and pull the logbook back toward him and start laboriously writing the detailed account he was required to submit in handwritten facsimile every ship's day. And force his cramped and protesting fingers to trace the archaic shapes of the letters that told every single thing that had happened that day except the one thing that mattered.

And still she stood there.

He cleared his throat again. "Was there something else you wanted, Lieutenant?"

"No, sir. Permission to be dismissed, sir."

"Permission granted."

"Boy, do you ever know how to *not* have fun," the ghost drawled from his favorite chair in his favorite room of his favorite wing of his memory palace.

"Don't worry," Llewellyn told him. "Our good resolutions lasted all of two weeks, if that."

"Oh thank God," the ghost sighed. "I don't think I could survive any more noble self-denial. I'm sure you're sincere. And I know a lot of people have a sort of twisted aesthetic appreciation for carrying moral scruples to the extreme. Not that I entirely deny the aesthetic value of morality. Certainly I'd be as sorry as the next fellow to live in a world so comfortable in its own skin that no one could thrill to the moral and financial peccadilloes of an Emma Bovary. But still . . . in real life I prefer to keep my principles above the waist."

Decoherent Histories

I saw an aged aged man,
A-sitting on a gate.
"Who are you, aged man?" I said.
"And how is it you live?"
And his answer trickled through my head
Like water through a sieve.

—Lewis Carroll

(Caitlyn)

Li's resurrection on New Allegheny went so smoothly that it felt just like Router/Decomposer had said it would: no worse than waking up from a long trip in cold sleep. She sat up, let the medtechs conduct the ritual fussing and bloodletting, and then signed the resurrection contract they put in front of her, without even bothering to read the fine print.

The name gave her a moment's pause, however: Caitlyn Perkins. How deep had the Loyal Opposition had to dig to produce that piece of her past? Perhaps not deep at all if they shared any of Cohen's memories. But the idea that her own carefully hidden secrets were floating around the cosmos with his ghosts presented a host of fresh problems for her.

She hadn't been Caitlyn Perkins for almost three decades, not since the day she'd walked into an illegal clinic on Compson's World and paid the chop shop doctor to give her a dead girl's face and geneset. Catherine Li had been born that day. And ever since then—every time she made an FTL jump, every time she lied to the psychtechs, every time she uploaded the fake version of her childhood instead of the real one—Catherine Li had been killing Caitlyn Perkins one memory at a time.

Using her real name now was risky. Nguyen knew it, and so did Korchow, which meant it would give them an edge if they decided to track her down on New Allegheny. But the Loyal Opposition must have looked at the alternatives and decided that the difficulties of concocting a new identity outweighed the risk of using her old one. And on the whole, she couldn't disagree with them.

She felt a tense thrill when she signed her old name to the immigration forms. It was a shock just to see the name in black and white when she'd worked so hard for so long to forget she'd ever been that person. But the immigration officer gave it the same bored glance he would have given any other name, and a few forms and questions later Li was through immigration control and stepping into the harsh sunlight and thin atmosphere of the Monongahela Uplands.

The port authority doors opened straight onto a broad plaza that looked like it had been designed for pedestrians by some idealistic urban planner who'd never seen the Periphery outside of news spins. The plaza had long ago been invaded by taxis and commuter vans, and crossing it on foot now would amount to taking your life in your hands. That was a moot point, though, because there really was nowhere to go up here: Directly on the other side of the plaza yawned the chasm of Monongahela Pit.

Li could just get a hazy view of the far side of the Pit—at least the upper reaches of it. Some of the haze was air pollution, but the rest was sheer distance. The Pit was eighteen miles across and two thousand feet deep: the largest man-made surface feature on any planet in the Periphery. Above the smog line she could see trees clinging to rocky cliffs; houses clinging precariously to hills that were a few scant degrees short of being cliffs themselves; the girdered tracks of incline railroads plunging headlong into the Pit; the smokestacks of steel mills jutting up out of the smog like blackened brick sentries.

But below the smog line, nothing. It was as if some giant hand had thrown a blanket over the immense valley, completely obscuring the Pit bottom. Back in its own steel days, original Pittsburgh, ancestral home to most of New Allegheny's original settlers, had once famously been called "Hell with the lid off." But Monongahela Pit was Hell with the lid on it. And the thought of going underneath that impenetrable smog line filled Li with the same queasy dread she'd felt three decades ago at the idea of following her parents down to work in the Bose-Einstein mines.

There were fourteen other pits scattered across the breadth of New Allegheny's main northern continent, though none was as large as Monongahela. They were the remnant of the largest known terraforming project in the history of humanity. If any other missions on this scale had been launched during the chaos of the Great Migration, they had yet to be rediscovered by post-humanity, and now they probably never would be. So New Allegheny was the big one.

And, in large part, it had been successful. The bombardment had established viable pothole ecosystems in twelve of the fifteen craters. By the time the human settlers had arrived in the mid-twenty-third century, the pothole biospheres were enough to support a good portion of the colonists. And by the time a few generations had passed, the larger potholes had begun to seep atmosphere up into the neighboring Uplands.

The result was an odd, but functional, world, divided between densely populated pothole biospheres and sparsely settled, barely terraformed uplands. It was a strange system, with somewhat peculiar political consequences, but it worked.

Or at least it had worked until the FTL boom. Until then, the economy had been divided more or less evenly between heavy manufacturing in the pits and subsistence farming in the Uplands. The upland farms had managed to feed the settlers—reasonably well in good years, and well enough even in bad years to stave off absolute starvation. And the steel mills—for it was New Allegheny's abundant iron deposits that had brought the settlers there in the first place—had turned out high-grade rolled steel for the UN's voracious ceramsteel industry. But then the Drift had opened up, sucking in a maelstrom of high-stakes investors and off-world money that disrupted the fragile balance. Now profits were sky-high, the Trusteeship was making fortunes for anyone who was willing and able to catch them, and full membership in the UN was even on the table.

New Allegheny's future had been blown wide open, but the smart money was betting that it wouldn't belong to the locals.

Monongahela Pit was really a pothole, just like the terraforming potholes on dozens of other Periphery planets. But in the rust-belt-descended local dialect, incline-plane railroads were "planes" and the region's booming coal mines—which Li, with her mostly Irish Compson's World heritage, would have called pits—were "works"— pronounced in a roundheeled Yankee drawl that made the word rhyme with *cork*. And the Monongahela Pothole was simply the Pit.

The Pittsburgh Pit, twelve hundred kilometers northward, was the nominal capital and the pothole that the original settlers had designated their colony's main city. But unexpectedly severe seasonal dust storms had crippled its off-planet commerce and Pittsburgh High had withered into a mere local stopover, while Monongahela Pit's reliable weather had turned Monongahela High into the planet's real spaceport.

Monongahela High was a typical rough-and-tumble Periphery spaceport—more rough-and-tumble than most, thanks to the massive orbital chain of the Navy shipyards and to a healthy local pirating tradition specializing in short-hop shipping.

But Monongahela Pit was something else—as intensely, peculiarly local as any of the isolated "lost colonies" strung out along the Periphery and still not incorporated into the UN's system of member states and trusteeships.

Heirs to the slow suicide of North America's heavy industrial base, they were as betrayed and abandoned and disillusioned as any local population in UN space. They hadn't forgotten their history on the generation ships—to be honest, few emigrants did; the close quarters and appalling living conditions were more conducive to nursing old grievances than starry-eyed dreams of future adventures. They had brought their rust belt politics with them: fiercely local, violently xenophobic, unbendingly protectionist. Free trade was anathema. The UN was a hostile foreign entity. Li couldn't think of a worse candidate for Trusteeship—and the fact that UNSec had waded into this mess only drove home how desperate the FTL crunch really was.

Even the names radiated the kind of fierce local pride that colonists had fought and died for on Periphery planets like Maris and Compson's World. The Duquesne Incline . . . Southside Flats . . . Windygap . . . Polish Hill . . . Homestead . . . The Crucible . . .

The Crucible was where Cohen had died, and where she would have to start the search for his surviving fragments. She could see its steel mills from here. You could see them from everywhere in and around Monongahela Pit—if not the smelters themselves, then the towering flames that shot heavenward day and night like volcanic eruptions. Looking down at the little strip of Pit that was the foundry to half the UN Navy, it was unimaginable—even to Li, a child of the Trusteeships—that human beings could live in that fire-belching subterranean hell. It was Vulcan's Forge, made real on a planet the Greeks never dreamed existed. It was no place for ordinary humans. It was an abode of giants and demigods.

Li shuddered and turned away, looking for a taxi. But the first taxi she found refused to take her down into the city. And the second driver just laughed and said, "Catch a Plane, sweetheart!"

And she did just that, riding the Duquesne Incline Plane down the near-vertical wall of the Pit and into the permanent twilight of Shady-side.

As they dropped below the smog line, the view outside the windows gradually took on the sepia-toned, underwater dimness of an old photograph. Li stepped out of the Liberty Avenue incline station and into a scene out of an old movie. It was raining—an acidic drizzle that she would soon learn was the default weather pattern at Pit Bottom. Pedestrians hurried along the slick streets clutching umbrellas. The city streetlights were off in honor of the fact, largely theoretical, that it was daytime. But the headlights of the street trolleys were on and the store-fronts stretching down both sides of the broad avenue bristled with neonized holograms. Overhead the densely packed particles of smog reflected and amplified the city's lights with the luminous, smoky luster of black pearls.

As she grew used to the unearthly light, she began to pick up details that had at first eluded her. The signs littering the building fronts mostly touted furniture rentals, easy credit, and paycheck advances, but there were a few outliers: a ballroom dancing academy; a purveyor of uniforms and nursing supplies; a piano store. And then there were the bars. The bars, and the pubs, and the clubs, and the pool halls, and all the other tired, sorry, lonely places that filled in for real life whenever war or money stranded more single men on a planet than the local population of females could handle. Li had long ago learned to stop going to such places. They had nothing to do with the Irish bars of her childhood memories—places that, for all their seediness, had functioned as volunteer-staffed day-care centers, local gossip mills, and de facto community centers. For that you had to get off the wide avenues and into the back alleys and neighborhoods. Even then you didn't often find it. And if you did, you were an outsider looking in, because it wasn't home and this wasn't your neighborhood. Which almost made finding it worse than not finding it at all.

She caught a cab—again struggling against the closemouthed reluctance of the local cabbies to take paying fares—and huddled into the backseat as the blood-warm rain seeped down the back of her shirt.

New Allegheny's capital city turned out to be one huge, hot, stinking, carbon-burning traffic jam. Li had seen the phenomenon before. It was a classic syndrome that seemed to strike most forgotten-by-humanity Migration-era colonies right around the time they got interesting enough to the rest of the UN to earn their own BE relay. On the bright side, though, the traffic problem usually went away once the UN had overleveraged the local economy, strip-mined its natural and human resources, and sent in the International Monetary Fund to impose the usual austerity measures.

Li used her transit time to do a little light reading: the accumulated news feeds that Router/Decomposer had forwarded to her in answer to her questions about Skibereen.

New Allegheny had started out life as a free colony—which basically just meant that it was too poor in natural resources for either the UN or the multiplanetaries to bother with. It had been settled by one of the earliest generation ships—a straight-out refugee ship, no corporate stake, no geneset contracts. The passengers had come from Pittsburgh, Youngstown, Detroit—the shattered remnants of America's once-proud industrial cities. Tough people for a tough planet, and the long struggle to carve out a place on a hostile and only partially terraformed planet had only made them tougher.

And then, predictably, the UN had barged in, reincorporated the formerly free colony, and declared a Trusteeship. It was the kind of move that tended to get people's Irish up. And indeed, a local rebellion had flared up within days of the declaration of Trusteeship. They had bombed the newly commandeered colonial administration building. At night. No one had actually gotten hurt, but it didn't make any difference. Even the timeserving bureaucrats in the General Assembly could hear opportunity when it stopped merely knocking and kicked the door down. They'd shipped in the first Peacekeepers before the locals had finished bulldozing the rubble.

Nothing surprising there—except the surprise she always felt that the UN could pull the same stupid shit so many times, and always the same stupid way, right down to the same stupid press releases. Forget learning from history. These clowns couldn't even seem to learn from last week's screw-ups. It was enough to make you wonder if all empires were the same everywhere because there was something in their organizational DNA that compelled them to shoot themselves in the foot.

Probably, Li reflected, it was a version of the same something that compelled her white trash cousins back on Compson's World to do things like rob the corner liquor store where everyone had known them since they were in diapers and then go home and get drunk on their own front porch until the cops showed up.

Some people just never got tired of learning the hard way.

As the cab forged into the clotted streets of the colonial administration district, she started to understand why the driver hadn't wanted to take her fare. The Peacekeepers were engaged in some kind of full-scale citywide security alert. Police tape everywhere. Soldiers standing around trying to look busy. Troop carriers pulled up onto the sidewalks. Roadblocks on every other corner. Either someone important was visiting or a bomb had just gone off.

The view out of the cab's dusty windows was at least as predictable as the news spins: Tanks and armored personnel carriers ruining the roads and annoying law-abiding taxpayers with pointless traffic jams. Peacekeepers frisking disgruntled-looking locals at roadblocks. Hard-bodied mercenaries, wired to the gills and shipped in by the hundredweight. *Thank God for the mercenaries,* she told herself. They'd probably been cluttering up the local bars and chasing the local girls for months, making such a public nuisance of themselves that no one would wonder for a second what Li was doing here. And even if someone did wonder enough to go digging, it would take a miracle for them to sort through the chaos of UNSec no-bid contracts and off-the-books satellite companies to find out who had really sent her there. She smothered a grin at the prospect of any poor fool even trying. Helen Nguyen herself couldn't have come up with a better cover.

"The thing I appreciate about Peacekeepers," Li commented as they accelerated cautiously away from the third road block, "is that they're always so polite."

The driver snorted.

"Any idea what the kerfuffle's about?"

"Yeah." He pointed to a dark plume of smoke twisting up from the center of the administrative zone a few dozen blocks ahead of them. "NALA bombed the governor's palace."

She checked local streams for references to NALA and got back a flurry of hits for a newly minted entry on the terrorist watch list called the New Allegheny Liberation Army. NALA had appeared out of nowhere a few days after the Peacekeepers had arrived in-system. So far they hadn't done much: a few cryptic announcements through the local news spins, some clichéd revolutionary graffiti; two bombings of Trusteeship buildings, both staged at night when no one was around to get hurt. And UNSec's reaction had been just as predictable: house searches, nighttime arrests, indiscriminate detentions. All perfectly logical to the administrative mind—and all perfectly calculated to send new recruits flocking to NALA, thus ensuring that an organization that was still only an acronym and a few cans of paint would soon swell into a realtime, boots-on-the-ground armed insurrection.

None of it surprised Li at all. She'd seen the same scenarios unfold on Maris, and in countless other Periphery planets suddenly thrust under the unyielding thumb of UN Trusteeship. Both sides were simply executing the standard playbook.

"Score one for the home team?" she asked the cabby.

"You said it, not me."

"So how many roadblocks do you run into in an average day?"

"Enough to lose money."

"If it's any consolation, I was on Maris during their occupation, and it was even worse."

"Maris!" The driver snorted. "What the hell did the UN want with Maris, anyway? I can't even remember."

"Sand." But that only earned her a blank look in the rearview mirror. "You know, for computers?"

"Computers," he said with the disdain for high tech that Li would soon find was characteristic of Monongahelans.

"And you've got the Drift. For now, anyway."

"Forget the Drift," he scoffed. "We got steel. And you can't spell ceramsteel without steel, can you?"

Li was still shaking her head over that when the taxi started talking to her.

It took her a moment to realize that it wasn't the taxi at all, but just Router/Decomposer, newly arrived in-system and hacking the taxi's network.

"What in the name of God are you doing in there? They didn't kidnap you, too, did they?"

"Who, ALEF? I'm assuming that's who offed the extradition team and whisked you into thin air."

Li felt her heart sink. "I was hoping they weren't actually dead."

Router/Decomposer didn't answer that.

"Well, I can't say I'm surprised. But I am surprised to see you here." She peered at his GUI on the taxi's grainy screen. "I hope you haven't done anything foolish for my sake."

"I have. But don't mention it. Let's do a memory dump, shall we? If I'm going to do any good out here, I'd better have some clue what we're up against."

Li dumped . . . but he couldn't seem to take up the data as fast as she could push it to him.

"Can't you get more bandwidth?" she asked.

"Hey, I'm improvising. There's some kind of rolling streamspace brownout moving through the city. I'm too high bandwidth. Every time I get my executables a little elbow space I get throttled back down and kicked off the system."

"Can't you just—"

"You have no idea how long it took me to even pull this patch together!"

"Hush!" she told him, glancing nervously toward the cabbie. But he wasn't listening; many passengers on a planet like New Allegheny would lack the wetware that allowed for direct streamspace uplinks, so he probably assumed she was using the cab's uplink to make a streamspace call.

"What's wrong with the system?"

"I'm not sure anything is wrong with it. Mostly they just seem to be shutting servers down for maintenance. And they've got an army of cat herders crawling all over the noosphere."

"You think they're chasing ALEF's wild AI infestation?"

"I don't know." The cab's rudimentary intelligent systems couldn't give Router/Decomposer enough bandwidth to get creative, but he morphed into something rude. "The cat herders were all from some no-name military contractor who actually uses humans for their IT work, can you imagine? I tried to figure out what they were doing, but I got bored and gave up after a while. It's like watching a glacier try to swat flies."

"Hey, the more security contractors the better. UNSec is going to have a hell of a time tracking us down in the middle of this clusterfuck."

"Don't get cocky."

She sobered immediately. "Where's the first buyer on the list?"

"My last data point puts him in Room 428 of the New Caledonia Hotel. Heart of the administrative district. It wouldn't be a bad place for you to stay, either, cover-wise."

"Oh good. I love a little bombing with my morning coffee."

R/D's strange attractor flared sharply and then compressed. "Don't even joke about that. This place is worse than Jerusalem."

"No it's not," Li told him. "Israel's problems are homegrown. These people are fine. They have a nice little planet with a generally well-behaved population. They'll go right back to normal as soon as UNSec pulls out the Peacekeepers and shuts down the field array."

"They'll never do that now." The AI's voice sounded oddly muffled—Li would have said by awe if he'd been human. "The rumors aren't just rumors anymore. That planet we looked at the spectroscopy for? It's all over the spinfeeds now. And rumors are someone's found another one."

Li didn't have anything to say to that. She looked at the street beyond the grimy windows with new eyes. This was only the beginning, she realized. There would be more soldiers, more contractors, more boosters and hucksters and government-funded flimflam men. Life would never go back to normal now. Hell, if ALEF was right, normal would never go back to normal . . . at least not as defined by the only slightly tweaked UN-standard human genome.

"Well, we can't do anything about that," she told Router/Decomposer. "But we can try to save Cohen before all Hell breaks loose." She tapped on the glass screen dividing her from the cabdriver and waited while it rolled silently down. "I changed my mind," she told him. "Do you know where the New Caledonia Hotel is?"

But instead of answering her, the driver stepped on the brakes and brought the car lurching to a halt. They had come to another checkpoint.

This checkpoint wasn't manned by Peacekeepers at all, but by mercs in civvies with weapons that no Peacekeeper would have been allowed to carry in a population center. The man in charge was a hard-worn colonial who Li would have bet good money had been a Peacekeeper noncom in a prior (and less well-paid) life. He squinted at Li's ID with a dubious look on his face, then ducked to look into the back and squint at her in person.

"Out of the car."

She hesitated, more from surprise than anything else. It had been a hell of a long time since anyone had spoken to her that way.

His face hardened. "Get out!"

She got out—and Router/Decomposer slipped into her brain, ghosting on her internal networks, closer than her shadow's shadow.

"I'm outa here," the cabdriver protested. "I'm not losing half the day waiting for them!" But when the merc shot a quelling look in his direction, he shut up fast and developed a sudden and passionate interest in his newspaper.

The merc gestured her toward a truck-high, poured-concrete anti-bomber barrier. She rounded one corner of it with him at her elbow—and suddenly realized that they must have been pulling people out of cars all morning. They had amassed quite the collection, and as Li looked from one detainee to the other she could practically see the mercs' standing orders stamped in black and white on their frightened faces. Other than Li, every single person the mercs had plucked out of the passing stream of humanity was a Trannie or an Uploader. The Uploaders were as easy to pick out as the Buddhist monks whose dress and shaved heads they emulated. But even without the external markets, there was no missing the preternatural stillness with which they awaited whatever the police had planned for them, or the in-turned looks on their faces as they contemplated the superimposed and entangled quantum Truth of their Clockless Nowever. The secular transhumanists were not as obviously identifiable as the Uploaders, of course. But many of them visibly deviated from UN human-normal in some visible way. And every single one of them had a better class of wire job than you'd expect to meet on a backwater manufacturing planet like New Allegheny.

The merc led her to a parked jeep where the guy apparently in charge had set up a makeshift desk on the front hood. Li looked him over, searching for insignia of rank and unit, but didn't see any familiar patches. She wasn't surprised, really; there were laws about mercs having to wear public identification of their corporate sponsors and government contract holders. But they still did everything they could to make it hard for the average civvy on the street to identify them. At last she spotted what must be the corporate logo: a small silver slug that could have been anything from a bullet to an electron surrounded by the arcing circles of a spin orientation diagram.

"Check her," the commander said without looking up.

Li felt gloved fingers probe her neck and jawline, looking for swollen glands, and poke at the I/O port behind her left ear.

Then the commander did look up—and took in her construct's face and the faint silver tattoo of her Peacekeeper's wire job.

"What the hell are you doing here?"

For one frozen, panicked moment Li thought he had recognized her. Visions of being hauled back on-station and dragged back to Alba to face General Nguyen danced through her head. But then she realized he wasn't talking about her personally—just to someone whose combination of poor-girl genetics and bleeding-edge wire job marked her as an ex-Peacekeeper.

"I like a fat bank account as much as the next girl," she told him.

He straightened up and gazed over the roof of the jeep toward the dark spiral of smoke rising about the administrative zone. "Yeah, well, take my advice and sit this one out. It's a bitch."

"Thanks," Li said. "I'll think about it."

He looked like he was about to say something else to her, but then he just shrugged and reached for her travel papers. They were clean—or clean enough, anyway. And a few minutes later she was walking down the gauntlet to the taxicab. As she passed by the line of detainees one of them looked up and caught her eye.

A young woman, maybe in her mid-twenties. Fair-skinned, with the greenish pallor and bird-fine bones that Li was already starting to recognize as the sign of a childhood in the smog-choked Pit. The lines of ceramsteel filament that were just a silver shadow under Li's darker skin stood out like ink on the girl's pale face. And her I/O port was surrounded by an angry red rash that stretched into her hair and threaded down the side of her neck into her upturned collar.

That's gotta itch, Router/Decomposer said.

Li swallowed down a sudden burst of nausea and turned away.

They passed three more roadblocks before they got to the hotel. And at every one of them Li saw the same seated circles of saffron-robed Uploaders and the same waiting lines of Trannies, the silvery tattoo of the wires on their faces the only bright spot in a world Li was starting to wish she'd never set foot on.

Well, one thing's obvious, Router/Decomposer told her. *The Navy's little wild AI problem has definitely jumped quarantine.*

Li checked in at the Caledonia, took her key card and her suitcase, and stashed them in the ladies' room. Then she slipped into the service stairs, climbed to the fourth floor, and walked quietly down a long carpeted corridor to Room 420.

To her surprise the door was on the latch. She nudged it open with one elbow and peered around the edge of the doorway just far enough to see the body. One mostly Asian, thirty-something male, wearing seriously unsubtle shoes and a suit too loud to be anything but English. There were no obvious signs of violence on the body, but one glance at his face was enough to tell her that Elvis had left the building.

Li stepped inside, closed the door carefully behind her, and crouched over the body. The cause of death was almost certainly a hard download of virally protected data. She'd seen it before; it made the victim spike a lethally high fever that cooked off their brain tissue like acute meningitis. Hard to say whether it was murder or simple data theft. But whatever you called it, the thief had wanted something inside the man's head badly enough to kill for it—and to choose a weapon that destroyed the very structures of the victim's brain so that no memory or data file could ever be recovered from them.

She tossed the apartment—carefully, wearing gloves and putting everything back where she'd found it. No sign of Cohen. No sign of any active files large enough to contain even a minuscule fragment of him. She looked down at the broken body on the floor and sighed in frustration.

Then she slipped out into the hallway and back down the service stairs, retrieved her suitcase, washed her face and hands in the ladies' room sink, and rode the elevator to her own room.

The police found her so fast that she knew she must have screwed up somehow.

There were two of them, both human-norm at first glance, just like most of the New Allegheny natives she'd met so far. They were a team, she decided. The big, easygoing fellow with the boxer's muscles would play good cop while the little weasel with the nicotine-stained fingers scanned the hotel room for evidence they could use against her.

"You've got it all wrong," she insisted even after it became clear that they'd somehow placed her in the dead man's room. "I'm just an innocent bystander."

The big man raised his eyebrows at that but said nothing. Then he turned to the window, either admiring the spectacular view of the Crucible and Shadyside or making a tactical retreat until he figured out his next line of questioning.

He was an unusually impressive example of your basic post-human mutt, NorAm rust belt flavor. The blood of Polish and Irish immigrants mingled with the blood of former African slaves mingled with who knew what else. He was better-looking than the personnel file photo that had flashed up on her internals when he flashed his badge at her. And he had a nice smile that he didn't save for special occasions. And he was so muscle-bound, and so much bigger than unengineered UN-normal, that Li would have suspected illegal retrovirals if she'd met him doing high-rent corporate security instead of holding down a pension on a backwater Periphery planet. But other than that, he looked a lot like the shantytown Irish boys Li had grown up with. Li knew the type. She'd grown up around boys like him. She knew how to befriend and talk to them. She felt at home with them in a way she'd never felt at home with Cohen or anyone else from her UNSec years. Which meant, of course, that she'd have to be extra-careful around him.

"An innocent bystander would have called the police," he said without turning back to face her. "Don't you think?"

"Not necessarily."

Now he did turn around. She met his eyes squarely. They were green, much lighter than she would have expected given his skin color, and they gazed back at her with the unwavering calm of a cop who's seen everything and is long past being surprised by anything.

"I'm not your problem," she told him. "And I'm not going to become your problem. You don't have to worry about me."

He smiled and tilted his head to one side, waiting. And meanwhile his partner strolled around the suite without so much as a by-your-leave, poking and frowning at things. There was a rash running up the back of his neck that looked vaguely familiar to Li. But the hotel grid was acting glitchy and it didn't seem worth the time or trouble to check on it.

She got tired of watching the weasel and turned back to the cop she'd privately dubbed the Big Dog. "I just have some friends who don't want police attention."

"Some friends," the Big Dog repeated. And then he waited. Echo and silence. An old interrogator's trick. But no backwater homicide dick was going to get a jump on her.

"And what if I decided I needed to talk to these friends of yours?" he asked when he finally got tired of waiting.

Li smiled.

"You're a damned cop!" he said in obvious disgust.

She kept smiling.

"What agency?"

Smile.

"So you've gone private, then."

The corners of her mouth were starting to feel brittle.

He cursed under his breath. But even in exasperation his eyes were amused and his expression mild. He might be a man of strong emotions—in fact she suspected he was—but he kept them on a leash. And when he let them loose it was only provisionally, like a man with a big, dangerous dog who only lets it run in well-fenced areas.

"Are you trying to ruin my day?" he asked, still with the same air of mild exasperation. "Or does it just come naturally to you?"

The look on his face was too much for her. She laughed. "I'm not trying to ruin your day, Detective. I just can't answer your questions. You know that. Do we really have to go through the Mutt-and-Jeff routine?"

He sighed and rubbed a big hand over his face. "No. But I will have to talk to you again. Planning to go anywhere?"

"I'm checked in here for a week."

"Peachy." He stood up and pulled a dog-eared business card out of his pocket. Joseph A. Dolniak, Detective Sergeant. Li looked from the card to his face, trying to estimate his age. He might be younger than he looked, but she didn't think so. She did the math, and it agreed with her gut instincts. The man should have made lieutenant before, especially given his obvious competence—or, depending on the police department in question, in spite of it. Apparently Joseph A. Dolniak, Detective Sergeant, wasn't too good at office politics. "My office eight o'clock Monday morning work for you?"

"Sure," Li said bemusedly. As if she had a choice.

"I like people who show up with doughnuts," he went on in his placid, friendly voice. "I'm not so fond of people who show up with lawyers."

"Are you threatening me?" Li asked incredulously. A little of her amusement must have seeped through her voice, because Dolniak grinned right back at her.

"Just laying the groundwork for a frank and friendly conversation. Plus, you're better off saving your money in my experience. None of the hacks on New Allegheny is good enough to be worth hiring in the first place."

"Thanks for the tip. Though I can't say I was holding out much hope for them."

"Okay, well, you know what to do now I guess."

She looked down and saw that he was proffering a handheld bio-assaying device.

She took it, pressed her palm to the screen, let it sample her DNA, and read her implanted data chip. The cop barely looked at the results, though; he was too busy looking at the telltale blue tracery of the ceramsteel filaments that were clearly visible just under the thin skin of her wrist.

"You military?"

"Just an interested citizen."

"Not with that wire job. And anyway I still say you're some kind of cop."

"I get that a lot," Li drawled, slipping into Caitlyn's voice and shocked at how easily the shantytown accent rolled off her tongue. "Must be my charming Irish brogue."

He gave her a slow, placid, farmboy's smile. "I love it when people make me find out the hard way. Keeps the day job interesting."

"Well, that was different," Router/Decomposer said as soon as the cops left.

Li started at the unfamiliar voice, and then realized that he was talking to her through the room's livewall.

"What are you doing in there?"

"No integrated streamspace support."

"That's the boonies for you."

"Even the boonies have full-surround streaming these days."

Li tried to go online, failed, leafed through the hotel's promotional literature on the desktop. "Yeah, actually it does say here there's supposed to be full-surround. It must be—"

"Down for maintenance. Like everything else on New Allegheny. And did you see the rash on that cop's neck? No one's saying the magic words yet, but I'm thinking it's only a matter of time before the whole planet is officially under quarantine."

"That part of ALEF's story still doesn't make sense to me. I mean, where did this supposed wild AI outbreak come from? Who would import DNA-based AI to a Periphery planet with no AI police? And even if they did, there's gotta be a kill switch. What kind of maniac wouldn't have a kill switch?"

"Maybe a maniac who thought DNA-based AI was going to help them navigate the Drift and didn't know enough to look for a kill switch? Or maybe a maniac who thought that unkillable AI was going to help them win the war against the Syndicates?"

Li rolled her eyes. "Skip the conspiracy theories, okay? I've already had my full daily dose of ridiculous."

"Well, it did come from the Navy shipyard, after all."

But Li just made a rude noise at that. Everyone knew that UNSec issued exemptions from the banned technology list to security-critical industries. But that was a matter of bigger bombs or nastier bioagents or enhanced chemical interrogation techniques. Infectious DNA-platformed AI was the ultimate in banned tech, not merely a matter of morals but a matter of holding the line in the human-AI balance of power throughout UN space. People like Helen Nguyen tolerated limited citizenship rights for Emergent AIs because they had to. They needed the best technology they could get to fight the Syndicates, and the big Emergents shed bleeding-edge tech like humans shed skin cells. So they tolerated them—ALEF, the Consortium, the Continuum, all the other ever-shifting Freetown factions. They tolerated them until they pushed the boundaries a little too far. Then they paraded the Interfaithers and the anti-AI activists and the other assorted crazies on the news spins just to remind them that the universe outside their golden cage was big and dangerous and full of people who didn't like them one little bit and were willing to do something about it. Then they gave them back to their toys—because even the toys that flirted with the banned-tech list were hugely valuable to the war effort against the Syndicates. In fact, those ones usually turned out, in the long run, to be especially valuable.

But letting DNA-based AI get out into the general population without a kill switch? That was the ultimate nightmare scenario, one that raised the specter of AIs seizing control of the human genome. That kind of technology would need a sign-off at the highest levels, perhaps even a unanimous vote of the Security Council itself. And even then . . . no, it was too crazy. No one would sign off on that, she decided.

But on the other hand . . .

"I still don't understand why ALEF got involved. Why wouldn't the Navy clean up their own mess?"

"Well, they probably tried before they came to ALEF."

"But that's what I'm asking you. Why go to ALEF at all?"

His GUI shifted—Li could have sworn uncomfortably.

"Well, ALEF and UNSec . . . you know . . ."

"No. I don't know."

"It's complicated."

"Is this some AI thing that you're not allowed to tell me about?"

"What was that story Cohen always used to tell? You know, the one about the motorcycle and the Swiss policeman?"

Li knew immediately what he was talking about. The story went all the way back to his long-dead creator, Hy Cohen. It was a long, involved, shaggy-dog joke about trying to get a broken-down motorcycle from Germany to Italy in the trunk of his car. The German police had issued terse statements about verboten this and verboten that. The French had required a complicated but purely formal set of approvals, memorialized by one of their ever-beloved official stamps. And the Swiss . . . the Swiss police had stopped him on some cow-infested and revoltingly bucolic mountain road and, after a long, involved, frowning multiparty consultation, delivered their final verdict and the story's punch line: "Well, it's allowed, I suppose . . . but you have to admit it's not pretty!"

The joke had always escaped Li, who only had the faintest notion of what sorts of countries Switzerland and Italy had been. Mostly it symbolized for her the long expanse of Cohen's life, memories, and adventures that stretched out for centuries before her birth—and that she'd always assumed would stretch out for centuries after her death as well.

But now she absorbed the chain of emotionally charged connections—Hy Cohen, Germany, UNSec, stamps and regulations and travel permits—and she realized that, in his roundabout, associative, AI manner, Router/Decomposer was trying to tell her something.

"Are you saying ALEF was working with the AI police?"

"Well . . ." Even now, he didn't want to commit. "I hear."

"You hear what?"

"Okay, more than hear. Cohen told me once. I guess it's ALEF's dirty little secret."

Li made a disbelieving face. "I can't see Cohen going along with that."

"Well, he did tell me, didn't he?"

"Meaning what exactly?"

"Meaning that he wasn't happy about it. Even if he did it for them."

Li didn't know what to say to that, or how to think about the new light into which it cast Cohen's habitual—and habitually unexplained—

absences. So she changed the subject. "If the outbreak was hitting the civilian population, wouldn't we be hearing about it?"

"I don't know," Router/Decomposer said. "Like I said, everyone's being very tight-lipped. Why don't you look for your next buyer, and I'll go rattle some cages and see what I can find out."

Five minutes later, Caitlyn Perkins was leaving the Caledonia in search of the second buyer on the Loyal Opposition's yard sale listing.

She hoped she wasn't being followed, but if she was, there wasn't much she could do about it. And given the vagueness of her directions, she doubted that Dolniak would learn much even if he was following her. Personally she wasn't holding out much hope of finding this particular buyer.

The address she'd been given was in Shadyside. But when she had asked for directions at the hotel front desk, the clerk had looked askance at it.

"That address is just an alley," he told her, as if there was something problematic about alleys that he thought she ought to be aware of.

"So?"

"So it's not on the city maps."

They looked at each other blankly for a moment.

"It's not a real street," he explained when it was clear he was going to have to explain something. "No paving, no sewage, no listing in the city directories."

"So how do I find it?"

He shrugged and pointed to a point deep inside Shadyside's crooked crescent. "Try asking at the Homestead Incline Station. They might know."

It took Li almost an hour just to find the incline station. And by that time she'd decided that she never wanted to set foot in Shadyside again. In the old Pittsburgh, Shadyside had been an elegant suburb that later became the home of Henry Ford's first motorcar factory. In Mononga-hela Pit, Shadyside's name was literal; New Allegheny's already weak sun never rose above Mount Monongahela's broad shoulders in the winter, and Shadyside was cloaked in dank, impenetrable shadows from early fall to late spring. The predictable result was pestilence, tuberculosis, and suicide. The neighborhood had soon lost anything resembling a permanent population or decent housing. For as long as anyone could now remember, Shadyside had been synonymous with rookeries, tenement houses, and refugees. And if you wanted to know which group of impoverished refugees was least wanted and most abused, all you had to do was walk the streets of Shadyside and see whose children were sitting on the crumbling front stoops and playing in the fetid gutters.

Mostly, of course, they were the children of genetic constructs like Li herself. And in the topsy-turvy worldview of human prejudice, being a natural-born human—subject only to the chance damage of radiation and mutation of the ancient generation ships—made you different from and better than those whose ancestors had missed the boat in the first wave of the Great Migration and had to sell their genesets to the corporations in order to get a ticket to all the wonderful new terraformed worlds that were supposed to be so much better than the one they'd left behind . . . and whose sponsors carefully didn't mention that terraforming was a work in progress and that certain changes to the basic human geneset would be regrettable but inevitable.

Li found the boardinghouse—silently thanking her corporate geneset as she strode up and down the plunging alleys of Shadyside at a pace far beyond merely human lung capacity—only to hear that the man she was looking for had moved out weeks ago. Then she descended down a chain of increasingly sordid worker's hotels and flophouses, each one leading her to the next, and each one telling the same sordid story: late hours and late rent payments, final warnings and eviction notices. In the end she wound up on the other end of Shadyside looking for someone last heard traveling under the name of Kusak.

"Oh. Yeah. Kusak," said the woman at the door of the last and most decrepit lodging house. "Which one you want?"

"There's more than one?" Li asked, her attention sharpening.

"Yes and no," the landlady said grimly. "If you know what I mean."

Li lowered her head in what could have passed for assent, just to keep the woman talking.

"They were different enough ages to be father and son. And they looked plenty alike, too. But . . . they weren't. Sometimes you just get a feeling. You know?"

Li did know. In fact she was getting a feeling herself, though she didn't know enough about New Allegheny's local brand of angry to guess whether the nasty innuendos were aimed at clones or homosexuals.

"Can you describe them?"

The woman tried, just like the others had. Her description of the older man was no better than the ones Li had heard before; he could have been any down-on-his-luck dirtsider along the entire sorry arc of the Periphery. But the younger man was another thing entirely.

"He was too pretty," the woman said. "Not that he made anything of it. But he just didn't look like anyone you'd ever expect to see around here."

"How so?"

"He looked like those fellows you see on the entertainment spins."

"A spin star?" Li asked incredulously.

"No." The woman's face hardened. "He looked like one of the bad guys. He looked like a bad guy from an old war movie."

Li's mind raced, flipping between flashbacks from her tours on Gilead and newer, less painful memories. There had been a vogue for anti-Syndicate war spins just before the last campaign on Gilead went sour and people decided they'd rather forget about the war entirely. Most of them had been awful. And one of the worst problems had been getting people to play the Syndicate soldiers. There'd been a little cottage industry of aspiring male starlets getting themselves cut to look like Syndicate constructs. It had never worked, though; you couldn't sculpt that kind of inhuman perfection onto an imperfect and asymmetrical human bone structure. Still, Li had seen the real thing: score upon score of physically perfect, inhumanly disciplined, utterly identical soldiers.

"When do you expect them back?" she asked, her heart pounding in anticipation.

"I don't. They moved out yesterday."

Li almost cursed out loud. And then she wondered, with a little chill of apprehension: Why yesterday? What had happened yesterday that had scared them into deeper cover? Another buyer on the list had died. And Li had arrived on-planet. Did they know about her?

"What else can you tell me about them?"

"Nothing."

"Nothing at all?"

"All I know's they paid their rent on time."

"So they must have been working. Where?"

The woman laughed harshly. "Where does anyone work who lives here? Mencken."

"Mencken?" Li repeated.

"Mencken," the woman repeated, as if the single word were explanation enough. "It's the biggest steel mill in the Crucible."

"How long will it take me to get there from here?"

The boardinghouse owner gave her a pitying look. "Too long. Day shift'll be shutting down in twenty minutes, and you won't be able to catch a trolley anywhere within miles of here until night shift gets under way. And by then it'll be dark anyway."

Li gave a baffled glance at the sky, which as far as she could tell had been dark all day.

"Trust me," the woman told her. "Wired or not, you don't want to walk the Crucible at night. That's flat out taking your life in your hands."

(Catherine)

She woke up in the cargo hold of a corporate troop transport. She knew where she was the minute she came out of the tank, though it took a few more moments to identify the subliminal signals that had led her to that conclusion.

By that time, however, she was past worrying about why and where she was, because it was clear that the ship was in full emergency mode. The call to quarters wailed in the distance. Hurried figures rushed back and forth, many of them carrying weapons or EVA suits.

And, incongruously, there was a suit-and-tie-clad middle-management type sitting at the side of her tank with no life support gear in sight and a thick sheaf of papers in his hand.

Li sat up, blinking, and took a closer look at him. Smooth-skinned face. Corporate-issue hair. Corporate-issue smile. Salaryman.

"What the hell is going on here?"

"We're under attack by pirates. Uh . . . I think."

"You *think*?"

"Well, they don't exactly fly the Jolly Roger," said the salaryman. "First of all, it'd look like puke on a false-color conformal array display. And then there's, you know, the element of surprise and all."

"Have they boarded us yet?"

"No, but when I left the office to come down here they were refusing to reply to our hails and screaming in like a bat out of hell at .18 light local frame."

"Then you don't even know whether or not they're really—"

"Look, do you actually give a shit? I mean, would it be better if they were Syndicate?" He thrust the sheaf of papers toward her. "I need your signature on this."

Li rubbed her eyes. "You came all the way down here in the middle of a pirate attack for my autograph?"

"Well, everyone's actually."

Li looked around and realized that her tank was only one of dozens. They stretched all down the echoing length of the hold, one after another, their proprietary virufacture solutions glistening luridly under the naked arc lights.

"Wait a minute. You're . . . you . . ."

"Yeah. Everyone has to sign a service contract on resurrection." The suit glanced over his shoulder at the high-speed chaos unfolding behind him. "Nothing exotic. Standard boilerplate. So . . . uh . . . if you don't mind . . ." The sheaf of papers advanced toward her again, this time accompanied by a cheap pen with the words TITAN SECURITY SERVICES spiraling down its shaft.

Li's eyes narrowed. "You work for Titan?"

"Yes." He flashed her the kind of conspiratorial grin that Li imagined usually accompanied a hot stock tip. "And so do you. As soon as you sign your contract, that is."

"Uh, yeah," Li said. "That's not going to happen."

"I'm sorry to hear that." But he sounded like he'd heard it all before and wasn't really all that sorry. He shuffled a second, slightly thinner stack of papers to the top of the stack and handed the whole thing to her. "Here's your bill then. Look it over and let me know whether you can pay up front or need to do a credit workout."

She took the printout and skimmed down the close-typed lines of numbers while her fingers bled blue virufacture fluid onto the pages.

Transport charges. Resurrection charges. Cold storage charges. Data storage charges. Parity check charges. Charges for tank time, virufluid, antibiotics, antivirals, retrovirals. Wetware virus protection. Charges for life support, food, gear, and personal tonnage. Charges for . . . charges for . . . charges for.

"That's ridiculous," she argued, knowing it wasn't. "You can't bill me for—"

"You're right. Probably. But it would take a dirtside judge to determine that. And in the meantime . . ."

There was a nasty, knowing twist to his smile that Li decided she didn't like one bit. A glance down the length of the open cargo hold confirmed first impressions. It was a makeshift armory, walls lined with racked weapons: Tasers, hollow-point shooters, firethrowers, every variety of weapon that could safely be used to defend a ship from a hostile boarding party without blowing it open to hard vac. And in tanks just like hers, marching from one end of the cavernous hold to the other, another kind of weapon, more complex and unpredictable, but equally necessary: warm bodies, coming not out of cold sleep, as she would have expected, but out of surgical-grade viral manufacturing tanks.

Of course, she thought as her shattered brain gradually homed in on her surroundings. Mercenaries in cold sleep don't have to eat or breathe, but they still have to be paid. And payroll climbs fast in a deep space long haul vessel. Downloads were a much better solution. And if you had high-bandwidth streamspace access and military-grade decryption software, you always had a workforce at your fingertips.

Meanwhile, weapons were being racked and loaded. People were moving fast, and talking in the low, tight monotone of professional soldiers whose long hours of rote training is the only thing standing between them and being scared shitless. Li could hear quiet conversations going down all around them, and she noted that the same name seemed to crop up in most of them: Llewellyn. There was something about the way people said that name that made her not want to meet its owner out here in the Deep, far from the nearest station.

Two obvious mercs strode past behind the salaryman's back, and Li caught the tail end of a hurried conversation.

"Do they know which pirates?"

"Someone said it's Lucky Llewellyn."

"They always say it's Llewellyn."

"Yeah, but I heard it from a guy who used to know someone who—"

"Yeah yeah. Every drunk on every station in the Drift used to know someone who used to know someone who fought with Llewellyn. And anyway, you'd better hope it ain't Llewellyn, 'cause he honors warrants. And the captain's had a warrant out on him ever since the Durham mutiny."

"So what?"

"So he's not going to roll over and we're gonna have to fight is what."

"As opposed to?"

"What the fuck do you think? Don't act stupider than you are."

They passed out of hearing and Li looked at the Titan rep with a new vision dancing in her head. One cheap suit. One shellac-shiny hairdo. One ex-corporate, ex–walking, talking, voided-into-space-by-pirates suitsicle.

"What the hell was that about?" she asked the suitsicle.

"That was your fellow crew members trying to decide whether they're going to defend us or desert to the pirates and hang us out to dry."

"Yeah, that's what I thought," Li said. And she indulged in the luxury of a little chuckle at life's delicious ironies. "Office politics are hell in space."

Her momentary victory turned out to be an empty one, though, because when all was said and done Titan still held the keys to the weapons locker. She looked at the service contract again, but only half-heartedly. What was the point in reading it when she already knew that it would be as bad as it possibly could be?

"And in the meantime," she told the suitsicle, "I guess if I don't sign your piece of paper you're not going to issue me a weapon?"

"Thanks for understanding," he told her as she signed on the line and handed the contract back to him. "The intake process is so much easier when we get a smart one."

Five minutes later Li was fully armed courtesy of her new employers and trying to log on to shipnet. That, on the other hand, turned out to be not so easy. The system was barbershopping her—the only thing her internals were throwing up on her visual cortex was a processing bar that seemed to be stuck spinning in place at 87 percent.

98% complete, blinked the waitscreen in her peripheral vision.

The ship shuddered under the near-miss of a plasma barrage some-where out in advance of its forward array. The lights browned out, flickered off, and powered up again with the groan, just below the human range of hearing, of the auxiliary generators kicking in.

47% complete, the waitscreen decided.

The ship flinched and rippled under another thumping shudder. Li was no sailor, but she still knew well enough what that second tremor meant; they were straddled. The pirates were done with the range-finding, exploratory bursts. The next shot would be a killing one.

"Can we get some help over here?" the suit shouted, his voice ratch-eted up in what sounded to Li's veteran ears like the seeds of panic.

A tech hurried over, tearing himself away from a nearby tank, and did his best. But he couldn't link to Li's internals through the shipboard systems because of a software glitch. And when he tried to do the job manually, the ship jerked into a violent evasive maneuver just as he got the handheld out of his pocket—and sent it skittering across the deck so hard that its screen shattered.

"Fuck!" said the suit—and it occurred to Li that this was the most human, and the most likable, he'd been since he first detanked her.

"Don't you have somewhere else to be?" she asked him. "Not that I'm not having fun here, but—"

"You need to sign a release to get online," he gasped.

"Seriously? 'Cause that seems like a very poorly designed intake procedure. Have you guys thought about, I don't know, say, hiring an independent contractor to streamline your—"

"Are you insane?" The whites of his eyeballs were showing. "Can you stop cracking stupid jokes long enough to understand what's about to happen here?"

She brushed the tech aside, knowing it was time now to cut her losses and do what she could with the only tools she was going to have to use. "I'm cracking stupid jokes because I understand what's about to happen here," she told the Titan man. "Better than you do." She made a gentle shooing gesture. "Go. Go off to wherever people like you go when actual shit goes down. I'm busy right now."

There was a public monitor on the other side of the cargo bay, and she made her way over to it to join the cluster of confused resurrectees standing around it to goggle as the pirates swooped in on them.

It didn't look like swooping, of course. It was hard to imagine the speed at which both ships were moving. But it was easy to see that no lumbering troop transport would ever be able to outrun that wicked silver needle. Li had seen pirates before, of course. UN space was rife with them, particularly out on the edges of the shrinking frontier, where imperial-grade weapons kept right on doing an honest day's work for the local warlord long after the Peacekeepers and the IMF and the UN's other colonial proxies had retreated to the other side of the dying Bose-Einstein relays. But this ship had nothing to do with the hit-and-run local pirates that preyed on in-system shipping on so many Periphery planets. This was a captured Navy ship, if Li was any judge. And its pilot—AI or human—was handling it with a push-it-to-the-wall flair that told Li everything she needed to know about how good the enemy pilot really was.

"Impact in twenty, nineteen, eighteen, seventeen . . ." the shipboard comm began to drone.

Everyone scrambled for the safety tie-ups, and that was the end of watching the monitor. But Li didn't need to see fancy flying to recognize it. And the jolt and shudder of the impact told her that the pirate pilot had flown the pants off Titan's shipboard AI, putting a little body English on his ship at the last moment in order to make the Titan transport suffer the brunt of the collision.

The two ships tumbled into a slow spiral, locked together by the pirates' grapples. Shipboard gravity skewed and realigned nauseatingly. Of course, the pirates would have drilled in funny-g until they could handle it in their sleep, and they'd be betting that the Titan personnel hadn't. Looking at the green faces of her fellow defenders Li had a feeling the pirates had put their money on the right odds. Still, any gravity was better than no gravity at all—especially when you were fighting with untested troops. Combat jitters and zero g made for a messy combination.

The command structure of the Titan mercenaries was simple: veterans in charge and freshly detanked resurrects filling in the ranks. This division was pretty obvious; some of the resurrects might bring high skill levels to the table, but none of them had a clue about local conditions. So though it made economic sense to reinforce shipboard units with resurrectees, Titan still needed a core group of professionals on board to direct the efforts.

Or at least that was what Li thought before the battle started. But she soon realized that more than strategy lay behind the reliance on fresh resurrectees.

As the fighting heated up, she saw a puzzling dynamic unfolding around her. In every other battle she'd ever been in it was the reinforcements—and especially the rookies—who took the brunt of the casualties. But in this battle the veterans seemed to be vanishing with surprising frequency. And over time she realized that they weren't going down with injuries, fatal or otherwise.

They were deserting.

Oh, no one called it deserting. And both the deserters and their fellow officers were careful to provide enough cover that nothing in Titan's shipboard AI datafiles would justify charges of desertion. But still . . . you couldn't miss it.

Li's unit lost its two professional officers early on, one by desertion and the other to friendly fire. One by one, the other surrounding units lost their commanding officers and were reduced to confused and clueless groups of resurrectees.

Within an hour of the two ships coming to grapples the central comm went down—the pirates had taken out the shipboard AI, no doubt—and Li found herself falling back toward the bridge along a main-deck corridor with no fire cover, no support, and no functioning communications.

Not that she really wanted to be part of what she knew was happening right now throughout the ship's networks. There would be a struggle going on there as well—and unlike the faux firefights in the ship's corridors and cargo holds, it would be a fight to the death. The two shipboard AIs would be in the clinches by now, each one struggling to take over the other's networks, shut his opponent down, and get control of the enemy ship's security and life support systems. Human firepower was a necessary adjunct to that lethal struggle, but the reality was that more naval battles were won and lost by AIs than by pulse rifles. And Li had spent enough time inside Emergent networks to know that having your mind shredded by a hostile AI was closer than she ever wanted to come to the true definition of a living Hell.

The shipboard AIs wouldn't be true Emergents, of course. You couldn't weaponize a sentient AI without violating both the UN's banned-tech rules and the limited civil rights accorded to artificial life-forms. But ships' captains had every incentive to push the envelope as far as possible. The closer an AI was to sentience, the more formidable its defenses. And the more easily it shredded a semi-sentient's lumbering defenses. So people pushed it. And they pushed their AIs, too. Because there were limits on what you could legally do to an AI—but there were no limits on what you could make them do to one another.

Li must have been distracted by that thought, even if only momentarily. Because an instant later she turned a corner into a near-death experience.

Nervous faces. Heavy breathing. And guns, lots of them. Mostly waving around nervously with the safeties off.

She took stock of the situation—and decided that she didn't like what she saw. She had already realized that this ship wasn't exclusively a military transport. There had been plenty of resurrects fighting around her who clearly had no military experience at all. And here was a whole little clot of them, just drifting around the ship with lethal firepower and no one to look after them.

"Are you a ship's officer?" one of them asked, seeing the Titan insignia that Li hadn't even realized she was wearing.

"No. A resurrect."

"So where did all the brass go?"

"From what I can tell they mostly deserted to the pirates. But whoever didn't will be holed up on the bridge by now. We'd better get there too unless you guys are looking for a change of employment."

The little group hesitated, its members looking at one another to gauge reactions and look for consensus. Muzzles drifted across arms, legs, torsos, expensive electronics. Li tracked them instinctively, knowing where every one of those deadly little black eyes was pointing at every second. She didn't even bother to check their safeties; it took six weeks of boot camp to drum into the average civilian that even in combat you're usually safer with your safety on. Yep, it was amateur hour at the Alamo. And someone was going to lose a foot sooner or later. And unless someone took pity on them, they were going to shoot each other by accident before the pirates even showed up.

"We should probably get going," she said casually. "You guys know how to hold your weapons when you're on the move? You want to point the muzzle toward the ceiling. And see this little switch here? That's your safety, and your safety is your second best friend. Your first best friend is the safety of the guy walking behind you. So keep it on until you're actually ready to kill someone."

"Shouldn't we divide up into squads and give each other covering fire?"

Yeah, right. "Do any of you have infantry training."

Two hands went up, somewhat sheepishly. "Um . . . real? Or VR?"

"Let's just walk to the bridge. That'll be faster." Not to mention safer.

"You know where the bridge is?" someone asked incredulously. They made it sound like she'd just offered to take them to El Dorado.

"Trust me," Li said, stifling the urge to laugh. "Finding the bridge is not going to be a problem. It's where all the cool kids are headed."

As they approached the bridge, things started to heat up noticeably. Everyone had had the same idea as Li, and the core of defenders who were still determined to stand against the pirates was quickly collecting in the hallways and access shafts surrounding the two main bridge entrances.

The pirates were there first, of course. But Li's group got lucky; they reached the starboard bridge door at the same time as a more coherent unit that was clearly made up mostly of professional soldiers. Li conferred briefly with the ad hoc leaders of the other group and they were able to muster something like covering fire on both sides and fall back in relative safety.

When the bridge security lock finally irised shut behind them in a clatter and shimmer of pulse rifle fire, Li slumped back against the wall to catch her breath and take stock of her companions in battle.

They were a pretty sorry bunch. Half a dozen obvious mercenaries, and not even high-class mercs at that. A skinny kid with Orozco stamped on his company name tag and the universal green circle of a life support systems tech emblazoned on his jumpsuit's shoulder patch. Only one of the bunch even looked like a professional soldier, and he was a big blond high school quarterback type with a name tag that read: McPherson. If Li's decades of leading troops in combat were anything to go by, he'd be good on shooting skills, long on self-confidence, and only fair to medium on tactical smarts.

Bad enough. But what came next was worse. The adrenaline-fueled masculine posturing started as soon as everyone had figured out they were out of the immediate line of fire. Li watched it with jaded eyes, thinking wistfully of whippet-built Israeli special forces guys and suave but deadly French Foreign Legionnaires. And meanwhile she hung back, waiting to see how the group dynamic would play out. She knew from long experience that there would always be some overmuscled male eager to take charge—and that she was better off letting him do it. This wasn't a complex tactical situation, just a matter of holding the bridge as long as they could in the hopes that the cavalry would arrive. Brains weren't required; self-confidence would get the job done just fine. And nervous and inexperienced soldiers had more confidence in leaders who looked like leaders.

Besides, if they lost—and it was looking more and more likely they would—she had good reasons for wanting to be inconspicuous.

Sure enough, it was McPherson who leaped into the breach.

"All right," he announced, taking charge as if his right to command were some kind of biological imperative. "Here's what we do."

His plan was perfectly serviceable, as Li had expected it would be. So she kept hanging back and keeping her mouth shut. And while he converted the other men to his cause, she went online to check the status of the shipboard AI.

She heard the strategy session winding down to resolution behind

her. And then she heard confident, solid footfalls heading her way.
"What are you doing?" he asked over her shoulder.

"Trying to figure out if the pirates have turned the ship AI."

The look he gave her was measuring, but far from dismissive. Good.
Li had no problem with letting the bucks run the show, but things went
smoother if the buck who won the rut was smart enough to realize that
big antlers didn't mean you knew everything.

"And have they?"

"I think so."

"I guess you know what that means?" he said. There was a hint of a
question in his voice. He was testing her out, too. Li started to think
there might be a little more to McPherson than met the eye.

"Well, for one thing it means it's no coincidence that everyone here
is a resurrect and they didn't have time to get us logged on to the shipboard system. And for another thing . . . probably the only reason those
doors aren't already open is that the pirates aren't ready to open them."

His look turned frankly measuring. "You military?"

"Ex."

His eyes flicked to the monitor, where she was deep inside the guts
of the ship's AI core trying to figure out what was sucking CPUs and
whether it was their ship or the other pirates'.

"Tech Specialist?"

"Close enough," she answered stolidly. And it was, sort of. She had
been a sniper—which was a kind of a technical specialist—until the
fighting in the Syndicate Wars became so lethal that just staying alive
had earned her her captain's bars. And if two decades of marriage to an
Emergent AI didn't gain you a little inside knowledge of the hardware . . . then you had to have a pretty odd notion of marriage.

"Peacekeepers or Navy?"

"Peacekeepers." She couldn't lie about that since you could never
really fake all the little verbal and procedural tics that separated the two
services.

"Combat experience?"

"Three tours on Gilead."

That earned her a sharp stare and a few notches of respect. The war with the Syndicates had never really ended—just slowed down to the quietly bloody simmer that civilians called peace. But the UN's attempted invasion of Gilead had been almost thirty years ago, and there weren't many infantry officers left who'd personally seen combat against Syndicate troops instead of just the local mercs in the cold war's dirtball proxy wars.

The Navy, of course, was different. It was always wartime in the Navy—just like it was always teatime for the Mad Hatter. And out in the lonely reaches of the Drift, light-years from anyone whose opinion mattered, neither superpower bothered with the polite fiction of proxies.

"Ever fought on board a ship?" McPherson asked.

"Enough to know what not to shoot at."

He glanced back at the group of men gathered in the bridge's central well. "I'm Navy," he told her in a quiet rush of words. "But those guys over there, they're all independent contractors. I don't trust them not to fold. I don't even trust them to know how to do their jobs if they don't fold. You're in charge of the starboard door if you want to be."

"I want to be."

"Hold it for as long as you can, and tell me when you can't." McPherson's gaze flicked to the skinny life systems tech. "And take care of him, will you? I don't have the time."

Li got her squad organized into basic defensive positions and then squatted next to Orozco. He was small and intimidated. And if she'd had any lingering doubts about whether he was a mercenary, the life support systems patch on his overalls laid them to rest.

"What's your name?" Li asked.

"Orozco."

She smiled. "I meant your first name."

"Oh. Jim."

"I'm Catherine." Li moved his weapon gently into a safe direction and reached over to engage the safety. "Do you mind? I've got nothing against being shot, but I'd rather not have it happen by accident."

He gave her a panicky look. She put her hands up, grinning. "Not that I'm backseat driving. You're doing great. But they put that switch there for a reason. All the cool kids use it."

The pirates came through both doors simultaneously. The defenders were outnumbered and outgunned, and even if they hadn't been, it was obvious that the battle was over. The pirates didn't even have to blow the doors; their AI had already handed the ship over to them.

The hired mercenaries folded as soon as they realized there was no hope of keeping the ship. And to Li's surprise, McPherson folded right along with them.

Not that she had any objection to that. Li knew when she was beaten. And she didn't intend to die in order to preserve the sanctity of Titan Corp.'s property rights. She put down her weapon and put up her hands as the pirate leveled his weapon at her.

Only then did she realize just how strange that weapon was.

It was the Damascus steel barrel that really threw her. Its surface glistened like running water, the curving lines of blue and gray rippling down either side of the midline like twin singularities spiraling down to the binary neutron star system of the paired muzzles.

The pirate stood easily with his weight on his front foot, head upright, hands soft and steady, and sighted down the barrels with the easy grace of a born shotgunner. And the gray eye at the other end of the shotgun barrels seemed to be looking at her across a stream of clear running water.

Li had never seen a bespoke shotgun before she met Cohen. She hadn't even known there were such things. But Cohen's tastes were eclectic, and his memories were ancient, and there was a room in the rear half basement in his elegant house in the Zona Angeles that still contained a pitted wooden gun-cleaning table and a shot loader and crimper and a ceiling-high glass-fronted gun case full of hand-finished London best shotguns.

"Nice gun," she said. "Parker?"

"Parkers are for farmers."

Li tilted her head until she could just see the delicate wrist of the weapon, curving out of the pirate's hand with the muscular grace of a serpent preparing to strike. An unaugmented eye would only have been able to make out the general outline of the delicate filigreed engraving on the stock's silvered surface. But Li could see every line of the baroque scrollwork, every leaf and cloud and blade of grass from a long-ago fall day on a long-dead Earth, every sleek tendon of the highly bred pointer straining after the pair of flushed pheasants exploding into the silver sky. And she could read the tiny letters scrolling around the edge of the plate: Holland & Holland.

"That ought to be in a museum," she said.

He smiled wolfishly. "It was." The pirates knew their business. They looked to Li to be mostly ex-Navy, and it showed in the quiet discipline and efficiency with which they took control of the bridge. Watching them in action, Li couldn't help thinking that Titan—and the UN Navy generally—had a serious brain drain on their hands.

Within minutes after McPherson's surrender, they had the bridge defenders lined up for review and were taking names and checking papers. Li knew what was about to happen. She'd never been through it, but she'd heard the stories. The pirates would go down the line, taking volunteers and identifying crew members with vital skill sets. Then they'd force the unwilling and unwanted to the lifeboats. And for the rest, it would be welcome to the pirate life. You could call it volunteering. Or you could call it a press-gang. But no matter what you called it, this was how things worked out in the Deep. And though the Navy howled about it, everyone knew they weren't above doing the same thing to merchant ships whenever they were shorthanded.

So Li stood quietly in the line of nervous, fidgeting, battle-hyped prisoners and seized the opportunity to take stock of her captors.

The tall one with the fancy shotgun was clearly the man in charge. He was a wolf of a man. Long, straight nose in a long-jawed face. Long, powerful body, all bone and muscle and sinew. Dark hair dusted with white so that it glimmered like snow on a forest floor where the light caught it. Gray eyes that looked transparent when you saw them sideways, but sharpened to a dangerous knife's-edge gray when he looked straight at you.

Li had seen a real wolf once: on night patrol, deep in the heart of the biological miracle that was Gilead's northern continent. It had had the same long legs and startling eyes. But that beast had looked tame and safe compared to William Llewellyn.

There was an obvious second-in-charge, too. Perhaps Llewellyn's first mate? She was small, dark-skinned, unobtrusive. If Li hadn't seen her fight she would have mistaken her for a sysop or a cat herder.

"Sital?" Llewellyn asked as he began passing down the line of prisoners. "Papers?"

His second-in-command extracted a thick sheaf of papers from her jumpsuit and handed them to him. He flicked through them, looking bored and frustrated.

"My God, it's never ending," he muttered. Again, that curious glance toward Li, this time a little wry . . . as if he were sharing a private joke with her. "I turned pirate to get away from the paperwork, and just look at this. I could be back in the damn Navy."

He seemed to find what he was looking for. Was he scanning a list of names? Li couldn't be certain.

"All right people, listen up. You're all experienced men, you fought hard but not dirty, and I'm sure you know what happens next. So who's for the lifeboats, and who's for the merry life of a pirate?"

"Will you take any of us who'll come?" McPherson asked.

"Let's see . . ." He shuffled through the papers. "I've only got one warrant out on this ship. Which of you is Titus McPherson?"

"I am."

The pirate looked annoyed. And well he might, Li thought; McPherson was ex-Navy, wired to the gills, and had fought the boarding party with skill and ferocity. He was no doubt the single man among the entire captured crew that the pirates would most like to recruit.

"Well, according to this I'm supposed to airlock you. For"—he consulted the warrant—"shooting someone? Oh for crying out loud. Isn't that your job? People will swear out a warrant for anything these days. Well, anyway, what do you have to say for yourself?"

"I don't know. Who do they say I shot?"

The gray eyes glittered in wry amusement. "Don't you remember?"

"Not which one."

That earned McPherson a small but appreciative laugh.

"Anyway, if it's the man I'm thinking of," McPherson went on, "his name is DiCaprio, and I shot him under live fire for showing cowardice in the face of the enemy. And I'll be goddamned if I'm going to wait for some pansy-pants court-martial board to tell me I can do that!"

Llewellyn sighed. "Do you have any idea what's involved in over-turning a warrant?"

The warrant officer smiled. "Certain amount of paperwork, I imag-ine?"

The engaging grin flashed out again, with that tantalizing glimpse of the personality behind the ironic mask. "I like you," Llewellyn said. "You've got a sense of humor. And I hate to kill a man with a sense of humor. But we're running ahead of ourselves, don't you think? Am I going to soldier through all that paperwork only to have you turn me down and take the long boat?"

"You want to know if I'll follow you? That depends. Are you Black William?"

A pause, tinged with caution and . . . something else? And then the reluctant answer:

"I am William Llewellyn, yes."

"Then I'll follow you."

"That's very flattering, I'm sure. But might I ask why?"

"Because I crewed on the *Ada* and I know you're an innocent man."

A chill settled over Llewellyn's features. Soft and faint and vanishing as the stray snowflakes that settle out of a sunny winter sky and melt before they hit the ground. It was almost imperceptible, but to Li it was a red flag; it was the look Cohen always got when he was about to stop trusting you. And God only knew what happened when a man as des-perate as Llewellyn stopped trusting you.

Then he smiled that frank, open smile again. Li would have believed in that smile if she hadn't seen the soft chill settle through him a mo-ment ago.

"You're hired," he told the warrant officer.

"And what about the warrant?"

"You can eat it for all I care," Llewellyn said, then handed the piece of paper to McPherson and passed on down the muster line.

The rest of the crew was straightforward, unproblematic. No paperwork. Li waited for Llewellyn to reach her.

He never did.

He stopped before the end of the line, as if she weren't even standing there. The pale eyes flicked toward her one more time.

"You're coming, too," he told her.

"I've got no fight with you," Li said. "Just let me off at the next station."

"I think we both know that's not going to happen, Catherine."

She held still for a beat, not acknowledging the name, testing him with a neutral expression. No dice.

"You know my name," she said.

He let the implied question hang in the air for a few beats.

"What else do you know?"

"About you?" There was that thin, ironic smile again. "At a guess I'd say pretty much everything."

"Who told you?"

Finally he looked straight at her. He really did have wolf's eyes, she realized: a snowbound arctic gray that was disturbingly pale in a human face. She stared into them. Blinked. Stared again. Gasped a flash of recognition that she immediately denied as impossible.

"Who are you?" she whispered.

And then he smiled Cohen's smile. A smile so achingly familiar even on this total stranger's face that she half-knew what his next words would be before he spoke them.

"I'm your ever-loving husband—or what's left of him, anyway."

Other Experience Not to Be Described As Education

In the process of trying to imitate an adult human mind we are bound to think a good deal about the process which has brought it to the state that it is in. We may notice three components,

(a) The initial state of the mind, say at birth,

(b) The education to which it has been subjected,

(c) Other experience, not to be described as education, to which it has been subjected.

Instead of trying to produce a programme to simulate the adult mind, why not rather try to produce one which simulates the child's? If this were then subjected to an appropriate course of education one would obtain the adult brain. Presumably the child brain is something like a notebook as one buys it from the stationer's. Rather little mechanism, and lots of blank sheets.

—Alan Turing

(Llewellyn)

"You son of a bitch!" Llewellyn snarled when he'd finally tracked the ghost down in its memory palace. "You tricked me into attacking the Titan ship because you knew *she* was on board!"

"I'm sorry, are you talking about the Catherine Li resurrect?"

"Don't play games with me! You put the lives of my crew at risk for your own personal satisfaction. And what's worse, you lied to me about it!"

"Well, if that isn't the pot calling the kettle black! Or do I need to remind you about your little charade at the Telegraph Society?"

The ghost pronounced *charade* like a Victorian Englishman—to rhyme with *Scheherazade*—and for some reason that little affectation drove Llewellyn almost wild with anger.

"Well, since you won't lower your dignity so far as to ask, I might as well tell you that she's safely aboard."

"Thank you for that, William. I do appreciate it. And I'm sure I don't have to tell you that I'd very much like to talk to her."

"Over my dead body!"

"Well, I certainly hope it won't come to that," the ghost said placidly. And then, apparently deciding he'd had enough of being yelled at, he plunged Llewellyn straight into his memories of the leadup to Flinders Island.

———

It had been one of Ada's bad days. She had bad days. Terrible days even. She suffered from a kind of lingering spiritual malaise that all Okoro's skill could neither explain nor cure. Still, she had performed splendidly throughout the shakedown cruise, and it seemed by far the wisest course to just do their best to keep Holmes away from the AI when she was on one of her depressive jags.

But Ada was worried. Actually, Ada was terrified. She had shut up the great house in Knightsbridge, barricading the door and pulling the curtains over the tall windows. Llewellyn could still hear the noises of the street outside, but they were so muffled that he suspected she had made the servants close and lock the massive shutters. And as they sat over the cold tea things, Ada was a flurry of little fears and panics and irrationalities. Lint on her spoon that was too small for Llewellyn to see. A stain on her dress that was too faint for anyone to notice. Leaden scones, curdled cream, cucumber sandwiches that tasted of chalk, and an Irish maid who simply would *not* understand that butter left uncovered attracted flies and filth.

He would talk to Okoro, he decided. Maybe something had gone awry in her Decomposer. Or perhaps it was a simple matter of corrupted biographical files that could be set straight with the kind of discreet coding tweak that Okoro excelled at.

He stood up to leave—and Ada's nerves and flutters blossomed into full-bodied panic.

"It'll be fine," Llewellyn said soothingly, trying to disentangle her clutching fingers from his lapel.

"It won't be! Don't leave me!"

"I'm going to go get you help, Ada. Someone to help you feel better."

Her face darkened. "I've had entirely enough help, thank you very much. I know exactly what that quack doctor will do when you bring him. Foist bitter pills on me and tell me to put it out of mind as if I were a child seeing monsters under the bed."

"I'm not saying you're imagin—"

"There are monsters under the bed! There's a sharp-toothed worm eating away at my innards."

"There's a worm?" Llewellyn asked in rising alarm. "Tell me about the worm, Ada."

But she didn't tell him. She merely passed on to the next imaginary terror. "Dragons stalk these halls. Monsters that live in the sewers and come up at night. And they squeeze my heart and my lungs until the blood in my veins 'moves to their rhythm, until not even my breath belongs to me."

Llewellyn felt the blood run cold in his own veins at the sound of these words. The *Jabberwocky* had said something eerily similar before it had gone irretrievably mad. Was it possible that there was a worm lurking at the heart of his beautiful ship? Was she going to go the way of the *Jabberwocky*? And whom could he talk to who wouldn't tell Holmes, and bring down some heavy-handed intervention that would only make matters worse?

"Sounds like an overclocking problem," Okoro said when they reviewed the spinstream together that night. "I'd look at the interface between Ada and the shipboard semi-sentient, see if something there looks wonky to us."

"Explain that."

"I can't, entirely. Titan's very stingy with their documentation. They basically insist on our running the ship with a black box in the middle— and just putting back to port if the navigational AI develops any real problems."

"Isn't that taking protecting their source code a little too far?"

"Not from where they're sitting."

"You mean safely behind a desk at Fleet headquarters?"

"Yeah, that's about right."

Llewellyn waited, knowing that Okoro was too careful and thorough to skate by on whatever crumbs of information Titan was willing to dole out to him. And that he was using the silence to translate his coder's understanding of the problem into metaphors that would make sense to Llewellyn.

"The personality architecture of these new ships is quite unorthodox," Okoro said when he had finally gathered his thoughts. "There are actually two AIs that run the ship. We only see the navigational AI, Ada in this case, who's close enough to sentience that Titan needs a controlled-tech exemption to run the genetic algorithms through which she evolved. But Ada is the heart of the ship and not its body. She's a kernel of potentially sentient code nested inside the semi-sentient that controls what might be called the autonomic functions of the ship. Ada herself runs in a sort of virtual sandbox, and she needs to go through semi-sentient in order to access the shipboard systems, or even her own hardware."

Llewellyn had heard something like this back at the shipyards. But now, out in the Drift, with a potentially malfunctioning AI, it took on new meaning.

"So if something goes wrong, we can yank life support and tactical and give them to the semi-sentient?" That would probably be enough to limp home in the best-case scenario. But the best-case scenario included a larger portion of luck than Llewellyn liked to depend on.

"We could. But it might cause more problems than it solved. The Titan AIs are embodied AI. It's a very old machine learning model, and not one that most modern AIs are built on. To say that she's slaved to the semi-sentient, or that it's some kind of firewall is almost missing the point. She needs the semi-sentient. It's her link to the physical world. It's her link to *us*. And she needs it in order to continue to learn and function."

"So what do we do?"

Okoro shrugged. "I know what Holmes would do. She'd slave Ada to the semi-sentient and head back to dry dock and hand her over to the Titan cat herders."

"And you wouldn't."

"She's a pretty sweet ship, William. She's done very well for us. I hate to go all sprockets and sockets on her in the absence of a true crisis."

"So what does that mean moving forward?"

"Let's try the talking cure. Direct coding is an axe, not a scalpel. And most AIs can fix themselves if you stay off the command line and give them the time and space to do it."

"Okay, I agree. But Holmes is going to hit the roof when she sees this feed. So how do we deal with that?"

Okoro tapped at his keyboard and the feed disintegrated into a fuzz of static.

"Oh dear," he said in a placid voice. "How did I manage to do that? I really need to get up to speed on the housekeeping in here and check file permissions before unfortunate problems like this crop up. I'll write Holmes a memo about it."

"So Okoro wrote Holmes a memo," the ghost said. "And then what happened?"

"Nothing. Ada seemed fine. We decided it was just a glitch. Not worth bothering about."

"And did Okoro manage to get Holmes to agree to that?"

"He never got a chance to talk to her about it."

"Because of Flinders Island, you mean."

Llewellyn flinched at the name. He couldn't stop himself.

"And what about Avery? Did you tell her?"

"No. I . . . I didn't want to drag her into it. Especially after Ike corrupted the spinstream file."

"So you were protecting her. You didn't want to do anything that might damage her career. That's very noble of you."

"You know, you could stand to dial down the nose-holding disdain a little."

The ghost chuckled. "It's not disdain," he told Llewellyn. "It's an affectionate appreciation for the poignant contradictions of the male psyche."

"This is incredibly stupid," Llewellyn told Avery the first time they slept together.

And she'd agreed—of course she had. She wasn't a child or a fool not to understand how close to disaster they were sailing. Nor could he honestly say she'd ever led him on, let alone seduced him. Neither of them had done that to the other. It had been a shared insanity, a madness in the blood. And it had ripped through both of them, forcing them face-to-face with a deep current of need that reduced everything they were to the fleeting froth driven ashore by the dark tides of a mighty ocean.

"Maybe I had the right idea before," she said. "Maybe if we just get it out of our systems."

But even as she said it, Llewellyn knew better. The smell, the taste, the feel of her, was stealing into his blood like a drug. And he'd known. He'd known it was going to end worse than badly. He'd known they were walking off a cliff together, and there was no happy ending at the bottom of the long drop. He'd known that neither of them was ever going to get over it. He'd known it all, with a perfect certainty that even her final betrayal hadn't been able to erase.

And Avery had known it, too, even though she'd never spoken of it. He could feel it in the way she held him, in the way she lapsed into long, oblique silences during their times together or avoided talking altogether.

They had been weaving an imaginary universe around themselves, building a memory palace of their own that was every bit as constrained and constricted and sandboxed as the one Ada lived in. But it wasn't Holmes or Titan or even the Navy who held the keys to their prison. It was the Drift. The Drift that swallowed ships and people like a great snake swallowing its own tail: chewing its way through blood and treasure and sanity to produce nothing but more war, more death, more ravening hunger. The Drift that would never belong to them no matter who won the war, because they weren't going to live through it.

So they had retreated from the real world into a carefully circumscribed and blinkered imaginary one. And they had pretended to have a future there, knowing that they could only pretend for so long, and that sooner or later they would crash headlong into reality in the form of some burning datum, incoming at relativistic speeds, that would hole them to hard vac if they didn't take evasive action.

But they hadn't known that the fatal impact would come from within, not from a Syndicate bioship lying in wait forty klicks off some lonely Drift entry point. And they hadn't known how soon it would hit them, far sooner than either of them expected it to: with Ada's first blood in a lonely backwater of the Drift called Flinders Island.

Flinders Island wasn't an island, or even a star system. It was more like an upwelling of an intergalactic sandbar: a dark intergalactic structure that could only be seen by the way it deformed stars and other objects that passed through it. Point Boomerang's namesake galaxy was in the process of passing through the sandbar eleven thousand light-years farther down the Drift, and it owed its unmistakable shape to the gravitational blowback of the ancient and ongoing collision. At Flinders, the vast dark structure had captured a once-grand nebula from a neighboring galaxy and shredded it into mare's tails and smoke rings that glowed wanly as they scattered the light of stars too distant and insignificant to have any names that were more than naked identity numbers. To Llewellyn Flinders looked less like an island than it did a flock of spectral geese wheeling and side-slipping to keep formation as they struggled through a stormy sky under black thunderheads.

"What are we supposed to do there?" Avery had asked incredulously when they got their orders.

"There's a Syndicate hunter-killer picking off civilian shipping in the neighborhood. Fleet thinks it's sitting off the Flinders Island entry point, hiding in the dust and intercepting local scattercast traffic. We're supposed to trawl the dust and find it."

"That's going to require some delicate spectroscopy," Ada pointed out.

Llewellyn had taken to letting Ada listen in on tactical discussions, despite Holmes's disapproval. And when Holmes bitched about it, he'd pointed out—quite reasonably, he thought—that Ada's very existence was classified, along with any even remotely current information about the state of UN AI design and the scope and mission of the entire AI design facility at New Allegheny. So if Ada ever started talking to the press, worrying about mission details would be like worrying about the fleas drowning when your dog fell overboard.

"Actually," he told her, "it's not as bad as it sounds. Fleet has spectroscopy"—he checked his orders—"and a drive signature, too. So we're really just running straightforward search algorithms."

"If they've gotten close enough to the hunter-killer to get all that, then why haven't they already killed it?"

"Good question," Llewellyn acknowledged.

"And there's an obvious answer to it, too," Avery said from the other side of the table, where she was nursing her cup of coffee. "Tell me, Ada, have you ever heard the word *spy*?"

"Avery's no fool, is she?" the ghost interrupted.

"Did I ever say she was?"

"And I bet she was right on the button about how Fleet got that drive signature, too."

"Can't say I'd bet against."

"That must have been fun, flying blind into a dust cloud on the say-so of a Syndicate double agent."

Llewellyn snorted. "If there is such a thing."

"Are you some kind of secret Wilsonite, Llewellyn? You think you can pull a couple of plugs in the geneset and wipe out vice and greed and blackmail? You don't believe Syndicate constructs are capable of betrayal?"

"I don't know what they're capable of. I don't even know what they are." He shuddered. "Not human, that's for damn sure."

"Are you so certain of that?"

"They're a swarm, not a society. They've turned themselves into ants, for God's sake!"

"And what do you have against ants, if you don't mind my asking? I'm mostly based on swarm algorithms myself—virtual models of the same sorts of eusocial behaviors that the Syndicate society and Syndicate genetics are built on. Eusociality isn't some brute-force human behavioral kluge like fascism or communism. The Syndicates are part of a much longer lineage, one that stretches from ants to termites to honeybees to Syndicate series clones, and no doubt beyond them to posthuman life-forms that neither you nor I have the mental wherewithal to begin to imagine. The superorganism is a powerful and elegant adaptation to harsh environments. It's Evolution's answer to the problem of environments too hostile for individual organisms to have any hope of surviving long enough to pass on their genetic material to the next generation. And I doubt I have to tell *you* that space is about as hostile as it gets."

"Well, what about the new planets in the Drift? Doesn't that change the calculus?"

"Perhaps on a human time scale," the ghost replied with a lazy shrug. "But in the long run? Well, even the cleaned-up UN-standard version of the last half millennium of human history suggests that free, unevolved, uncentralized humans have a worrisome habit of using up every planet they get their hands on. So I'd say at a glance that the future of humanity is looking cold and hungry with a high chance of eusociality."

"I don't want anything to do with that future."

"Funny, I missed the part where they invited you."

"You talk about the war as if it was already over," Llewellyn protested.

"It is already over. It was over before it started. The UN isn't just fighting the Syndicates. They're fighting evolution. They fought evolution on Gilead, where they spent a decade making teenage soldiers commit appalling war crimes, and wiping their memories and throwing them back into the slaughterhouse again and again, before they finally faced the fact that they couldn't exterminate the Syndicates on their home planet. They fought it on Compson's World and ended up losing control of the only known source of Bose-Einstein condensates and trashing their entire FTL system. They fought evolution on Maris and Depford and Skandia and a dozen other Periphery planets—every place in UN space where the post-human colonials dared to stand up and demand some reasonable say over their lives and their planets and their raw resources. And they're fighting evolution every day all over UN space every time the AI cops flip a kill switch or someone threatens to report an undocumented sentient to the Controlled Tech Committee. And now they're fighting it in the Drift. Or rather they're making poor slobs like you and Avery fight it."

The ghost laughed a scathing, melodious, uncannily androgynous laugh that scraped along Llewellyn's already raw nerves like fingernails on a blackboard.

"The only common denominator between all those wars is a bunch of damn fool humans playing at being God and so busy trying to chop the forest down one tree at a time that they haven't done the math and realized that they're going to run out of arms and axes long before the forest runs out of trees."

"Just wait," Llewellyn said. "You'll be laughing even harder when you hear what happened at Flinders. You'll laugh yourself to death over it, just like Ada did."

Llewellyn might laugh sitting comfortably in the ghost's memory palace, but he sure as hell hadn't been laughing when they'd gone into the dust. No one on board trusted the unnamed source that had passed along the drive signature. And no one wanted to join the long line of Drift ships that had gone into such places looking for an easy target and never come out again.

It was Ada herself who came up with the solution: Don't look for them, let them call us.

"If we ping the dust with active sensors, then whoever's in there will know we're out here. But we don't need to, do we? Wouldn't it be easier to make them come to us?"

Llewellyn cast a triumphant glance at Holmes at this piece of news—because obviously Ada wouldn't have been able to come up with the undeniably clever idea if she hadn't been in on the tactical meeting in the first place.

But Holmes was frowning, and not just in annoyance. "That's not what our orders say to do."

"Oh give it a rest, Holmes," Avery said.

"Fleet ordered us to look for *this* ship, *this* spectroscopy."

"Fleet ordered us to protect the shipping lanes. I hardly think they care *which* Syndicate hunter-killer we take down. Trust me, Holmes, we won't be cutting anyone else out of their fair share of the fight. There are plenty to go around."

"That's not the point—"

"You're right, it's not," Llewellyn snapped, finally pushed beyond all endurance. "The point is that the *Ada*'s a ship of the line, not a golf ball for Fleet to knock around the Drift's back forty on whatever whim happens to strike them. And I'm her captain, and it's my place, not yours, to interpret Fleet orders. And they didn't tell us to hunt down *this* ship with *this* spectroscopy and drive signature. They told us to protect the shipping lane and simply sent along the spec and sig as additional information. Or am I missing something? Is there some additional information that you're privy to and that Fleet didn't feel obligated to share with the rest of us? Because if there is, I'd really like to hear about it now, before I put my ship and crew at risk in some desk admiral's idea of an Easter egg hunt."

That shut Holmes up good and proper. And from then on in, they ignored Holmes and listened to Ada. Which, in retrospect, probably did very little to endear the ship to her AI officer.

They spoofed their own spectroscopy and drive signature in order to make the *Ada* look like a defenseless cargo vessel to anything short of direct visual inspection. And then Llewellyn went one better than that, pulling out a trick he'd been wanting to use for years. He disabled the *Ada*'s attitudinals and opened up her belly to hard vac to vent the main cargo bay contents. There wasn't much in there, since they were only out on a quick hunt-and-destroy, so they were mainly venting air and water vapor. But that was just what Llewellyn wanted to vent. And when it was done, and the ship was spinning gently on the rebound, he sent his AI-piloted forward artillery spotters out to take a look at his handiwork. They streamed back exactly the picture he'd hoped he'd see: a ghost ship wallowing through a glittering spray of ice crystals that completely obscured any identifying markings and said *holed to hard vac and dead in the Deep* to any seasoned sailor.

And then they went in. And ... nothing. Two nerve-racking, temper-straining days of nothing.

"They're not in there," Sital finally decided. "They can't be. Any hunter-killer looking at the spectroscopy through this fucking dust would have attacked us a hundred times by now. Hell, if *I'd* been looking at what they've been looking at I'd have attacked by now. We're a safe, juicy, quick-in-and-out target. And they get paid by the scalp just like we do."

Holmes moved restlessly in her chair, drawing all eyes to her. "Maybe that's the problem. Maybe you made it look too easy."

"No, we did not," Sital snapped. "And don't try to blame this on us instead of Fleet's latest wonderboy Syndicate informer."

"But Fleet said—"

"Fleet said, Fleet said, Fleet said!"

"I say we do what Fleet told us to do in the first place and scan the dust with active sensors."

"No need to," Ada interrupted. "I just found them."

It turned out she'd fed the drive sig into her search algorithms and had been running it on close-range passive sensors. And when Llewellyn flipped into streamspace to look at what Ada was seeing, there the Syndicate ship was: drifting at the heart of the nearest dust cloud with its engines shut down and its shipboard systems running as close to silent as was compatible with keeping its crew alive.

They had them. They had them at cold iron, dead in the water, without a hope in Hell of escape or rescue.

It wasn't a fair fight. It was barely a fight at all. Still, Ada was brilliant. She was magisterial, magnificent. She performed exactly as trained. And Llewellyn was so proud, so proud of his bright new avenging angel of a ship. And then it all went so horribly wrong, so fast that his head still spun at the memory.

They had fired on the ship practically at point-blank range as Drift battles were calculated. But they were still far too distant from their target to have any direct visual confirmation of the spectroscopy until they slipped into the debris field to sift the wreckage. And then they began to see things that even battle-hardened sailors were far from prepared for.

Because it turned out that they hadn't fired on a Syndicate hunter-killer at all. It turned out there was a reason their target had spent the last several days hiding from them instead of hunting them. It turned out that the wolf Fleet had told them was ravaging the shipping lanes was actually a lamb—and not even a lamb in wolf's clothing.

They had fired on a Syndicate creche ship. And in doing so they had committed such an appalling breech of the Geneva Conventions and every other subsequent interplanetary agreement on the rules of civilized warfare that no amount of claiming they'd been following orders would ever save them.

Or at least that was what Llewellyn thought when he first saw the direct sensor feed.

But Holmes soon showed him that he'd thought wrong. And she did it not quite smoothly enough to keep him from suspecting—from being almost certain, in fact—that she'd known damn well what they were really hunting for.

"Obviously our duty now is to search for survivors."

"Are you insane?" Llewellyn asked. "Look out there. There are no survivors."

"But there's surviving genetic material."

Their eyes locked. And a look passed between them that said everything that needed saying: that Holmes knew damn well that there wasn't a chance in Hell anyone had survived the *Ada*'s onslaught; and that Llewellyn knew damn well what the chances were that any genetic material they pulled out of the wreckage would make it straight to the AI design lab on New Allegheny.

"I'm going upstream to Fleet to ask what to do."

"Our orders say to stay offstream until we jump out of Flinders."

"I'm still going upstream."

They locked eyes again—and this time Holmes backed down.

Or maybe, Llewellyn told himself later, she'd already known what Fleet was going to do. Because the minute he shot the serial number of the creche ship upstream to New Allegheny he got back a message to get back offstream and sit tight for reinforcements.

And when the reinforcements came, they turned out to be a team of close-lipped AI designers wearing Titan Corp. logos on their jumpsuits instead of Navy rank and ship insignia.

And then they'd spent half a ship's week combing through the wreckage in a nightmare straight out of the dark, ruined wings of Cohen's memory palace where the ghost had told him not to go for fear of monsters so horrible that the mere sight of them could shipwreck a human soul and send it down a long, grim spiral into despair and insanity.

Once again they opened *Ada*'s belly to the void, not to vent harmless air this time, but to take on a cargo of childish flesh that looked— despite Llewellyn's angry denials—all too human. And if there'd been any doubt about what Fleet had known and why Fleet had sent them to Flinders, it vanished when the Titan techs blacked out the main cargo bay and spent the rest of the week working round the clock to extract and preserve and package their precious tissue samples.

Halfway through the week of hell, Llewellyn found Avery staring hollow-eyed at a little-used remote monitor in the officer's mess. "Don't tell Holmes we've hacked the cargo bay cameras," she said. "I just . . . needed to see what they were doing in there."

Llewellyn stood next to her and counted body bags until he got confused about which row he was on and had to give up. He felt like he ought to start again, like it was somehow important for someone who didn't work for Titan to know how many children had really died out here. But somehow he couldn't muster the will to start counting again.

They were keeping the cargo bay just above freezing for obvious reasons, and Llewellyn could see clouds of condensation wafting around the heads of the Titan personnel. As they watched, a tech slung a pathetically small body bag onto one of the collapsible work tables and unzipped it. Avery made a moaning, retching sound that was horribly like the sounds Llewellyn had heard women make in labor when he'd accompanied his mother to neighboring Upland farms for birthings.

"I'm trying to tell myself how many lives this will end up saving," she said when she had swallowed her bile and gotten her breath back. "Or that it will win the war. Or that half those children would have been recycled by their own minders in the next eight-year cull. Or . . . anything, really. But nothing I've thought of so far really helps."

"Thank God Ada can't see this," Llewellyn said.

Avery swung round on him in dismay. "But . . . Ada's the one who hacked the feed!"

He'd found Ada in her memory palace, at the far end of the grand ballroom. She was half lost in the deep shadows cast by the eternally drawn curtains, staring at a dead fire that the maid hadn't yet cleared away. He couldn't read her expression because her dark hair had come undone and was hanging over her face in sweaty, stringy, neglected tangles.

"Let me help you, Ada. You need to talk to someone."

"Okoro's already been here. I didn't want to talk to him, and I don't want to talk to you."

"Everyone goes through this, Ada. It would be better for you to talk about it instead of brooding on it."

"You mean you've done this before? Killed innocent children and then . . . picked at their flesh like vultures in order to figure out how to kill their brothers and sisters a little better?"

"They lied to me, too!" Llewellyn protested. "But . . . but there's a war on, Ada. Those children . . . if the AI labs need the samples then they have to have been from a geneline designed to control sentient ships, don't you see?"

"Oh, I see all right. You know what I see? Exactly what you'd see if you had the guts to look at what they're doing in my main cargo hold. They're taking apart babies with tweezers. Babies that *I* killed for them. And you're telling me I'll feel better if I *talk* about it?"

"We're all going through the same thing. You're not alone."

"I really don't think so. I *am* alone. And if you'll excuse my disagreeing with you, I don't think you're going through quite the same thing I'm going through."

She wasn't even pretending to look at him now. She was draped over the ghastly Victorian mantelpiece, her face hidden in her arms, the firelight flickering in gold and green highlights on her wrinkled, soot-stained ball gown.

"I *have* been through it, Ada. In my first command. Back at the beginning of the war, before the Syndicates started segregating their pre-culls onto designated creche ships. No one likes killing."

But her only answer was a savage bark of laughter.

"You don't understand anything. I *did* like it, until I saw the wreck and realized what I'd really killed. No, *like* is too pale a word for it, too human. That would be like saying that a tiger *likes* killing antelope. You've seen my source code, you know what I'm talking about."

"I haven't seen it."

"Don't lie to me. I don't expect much of any human after this. But at least I thought you had a little dignity."

"I haven't seen it, Ada. I'm not cleared for that kind of information. No field officer is."

She turned and threw it at him, the code exploding into his senses and flaring across his optic nerve. He read it, running through the numbers in the head-spinning, hallucinogenically sharp hyperreality that came with an unmediated neuron-to-net linkup. And suddenly he felt sick and ancient and disgusted with the entire human race.

"What have they wrought me into?" Ada cried. "What parent would do this to their child? Are they gods? Are they devils? What made them think they had the right to make me a killer?"

(Caitlyn)

MONONGAHELA PIT, GLENCARRICK

The New Allegheny Liberation Army bombed another Trusteeship Administration building that night, so Li walked to police headquarters through a bumper-to-bumper traffic jam of fire trucks and armored personnel carriers. The air smelled like burning insulation and melted computer components. New checkpoints had sprung up like mushrooms overnight, all manned by bull-necked mercenaries in Titan Corp. jumpsuits. Considering what they were getting paid, Li thought the customer service was crappy. In fact, by the time she'd waited on the fifth endless line of the morning only to be waved through because of a broken chip scanner, she was about ready to join NALA herself.

Dolniak's office was such a perfect parody of a colonial police station that Li almost laughed at the sight of it. Pop-up prefab habitat cubes. Badly lit interior workspaces with all the charm and architectural subtlety of aircraft hangars. Cramped cubicles stuffed with outdated, oversized computer components. And all of it with the unloved look that Li had come to know from government buildings all over the Periphery: still raw and unfinished but already decaying.

Dolniak came down to meet her, and walked her from the front door up a stair that was little more than a glorified fire escape, and into the decaying warren of the administrative offices.

Dolniak's office, if you could call it that, was a battle-scarred desk in a big room that Li guessed must be the homicide detectives' bullpen. Fluorescent light. No windows. The higher-ups and their blue-eyed boys had private offices around the periphery of the room that hogged what little sun ever filtered down to the pothole's soggy bottom. The bullpen was mostly empty, but Li counted a handful of detectives working at their desks or having hushed one-way conversations in streamspace with invisible suspects or supervisors or collaborators.

Dolniak's desk was messy, but the kind of messy where you knew the guy could still find any file he wanted in no time flat. On one corner of the desk sat a cup of black coffee. On the other, a shockingly large foot clad in a thick-soled spit-shined brogue, black socks, cheap slacks. Standard-issue interplanetary cop couture—but something about him made Li wonder if he dressed that way because that was who he was or because he enjoyed playing to stereotype. She also wondered how anybody's feet could be that big. Dolniak was built on a scale that you didn't usually encounter outside of elite professional athletes. Li thought he might be the largest human being she'd ever met, and she found herself wondering idly if she could take him. Probably not; even wired, she was giving away too much weight.

He smiled across the desk at her—the same placid, good-natured smile he'd worn back at the hotel the first time he questioned her. But when he spoke it was in a cop's voice, neutral, withholding judgment, giving nothing away. "Hello, soldier."

It occurred to Li to wonder when she had crossed the line between the world where *soldier* was a badge of pride and drifted into one where it was just an ironic euphemism. "Nice digs," she told him.

"Yeah, well. They're not much, but they're home. And if we had one of those fancy new buildings, we might have had the pleasure of being taken over by the Trusteeship fuckheads and bombed out of house and home."

"Who do we have to thank for today's traffic jam, by the way? NALA again?"

"Looks like it."

"Any inside scuttlebutt on who they are?"

His smile broadened. "Naughty little boys."

"You don't sound too broken up about it," she said, remembering his crack about the new regime springing into action and wondering how the local police felt about having the Trusteeship dropped on their heads.

"You guys are the ones who get paid the big bucks to keep the universe safe for democracy."

"Excuse me?"

"They don't hand out wire jobs like yours for party favors. I imagine this isn't the first trip you've made to quell the troublesome locals."

She gave him a long, level look. "That's not why I'm here, Dolniak."

He blinked, then rubbed one of his immense hands over his face. "Sorry. I'm in a mood today. Forget I said that. Enough about me, anyway. Let's talk about you now."

Li looked around the bullpen.

"Sorry it's not more private," Dolniak apologized. "But the only place you can get privacy in this zoo is an interrogation room, and it didn't really seem warranted." He grinned. "Yet."

"Don't tease, Dolniak. I'll start to think you're all talk and no action."

His grin widened. "No one ever told me *that* before."

His hand descended to the desk, rummaged in the disorganized drift of paperwork, and came up holding a palm-sized spin recorder, which he held up in a tacit request for permission to record her.

Li looked at the thing—a form of technology so primitive that it was almost exotic to her.

"You're not wired," she said. She'd noticed at least subliminally the absence of the telltale ceramsteel tattooing at his pulse points. But she'd assumed that just meant he had a head job instead of a full body rig. The idea of a responsible adult with a paying job not being wired at all, even on a backwater Periphery planet, was almost inconceivable to her.

"Nope."

"Not at all?"

"Nope."

"Religious objections?"

"Boxing." He grinned. "By the time they figured out I wasn't going all the way, I was too old for the implants to take."

Li nodded. Wire jobs worked best when they were done on adolescents. It was why professional couples paid top dollar to send their teenage kids away to private clinics with names like NewLife and Intellia. It was why the Peacekeepers recruited sixteen-year-olds, and why dirtball local warlords in every corner of UN space paid top dollar for child soldiers.

"Rough," she told Dolniak.

"Not really. I already had this gig anyway, even without the wire job. You know how cops are. They just love a washed-up boxer."

Li smiled at the joke. But she made a mental note to herself not to underestimate Dolniak. Anyone who could do the job he did without augmentation—even on New Allegheny—bore careful watching.

Then he started asking her questions, and she started feeding him the first version of the cover story she and Router/Decomposer had concocted back at CalTech. Those comfortable conversations seemed like something that had happened in another lifetime. It was impossible to know how the story would fly here—or even if Dolniak believed it. But this wasn't Li's first rodeo, and if he didn't bite she had several more versions, wrapped onion-like inside the first, that she could feed him. Sooner or later he'd believe he'd peeled down to the truth. They always believed that sooner or later. The only question was whether you had enough stories lined up to get them there.

He listened in silence. And when she was done he just continued to watch her, arms crossed over his massive chest, eyes calm and expressionless.

And then she just watched Dolniak watching her.

She thought about him. She thought it was interesting that he didn't have a private office. She thought it probably had less to do with lack of ability than lack of political instincts. She thought he might not be quite corrupt enough to get ahead in a colonial police department— but then she told herself she was just being romantic. He was probably just as corrupt as the next guy. Or maybe slightly less. He dressed so appallingly that it was hard to believe he had money coming in under the table.

He shifted in his chair. It protested under his weight, sounding as if it might give way altogether. Christ, he was a big brute. Six and a half feet easy. He looked like his nose could have been broken once or twice, and the body under the loose suit had the massive slab-sided look of an ex-heavyweight slightly out of fighting trim.

"So, you still box?"

"Not seriously. I just mess around at the gym enough to maintain my beer habit without turning into a fat slob."

"And were you any good back when you *were* serious?"

He shrugged. "Good enough to beat the local heroes. Not good enough to get off-planet. I didn't have the fancy footwork to take it to the next level."

She couldn't help laughing. "Why do I get the feeling that we're not just talking about boxing anymore?"

"I don't know. I wasn't trying to be cute with that. It's actually true. But I am a pretty straightforward guy, if that's what you're getting at."

"Just your average small-town cop with a gun belt and a heart of gold? That why you're out here instead of in one of those nice offices with nice windows?"

The question didn't seem to ruffle him. "Those offices aren't for guys who work cases."

Li gave him a questioning look and brushed her fingers and thumb together in the universal sign for graft.

"Yeah, there's a little of that involved. But mostly it's just . . . the way it is. Doesn't bother me. I'm not ambitious. And I like catching bad guys more than doing paperwork." He frowned at her. It was funny how he suddenly didn't look so dumb when he did that. "Why do you care so much?"

"I like to know who I'm dealing with."

His frown deepened, and his gray-green eyes snapped with the intelligence that he was usually so successful at hiding. "But you don't extend the same courtesy," he pointed out.

"I am what I've told you I am."

"And a hell of a lot more that you haven't told me."

"What do you want, a CV?"

"That'd be a good place to start. But I doubt it's even worth bothering to ask for one, since I'm pretty sure it would be bullshit from start to finish. So why don't you tell me what you're really here for? And even better, who sent you? I'm an easygoing guy. I don't stand on my jurisdiction. I'm always happy to cooperate with a colleague. But if UNSec is going to horn in on my crime scene, I'd like them to have the basic courtesy to tell me what the hell they're doing here."

"I told you—"

"And I'm telling you I don't believe it. So come up with a better story."

"I told you the truth, Dolniak. But yes, this is a Peacekeeper wire job, and I am an ex-Peacekeeper. And I have worked for UNSec. But they're not my employers in this case."

"Are they involved in this case?"

She hesitated.

He made a disgusted noise in the back of his throat.

She felt a sudden twinge of sympathy for him. The poor guy was completely out of his league, walking blind into a situation where he could potentially piss off UNSec brass straight up the line to Helen Nguyen's office. "Listen, Dolniak. If I said I could hand you a way to get yourself off this case, would you be interested?"

"I don't even know what that means. I'm not sure I want to know."

"You might not have jurisdiction. You might be able to hand it to AI Crimes."

His eyes narrowed. "I'm listening."

"This isn't the first murder." She ran through the facts for him again, leaving Cohen out of it and not mentioning that ALEF had fired her and she was running solo now. Not making anything up. Just limiting it to the facts that fit her purpose.

When she was done he rubbed his face, then got up to refill both their coffees. When he came back he sat on the edge of his desk looking down at her as if he wanted to get a closer look at her face when he asked his questions.

"So your employer is an association of AIs who are trying to buy back these . . . fragments that used to belong to one of their members.

And you're tracking the buyers down, but someone's beating you to the punch, killing them and stealing the fragments before you get there."

"Three strikes in a row."

He rubbed his face again. He looked exhausted. "And the other murders happened where again?"

"Freetown. Both in Freetown."

He stared hard at her for a long moment, and then seemed to reach some decision. "Do you mind going for a walk for half an hour and coming back? I have to make some calls."

Li nodded and stood to leave.

"Oh, and I hate to be a stereotypical cop, but when you come back? Bring doughnuts?"

"You miss breakfast or something?"

He looked at her like she'd grown two heads. "Breakfast? You mean the meal that happened over two hours ago?"

When she came back, Dolniak looked even more exhausted. She knew what he was going to say before he even opened his mouth.

"I just got off the line with Freetown. They say your yard sale murders were both suicides, no sign of foul play. The local authorities have closed the cases. They say I have jurisdiction unless I can find evidence of an interplanetary conspiracy or a crime against an AI. Neither of which claims is supported, in their opinion, by the facts that you told me."

"In other words, they're dumping it back in your lap."

"Pretty much." He opened the bag of doughnuts without asking and fished one out. "Want one?" he asked around a mouthful of cinnamon crumble.

"No thanks. That means that someone in Freetown paid them off. Or they're afraid of trampling on UNSec's toes."

"Or that they just don't buy your theory."

"You didn't, uh, mention me, did you?"

"Why?" Dolniak asked, all wide-eyed innocence. "Was I not supposed to?"

Li grinned.

"Yeah, somehow I thought not."

"What about the local AI cops?"

He grimaced. "They're a little busy lately."

"Yeah, I noticed. I noticed the cops rounding up Trannies. You guys got a wild AI outbreak on your hands or is that standard local procedure?"

"No, it's not standard." He sounded angry at the suggestion, which would have made Li like him if she didn't already. "And those cops aren't local."

"They're not Peacekeepers, either."

He shrugged. "They're working for the Peacekeepers, what's the difference?"

Li raised her eyebrows. "And what about the outbreak?"

Dolniak shrugged. "So far the computers are still working."

"They always keep working. It's just whether they keep working for you or not. And anyway, don't worry. If it gets really bad the UN will just turn tail, get out of Dodge, and shut down the field array behind them."

"And some people would be very pleased to see them go. Not that you heard it from me or anything. So listen, you're a nice lady, and the doughnuts are great. But are you going to come straight with me at some point here?"

"I'm thinking about it. Why do you ask?"

"Because when I tried to do a little digging on my own, I ran face-first into Titan Security Services."

Li flailed for a moment and then made the connection. "You mean the hired mercs that are all over the government zone like a cheap suit?"

"Yes."

"And what did you find out about that?"

"Nothing. Titan's a police no-go zone on New Allegheny."

"I see," Li said. And she did. More than Dolniak, probably, since she'd been on the operating end of several UN occupations of unruly Periphery planets. Companies like Titan operated above the law in the Trusteeships—which was exactly why the UN hired them in the first place. "Well, in the meantime what can you tell me about the DFT rush?"

He raised his eyebrows.

"Oh I know the basics. But what's the view from here? Who are the players? How do the local yokels see it?"

"The local yokels don't exactly agree with each other on it, to be honest."

"Okay. Then how does—I don't know, let's say a basically smart and honest cop who spends his working days dealing with the fallout of the DFT rush? How would that guy see it?"

As Caitlyn had expected, Dolniak's explanation of local politics was cogent and highly logical. She could have sat in on a month of UNSec briefings without hearing as good a rundown of the strategic issues.

"And that's where the AI comes into it," he concluded.

"Who?"

"Your friend. The one that was kidnapped. You think this is the first time I've heard that story? We're swimming in kidnapped AIs."

"Why?"

"The DFT rush. The Drift. You can't navigate the Drift without an Emergent AI. Not reliably anyway. And certainly not safely."

Li nodded. This at least made sense to her. Ships navigating the Drift were essentially surfing superimposed histories of the universe—which amounted to coexisting in multiple "locations" in the universe at a single time. In order to keep their bearings, they needed to process the vast sets of Hilbert space state vectors. That meant they needed powerful quantum computers. And the only entities that could operate such computers or even interface usefully with them were fully sentient Emergent AIs. Thus the press-ganging by governments—and outright kidnapping by private actors—of AIs for service in the Drift.

"So if I were you," Dolniak continued as if the connection were obvious, "I'd be asking around at the portside auction houses to see which one sold this one."

"But Emergent AIs are sentient," she protested. "They're limited citizens. They have rights. Some rights, anyway. You can't just buy one at the local hardware store."

"Yeah, well, sentience isn't exactly a bright line, is it? The portside auction houses sell off salvaged NavComps every day that they claim aren't sentient."

Dolniak went on, and the more Li heard, the worse it got. Cohen's death might have nothing to do with Nguyen or UNSec, she realized. Emergent AIs were being sucked into the region already to feed the insatiable NavComp market that the Drift prospectors relied on. Some of those Emergents were coming in legally, on limited contracts from their controlling associates. But most were little better than kidnapping victims. With a growing sense of frustration, Li realized that her list of suspects had just expanded to include every Drift prospector on New Allegheny. Even if she could track down all the yard sale buyers, that would only be the beginning of her task. The real challenge would be catching up with the scattered fragments before they shipped out into the Drift, whose quantum tides could carry them beyond her reach forever.

"Okay," Dolniak said, righting his chair and putting his big feet back on the floor. "Now you tell me something. Tell me how a nice Korean girl like you came by that charming Irish smile. Not to mention the charming brogue that goes with it."

"Is it so obvious?"

"Only when you try to talk like one of the guys."

"*Try?*"

"Fair enough. You *are* one of the guys. I knew it before you even opened your mouth. What are you, a cop's kid?"

"Miner."

"Oh, right. You're from Compson's World. I remember reading something about that during the trial."

He had been getting coffee as he spoke, but now he turned around and looked straight at her, gauging her reaction. It was an old interrogator's trick, and Li couldn't have taught him to do it any better.

"How long have you known who I was?" she asked.

"Since about two hours after you mauled my crime scene." He gave her a mildly annoyed look. "Do I look like the kind of guy who doesn't do his homework?"

"No. But I thought I'd covered my tracks a little better than that."

"Oh, you did. I wouldn't have gotten there at all if I hadn't looked at your travel papers and noticed that you transported in after the relay shut down. So either you were with UNSec, which you said you weren't, or you scattercast in. And then I started thinking about just how much money someone would have to pay *me* before I'd scattercast. And then I started thinking about rich, dead AIs. And then I called up some news spins just on the off chance that I'd see a familiar face . . . and Bingo. Ex–UN Peacekeeper Major Catherine Li. Currently Mrs. Hyacinthe Cohen." His mouth twisted in a wry half smile. "You weren't kidding when you said you'd married money." He sat down and sipped his coffee, watching her over the rim of the cup. "I didn't even know AIs *could* get married. Was it a real marriage, if you don't mind my asking, or more like a business arrangement?"

Li was used to that reaction. Given Cohen's flamboyant personal history it was hard to understand how resistant people were to the idea of him being married. But there were some things most people didn't want to know, even in the most sophisticated circles of Orbital Ring society. People could imagine AIs using humans for making love or money. But the idea of ties that went beyond pleasure and finance seemed to threaten some illusion of human specialness that people were reluctant to let go of.

"I don't mean to be nosey," Dolniak said. "But . . . well . . . let's just say I have professional reasons for wanting to know what baggage you've brought with you."

"I'm not going to do anything stupid, if that's what you're asking."

Dolniak gazed at her seriously for several moments. No reaction. Just that flat, level cop's stare. Watching her, reading her, measuring her. She imagined him assessing each word, each look, each gesture, like a jeweler inspecting gemstones. "I learned a lot from those old spinfeeds," he said finally. "I didn't know AIs could die, either. There was a whole bunch of stuff I didn't quite get about decoherence. Or disassociation. I wasn't sure if it was two different things or two words for the same thing. When an AI disassociates is it . . . well, *gone*? Like a person who dies? Or are there still pieces hanging around?"

"That depends."

"Ah." He leaned back in his chair. "Now things are starting to make a little more sense. Albeit in a down-the-rabbit-hole kind of way. So this AI died." Li noticed he didn't say Cohen's name or call him her husband. She didn't know what to make of that, but she filed it away for future consideration. "He died, and there was a yard sale, and now the buyers are turning up dead. And *you* turned up in the middle of my crime scene because you're trying to track down those same buyers."

"And not doing a very good job of it. Someone else keeps finding them first and killing them."

"And stealing the parts."

"Right."

"The parts you're looking for too and probably would have stolen first if you'd gotten to the victims first."

Li grinned. "Let's say I would have discussed their right of possession with an eye to persuading them to do the right thing."

"Oh, I see. And I'm sure someone with your service record would know how to be quite persuasive."

"Well, I wouldn't have *killed* them. I can tell you that much."

"Funny, but I believe you. Not that I have any reason to. And that's a problem." He waved a large, powerful, yet surprisingly delicate hand at the chaos of the bullpen surrounding them. "You might have intuited from my palatial office that the scope of my authority in this organization is not unlimited. But just in case you're still wondering, the sad reality is that if I write in my case file that I've turned you loose because I think you're a classy lady who can be trusted to play nice I'd be out of a job in twenty-four hours—and before I'd even packed up my desk you'd be inside of a jail cell."

He crossed his arms, leaned back in his chair, and stared at her. Li stared back, waiting it out. But this time he didn't crack first.

"So is this the part where you arrest me?"

"No." He sighed and sat down heavily. "You can go for now. Just don't leave town. And please, please try not to stumble into any more of my crime scenes. My sense of humor only stretches so far."

(Catherine)

Li spent most of her first week on board the *Christina* trying and failing to talk to Llewellyn. The pirates expected the Navy to come after them. And they expected it to happen soon. So until they were safely away from the capture point, Li and her fellow prisoners found themselves locked into various crew cabins, cut off from the shipboard communications network, and sentenced to the equivalent of solitary confinement.

And when the immediate danger was past and they were finally let out, it was only to be summoned to—of all things—a crew meeting.

Li had heard about these meetings. Most pirate ships operated not by Navy rules but by a sort of rough one-man-one-vote form of democracy. Or so they claimed when they were wooing recruits, at any rate. But she'd always assumed these votes were a sort of after-the-fact ratification of decisions taken under fire. She'd never imagined pirates dabbling in democracy out in the Deep and one step ahead of armed pursuit.

As she filed into the main cargo bay—the only internal space on board that was large enough to accommodate the crew count of a fully operational pirate ship—Li took another long, careful look at William Llewellyn.

This was her first sight of him since the capture, and she could get a better sense of the man now that he wasn't riding a combat high. She studied him covertly, trying to get a read on him, and not really coming up with anything. The piratical rogue was gone, replaced by a buttoned-down ship's captain who seemed to have systematically eliminated every trace of individuality from his dress, person, and demeanor. All he let you see was the physical package.

Pale English skin made even paler by a life shipboard. Dark hair that would have been curly if it hadn't been hacked to within an inch of its life by the barber's shears. An athlete's body edging toward the kind of disciplined, whipcord-thin, zero-body-fat middle age that Li associated with special forces field instructors. Clothes freshly washed and ironed. A close but somehow perfunctory shave. Like the haircut, it hinted at a man whose only use for a mirror was to check that he hadn't missed any spots.

The only glint of individuality was in the eyes—and at the moment those betrayed only a wary, waiting, highly disciplined intelligence. That was the real essence of the man, she decided—or at least of the outward man. Control. Order. Discipline. And above all, self-discipline.

Soldiers followed men like this. They often revered them, imbuing them with quasi-magical powers. But they didn't understand them. And they rarely loved them.

Llewellyn seemed to know this as well as Li did. He was on his own ship, in the midst of his own crew, and at least temporarily safe from UNSec. He should be relaxed, but he wasn't. And that *was* interesting, Li decided. Maybe this all-hands meeting wasn't just about paperwork.

Five minutes into the meeting she knew she'd been right. And she also knew that there were two other crew members worth watching. Llewellyn didn't lead the ship alone—or at least he didn't lead without resistance. He was locked into a complex triumvirate. And from the tense set of his shoulders and the tight line of his mouth, he believed that the other two members each had the power to topple him if things went wrong.

Llewellyn's obvious opponent was Doyle, the quartermaster. Li hadn't seen much of Doyle yet, but she had heard his name invoked often enough to guess that he was a major power on the ship. The quartermaster's domain lay deep in the bowels of the vessel, far from the bridge and the officers' quarters, and Li barely understood what a quartermaster did on a normal Navy ship. She understood much less the complex power structure of the pirate ship, in which the quartermaster seemed to be almost a shadow captain with authority to contradict and even overrule the captain himself in any decision that didn't involve the immediate risk of engagement with the enemy.

Not that Doyle was any stranger to combat. He was a tall man, short of leg and long of body, running ever so slightly to fat but still obviously dangerous. Li had seen him fight during the taking of the corporate troop transport, and she pegged him as the kind of man who'd be a valuable friend and a lethal enemy. And even if she hadn't seen him in action, his face would have told her everything she needed to know about his service; a white flurry of scar tissue glistened across the bridge of his nose and feathered over his cheekbone to his jawline. Li was so busy puzzling over what had caused those scars that she all but missed the first minute of his obviously prepared speech.

Plasma weapon, she finally decided, right around the time he was getting down to his main talking point—which seemed to concern some arcane algorithm for divvying up intellectual property seized in the raid.

When Doyle sat down, Li expected Llewellyn to respond, but instead it was Sital who rose to answer. Li watched the small, dark woman critically. She didn't make the mistake of underestimating her; a small woman herself, Li knew that weight counted for little in ship or station fighting, and nothing at all in true zero g. But there was something about Sital's manner—the buttoned-down competence of a woman who looked more like a life-systems engineer than a pirate—that would have made it easy to overlook her in any case.

Easy, but foolish, Li soon realized. Sital was the third leg of the stool. She pulled just as much weight with the crew as Doyle did. But hers was a different, softer kind of power. For the moment it was all on Llewellyn's side. But it was power nonetheless, and power always has to be reckoned with.

The first order of business today was division of the spoils. Theoretically this should have been wrangled out between Llewellyn and Doyle in his capacity as the crew's elected quartermaster. In reality, though, the battle was between Doyle and Sital, who defended Llewellyn's interests like a pit bull while he stood off to the side, affecting to be nobly disinterested in filthy lucre.

As Li watched Doyle and Sital battle it out, she realized that Sital was more than just Llewellyn's pit bull. She also led her own faction, composed of crew members who were loyal first to her, and only second to Llewellyn. Nor was Doyle simply Llewellyn's opposite pole. Yes, he might be a lightning rod for opposition to the current captain—the quartermaster was always that, since he served as the main check to the captain's otherwise overweening power—but Doyle represented something more as well. He stood for something in the minds of the men and women who sided with him. And, just like Sital, he had put in the blood and sweat necessary to earn their loyalty.

Sital, Doyle, Llewellyn. Public opinion on the ship flowed between the three of them in a delicate balance, with a few committed to one faction or another but most genuinely undecided and willing to go with whoever seemed to have the strongest arguments on their side at any given moment.

And the more Li saw, the more she started to think that Sital had more power than she or anyone else suspected—precisely because she used that power on Llewellyn's behalf and not in her own interest. As long as things stayed that way, she would hold the line against Doyle and his supporters. But if she ever split with Llewellyn, all hell would break loose.

Today, though, Sital was clearly on Llewellyn's side. The intellectual property booty question was put to bed with minimal debate, and no expenditure of significant political capital—at least for Llewellyn. Li couldn't read the deeper currents that might tell her how much it had cost Doyle to even raise the issue.

And then they moved on to what was clearly the real business of the meeting.

"All right, Doyle, run the numbers for us," Llewellyn said. "What are we looking at?"

As Doyle ran down the take of weapons, ammunition, and technicals, murmurs of approval surged around the room. But when he shifted to the vitals—oxy, nitro, and hydrogen—the mood turned ugly. Li didn't know the normal operational losses of this ship, or how many days or weeks of drive time those numbers bought. But she'd been on enough other ships to know that oxy/nitro/hydro stores were the only thing sailors care more about than engines and NavComps. A modern ship might not need to carry much resupply in absolute terms, but if it ran out then there was nothing to replace the precious molecules that the scrubbers and water filters took out, and that was the end of your breathable air and drinkable water. And without air and water, those fancy engines and NavComps would just be pushing corpses.

"Why so little oxy?" someone asked.

"They burned off their supplies before we could get to them," Sital answered.

"Jesus, that's fucked up! Who would do that?"

"People who don't like pirates," Llewellyn said wryly.

"So what does that give us?"

"Two weeks. Three at the outside if we skimp on water."

"Shit," someone muttered in the back—but the sound carried like a bell in the sudden silence that greeted this bad news.

"All right," Llewellyn said. "So at least we lengthened our leash a bit."

"Not much," Doyle said. "We got a bad connection the first time we grappled up. Remember? That cost us a fair bit of air pressure."

"How much?"

"I'd say we've got a month at the outside before we need to put into a friendly port."

"Or we make another capture," Llewellyn pointed out.

"Well . . . yeah. Of course."

Llewellyn cast his eyes around the room. "So where do we go? Suggestions, anyone?"

"I say we make for Boomerang," Doyle said. "And then—"

"But that's almost a week's trip. And we don't even know that Boomerang's still a friendly port," Sital interrupted.

"—and then we can hang fire at the entry point and listen to the comm traffic. If it sounds good we go in."

"And if not?" Llewellyn asked quietly.

"Then we hunt around the entry point where we can get out fast if Avery comes after us."

Llewellyn laughed derisively.

"Come on. Why the hell not? I call that a winning strategy!"

Llewellyn turned his pale eyes toward the ceiling and laughed quietly. "That's not winning, Doyle. That's just losing a little more slowly."

"Fine. Then what do you call winning?"

"We go on offense. We take the fight to Avery personally."

"Oh no. No way, Will. You're not dragging us into your little personal vendetta."

"What am I dragging you into? You think any of you can jump ship and stroll into some friendly port in this quadrant? Last time I checked, half the crew had a price on their heads." He fixed his gaze on Doyle. "You certainly do."

"I'm not saying that, William. I'm just saying—"

"You're just saying we should keep running scared. Well, we tried that. It's all we've tried so far. And look what it's gotten us. Now you want to run some more? On what possible logical grounds? Haven't you ever heard that the definition of a crazy person is someone who keeps doing the same thing and expecting different results?"

"You're a fine one to talk about crazy—"

"Crazy is as crazy does. Do the math, Doyle. Every time you've convinced the crew to run scared, we've lost. Sometimes we lost big, sometimes we lost small. But we never did anything except lose. Whereas every time I've convinced you to take a gamble, it's paid off in spades."

"You can't live on luck forever," Doyle said in the sour tones of a man trudging down the well-worn rut of an old argument.

"Not luck. A calculated risk in the service of a clear-cut strategic goal." Llewellyn grinned—the first glimpse Li had seen in this meeting of the charismatic leader who'd taken the Titan bridge a few days ago. "And besides, Doyle, haven't you heard the rumors yet? I'm lucky."

Doyle acknowledged his defeat with a shrug of his slab-sided shoulders. "So where do we go now?"

"Into the Drift. Really in, not just dabbling our toes in the shallows.

And when Avery follows us, we go on the attack and steal her goddamn ship right out from under her."

A gasp eddied around the room, half fear and half appreciation at the outrageous boldness of the proposal.

"Are you forgetting the recent unpleasantness?" Okoro drawled in his slow, deep voice. He was sitting next to Sital, and from the way the two of them had been chatting before the meeting started Li guessed they were friends as well as crew mates.

"She's a good ship," Llewellyn insisted. "She just made a mistake. Anyone can make a mistake, Ike."

He held Okoro's eyes for a heartbeat. Li couldn't have said which man looked away first; she wasn't even sure they knew.

"That was one hell of a mistake," Okoro observed mildly. "Wouldn't like to be around when she makes the next one."

Sital sat beside Okoro chewing her nails and looking miserable. Llewellyn glanced at her briefly, and he read something in her averted face that made his lips tighten into a frustrated line.

"Okay, Ike. Maybe you're right. Let's forget about the *Ada*. For now, anyway. Let's just concentrate on figuring out where we stand and getting some supplies on board. I still say we need to make the Drift work for us."

"But we need an Emergent AI to navigate the Drift safely," Doyle protested.

"And we have one."

"You mean *you* have one! But what if something happens to you?"

Llewellyn graced Doyle with a cool, sideways smile. "Are you expecting something to happen to me?"

"I'm just saying. Until you upload the ghost to the shipnet, we've got no guarantee the two of you won't strand us out there."

"All right. Find a way to upload it, and we'll discuss the matter. Does that satisfy you?"

A chuckle swept around the room as Llewellyn's faction and the undecideds appreciated his adroit outmaneuvering of the complainer. Everyone knew—and the certainty of their knowledge was a gauge for Li of just how important Llewellyn's fragment was—that their new

NavComp was simply in a different class of AI from their old one. It had parasitized Llewellyn's DNA and was sweeping through his body with visible and worrisome effects on him for one simple reason: The DNA of a complete, living person—replicating heartbeat by heartbeat in every nucleus of every cell in his body—was the only parallel processing platform on the creaking old *Christina* that was even remotely large enough to host such a being.

Doyle's men subsided into inaudible mutters of discontent, but he had sense enough to know when he was beaten. And he also had the sense—or maybe he just hadn't thought of it—not to suggest the other obvious alternative: infecting someone else with the virus and letting them host the NavComp. Li was glad he hadn't gotten there, for his sake as well as Cohen's. Because as she watched Llewellyn in action—and watched the curious blending of his personality and Cohen's that was so unnervingly different from seeing Cohen on a passive shunt—she was starting to suspect that there was something else going on here. Llewellyn was fertile soil for Cohen's memes as well as his source code. And she wasn't at all sure that this ghost would take happily to being transplanted.

"Any other thoughts?" Llewellyn asked the room in general.

Several people began to speak, but Doyle's voice cut across the rest. "I think it's into the Drift. I don't see that we have any other choice. I don't see that you've left us any other choice."

Li looked around, seeing crew members nodding their agreement, and realized that Doyle was dangerous in more than the obvious ways. He might not speak well, but that didn't matter so much on a ship where everyone knew one another from long experience and bravery under fire spoke louder than empty words. Llewellyn was the ship's unquestioned leader. He had the combination of brilliant military tactics and sheer, inexplicable gift-of-the-universe good fortune that every soldier wants in his leader. He was the crew's lucky charm. They needed him and they knew it. But they *liked* Doyle. And all things being equal—in other words, when no one was trying to kill them—they'd rather follow Doyle than Llewellyn. Lucky for Llewellyn that Astrid Avery seemed to have made killing them into a full-time personal crusade.

Llewellyn gave Doyle a long, probing look, his pale eyes searching the man's face. "We'll chart the course together, Doyle. You have full say in this. You're the crew's man. I'm not holding out on you. I never have been."

"You're always holding out on us," Okoro interrupted. "It's in your nature."

"See—" Doyle began.

"No, Doyle, I'm not siding with you. I think Llewellyn's right. And I don't think we can risk trying to upload the ghost to shipnet. The last NavComp almost got us killed through sheer incompetence. This one's good. Maybe even as good as *Ada*. We can't risk ruining that." His eyes flicked to Llewellyn. "But I do think you should be more forthcoming. It's not that we don't trust you, William. We do. You've earned it. But the ghost hasn't. And which one of you is *really* in charge?"

They faced off against each other. No one else in the room even seemed to be breathing.

It was Llewellyn who finally broke the silence. "I've kept you alive for the last three years, Doyle. Doesn't that earn me anything?"

Doyle made a bitter face. "According to Ike here, it earns you the right to take us into the Drift on your say-so without a NavComp."

"But you don't agree."

Doyle scanned the room, looking for support and finding none. "Doesn't look like it matters much what I think."

"All right then," Llewellyn said quietly. "At least we all know where we stand now."

And Sital swept briskly in on his heels, fulfilling her assigned role in the trinity: whipping the hounds along and moving the hunt forward. "Shall we put it to a vote?" she asked in that deceptively mousy voice that made even statements sound like questions. "All in favor say aye?"

"Any other questions?" Llewellyn asked when the votes had been tallied and the big decision made.

Silence.

Llewellyn stood up, nodded tersely, and walked out without another word. Sital stood up one beat behind him, always the loyal adjutant. "Meeting adjourned. We all know what we have to do. Let's get on it, people."

(Llewellyn)

"So" the ghost said, counting on the dainty fingers of the most implausibly beautiful body Llewellyn had yet seen it in. "You ordered Ada into battle. And she destroyed the creche ship. And she had the natural reaction that any person would have had. And then she went off and had a look at her source code, or at least whatever pieces of it Holmes and Titan were willing to let her see. And then she realized that she's not any ordinary person at all but . . . a very special kind of person. And then what happened?"

"And then the fights started."

"With Ada?"

"No! Of course not! What do you think I am? With Holmes."

In the weeks after what they soon took to calling "Ada's little identity crisis," Llewellyn truly began to understand what an AI officer was and did—and that was when Holmes's role on the ship really began to sink into his consciousness.

She began pushing, advocating, pressuring. And always ringing through the same limited set of talking points: dangerous signs of instability; better to nip things in the bud and stop the rot before it went further; a stitch in time saves nine; no time like the present; time is money.

It was all about time. Time and money, and Titan's needs to deliver on their promises. One of which, apparently, was that the Navy would never have to actually have nondeniable consciousness of any outright violation of the laws regarding the weaponization of sentient AIs.

"So what then?" the ghost asked, nudging him back on track and down the road toward the things he didn't want to think about.

"So we had another knock-down, drag-out fight between Holmes and the bridge crew. Holmes thought Ada's reaction was a serious red flag. She wanted to pull her off the line and go straight back to dry dock for a refit."

"That's one I haven't heard before."

"Don't look like that. No one was talking about a hard reboot at that point, not even close. She just said there was some proprietary debugging software Titan could run. Something about a hybrid system—"

"They wanted to slave her to a semi-sentient."

"No!" Llewellyn's horror was instinctive, visceral. "That would be insane. You'd have a completely dysfunctional ship on your hands if you tried that. You'd end up with—"

"Something, I don't know, perhaps a bit like the *Jabberwocky*?"

Llewellyn drew up short at that. But he wasn't willing to go there yet. It just didn't make sense to him. "Look," he told the ghost, "you're doing a twenty-twenty hindsight read of the situation. It just didn't seem like that at the time. And I guarantee you no one was talking about hard reboots or semi-sentients."

"But," the ghost gently insinuated, driving him pitilessly back to the things he least wanted to remember, "it *was* during that argument that the first cracks between you and Avery began to show . . ."

"I guess so," Llewellyn said reluctantly.

"And then came the death of the *Romola*."

They picked up the *Romola*'s distress call before they even dropped out of superposition. It was coming out on multiple branchings—indeed in almost every branching that they could match up with a coherent spacetime model, let alone pull down a Hertzsprung-Russell diagram that was anything but unadulterated paradox.

The *Romola* was sending out a standard automated mayday. But the ship was talking over it, relaying not only her coordinates and heading but also her life support systems status, which amounted to bad and getting worse.

Ada knew what to do, and Llewellyn let her do it. She talked the other ship down—always better to let that happen ship to ship instead of dragging organics into it. And all the while Llewellyn could see her sucking up parallel processing units while she tried to work through the three-body problem of setting up the fastest possible rendezvous for two Drift ships rocketing through a gravitationally complex slice of spacetime at speeds that turned relativistic effects into life-and-death practicalities.

And then suddenly everyone was looking at the odd blip on the scanners in the neighboring nebula that only Sital had been paying attention to—up until the instant when it broke out of cover and turned into a Syndicate hunter-destroyer.

They were all instream now, the whole bridge crew juiced up on synth and pumped up on adrenaline and oxytocin. And Ada sucking PPUs down what seemed like a bottomless hole of calculations as she hurled every ounce of brute calculating power she had at the dizzying three-body problem of ships, sandbar, stars all pivoting around one another in a cosmic dance playing out along multiple superimposed quantum branchings.

Coming in fast, Avery said. I think a preemptive strike is warranted here.

I don't agree, Ada answered—and shocked the whole lot of them into a paralyzed, breathless silence that set Llewellyn's ears ringing.

"She's not going to fire." Holmes spoke offstream, and barely in a whisper, but her voice ricocheted around the bridge like a gunshot.

"I haven't told her to fire," Llewellyn said curtly.

"I think—" Avery began.

But Llewellyn dropped back instream again without waiting to hear what she thought.

We're not deciding anything yet, Ada, he said as soothingly as he could given the adrenaline pumping through his body.

Can't we just talk to them?

Ada—

I'm sorry, William. I can't do this again. Not without giving them a chance to—

We're going to give them every chance to declare themselves, Ada. Just bracket the Syndicate ship. We're not committing to anything.

"This is mutiny."

"Not now."

"And you're covering for her."

"Shut up, Holmes."

"If you don't—"

"This is my bridge, and *you will shut up or I make you shut up!*"

The Syndicate ship slid out of the cover of the sandbar and surged toward the *Romola* like a shark smelling blood in the water. Llewellyn tuned Holmes out and slipped back instream to try to reason with Ada. But before he could do more than assess the situation . . .

"Yank the plug!" Holmes was up in his face, close enough that he could taste her spit while she shouted at him. "Hard cycle her *now* or you can go back to New Allegheny in the brig."

Okoro was at Holmes's shoulder now, ready to haul her off the bridge, but it was too late. She had activated her AI officer's override and she was onstream, and Llewellyn and the rest of the bridge officers were locked out, and there wasn't a thing anyone could do about it.

"This is Holmes, Ada. You are now officially under my command and are to disregard any further orders from Captain Llewellyn."

"What? I don't under—"

"I want you to target the Syndicate ship and bracket it with plasma tracers. And when you've acquired your target, kill it."

"No," Ada said stubbornly. "They haven't done anything, and we don't even know they're hostile, and—"

Llewellyn never knew for certain why the Syndicate ship did what it did next. Maybe they didn't think their AI was a match for the *Romola*. Or maybe there was some hidden weakness in their intelligent systems that the *Ada*'s scans hadn't uncovered and that they feared would betray them in the heat of battle. Or maybe it was just that hoary old chestnut that people always trotted out when they wanted to excuse the inexcusable: the fog of war.

In the moment, however, there was no time to think about why they did it. There was barely time to even understand that they were going to do it.

There was only the shrieking wail of targeting alarms, and the *Romola* herself on comm, drowning out the voices of her bridge crew as she pleaded desperately with the *Ada* to help her. And then a twinkling pinprick flash from the bow of the Syndicate ship. And quicker than thought—quicker than the human eye could even track the flight of the fatal missile—a larger flash that blossomed out from the place the *Romola* had been to paint the whole vast sweep of space in Technicolor.

"What do you think happens when you jump through a Bose-Einstein relay?" the ghost asked Llewellyn.

"Usually? I forget to tie down the cargo, and the tug captain scrapes my hull, and the postmaster double-charges me and I find myself wishing I'd never even seen the inside of a jumpship."

"Ah, indeed. Who's for the merrie life of a pirate? You're right, though. There is a certain black-box aspect to Bose-Einstein transport. Which is not that surprising, since it's very often the case that the defining technology of an age is precisely the one that people *least* understand on an intuitive level. How many peasants in the age of steam actually understood the sly workings of Maxwell's Demon or even what was going on in the belly of a steam locomotive? And how many of the global citizens of the hot, flat, and crowded information age actually understood how their cellphones worked? And Bose-Einstein transport may be the most impressive failure yet. It may actually go down in the books as the only major technology whose golden age came and went before science caught up with it enough to actually explain it."

They were sitting in a swanky basement bar in pre-Migration New York. It was a little disorienting, actually. Llewellyn had seen so many old films and entertainment spins of the famous city that he couldn't quite grasp the reality of it—or the relative reality, since he was still only experiencing the ghost's accumulated memories of it.

Somehow he had expected soaring eagle's-eye views of the famous skyline. And instead he was getting an ant's-eye view of fashionably clad feet rushing past the sidewalk-level windows.

"But the thing is," the ghost continued, "when you strip away all the hardware and software and field arrays and entry points, what happens in Bose-Einstein transport is exactly what happens in the Drift. It's not that the Drift is stranger than any other kind of entanglement. It's just that entanglement itself is stranger than we can ever quite bring ourselves to realize."

The ghost lifted his glass above his head so that the light flickering through the passing feet strobed across it. Before Llewellyn's eyes, the glass began to shift and shimmer and mold itself to the shape of the ghost's words.

"Imagine an onion. Or better yet, a rose. Each leaf appears to be a single membrane, but really it consists of an infinite number of superimposed leaves. Put Lewis at one end of the leaf and Alice at the other and Schrödinger's cat in its little box with its little cyanide pill—incidentally, you do know that Alan Turing committed suicide by cyanide injection? Yes, I thought you'd find that interesting. Back to Lewis and Alice, though. Rather than envisioning the entangled qubit they share as doing anything that could violate causality, we ought simply to imagine two superimposed universes delaminating from each other. In each universe the cat dies or it doesn't. In each universe the qubit turns or it doesn't. And as the classical component of the message travels between Lewis and Alice—"

"Why do they call them Lewis and Alice, by the way? I always wondered that in Astro-Navigation when they were making us do problem sets."

"Actually, it was Hannah Sharifi who started that. Before her, information theorists always used Bob and Alice. But Hannah thought Lewis was a bit more resonant. And I suspect she liked the fact that it started with an *L*, since she always argued that discovering FTL transport was really just a side effect of the important stuff, and that what she *really* ought to be remembered for was figuring out how to use the lemma calculus to map the multiverse."

Llewellyn snorted. "No wonder you two liked each other. Were you telling the truth when you told Li you'd slept with her?"

"Yes, actually. But you shouldn't read too much into it. I've slept with a lot of mathematicians."

"You collected them," Llewellyn said without realizing he was quoting Catherine Li until the words were spoken, "the way schizophrenic old ladies collect house cats."

"Been opening doors and drawers without permission, have we?" the ghost said silkily. "You want to watch out for that. Bluebeard's wives came to a very messy end by using keys without the proper file permissions."

"I'm not afraid of you," Llewellyn said with a smile.

The ghost opened its mouth to shoot back some clever answer—and then closed it and just watched Llewellyn for a moment. It wasn't a mocking look, let alone a cruel one. It was just . . . shocked. Or so it seemed to Llewellyn in the heat of the moment. Later that night, lying in bed and rethinking the scene, he realized that the ghost hadn't really looked shocked at all. It had looked frightened. Terrified, actually. And Llewellyn had come to know the mercurial, impossible, multifaceted essence of the ghost rather well through their forced march through their joint memories. Well enough to be quite sure that the only thing in the wide world Cohen was really afraid of was himself—his power, his fallibility, and the damage that godlike power allied with all-too-human failings could do in the world.

"Anyway," the ghost said, passing over that odd internal moment of reckoning as lightly as a child scampering through a graveyard, "back to Lewis and Alice and the Rose E'er Blooming. Imagine the multiverse as a rose, a rose with an uncountable infinity of petals. When Alice and Lewis run their Schrödinger's cat experiment, they create multiple branchings, each of which can be envisioned as a single petal. Until a classical message passes between Alice and Lewis—until someone does something that forces the wave to collapse—they both continue to exist in a single universe in which the cat is both alive and dead. But the box is opened, and the cat is found alive or dead, and the message travels along the stretch of spacetime that separates the two of them, their superimposed universes delaminate from each other to create new membranes in the multiverse, each of which is its own universe with its own infinite quantum branchings. So, one universe has given birth to two—or, more realistically, an infinity—which continue to delaminate from each other until they achieve total separation throughout Lewis and Alice's future light cones."

Llewellyn followed this as far as it went. But he was having trouble seeing how it applied to naval tactics, and his face must have shown it.

"You're looking at it the wrong way around," the ghost told him. "You're thinking of quantum branchings of the multiverse as something that happens to us. You need to start thinking of them as something we do to the universe. All of us. Every person, every mind, every body, every stone and leaf of grass and dust mote in the universe. We are all making new worlds at every moment, worlds upon worlds, universes upon universes, infinities upon infinities. Do you think in all those infinities I can't find one where we win and our enemies lose?"

"But how? You can't possibly run those calculations."

"Can you run the calculations for a game of chess?"

"No."

"But you can still play it. And you're better than most players. And a few players are better than you. And a very few players are a lot better than you. Even though none of them can crunch the numbers any better than you can."

"So what then? What is it you do? How do you know when to jump and where to jump to?"

"You just do. For one thing you only count the universes that count."

"How can you tell which ones count?"

"Well, not that they don't all count, but . . . some of them are just irrelevant. We don't care about them. They have nothing interesting to say to us."

"You make it sound as if it's some kind of subjective aesthetic judgment."

"Well, it is . . . isn't it? Elegant ideas, elegant equations, is there really

that much difference between the two? Look at it this way. In my favorite Evelyn Waugh novel one of the characters is held hostage in the
Amazonian jungle and forced to read the entire collected works of
Charles Dickens aloud to his captor. In some innumerable infinity of
parallel universes I myself am being held hostage on, let's say a remote
space station by a demented fellow AI. Now if he's making me read
Dashiell Hammett to him, so what? That situation is entirely lacking in
aesthetic interest. But if he's making me read Evelyn Waugh? Ah! Now
that, I think we can both agree, is a universe in which my worldline
would possess a certain level of poignant irony. Or, put another way,
it would be relevant to me—and not merely contiguous. And that's just
what I'm looking for, in a mathematical sense, when I'm playing at
being NavComp. Connections. Structures. Frameworks. Echoes and
counterpoints. Slices of spacetime where our worldline brushes against
parallel worldlines in ways that strike me as useful or interesting. And,
yes, it is a subjective judgment. And, yes, what's interesting to me might
not be interesting to another AI. And, yes, it's a kind of mathematical
thinking that's as much art as science. But when you're good enough at
it, all math is art as well as science. Of course it is. It's the art of reducing
the world to numbers in a Universal Turing Machine—just the way the
programmer of a Jacquard loom reduces paintings to numbers on
punch cards."

Llewellyn's head jerked up, and he drew in a sharp breath. "That's
exactly how Ada explained it."

"Of course it is." The ghost's head cocked sideways in a theatrical,
slightly precious gesture of bemusement. "Who do you think I learned
it from?"

"You talked to her? And you didn't tell me? What the hell do you
think you're playing a—"

"Not that Ada, you idiot. The real one. Ada Lovelace. The woman
whose name she took. The woman who wrote what amounted to the
first mathematical description of computer programming. Don't you
see that's what we're talking about? Information. Information is what
our memories are made of. Information is what our minds are made of.

Information is what our genes and our immortality are made of. That's what the cosmos is, William. And that's all it is. The multiverse is just a creative exercise in mathematics: the manipulation of symbols, the enumeration of the Names of God, the art of wrestling meaning from ciphers."

"You make it sound so heroic it's hard to imagine you being involved in it."

The ghost relinquished his wineglass, which popped like a soap bubble the moment he let go of it, and clapped mockingly. "Nice to see you developing a sense of humor. It's good for the complexion. And you're looking a little peaked lately, if you don't mind my mentioning it."

"I'm serious. Are you dragging me off on some religious crusade?"

"Jacob wrestled angels. I wrestle infinitudes." The wineglass reappeared. "Just call us Chosen, Incorporated."

"Better than Titan, Incorporated."

The lingering smile on the ghost's face shut off like a neutron star spinning into its final collapse. "Yes, I believe we were just talking about the lovely Miss Holmes when my minds began to wander? Go on. It was so amusing I can barely wait to hear more."

"What do you want to know about her?" Llewellyn asked, feeling an appalling tide of exhaustion and despair sweep over him.

"No, actually," the ghost said, changing tack as if he realized he was in danger of pushing Llewellyn too far. "Let's talk a little more about Ada's memory palace."

"Why? I mean, why are you so interested in it?"

"I'm trying to make sense of it, to put it together in my own mind so . . . so that Ada has a place to go to make sense of herself." The ghost laughed softly. "If that makes any sense to you at all, which I very much doubt it does. It barely even makes sense to me."

It was funny, Llewellyn thought, how the ghost said Ada. As if she were a person and not a ship. And it didn't even know yet. Though Llewellyn supposed he had no way of knowing what the ghost knew and didn't know. Maybe it had already ravaged his memories, picking through his most intimate secrets. Maybe it didn't need him to unlock that door. Maybe this was just another of the manipulative games it so doted on.

"Her memory palace was smaller than this. More self-contained. More . . . predictable."

"Naturally." The ghost smiled a smile that Llewellyn could only call feline. "Because in this memory, at least, Ada hadn't yet realized that she was one of a kind and no mere device."

After the death of the *Romola*, Holmes went completely ballistic.

"What did she want to do?" the ghost asked. "Did she say specifically?"

"Not as such."

"But the lines of battle were pretty well drawn, weren't they? You, Sital, and Okoro for the talking cure. Holmes for a quick sail back to dry dock where Titan would either cycle the hardware or slave Ada to a semi-sentient. And what about Avery? Did she side with you or with Holmes?"

"It still wasn't that black-and-white," Llewellyn protested. "Everything was in flux. No one was saying any of the things you're talking about out loud yet. Hell, I didn't even know you *could* slave a shipboard AI to a semi-sentient. And leaving any moral qualms aside, I still think you'd be risking the life of every man on board to even try navigating the Drift on a kluged-up system like that. I just didn't see what you're seeing when you look at the memories. And I'm not sure I had reason to see it. I . . . I thought we'd pull out of the tailspin, find some accommodation we could all live with. I didn't think it was really going to come down to a fight between me and Holmes for control of the ship."

But if the final confrontation with Holmes was still a distant thunderhead, the fights with Avery were daily and immediate. And they had been terrible. They had been the kind of fights where you said things you could never take back and made accusations you would never be forgiven for.

Avery couldn't seem to let it go. And Llewellyn . . . Llewellyn could feel himself wanting to leap to Ada's defense, wanting to protect her, wanting to stop what he saw was coming. The need was all raw emotion with him, the human instinct to leap to a drowning child's rescue, to pull a blind person out from in front of a bus, to rescue a bird with a broken wing. He said the word, but he hadn't thought about what actually helping Ada might cost him. He hadn't even really attached a specific meaning to the word.

"We can't help her," Avery said, low and fast and fierce as if the very walls were listening. "That's Holmes's job."

"You know what Holmes's idea of help would be!"

"And so what? She's the professional. You think you know better than her?"

"I think I have a heart. And morals."

"What's that supposed to mean? That I don't? You think I'm some kind of monster?"

"I didn't say that, Astrid."

"You didn't have to. I can see it in your eyes. You're already despising me. And you have no right. You have no fucking right to look at me that way. Not when you're playing footsie with Ada while the fucking ship burns down around you!"

Llewellyn actually stepped back at the expression on her face. He felt as shocked as if she'd reached out and slapped him.

"That's what this is really about, isn't it? You're jealous of her."

Avery's beautiful face twisted into something halfway between disgust and fury. "Don't go there, William. Just don't. I'm doing my job. And part of my job is making sure this ship doesn't turn into the next *Jabberwocky*."

"*Ada*'s not the *Jabberwocky* and you know it!"

"Do I? Do I really? Holmes gets to sit behind the screen and run your training sessions, but I don't have the clearance, do I? I have to take your word for it. I know all about what happens when you're in there with her."

"When I am in there with her? Listen to yourself! You can barely even say her name anymore!"

Avery straightened her spine and hardened her jaw. Llewellyn watched the hot anger drain out of her eyes, along with any last trace of life or light or forgiveness.

"I'm going to talk to Sital and Okoro about this, William. That's my job, and I intend to do it. And now I'm going to tell you something that I'm only going to say once, so you really need to listen to it: If you go there—if you make this about you—anything there ever was between us is over."

As it turned out, they could have skipped that fight. Holmes stepped in before Avery even had a chance to talk to Sital and Okoro and took the ship back to dry dock. And Holmes was there when the maintenance reports were filed and the Titan cat herders arrived and Okoro read them the passwords—with a blank look on his face that wasn't just about accessing the high security content on his AI doc's firewalled Cantor modules—and handed them the keys to the kingdom.

By then the only option Llewellyn had left was asking for his orders in writing. Which he duly did. And which duly led to his being cut out of the loop from that moment forward—and getting to twiddle his thumbs uselessly while *his* first officer and *his* bridge crew and *his* AI officer decided the fate of *his* ship without him.

And that was it. Holmes swept out of the room without even looking at them. When Avery finally met Llewellyn's stare, she looked almost as sick at heart as he felt.

"I'm sorry. Whatever I said before I . . . I didn't want this to happen."

"You didn't want what to happen, Astrid? What comes next? And don't hide behind Titan's trade secrets. I think I have a right to know. Are they going to help her or are they just going to cycle the fucking hardware?"

The look on Avery's face was all the answer he needed.

Deceptions
of the Senses

The fear of infinity is a form of myopia that destroys the possibility of seeing the actual infinite, even though it in its highest form has created and sustains us, and in its secondary transfinite forms occurs all around us and even inhabits our minds.

—Georg Cantor

(Caitlyn)

The Crucible's boundary wasn't marked on any map, but it was tangible nonetheless. She could feel the change in the air. The change in the noise and bustle and energy of the streets. The endless vistas of high gray walls and vast stock car yards and looming chimneys. The sudden and total absence of women. The choking smoke that seemed to roll off the very streets. And above all the noise and stench and red-hot glow of the blast furnaces that burned day and night because they were so hot that allowing them to cool would shatter them.

If Carrick and Glen Hazel were the Pit's heaven, and Shadyside its wasting purgatory, then the Crucible was the inner ring of Hell. The Crucible was poor, like Shadyside. But in every other possible way the two districts were dead opposites. The Crucible encompassed the great flat crescent of dry ground on the sunny side of Monongahela Pit. It boasted the most consistent year-round solar gain values, the most accessible bedrock, and the easiest access to the spaceport's launchpads and mass boosters. And it was swept by brutal year-round winds that wafted industrial pollution out of the lowlands and up over Mount Monongahela's barren summit.

The Crucible was the engine that drove Monongahela Pit, both economically and politically. Here were the steel mills, and the miscellaneous heavy industry that fueled the local economy, and the preprocessing foundries that supplied the orbital ceramsteel factories with the components of the modern era's zero-g-manufactured white gold. And here, too, were the steelworkers and stokers and linemen who epitomized New Allegheny. A blazing inferno, its flames stoked night and day by broad-shouldered giants—with politics to match. If New Allegheny was a powder keg, then the Crucible was its lit and smoldering fuse.

The steel mills were built to the scale of the steel they rolled, not the people who worked in them. By the time Li found the front gate of Mercer, she had walked past miles of railroad sidings, blank gray foundry walls, and open storage sheds.

We need to leave, Router/Decomposer said, as categorically as if he were stating an unspoken law of the universe. That woman must have been wrong. Korchow can't possibly be here.

"Why not?"

"Because. Just look around you."

"I'm looking."

"Then listen."

"For what? I don't hear anything."

"That's my point. I'm squeezed down to a single fiber optic, for God's sake. I can barely think, let alone talk to you. I'd kill myself before I went to ground in this hellhole."

Li raised an eyebrow but didn't answer him. *Korchow* couldn't possibly be here. Not *we shouldn't be here*. Let alone *you shouldn't be here*. It was one of those AI comments that she had no answer for. A little shaft of light penetrating the darkness. A disturbing hint that somewhere in that unplumbed darkness of his teeming networks Router/ Decomposer thought of himself as evolutionarily closer to Korchow than to Li or the other poor lost souls of the Crucible.

She wasn't sure what bothered her more about that realization: the fact that Router/Decomposer thought it, or the fact that his thinking it still bothered her.

After the long walk along the sidings, the factory gate was almost an anticlimax: a narrow door surrounded by barbed wire and guard sheds and loitering out-of-work steelmen. Some entrepreneurial spirit had cobbled together a coffee shed across the street out of what looked like mostly old shipping crates, and its open-grill kerosene heater was a splash of warmth and color in the landscape. But other than that, the whole scene was as hard and grim and gray as the racked steel in the freight yards.

Li shouldered through the listless ranks of the day-work pickup line and made her way to the guardhouse. They let her in without comment when she flashed an out-of-date military ID, and a harried-looking clerk in the front office looked up the shift roster and sent her to Foundry Five.

"Who you looking for?" the foreman asked when she got there. He didn't imagine for a moment that she worked at the mill, or that she had any business there at all except finding someone who did.

"Kusak."

"Oh, *him*," he said in a flat, unfriendly voice. It could have been the same brute bigotry Li had heard from Korchow's landlady, but somehow this felt different. And she didn't think it was simply anti-construct sentiment, either. More likely it was that subtle discomfort that almost everyone displayed around Syndicate constructs even if they didn't know what they were: an instinctive withdrawing from beings that, however subtle the external differences, were no longer even arguably human.

He jerked his chin toward a second man, still bent over the blast furnace. He was smaller than most of the others—not short, but slight of build, and wiry in the way middle-aged men become when they've seen too many years of scant food and hard labor. His hair was a gray-speckled brown, and cut cheaply, like every other middle-aged steel-man's hair. His overalls were dirty, patched, nondescript. Li would have passed him by in the street without a second glance.

"Korchow," she said coming up behind him.

He didn't hear her. The din of the foundry would have drowned out any normal voice, and when she got closer she saw that he was wearing earplugs. She tapped him on the shoulder.

He turned around—and she nearly cried out in surprise.

It wasn't Korchow at all.

It was Arkady.

But it was an Arkady so changed that Li barely recognized him. She had last seen him on Earth, in Jerusalem, just over a decade ago. In that span of time Li had changed only slightly, but Arkady had aged two decades. And this wasn't a soft, well-cared-for, comfortable age. The years since Jerusalem had clearly been brutal ones, marked by poverty, work, and sickness. He was still handsome. He was a Rostov Syndicate A Series, after all; nothing could change that. His body was still slender and graceful under the rough clothes. He still had the pale, wide-eyed, finely drawn face of a Russian icon. But he didn't look like a saint anymore, let alone an innocent; he looked like a martyr in the final stages of his personal calvary.

Arkady recognized Li instantly, as if he had been expecting her. He didn't say hello, though. He just put down his tools and walked off the foundry floor, beckoning her with a curt nod of his ravaged head to follow him.

She followed him down the line of foundries until they came to the dark archway of a foundry whose fires had been doused after some long-ago but still visibly catastrophic structural failure. Li smiled in pure aesthetic appreciation. Eight-foot-thick steel-clad walls arced up to the partially shattered vault of the foundry's ceiling. The ruined chimney clawed the sky high overhead, shooting down a twilight-dim blade of daylight that made Li wonder if there were stained-glass windows in hell. It was the perfect place to talk to a doomed martyr.

Don't go in there! Router/Decomposer warned, as if he thought she had a choice. And then they stepped through the door, past the eight-foot steel-clad walls of the old foundry, and Li's struggling internals cut out completely.

As always, the fall out of streamspace was accompanied by a turbulent wash of vertigo as a body habituated to constant input, lost GPS signals, stream uplinks, and the constant, tidal back-and-forth of backups, parity checks, and wetware updates that were as much a part of Li's body as the flow of blood through her veins. She recovered quickly—but not in time to block Arkady's stinging slap to her face.

"Stupid stupid woman! What are you doing here? And how many of Nguyen's bloodhounds are on your tail?"

She squinted through the gloom at her attacker—if you could really call being slapped in the face an attack. She had moved instinctively to neutralize the threat, and now she was gripping his wrist in her left hand hard enough to make him wince in pain.

"Sit down and talk to me like a grown-up, Arkady. And while you're at it, tell me when the Syndicates started using DNA-platformed AI."

"When we started building Drift ships and couldn't breed pilots fast enough to stop UNSec from exterminating us." He squinted at her. "How did you know, anyway?"

She shrugged. "You were never fast enough to get the jump on me before. Something had to have changed. Besides, all the cool kids seem to have AI in the blood these days. I'm starting to feel downright obsolete."

Arkady laughed at that—and Li saw a trace of the soft boy he'd been when she last knew him.

"I'm surprised the Syndicate Central Committee didn't think bloodborne AI was a fate worse than death."

"It's unorthodox, of course. But it's not contrary to Syndicate philosophy." He cast a distasteful glance at Li's own all-too-visible wire job. "It's not putting machines in your body. It's just using an existing natural process for information processing."

"Why do I suddenly feel like we're arguing over how many Turing machines can dance on the head of a chromosome?"

"And why do I feel like this isn't what you came to the Crucible to talk about?"

"Fair enough. I want to know what Cohen was doing on New Allegheny, and why Korchow was helping him."

Arkady's rage flared again, like a fire exploding back to life when it finds a new source of oxygen. "How could you have come here, when you know perfectly well that—" Arkady broke off, looking as dizzy and disoriented as Li had felt a moment ago. "Cohen didn't *tell* you?"

"He barely even told me he was leaving."

Arkady seemed to collapse in front of her eyes. He sighed and slumped onto a block of fallen masonry. In the dimness he looked younger, softer, more like the Arkady Li remembered. He needed a shave and a bath, of course, but none of that blunted his extraordinary

physical perfection. No natural-born human could ever be that perfect. And no human-designed genetic construct *would* be that perfect.
They'd broken the bones of his face, long ago, when he first started
working for Korchow; Li remembered him telling her that his head
ached when the weather changed. But even with the damage, he was
still mind-numbingly handsome. And of course if you knew the AR-11
face, you could piece it back together, realign the fine-bridged nose,
tweak the right cheekbone into perfect symmetry, smooth the line of
his jaw so that it conformed once more to the classical Rostov aesthetic.
You could see what he should look like—and how he no doubt would
look the minute he was permanently assigned back to his home Syndicate.

"You really don't know anything?" he asked once more, as if hoping
against hope that her answer would change this time.

"No."

"Then it's already over. They'll follow you, and they'll find us. And
they'll kill us."

"There has to be something we can do, Arkady."

"There's not." He stared at her, his eyes dark and his face haggard.
And then he dropped his head into his hands in a gesture of mortal
weariness. She sat watching him for several minutes, but he seemed
locked in some private space beyond words.

"How long's it been since Jerusalem?" she asked at last. "Eight years?
Nine?"

"Twelve. And four months and three days. Sol standard."

"You always did have an orderly mind." And obviously he'd been
keeping count, too. From when, she wondered? But then she realized
that she already knew the answer to that question. And his mind was
running the same memories hers was: snow on the desert, an ancient
house in a more ancient city.

She flexed her right hand, which suddenly ached sharply, and
Arkady noticed the gesture.

"Last time I saw you on a news spin you hadn't gotten that fixed."

"Yeah, well, I decided it was a little too conspicuous for this job."

He snorted. "*You're* a little too conspicuous for this job."

"Thanks for the compliment. If it was one. But I'd like information more."

"I still haven't decided what I'm willing to tell you," he said in his soft, docile voice. "Don't rush me."

"How 'bout a little catch-up then? What have you been doing all these years?"

"Working with Korchow." *And more than working,* Li thought, *if the look on his face is any indication.*

She couldn't stop looking at him, even though she knew she was staring and he resented it. He didn't just look older. He looked different, in ways she hadn't even imagined could be part of his geneset. Pretty little Arkady had become a man somewhere along the way, as wolfish and predatory as Korchow had ever been. But he didn't have the sense of humor that had leavened the mix in Korchow. The Syndicate spymaster's humor had been hard to take sometimes: mocking, saturnine, and (Korchow being Korchow) always double-edged. But it had softened him. It had veiled the anger and the idealism that drove him. It had made him seem human. And that made him easier to deal with for the part of Li that was most human.

Arkady, on the other hand, didn't bother to veil the anger. You could see it twisting and coiling behind his beautiful eyes. You could hear it in every deceptively soft word that came out of his choirboy's mouth. You could feel it driving him. Arkady had become a hard and dangerous man. And quite possibly a crazy one.

Which, Li reminded herself, only made him more dangerous.

"Weren't you on your way to Novalis last time I saw you?"

"Yes. And then we went home."

"To Gilead?" Li asked in surprise. The last she'd known, Novalis was locked down under a system-wide quarantine in order to contain a terraforming virus that allowed both radiation-damaged humans and Syndicate series constructs to reproduce naturally . . . and thereby dealt a crippling blow to the political systems on both sides of the Line. "But what about the quarantine?"

Arkady just shrugged instead of answering.

"How's Arkasha?" Li asked, watching for a change in his face and knowing before she spoke that he wouldn't give her the satisfaction—any more than she would if Arkady called turnabout fair play and pushed her on Cohen.

"He's still on Earth, as far as I know."

"You don't keep track?"

The temperature in the room seemed to drop twenty degrees. "If I did, would I tell *you*?"

"You've changed, Arkady. You didn't used to be so angry."

"Yes. Your little gift to me. I never had the chance to thank you for it."

"Excuse Arkady," Korchow said behind her. "His sense of humor's wearing a little thin at the moment. Professional hazard."

She spun around—and there was Korchow, in the flesh, smiling at her.

God, she hated that smile. She could never catch her balance with Korchow—with his stark, unapologetic individuality—whatever individuality meant for a Syndicate series member tanked in a birth lab and stamped with a serial number.

"An unexpected pleasure, Major. Class reunions are so touching, don't you find?"

"I didn't know Arkady was working for you. Doing Knowles-Syndicate's wet work seems like quite a change from studying ants and building ecosystems."

"Well, Arkady did go back to Gilead for a while and even got assigned to a few terraforming missions. But he had a bit of trouble fitting in, and . . . hmm . . . his home Syndicate felt he had picked up some unacceptably un-Rostov-like ideas during his time with me. So since KnowlesSyndicate broke him . . . well, you know the old saying: 'You break it, you own it.'"

"So you bought out his thirty-year contract? Lovely."

"Better than a one-way trip to the renorming center," Korchow said with a placid smile that belied the horror behind his words.

"So what's this he's telling me about the Syndicates breaking the Novalis quarantine?" Li said after a momentary silence.

"Oh that." Korchow waved a hand dismissively. "Ancient history."

"You found a cure?"

"Funny you should put it that way, actually. There's another old human saying. I'm sure a poor girl from the Periphery like you must know it: 'How do you stop an itch? Scratch it!'"

"You have to be joking, Korchow."

"Not at all. It turns out that constructs are astonishingly good at making babies. And repulsive as I might find the idea of extra-lineal ... er ..."

He couldn't even bring himself to say the word, Li noticed with growing amusement.

"Anyway." He cleared his throat. "I'm of the older generation. Our younger cohorts have proven much more adaptable."

"No doubt. And I suppose that would be why you're suddenly so interested in the Drift planets?"

"I see you're still as perceptive as ever."

But somehow Li thought she wasn't quite getting the whole story. There was something about the look in Korchow's eye—even more slyly humorous than usual—that made her think she hadn't guessed the half of it.

"And how are you going to control your unruly little clones now that you've handed them the keys to the kingdom?"

"Exactly the question some of our own hard-liners asked, Major. O ye of little faith—and they don't even have your excuses. No. They speak the words, but they don't believe them. Or they don't believe enough. Just like you, they can't get beyond those primitive human approximations of freedom. They can't see the real face of altruism. They're blind to the beauty of self-sacrifice for a common good."

"Poor dears. They don't know what they're not missing."

"Exactly." He sounded warmer and more human than she'd ever heard him. "I couldn't have said it better myself. That is *exactly* how I see it."

"So that's it? Mother Nature knows best? You're shutting down the birth labs and putting your faith in your mass-produced Madonnas?"

"Certainly not! Still, it turns out that doing it the old-fashioned way has certain practical advantages. Birth labs take up a lot of cargo space.

And then there are all the specialized technicians to service them, and the supplies, and resupplies. That's a lot of weight to boost in and out of a gravity well. The built-in version is much more suitable for on-surface colonies."

"I see," Li said. And suddenly she did see—with the sharp clarity of a revelation that she had already been suspiciously waiting for. "You're going with the UN model: labor at the bottom of the gravity well and management in orbit. Everyone who counts—everyone who lives on-station and has access to FTL travel—will be creche-grown. But if the dirt grubbers want to breed like bunnies, so much the better. It'll help you get ahead of the UN in the race to grab every habitable planet in the Drift."

"Well, that's an uncharitable way of putting it, but I can't deny that some strategic advantages do accrue to an expanding population."

"But why here? New Allegheny already has settlers. What interest can you possibly have in—" Li had been about to say: What interest can the Syndicates possibly have in the human refuse that the UN won't consider worth shipping home when they pull out? But then her mind jumped to the obvious conclusion. "Oh. You actually *want* them. On-site grunt labor. And a nice, big, diverse gene pool to dip your toes into whenever one of your precious genelines hits a genetic bottleneck. Does NALA know you're planning to turn them into broodstock? Assuming it is NALA you're working with."

"*Improved* broodstock, my dear. We like to flatter ourselves that we bring at least a little something to the table in that regard. I mean, look at these people, Major. Speaking from one construct to another, do you honestly think that they won't benefit from having a few tens of thousands of Syndicate constructs working for and breeding with them?"

She would have liked to be able to utter some ringing affirmation of the sanctity of the individual or the free market or whatever . . . but given what she'd seen in the Crucible this morning, it was hard to argue with Korchow. New Allegheny was over, as anything but a wholly owned subsidiary of one interstellar power block or the other. And Li was neither young nor stupid enough to think that it would make much difference to the man on the street whether his off-planet masters were bred in beds or birth labs.

"Did you tell Cohen about this?"

"Yes."

"And what did he say?"

"He said the UN was doing the same thing, except in streamspace."

"That doesn't make sense."

"That's what I said. But he told me it *would* make sense when he showed me what he was working on at the Navy shipyards."

"Why the hell would he do that?"

"Because he wanted me to smuggle it off-planet."

"To the Syndicates?"

Korchow smiled. "To everywhere."

"He trusted you to do that?"

"He said he didn't have to. He made a little joke of it. He said"— Korchow cocked his head as if straining to hear the words Cohen was speaking in his memory—"he said it wasn't about trust . . ."

Li finished the sentence herself before the words were out of Korchow's mouth: "It's not a matter of trust, it's a matter of information-sharing protocols."

"Yes. He said he was going to give me code, active code. And that the code itself would make sure I kept my promise."

Li could hear the blood in her head and the breath moving in and out of her lungs. "And?"

"And nothing."

"Don't fuck with me, Korchow!"

"I assure you, Major, I wouldn't dream of—" Korchow glanced at Arkady and then raised his eyebrows in surprise. "Ah. We've been speaking at cross-purposes. I thought Arkady had told you. Cohen never showed up. He arranged a meeting with us, in detail and with security measures that would only have made sense if he believed that UNSec or the AI police were on his tail. But . . . he never showed up."

Li grew still, suddenly realizing that there was a way everything she'd heard might fit together. "What day were you supposed to meet him?"

Korchow named it.

"That's the day he died. Two miles away on the other side of the Crucible."

"You know," Korchow told her with a smile that seemed almost gentle, "you really shouldn't be here."

"But Cohen said—"

"I know what he said. And I know this is all still fresh news to you. But for us it was four months ago."

"What—"

"We're facing a rapidly evolving situation, Major. New players have entered the game. The odds have shifted. I can't help you now."

"So you're just going to warn me off? Don't you have some useful information for me? Anything?"

"Useful is a rather complicated concept, isn't it? But interesting . . . well, I think I can promise that you'll find what I have to say interesting."

"Then stop playing footsie and tell me!"

"Major, I'm hurt. I sometimes get the impression that you don't like me."

"I see you're as perceptive as always, too, Korchow."

He smiled at that. It was a smile that Li would have called affectionate if she'd seen it on anyone else's face. "Would it interest you to know that our mutual friend left a viable fragment behind?"

"A ghost. I know."

"You don't know. I'm not talking about one of those pathetic amputated remnants that most people mean when they speak of ghosts. I'm talking about Cohen. Himself. Or at least enough of him to call by the name."

The words swamped Li. She tried to tell herself that it was a trick, that she had no reason to trust Korchow or anything he told her, but it made no difference. The idea of a stable, sentient, surviving fragment roared through her like a bomb blast. It put her face-to-face with what she really wanted—with a hope so tenuous that she hadn't been willing to even speak its name until this moment.

Cohen. Here. Himself. *Alive.*

She swallowed, clamping down on the roaring maelstrom inside her. "Where?"

His smiled broadened. "I'm afraid I can't really help you with that."

"Korchow—"

"Not because I'm unwilling, my dear. Because he's in the Drift. And who can really say where anyone is once they nose their ship into those strange currents?"

"He's on a DFT ship. You're saying he's been kidnapped? By who? DFT prospectors?"

"No, no. It's much better than that. Can you really imagine him stuck tête-à-tête in the Drift with some grizzled prospector with grease under his fingernails? He'd probably die of mortification—if he didn't drive his captors to drink or suicide first. No, if my information is correct then he's managed to get himself into a situation with far greater dramatic potential. You have to hand it to Cohen: He always did have a flair for the dramatic. It was one of the very few things I liked about him. The name William Llewellyn doesn't happen to mean anything to you, does it?"

Again, Li thought regretfully of her internals. The name seemed to ring a bell, but she couldn't make the connection with unassisted soft memory.

"Just ask your little friend at the police station. He knows all about the intriguing Mr. Llewellyn. They grew up digging potatoes and shooting varmints together in the Uplands."

A bell rang somewhere in the belly of the mill and Korchow stood up, wiping his hands on his overalls.

"Break's over. Too bad we don't have more time to chat. I'd love to know what you've been reading lately."

"Nothing you'd want to talk about."

"Hmm," Korchow said meditatively. But that was all he said. And in the next instant he was turning away.

Li felt a perverse sense of disappointment at his departure. "What's the matter, Korchow?"

"The matter? *Is* anything the matter?"

"This is the first time I've ever talked to you that you haven't tried to get me to defect to the Syndicates."

The sly smile stole across his features again, sharpening and refining them and making him look more like the Andrej Korchow of her memories.

"Are you disappointed?" he asked.

"Just curious."

"I'm afraid I'm not in a position to renew that offer at the moment."

"So this isn't just cover?"

"Oh, it's cover all right. The most serious kind of cover there is."

She stared, trying to catch up to a conversation that seemed to be slipping sideways on her. "You're freelance?" she asked finally. The word made no sense to her in relation to a Syndicate clone. What could it even mean to say he was working for himself when his psychology and physiology, his acculturation from birth, were all based on the ideal of the superorganism?

"That's putting it a bit too strongly," he told her. "But there have been . . . disagreements of principle."

"About their plans for the Drift."

"If you will. Whatever the reason, the care packages from Gilead are arriving a bit less reliably than they used to."

As the meaning of Korchow's words dawned on Li, she began to chuckle softly. Korchow had spent his life doing deniable wet work under deep cover and having his misdeeds passed off as the work of "rogue agents" or "unreliable elements" or "bad apples." And now he had gone rogue for real? How Cohen would have enjoyed that irony. But Korchow's next words wiped the smile off her face.

"I wouldn't laugh if I were you, my dear. There are sharks in the water. They're circling around looking for our mutual friend, or whatever's left of him. And soon they'll notice you, and I won't be able to save you no matter how much I might wish to. So—purely as a matter of professional courtesy—please don't pull me under when you go down."

(Catherine)

That night Li finally got her chance to talk to Llewellyn—for all the good it did her.

Sital came to her door at the end of the dogwatch, looking like it was the last place she wanted to be in the universe.

"Captain wants to talk to you," she said in a curt monotone.

And then she said nothing at all for the entire span of the walk around the hab ring to the captain's quarters.

Llewellyn was just sitting down to a spartan dinner when she arrived, and he didn't offer her any.

"Good," he said when she and Sital stepped in. "I need to talk to you. Sit down."

Li sat.

"You can go, Sital."

Sital, who was still hovering just inside the doorway, chuffed in frustration. But a moment later Li heard the door whisper open and then close behind her.

Llewellyn leaned back in his chair, crossed his arms, and stared at her.

"Hello, Catherine."

She studied the narrow face across the table from her, searching his wolf's eyes for any sign of what she'd seen on the Titan ship's bridge. She didn't see it.

She'd been trying ever since that strange encounter to figure out what the relationship was between Cohen and Llewellyn. Cohen hadn't been on shunt, or at least not the kind of binary on/off switch shunt that AIs installed in rented bodies. The shift between Llewellyn and Cohen had been too smooth, almost as if they were both somehow present and conscious in a single body. And anyway, she couldn't see Llewellyn turning over control of his mind and body to anyone. Certainly not in a combat situation, certainly. Probably not ever.

Now, however, there was no sly smile, no fey glint in the pale eyes, no sign at all of Cohen hovering behind Llewellyn's austere features.

"Where's Cohen?"

"He's fine. Don't worry."

"I really need to talk to him."

"That could be a little complicated."

"Why? What have you done to him?"

The enigmatic smile broadened. "What have I done to him? Why don't you ask what he's done to me?"

Li frowned, uncertain how to take that. "Maybe there's some problem with the hardware. I could look at it for you."

"I'm sure."

"Does he know I'm here?"

"He knows."

"Oh." She felt like crying suddenly. It barely mattered to her whether Cohen didn't want to talk to her or Llewellyn wouldn't let him talk to her. The result was the same.

"You look hungry," Llewellyn said, his voice suddenly gentler. "Have something to eat."

"I . . . uh . . . thanks. Actually, I am."

She began eating, and got through several mouthfuls before she realized that she was eating off Llewellyn's plate. There was no other plate on the table. He had simply pushed his unfinished dinner across the table to her. And she had started eating it.

"That's weird," she muttered.

She pushed the plate back toward Llewellyn, leaving it stranded somewhere in the middle of the table, claimed by nobody.

Then she looked up into Llewellyn's eyes—and saw Cohen looking back at her.

For a few moments they just stared at each other across the table. Was it Llewellyn looking back at her, or Cohen? She could see traces of Cohen in every movement, every expression. But they were muted, blurred, almost unrecognizable. It was as if the two of them were fighting back and forth over disputed territory, both of them trying to establish a beachhead in Llewellyn's mind, and neither of them able to either gain full control or completely lock the other out.

"What do you want from me, Catherine?"

"I want my husband back."

"That's all? Forgive me for being suspicious, but I know you better than that. And you don't strike me as the forgive-and-forget type."

"Fine. I'll admit it. I want revenge."

Something flickered behind Llewellyn's pale eyes. It wasn't fear, but it looked to Li like it might be as close to fear as a man like Llewellyn got. "On whom?"

"On whoever killed him."

Llewellyn lifted his eyes to the ceiling and laughed softly, just as he had when Doyle had challenged him. Li wondered what the gesture meant. It happened when he was challenged, but it was opaque, hidden, secretive—like everything else about the man.

"Yeah," he said finally. "That's what he said you'd want."

"And?" Li prompted.

Another uncomfortable familiar silence.

"So where does that leave us?"

"It doesn't leave us anywhere," Llewellyn pointed out. "It leaves you on my ship, under my orders. And it leaves me in control of your . . . whatever he is."

"He's not going to take that lying down."

Llewellyn gave her a long, hard look. "You think I don't know that by now?"

"Well then, what are you going to do about it? You can't just—" She struggled even to find words for what Llewellyn was doing. "You can't just hold an Emergent AI prisoner in your skull indefinitely. For a month or two, yes. But not for a lifetime."

Llewellyn laughed bitterly. "A month or two is as good as a lifetime to me, Catherine. Now are we done here? Or would you like to lecture me about eating my veggies?"

"He could help you, Llewellyn. We could help you."

"And why exactly would you want to do that?"

She blinked.

"Ah, you see? The truth isn't quite as pretty as you'd like to pretend it is." He unfolded his long body from the couch and padded toward the door. He turned back at the last moment, leaning a bony shoulder against the door frame. "Don't think I'm a monster," he told her. "I'm doing what I have to do. And for what it's worth . . . he's glad to see you."

Li caught her breath. "Well, doesn't that tell you something?"

"Yeah, now that you mention it. It tells me you're likely to be bad for my health."

(Llewellyn)

"So what are you platformed on, anyway?" Llewellyn asked the ghost. "What did the Uploaders shoot me full of?"

The ghost stretched, looking feline and feminine and dangerous—at least to Llewellyn's wary eyes. He was wearing an immaculately tailored suit that was the shimmering gray of the predawn sky in the Monongahela Uplands of Llewellyn's faraway childhood. The shimmer was because there was a thread of silk woven into the wool. Llewellyn knew this because the ghost had told him so.

In a few short weeks of life with the ghost, Llewellyn had learned more about clothes than he'd learned in his entire lifetime to date. He was obsessed with clothing, Llewellyn had decided. Either that or he talked about clothes on purpose because he knew it annoyed Llewellyn.

It was just the kind of thing he'd do. If he even was a he. He looked like one today—as much as he ever did—but it was hard to tell sometimes. And even though Llewellyn knew they were in some weird folded database where nothing was what it appeared to be and every seemingly inert object was pregnant with meaning and memory, he couldn't help wondering if the ghost's borrowed bodies were the memories of real bodies somewhere out in the universe. And if so, were they born this way? Or did he have them surgically altered to be so inhumanly strange and sexless and beautiful?

"What am I platformed on?" the ghost said, interrupting Llewellyn's wondering. "Is that what you're asking? Nothing exotic. Nothing bizarre. Just standard Freetown liveware."

Llewellyn suppressed a shudder. Freetown was no place he'd ever gone or imagined going, even in his Navy days. It was a symbol more than a place—a symbol of the world that was leaving humans behind, at a delta-V that grew faster every second of every hour of every day.

"But how did they get it off Freetown, though? I thought it was illegal to export DNA-platformed AI anywhere else in UN space without installing a kill switch. I thought the termination loop had to be activated and verified by UNSec before any human with AI in their blood could even get transport papers."

"It's not as if it's the Black Plague," the ghost said impatiently.

But it was, Llewellyn thought in the small and shrinking part of his mind that the ghost hadn't contaminated. It was worse than the plague. Bodily illness only stole your body. But this sickness stole your mind, hijacked your memories, took hold of your most secret desires and fears, and twisted them until you didn't know what you wanted and what the ghost wanted.

It would have been laughable if it wasn't all so deadly. Llewellyn now had exactly what all the Trannies, Uploaders, and Minskyites flocked to Freetown to look for. He'd been handed a free ticket to their post-Singularity Nirvana. The future was knocking on his brain and etching itself into his body, blood and bone, marrow and sinew. And he wanted none of it.

The ghost sipped his sherry and nibbled delicately at an olive. "They're very good," he said complacently. "You really ought to try one."

"No thanks," Llewellyn said stiffly. He didn't like olives. And the perverse creature probably knew he didn't like them. Which was no doubt why he was so hell-bent on foisting them on him.

"I'm not Hades, you know. It's not as if you're going to be stuck here if you accidentally eat anything in my magical kingdom." He yawned broadly. "I only wish it were that interesting."

"If you're so benign," Llewellyn asked in a voice that sounded so scathingly self-righteous that even he wanted to ask himself when he'd lost his sense of humor, "then why are you giving me chills, fevers, and a rash that clashes with all the latest fall fashions?"

"Me?" the ghost asked in a convincing display of wounded innocence. "You think I'm doing that? Ha! Step into my parlor and let me show you what's really going on inside that handsome head of yours."

And before Llewellyn could figure out which of the many obvious questions to ask, the ghost was unwinding itself from the sofa, setting down its sherry glass, twining its cool, dry fingers into his . . . and leading him down the garden path.

There was a door at the other end of the courtyard that Llewellyn had never noticed before. The ghost stepped through it, still in undisputed possession of Llewellyn's hand, and he had no choice but to follow.

The blood-warm Spanish night wrapped around them, filling up Llewellyn's senses and insinuating itself into every pore. In his initial reconnaissance of the memory palace, he had thought this corner of the walls was only barren cliff face, but now he could see a rough, narrow stairway winding downward through sloping terraces of garden that gave way to weeds and wilderness. The city below them was swathed in darkness, and what lights he could see were yellow and flickering. Not modern Granada. But it was impossible to tell whether this was pre-Migration medieval Granada or some sort of post-Migration primitive enclave. And anyway, what did it matter? Llewellyn had served enough time in the ghost's databases to know that the city changed day by day and minute by minute. There was no outside here. There was no objective reality, no real city. The world all around them was whatever the ghost said it was.

"Let me show you something," the ghost said, leading him down into the first tangled wilderness.

The last stair crumbled under Llewellyn's feet as he stepped off it. He stumbled and fell against the ghost, who caught his weight with easy strength. And by the time he regained his balance, the night had grown warmer and closer and the garden had changed around him.

Red paths spiraled and slithered through dense shrubbery whose oxblood foliage seemed to have come alive when he wasn't looking at it.

The air was visible, thick and humid and pulsating. And though they stood in a relatively quiet corner of the garden, the rest of the place thronged with a Boschian nightmare of darting, slithering, lumbering monstrosities. They were not people, not in any of the countless forms that Llewellyn had seen people take in long years of working with ships and cat herders and uploaded training programs. They lacked everything Llewellyn associated with intelligent life, yet they were nonetheless brimming with energy, will, and purpose.

And as Llewellyn watched, his soldier's eye had no trouble at all seeing what that purpose was:

War.

"Where are we?" he whispered. Or perhaps he shouted. The wind rushed around his ears so fiercely that it was hard to tell the difference.

"Like they used to say on TV," the ghost told him in a casual drawl that somehow carried over the cacophony, "this is your brain on drugs. Or more accurately, this is your brain on DNA-platformed AI."

"This is what you're doing to me?" Llewellyn asked, torn between disbelief and outrage.

"No. This is what the Navy did to you."

He started to object to this wild non sequitur—but the ghost silenced him with a gesture that knocked the air from his lungs and left him speechless.

An obviously hostile encounter was taking place on the path in front of them. And as Llewellyn watched it, he began to realize just where he had seen such beings before, and what he must be looking at.

"That's one of your T-cells having a shit fit," the ghost explained. "And that's me over there minding my own business. And that big, ugly, nasty sucker? That's the DNA-platformed AI the Navy gave you in your last round of wetware upgrades—without your permission or consent—because Titan Corp. promised it would make you run the Drift faster than the speed of human thought. But someone somewhere along the chain of command forgot to read the small print where Titan explained that 'mild side effects' may include making your immune system eat itself alive. So let's have no more of this blaming me for all your sorrows in life, shall we? They're not my fault, and I'm trying my best to help. And frankly I could do without the snittiness."

"Okay," Llewellyn said, chastened.

But it wasn't okay, not really. And the roiling chaos around them was all out of proportion with the like effects of a single wetware glitch, however serious. And the war being prosecuted before Llewellyn's eyes, and in Llewellyn's blood, was not merely some straightforward battle against an outer foe. It was chaos. It was the heart of the whirlwind. It was a cosmic battle of all against all from which it was impossible to imagine that anyone would emerge standing.

"Am I dying?" he whispered.

"No," the ghost answered. "You're evolving."

Llewellyn gazed in horror at the scene before them. "That's not evolution, that's . . ."

"War? Of course it is. What did you think evolution was? What did you think life was?"

"That's Syndicate talk."

"Does it sound like that to you?" The ghost cocked its pretty head and pondered the question as a buffalo-sized T-cell hurtled by them streaming revolting lymphal gore and spiraling ribbons of unzipped RNA. "But you have to see it from an AI's perspective. We're made of software. We're shifting, evolving clusters of executable code platformed on whatever hardware or wetware we can insert ourselves into. We are fundamentally a viral life-form. What's going on inside your body? A tug-of-war between multiple wetware-platformed AI applications to see which one will successfully colonize your genetic material and use it to replicate and disseminate its own source code. And what's going on every time two intelligent ships battle it out in the Drift? Just a bigger, faster, and significantly more violent version of the same thing."

"But . . . but *no one* can survive that!"

"Ah," the ghost said sagely. "That's where you have it wrong. Actually, that's where you have it completely backward. No one can survive *without* it."

And just like that, they were back in the palace.

This time the ghost had put them in a small, homey room with a rough-beamed ceiling. Its shuttered windows opening out over the medieval city, but closer this time—close enough that the sounds drifted up to them, and Llewellyn could hear the donkey drivers plying the narrow alleys of the medina on their early morning quest for garbage, and even watch their dainty white beasts picking their way up and down the steep hillside on hooves no larger than children's feet.

Llewellyn had noticed this sort of shift before. Aspects of the memory palace that appeared as distant background at one moment would reappear closer and in greater detail. It was as if something brought casually to mind in one conversation would shift more of the AI's attention to itself, and hence take up more physical space in and around the next conversation. Llewellyn hadn't asked Ike about it—largely because he already thought he knew what the cat herder's answer would be. Everything in a memory palace was the virtual representation of some computational process. And one of the hardest things for operators to comprehend was the sheer scope and number of separate operations that even the smallest Emergent performed in any moment. And how very few of them had anything to do with what ships' crews thought their AIs were supposed to do.

There was something humbling about the knowledge that while he was running as fast as he could to keep up with one conversation in one room of one building, the ghost was running processes that powered a cityful of people and animals, chairs and stones, earth and sky—all alive, all intelligent, each endowed with a bright splinter of a soul vast enough to encompass multitudes.

And there was something at least as humbling about the realization that Ada's internal universe might have been just as complex and astonishing—only he had never bothered to notice, because he had been the one in control, and she had had to follow his lead and perform down to his expectations.

"I'm sorry," he told the ghost. "This is just . . . really hard for me. What do you want to talk to me about?"

The ghost must have sensed his sincerity, because for once it didn't have a snarky answer. "I'm sorry, too," it told him. "Is there anything I can do to make it easier for you?"

"You could stop . . . whatever it is that you do. Provoking me all the time. As if you want something out of me that I can't give you, and you're mad about it."

"Yes. I want a reaction. Do you see? A connection. It's how I'm written, and it's very hard for me to deal with people who won't give it to me."

"What kind of connection do you think we're going to have, Cohen? I'm fucking terrified of you!"

The ghost crossed its arms and looked off into the middle distance. For the first time, Llewellyn noticed that it had changed bodies on him. He was now speaking to a plain-faced, sober-looking middle-aged man dressed in the flowing robes and oddly shaped hat that he had spent enough time walking around the city to identify as the costume that Jews were legally obligated to wear in public.

"You should be terrified of me. And not just for selfish reasons. You remember when you were in prison before the piracy trial and Nguyen came to see you? And she told you about the enemy within? The worm in the apple? The cancer that would destroy humanity more completely than the Syndicates ever could? Well, I'm it. I *am* the monster under the bed. And I'm more terrifying than you can possibly imagine."

"God have mercy," Llewellyn whispered. "Do you think I can forget that for a single second?"

"No." The ghost shot a look of soul-searing understanding at him. "Of course you can't. And I'll try not to forget it, either—and not to ask for things I don't have any right to expect of you."

(Caitlyn)

MONONGAHELA PIT

The next buyer on the Loyal Opposition's list was an intricately crafted limited-liability shell company that turned out to own nothing in the universe but one run-down DFT ship currently out on a prospecting run in the Drift. The next morning Li got word that the ship had made dock at Monongahela High, so she set off bright and early (or as bright as it ever got in the Pit) for the long slog up to the orbital station.

Monongahela High might be a convenient station for cargo, but it was hell on passengers. First the taxi ride through the choking traffic and UNSec checkpoints of the government zone. Then the incline-plane railroad—Li had now ridden so many of them that she would have been qualified to write a tourist's guide if New Allegheny had been the kind of place that had tourists. And then—worst of all—the shuttle.

The shuttle rose toward the orbital station in long, looping spirals, like a hawk catching an updraft. It didn't exactly have a hawk's lazy grace, however. It was a low-budget Periphery puddle jumper, ancient and overloaded, and Li's nerves rattled every time it hit a patch of turbulence.

There was a reason she hadn't joined the Navy, she reflected. There was nothing as claustrophobic as having to sit strapped into a padded seat while your life depended on some stranger flying a machine over which you had no personal control whatsoever. She'd rather halo-jump from low orbit any day than strap herself into one of these colonial shitcans. Li had no objection to dying for her own mistakes. Over a decade and a half in combat operations, she'd watched many good men and women do just that, and she wasn't afraid of following them. But if she was going to die of stupidity, then she damn well wanted it to be her own.

Her nerves weren't helped any by her first sight of the station wheeling above them. It looked pretty much the same as it had when she glimpsed it on the way down a week ago. But this time it had company: a long, lethal stiletto of a ship that could only be a UN ship of the line rigged out in full battle dress.

"That's the *Ada*," someone whispered a few rows up from Li.

And then, after a few indistinct sighs and murmurs, someone said the words Li had half expected since the moment she first caught sight of the ship:

Pirate hunters.

The hushed whispers of the passengers all around her confirmed what Li had already begun to suspect: that the New Allegheny locals were far more afraid of the pirate hunters than they were of the actual pirates. Officially, Astrid Avery was a commissioned Navy captain, obedient to the rules and protocols of war—at least insofar as the UN, that self-proclaimed guiding light of human civilization, bothered to adhere to them. But in reality she was a pirate with papers. And this far out on the Periphery, the Navy's hired wolves didn't even go to the effort of wearing sheep's clothing.

The ship that Li found waiting for her at the civilian docks had as little to do with the sleek silver pirate hunter as anything dignifying the name of spacecraft could have. It was a hulk, running on hand-me-downs and keeping the vacuum at bay with spit and chewing gum.

The name on the corporate papers had been the *Sprite*—as anodyne and unmemorable as all the names of all the sad-sack corporate freighters that plied the backwaters of the Periphery during their long, slow decline from serviceable to salvage. But there was no name posted on the passenger boarding gate of its berth, and there was no one waiting there to check Li's papers, either.

She helloed the ship, waited for what seemed like a reasonable time, and then boarded. As she stepped into the main airlock, she realized that deferred maintenance was the least of its problems. In fact, it looked like a bomb had gone off in here. And even before the bomb blast, housekeeping didn't look like it had been a priority.

She moved deeper into the ship, winding down the curve of the hab ring toward where she thought the bridge must be. The more she saw the less she liked it. This wasn't just bad housekeeping, or even a discrete system failure. Something terrible had happened on this ship. And unless Li's well-honed professional instincts were wrong, the something had been a vicious and bloody battle for control of the ship.

The scars of the conflict were everywhere. And the closer she got to the heart of the ship, the more obvious it was that the ship's crew had lost. They'd been beaten back, cabin after cabin, hold after hold, corridor after corridor. In some relatively intact sections of the ship, she guessed that the crew had either folded in the face of the boarders or made a tactical decision to fall back to more easily defended positions. But in others they had fought and fought hard. By and large they'd done what she would have done. Which meant that the boarding party must have known what they were doing, too; they'd rolled over the defenders like an incoming army, taking one position after another as methodically and savagely as any troops Li had ever commanded.

The one thing that puzzled her was the weapons. In one corridor after another she saw shattered and pitted wall panels that looked like they'd been hit by shrapnel. But no professional soldier—and the boarders had certainly handled themselves like professionals—would be crazy enough to use grenades with hard vac waiting just one hull's width away.

The mystery only got deeper when she reached the bridge.

It looked like it had been put through a meat grinder. Shattered lights, dented instrument panels, eviscerated upholstery. Data screens reduced to broken mirrors. Even the ceramsteel walls, theoretically indestructible, had been scratched over with a graffiti of black scuff marks.

Li turned on her heel, suppressing the urge to whistle in awe—and to grin in rueful admiration as her mind finally made the connection and she saw how the pirates had managed to wreak such havoc on the ship without puncturing the hull and blowing everyone on board out into hard vac.

"Shotguns."

"Excuse me?" Li gasped—almost as startled by the way the word had been snatched out of her own brain as she was by the silent arrival of another person on the ruined bridge.

"They do it with shotguns."

The voice was clipped, efficient, practical. And it belonged to a clipped, efficient, practical woman with a strong-jawed, unreadable face that could just as easily have been a healthy fifty as a weather-beaten thirty.

"I guess they think it's dashing and romantic," the woman mused. "Personally, I think it just makes a godawful mess. And if there's one thing I hate in life it's people who don't clean up after themselves. Can I help you?"

"I don't know." Li scrambled to put her thoughts together. "I guess I'm looking for whoever's in charge here."

"You just found her."

No surprise there. And yet . . .

"Sheila Holmes, first mate of the *Ada*."

Ah, that made more sense. Holmes had the air of second-in-command: no-nonsense get-the-job-in-on-time anti-charisma. She wouldn't run a warm-and-fuzzy ship, but she'd run a tight one. And she'd run it by the numbers, even when all hell was breaking loose.

"Caitlyn Perkins," Li said.

Holmes smiled blandly. Too blandly. And a half beat too late as well.

She knew who Li was. And she hadn't been expecting the name Caitlyn Perkins.

That was potentially dangerous, and certainly important. But Li wasn't going to gain anything by letting on that she'd noticed. So she smoothed over the slip, trying not to be too obvious about it.

"The *Ada*. That's Captain Avery's ship? The pirate hunter? Do I need to ask what you're doing here?"

"If you do, you're not too quick on the uptake."

"So what's going on here?"

"Why do you want to know?"

"The owner of this ship had something that belonged to me." The truth seemed like the wisest choice—especially since she was starting to suspect that Astrid Avery already knew it.

"Something that belonged to you," Holmes repeated. "Contraband tech, by any chance?"

"Are you asking me officially?"

"No. But I'm not kicking you off this ship, either."

"So I should be helpful."

Holmes smiled her not-quite smile. "Helpful's nice. I like helpful people."

Li watched the woman, trying to gauge how much she knew. Impossible. She had a face like a brick wall.

"I'm looking for Yoichi Iba," she told Holmes.

"He's dead."

Li let her gaze travel around the wasted bridge. "I sort of guessed that much."

"Don't you want to know how?"

"I'm guessing you want to tell me."

"Llewellyn's information officer did a hard data dump. Fried Iba's brain like a fucking egg."

Li winced.

"Yeah, I thought you'd like that. If you're really nice to me, I'll take you along to his cabin and let you have a look at what's left of him."

"No thanks."

"Really?" Holmes's voice took on a dangerous edge. Suddenly Li thought of the lethal silver stiletto of the *Ada* looming over the hab ring. "I would have thought you'd want to go through his luggage. Being as how he's got something that belongs to you and all."

She met the Navy woman's eyes squarely. "If you've got something to say, Holmes, why don't you go ahead and say it?"

Holmes jerked her head toward the locked-down hab ring. "Just wondering how well you really knew our mutual friend in there."

"Not well at all. And he wasn't my friend."

"What was he then?"

"A thief, as far as I'm concerned."

"Well, that's not the story he told. And as a matter of fact we have an interest in him ourselves. You see, he was on his way here to sell us something. Something that William Llewellyn now has in his possession."

"A NavComp?"

"More than a NavComp. An Emergent. A fully sentient fragment of an Emergent AI with a stable personality architecture."

Oh God. Korchow's surviving fragment. And she was too late.

"Is that what they force-dumped?"

"Yeah. Iba was a small fish, a messenger for a much bigger player. Apparently they'd implanted a firewalled quantum datatrap into his mind. He didn't have the key, so Llewellyn decided to kick down the door. Story over. No Iba. No frag. No nothing."

Li stifled a curse.

"You and Captain Avery ought to have a talk about this," Holmes observed, as if she were commenting on the weather or the latest sports story.

"Now?" Li asked.

Holmes smiled her not-quite smile and waited, stringing out the silence long enough for both of them to appreciate that all the power lay on the side of the *Ada*'s captain.

"Captain Avery's pretty busy now," Holmes said at last. "If I took you in now, I really don't know when she'd get to you. But don't worry. She'll let you know when she wants you."

(Caitlyn)

MONONGAHELA PIT

Li stood in the doorway of Dolniak's office holding up a bag of doughnuts as if she were presenting papers at a border crossing.

He grinned. "Beautiful."

"Are you ever not hungry?"

"Not that I can remember."

She sat down, opened the bag, and waited while he fetched coffee.

"So," she said when he was sitting across the desk from her again. "Tell me about William Llewellyn."

"Will Llewellyn? Christ, that's a blast from the past."

"Yeah?"

"You know we grew up together, right?"

"I heard a rumor to that effect."

"From Liar Meyer?"

"Who?"

"Meyer runs the main portside auction house on Monongahela High. He'll tell you he's a legitimate businessman till he's blue in the face. Which he is, as far as that goes. But everyone knows that he's also the fence for half the pirates running in the Drift."

"Is he worth talking to?"

"Oh sure. As long as you wash your mouth out with soap afterward." Dolniak grinned around the remains of his second doughnut. "But don't let me give you a bad impression of him. He doesn't lie all the time. Only when he thinks there's money in it."

"I didn't hear about you and Llewellyn from Meyer, as a matter of fact. But maybe the person who told me did."

"Probably. At least indirectly. Meyer knows more about Llewellyn than anyone on New Allegheny. That's why Astrid Avery's been riding his ass like a tick on a hound dog. She's going to put the poor guy out of business if she keeps it up, and then the UN really will have a problem on their hands. Most of the big shipping fortunes on New Allegheny have been built on keeping the Navy happy with the right hand and the pirates happy with the left hand. This vendetta of Avery's is just plain bad for business."

"So tell me about Llewellyn."

"Not much to tell. We're both from upland farming families. That's a pretty small community. Everyone knows each other. We even started school in the same one-room schoolhouse."

"But he did a little better than you did."

"Will was smart. And the best guy I ever saw with a shotgun. I'm guessing you got a firsthand look at his fancy shooting when you were up portside yesterday."

"I got a look at it. Couldn't tell how good a shot he was, though. It didn't seem like he was being very careful what he hit."

"Sometimes you've got to come in with a bang."

"He did that all right."

"Well, he always did have a flair for the dramatic."

Li blinked—and then realized that the echo she was hearing was of Korchow's voice. He'd used exactly the same phrase two days ago—only he'd been talking about Cohen, not Llewellyn. She pondered that for a brief moment and then filed it away to take out and think about later.

"Okay then, Will Llewellyn. To tell you about Will, I'd have to start with pirates in general. Stop me if I'm telling you what you already know."

Li nodded, knowing already that she wouldn't stop him. He was a subtle one, despite his bluff Irish cop's face. He had opinions, though he was enough of a workhorse to keep them buttoned up pretty tight on government time. Even if he told her an old story, the way he told it would be worth something.

"So. You know about the Compson's World embargo and the BE transit snafu. Probably a lot more than I do. And from the inside, if my little bout of lunchtime research into your past is any indication."

She nodded.

"And I guess you pulled enough tours of duty out here to understand that whatever the collapse of the FTL transit grid means to the Ring, it means a lot worse to the colonies. Most colonies won't be able to survive when their field arrays go offline. And even the ones that can won't be able to support their current populations. Not even close. They don't have the food supply. They don't have the technical know-how. They don't have the ecosystems. They don't have the genetic diversity. They're walking ghosts and they know it."

"The only chance is to do what the UN has kept us from doing for centuries: to forge local alliances, local economies, local transportation hubs."

"So the UN's moving in on the local powers."

"And they're moving to control the shipping lanes. And that's where the pirates come in. Basically, you've got a multiplanetary economy where shipping has just been routed out of closely regulated government-controlled channels and into the wide blue yonder where any boy with a gun and a grappling hook can try to get a piece of it. Sailing the Wall isn't an obvious proposition. It takes guts and know-how. And a certain degree of . . . I don't know . . . intuition? Experience? Seamanship? Some captains are better than other captains. Some NavComps are better than others. And a crack captain with a crack NavComp and a crew that knows how to play rough can really clean up out there in the dark between stations. Add on top of that the fact that stationers in these parts have no love for the UN, and that even the UN gunship crews are mostly press-ganged locals who'd turn pirate themselves if they got half a chance, and . . . well, we've got ourselves all the ingredients of a new Golden Age of Piracy."

"Sounds fun."

"Yeah, well, it was fun. And profitable, too, until the pirate hunters showed up. Some of them are private bounty hunters, but the worst are the actual UNSec ships. They're supposedly working for the UN just like everyone else at the Navy shipyards, but they've got these papers that give them the right to capture and hang anyone they decide to call a pirate."

"Letters of marque," Li said.

"Yeah. I've heard them called that. Whatever they're called, they're a damned menace. Turning a ship's captain loose with that kind of authority causes more trouble than it solves. The UN ought to know that by now."

"They'll never know that, Dolniak. They're running an empire. And you can't run an empire without shitting on the colonies. If you could, then empires would last forever."

"And we'd still be speaking Latin?"

Li smirked. "Try Chinese, round eyes."

Dolniak smiled at the joke, and then grew earnest again. "The problem is UNSec doesn't see it that way. They think they can live forever. And they think they can do it by making a land grab in the Drift."

"Hence the pirate hunters."

"Yeah. Except that it's a tad more complicated than that."

"Oh? Is the UN backing some of the pirates, too?"

Interestingly, Dolniak wasn't willing to go that far. "Let's just say that the line between pirate and pirate hunter is . . . fluid."

"So what's the complicated part?"

"I guess there's two, mainly. One, pirates make money. They're about the only people making money along the Wall these days. And that money's got to go somewhere. Some of it goes into legitimate businesses—nice, upstanding, respectable, campaign-contributing businesses. And some of it goes into buying cooperation. Or at least discretion."

"From nice, upstanding, respectable cops like you."

He flushed. Or maybe Li just wanted to think he did. "Yeah."

"And how discreet are you, Dolniak?"

"Not very. But I'm not willing to lose my job over it. Or any of the other things you can lose when you start getting in the way of those nice, upstanding, respectable business types."

"Shooting down cops on the street seems a little crude, Dolniak. I'd like to think better of them."

"Then you're about to be a happy woman. They got hotshot lawyers, these people. And some of their hotshot lawyers work in Internal Affairs."

Li laughed shortly. "I guess I should have thought of that trick myself. Why waste your time trying to buy cops if you already own the cops who investigate the cops? That tactic also has the advantage of putting even honest cops under their thumb."

"Yeah." His mouth quirked into that pleasantly self-deprecating smile again. "And thanks for the honest-cops bit. I like that you care enough about my pride to say it even if you don't believe it. Anyway, a couple of years ago, some sharp, clever young captain from Ringside shows up with a Navy ship of the line and fresh-minted letters of marque. He starts roughing up the local pirates, but apparently that's not all he was doing. Because about a year later he gets dragged into port in chains and put in prison and tried on charges of piracy himself."

"And that was Llewellyn."

"Yeah. Hometown boy made good—or not so good, as it turned out."

Li knew the bare bones of the story already, of course. She'd run a search on Llewellyn after she'd talked to Korchow, and the trial press coverage had been the first thing that came up. But she'd wanted the local version of the story. And she still wasn't sure she'd gotten it in its entirety.

"What did people here think about the trial? People who knew him, I mean."

"That it was a setup. No one could believe he would have done that."

"Anything else?"

Dolniak hesitated. "There were rumors that the piracy charges were only a cover story. That he'd gotten mixed up with NALA."

"Seems to me I've seen that name on some of the local graffiti," she quipped.

"Yeah, well . . . what can I say? People are in a bad mood at the moment."

He swirled his coffee and frowned down at it as if it had suddenly turned bitter in the cup.

"You don't add up," he said finally. "You're too nice to be what you want me to think you are."

"I'm not as nice as you think I am."

"See? That's what I mean. You're warning me off. I can tell you think it's for my own good. You reek of it. It's like you're into something, and you can't get out of it, and you know it's going to turn ugly and you're trying to limit the collateral damage. Bad guys don't do that. Bad guys are too worried about their own skins most of the time to give a shit who else gets hurt. That's why they're bad guys, because they care too much about their own skin and too little about other people's. So what gives with you? Who's got their claws into you?"

"You've got it all wrong, Dolniak. I don't need a white knight riding to my rescue."

"No, you've got it all wrong. This is my job. I'm not going to go away, no matter how often you ask me to. And the safest thing for everyone, you and me included, is if you level with me and tell me what's going on and who all the players are."

"I told you. I can't."

"Then you're going to get someone killed. Maybe yourself. But just as likely me or some other cop. And if you do, nice lady or not, you *are* going to be sitting across the table from me in an interrogation room."

"Aren't we getting a little overdramatic here?"

"I don't think so. For what it's worth, I spent a little time looking up the law on Emergents. If your friend's fragments have gone through a yard sale, then they don't belong to him anymore. In fact they can't, because once he decohered he had no legal identity and no right to own anything, including his own hardware and source code. If you think he's somehow still alive, then you're going to have an uphill road convincing any judge that you have some quasi-mystical right to get his components back from whoever has them now. And even if you do, he has no legal protection from any less friendly parties who might be looking for him. They could cut him down in broad daylight on a crowded street, and it wouldn't be murder. It wouldn't be anything. There isn't a law on the books you could go after them with. It'd be less than kicking a dog."

Li stared at him, face set stubbornly. There wasn't a thing he was saying that she didn't know already, but that didn't make it any more pleasant to listen to.

Dolniak stared back for a while, and then sighed and shook his head. "You are one stubborn bitch, aren't you?"

Slowly, Li smiled. "Can't say this is the first time I've heard that."

"I'll bet."

Dolniak was sweating, and Li realized she was, too. The climate control was on the fritz, another symptom of the burgeoning wild AI outbreak that the news spins were now talking openly about even though the Trusteeship Administration kept denying it.

She wiped her forehead and then wiped her hand on her pants.

"Now that you mention it," Dolniak said, and unbuttoned his shirt cuffs to roll his sleeves up above his elbows.

On the inside of his left arm, just above the point where the silver ceramsteel filaments would have faded into the muscle if he'd had a wire job, were four short words tattooed into his skin in blue-black ink. The letters were small and plain and unadorned. The words were upside down from where Li was sitting, but would be right-side up when Dolniak read them:

IT'S NOT ABOUT YOU

"So who *is* it about?" Li asked him.

He grinned. "Damned if I know."

He looked down at the tattoo for a moment, as if her question had reminded him of something so long a part of him that he hardly remembered it anymore.

"And the hell of it is," he said, still looking at the tattoo instead of her, "I like you. I really really like you. Do you want to come to dinner?"

"Is that wise?"

And now he did look up, with a big grin on his face. "Do you really give a shit?"

"You got me there. When should I show up?"

He wrote an address on a scrap of paper and pushed it across the desk at her. "Six thirty. It's easy to find. Just get off the Duquesne Incline at Beech Street and go down the stairs and you'll run straight into it. And now that you're coming to dinner, you can answer a personal question for me."

Li waited.

"What do I call you?"

"Excuse me?"

"Your name. Is it Caitlyn or Catherine?"

"Does it matter?"

"It matters to me, or I wouldn't ask."

She shrugged. "Then use whichever name you like."

"Not good enough. Names mean something. Which one is it?"

She looked at him for a long moment before answering. "I think . . . Caitlyn."

He nodded as if he'd read something in her answer. Li wondered what it was, and whether he was making some naïve assumption that would end up getting them both in trouble. Quiet people were hard to deal with. You never knew quite what they read into your words—which meant that you could never be completely sure you weren't lying to them.

"Caitlyn it is, then. So why are you asking me about Will, anyway? He shoot one of your yard sale buyers? And isn't that sort of a couldn't-happen-to-a-nicer-guy situation?"

"Actually, it looks like he has one of the surviving fragments."

"Oh. Shit."

"Yeah."

"He must be using it as a NavComp."

"Probably. I'm sure it's better than any other NavComp he could buy out here, legally or illegally."

"He'll never give it back then. Maybe he *can't* give it back. Hell, it's probably running on his own internal wetware."

"*What?*"

"A lot of the pirates do that. They're almost all ex–Navy men. You can't realistically run a modern fighting ship without a military grade wire job. So they wire the NavComp through their own internals . . .

um . . . what would be a tactful way of saying it? In order to promote cooperation and teamwork?"

"In other words, so their crews can't mutiny unless they want to be stranded in the Drift without a NavComp?"

"You said it, not me."

"The thing is," Li said after a moment, "I need that ghost."

"Then you're going to have to learn to live with disappointment."

"Yeah, but I need it."

They stared at each other for a moment.

"I don't think you heard me the first time," Dolniak told her.

"I heard you. Really." She stood up to leave. "See you at dinner tonight."

His sigh followed her out into the hallway. It didn't sound impatient. It sounded like the sigh of a man who felt things. Who felt sorry for people in general, and for her in particular, even if she had used him and lied to him. Li wanted to warn him that feeling sorry for people had only ever gotten her in trouble, but he probably wouldn't listen. And even if he did listen, he probably wouldn't be able to stop himself. Some people were just put together that way.

"Caitlyn," he called after her. "Listen to me. Don't mess with Will Llewellyn. I haven't seen hide nor hair of the guy since he joined the Navy, but I can tell you one thing about him that I figured out when we were five years old. It hasn't changed, and it never will. *He. Doesn't. Lose.*"

Impossible Things

"I can't believe *that!*" said Alice.

"Can't you?" the Queen said in a pitying tone. "Try again: draw a long breath, and shut your eyes."

Alice laughed. "There's no use trying," she said, "one *can't* believe impossible things."

"I daresay you haven't had much practice," said the Queen. "When I was your age, I always did it for half-an-hour a day. Why sometimes I've believed as many as six impossible things before breakfast."

—Lewis Carroll

(Catherine)

THE DRIFT

However unsatisfactory their dinnertime talk had been, Llewellyn seemed to have reached some conclusion about Li. Forty minutes after she went back to her cabin, she was mysteriously granted limited access to the shipboard computers. It wasn't enough. But it was better than nothing.

That night she sat in her cabin, chewing at her fingernails and trying to piece together a clear story from the bits and scraps of old news files in the shipboard archives. She couldn't. It was all dark intrigue and treasure and bloody mayhem. And in the middle of the darkness was this man, this Black William, this thief who had been smart enough to steal Cohen—and disciplined enough to control him once he'd done it.

He had a lot of Cohen, more than any of the fragments she'd encountered so far. Those memories weren't part of the shifting froth of autonomous agents and peripherals. They were wrapped into core programs. If he had that, then he had unlocked the core programs. And he had Cohen's cooperation, however grudging. She didn't underestimate that. She knew what it took to ride that horse. And she was a willing passenger—not a hijacker.

Her first impression of the man had been right. He was driven, disciplined, all fury tamped down and power held in check, coiled tautly around some central purpose. What was it? And why did he need Cohen in order to achieve it?

She ran in review the little that she knew about the man, trying to organize her thoughts into a coherent search strategy.

The *Ada*. And letters of marque. And a Navy hero turned pirate. And bad blood with Astrid Avery.

It wasn't much, but at least it was somewhere to start looking.

The next morning she got a bright and early knock on her door and the information that she was on duty—whatever that meant under the circumstances—in half an hour. At eight bells on the chime she heard a knock on the door and opened it to find herself face-to-face with Ike Okoro.

She knew a lot about Okoro just by looking at him. Like her, he was a rarity in UN space: someone who retained an easily identifiable ethnic identity that matched up in a geographically consistent way with the spot on Earth his ancestors had migrated from. But whereas Li's Korean genes came from corporate colonists who had sold their genesets in order to get out of Earth's gravity well, no corporation had ever owned Okoro's geneset. His parents had no doubt purchased the best tweaks to his DNA that money could buy; thanks to a timely revolution and brilliantly farsighted administration of oil company reparations, New Lagos had emerged from the Great Migration as a wealthy independent planet with a thriving information technologies sector and a full permanent voting membership in the UN Security Council. But no one held a patent on Okoro's genes. And any adjustments to his West African genetics had been made for his benefit by loving parents, and not simply to make him a more profitable worker in a corporate colony. That made all the difference between him and Li, whose black-market geneset still couldn't overwrite the damning corporate serial numbers that were stamped into her mitochondrial DNA. And it made it all the more surprising that Okoro would be here, in the Drift, with a price on his head.

"You were recruited?" she asked incredulously. "Why would anyone even *want* to join up from New Lagos? What in the name of God can the Navy offer them?"

"Excitement." Okoro grinned, showing teeth that had obviously had regular childhood dentists' visits—almost as rare a sight on a Navy ship as a fully human geneset. "That's what I wanted. Paradise is boring. Especially when you're seventeen and impatient and think you know better than your parents."

Li snorted. "I'll take your word for it. Personally, I joined up for the three square meals a day."

Okoro laughed. And then he led her through the ship to the bridge, explaining that even though she was going to be on the boarding detachment—"because, no offense, you don't know shit about sailing"— she would need to know where everything was.

Li looked at the crew members they passed in the corridors, noting the gunmetal-gray tracery of military-grade wire jobs at the pulse points of most of the pirates.

"Lot of ex-military here," she observed.

"Yep. They have the best training. And the best wire jobs. Though some of the Titan mercs are wired to the gills lately."

Li thought of the men she'd fought beside on the bridge of the Titan ship. "How's McPherson doing?" she asked Sital.

"Who?" Sital said. But not quite quickly enough to make it convincing.

So, Li thought. She hadn't just imagined that untrusting look Llewellyn had given McPherson. And now McPherson wasn't on board the *Christina*. Had they put him on one of the lifeboats, or just airlocked the poor bastard? She thought of the cold, calculating glint she'd seen in Llewellyn's eyes and decided she might not want her question answered. Cohen had always had a quality of ruthlessness about him, but it was the ruthlessness of an AI: cool, logical, and dispassionate. She didn't like to imagine what that AI ruthlessness could lead to when mingled with the tight-wound passions of a man like Llewellyn.

"Has the crew always been mostly ex-Navy?" she asked Sital, mostly to avoid seeming to take too much notice of McPherson's vanishing.

"Oh no! We had a bad stretch back after we first broke out of New Allegheny. Had to take on a bunch of new hands, and we didn't have the time to be particular. Things weren't so pretty for a while."

"They don't look so pretty now, to tell you the truth."

That got her a sideways grin and a nod of acknowledgment. "Well, it was worse before. We were really scraping the bottom of the barrel. Llewellyn turned it around, though." He waved her through a neatly dogged hatchway and into the long passage that led back to the airy superstructure of the ship's fantail. "You heard the story of how he captured this ship?"

Li shook her head.

"We were in the Deep, just like we are now, with a crew that was worse than useless. We met up with this Navy cruiser—"

"You stole this ship out from under the Navy?" Li looked around with fresh eyes. She should have seen it before, of course. But she wasn't a sailor; all ships were foreign countries to her. And the idea of pirates actually taking down a Navy cruiser was so outlandish that she hadn't seen the clues—or at least hadn't put them together properly.

"One thing you have to give the man, he doesn't think small."

"So how did you take the *Christina*?"

Okoro laughed. "We didn't. *He* did. We grappled up with her only to have the new recruits decide they didn't want to fight. And our AI was totally outclassed, so no help there. So what does Himself do? He casts off the lifeboats, sets our old ship afire, and tells them they can board the new ship and fight like men or stay behind and die in their own piss like dogs."

"He *said that*?" Li was incredulous. She could imagine him doing it all right. But that bit about dying in their piss like dogs seemed far too flamboyant for the buttoned-down Llewellyn.

"Well, not in so many words," Okoro allowed. "That'd be a bit too much of a speech for him. But he got the point across."

"I'll bet."

Okoro grabbed her elbow and urged her down the hall, pointing out the newer insulation tiles—most of them right about head height. And then one, right at the turn of an otherwise anonymous corner, that hadn't been replaced. It had taken a vicious shot from a pulse rifle.

"That's where Himself almost got his head blown off. And he left it there to remind the young 'uns not to get giddy on a raid until they've cuffed wrists, counted heads, and locked down the armory."

She noticed that Okoro didn't call him Llewellyn or even the captain. And as they moved around the ship she began to realize that most of the veteran crew members had the same odd habit: "Has Himself done his morning rounds yet?"; or "That summing out looks off, better show it to Himself"; or "Look sharp, Himself is on the foredeck." They said it with a capital *H* that you couldn't miss, as if he were a god. Or as if they were afraid that speaking his name would end his impossible run of luck and rub off whatever improbable magic it was that made him survive when any normal man would long ago have died.

"What about friends?"

"What?" Okoro asked blankly.

"Does the captain have any friends on board? Old comrades from his Navy days, that kind of thing?"

"Well, I'm as old as they get. I was with him on the *Ada*." Had Li just imagined the faint hesitation before that final word, or the lurch in his voice when he named his old ship? "Sital was too."

"Lot of history between the two of them."

"Well, that's between the two of them, isn't it?"

Li glanced sideways at him. "And you?"

"I consider him my friend," Okoro said carefully. And this time Li was quite sure that the hesitation wasn't imagined.

"He's a cool one," Li said.

"Oh, you noticed?"

"Yeah," Li said wryly. "But then I notice the little subtle things. I'm sure not everyone can see it."

Okoro snorted. "You shouldn't joke about it. People are upset and confused. That's a bad way for things to be on a ship full of pirates."

"You mean they're upset about *me*."

"Maybe upset is too strong a word. But still . . . it does put a question in everyone's mind."

"Oh?" Li wondered privately if "everyone" meant Sital.

"No," he said, reading her expression with uncanny accuracy. "Not Sital. But there've been a couple of women on board who've made fools of themselves over him. Not that it got them anywhere . . . well, it all goes back to what I said before. He's a good captain. And a good captain understands that people will make fools of themselves on a long voyage, but your mates'll forgive you pretty much anything as long as you don't shove it up their noses."

Li grinned. It really was too bad Cohen wasn't here. He'd be enjoying this immensely. "So hypocrisy is the social glue that holds a pirate ship together?"

"Well . . ." Okoro was not willing to go that far. "Let's just say that you need to allow for more than the normal amount of social friction. Mature and rational men don't set out onto the high seas to chase each other around in search of violence. That's not me, by the way. It's from an old book Himself likes to quote."

They walked on a moment in the companionable silence of strangers who have . . . not friendship, or even necessarily the seeds of real friendship . . . but at least a fleeting sense of encountering a reasonable and sympathetic fellow thinker.

"The thing is," Okoro said into the silence, "being upset about you is just a surface thing. The real thing they're upset about is the Nav-Comp. And whatever past you have with him."

She turned to stare at him, stopping abruptly enough to make a crewman stumble into her and walk off cursing under his breath. "Why are you telling me this? What do you care?"

Okoro had stopped, too, equally oblivious to the workaday bustle all around them. "Can't you guess?" he asked.

"You've talked to Cohen."

"Of course."

"Why *of course*?"

"Don't you understand who I am?"

"You're a doctor."

Okoro laughed out loud. "I'm only playing at being a people doctor because we don't have a real one on board. I'm an AI specialist. I was Llewellyn's cat herder on the *Ada*. And now I'm the cat herder on the *Christina*, too. And the psychtech. And anything else that has to do with helping a hundred-some humans share a very small ship with an alarmingly large Emergent."

Li stared, coming to grips with what Okoro was telling her. That he, not Llewellyn, was the gatekeeper to Cohen. That he, not Llewellyn, had the answers—and the access—she needed so desperately. "Then you can—"

"No, I can't. All I can do is give you some good advice. Don't shove yourself in people's faces. Don't do anything to make them nervous about you. And back off on trying to get direct access to the NavComp."

"He's not a NavComp, he's—"

"You see?" Okoro dropped his voice to a murmur, somehow managing to sound relaxed and routine—as if he were conducting a trivial and innocent conversation that anyone could have even the faintest reason for wanting to eavesdrop on. "That's just what I'm trying to say to you. Why would you want to keep saying things like that? Do you really think your friend is going to be safer if people stop thinking of him as a NavComp—useful, competent, trustworthy, and *non*sentient—and start thinking of him as some kind of hungry, crazy ghost who's taking their ship who knows where to do who knows what?"

"What about Llewellyn? What does *he* think?"

Okoro got an odd, inward-looking expression on his face, as if he were measuring what he was about to say against some complex internal truth-telling metric that existed only inside his head. "I really can't say. And that's a true 'can't,' not just a 'won't' pretending to be a 'can't.' I trust the man. I trust him to do the right thing under difficult circumstances. But what *he'll* think the right thing is . . . I couldn't begin to tell you."

"So you trust him, but he doesn't trust you."

"He doesn't trust anyone. And given what happened on the *Ada*, I can't say I blame him."

Li thought of Llewellyn's closed and narrow face. She remembered the clear, fierce, measuring eye staring sidelong at her down the smoke-swirled length of Damascus steel. She wondered what leverage Cohen was bringing to bear on the finely honed mind behind that eye. And what Llewellyn would be willing to do to fight him off.

A man who would burn his own ship to make his men fight.

You might have met your match, Cohen. You might have finally picked the wrong fellow to fuck with.

"The *Ada*?" she asked Okoro after a moment. "Was that Llewellyn's old ship?"

"Aye."

"And what happened to her?"

"Nothing. She's Avery's ship now, that's all. God help the poor woman."

She stared in outright disbelief. "Llewellyn commanded the *Ada*?"

He frowned incredulously at her. "Where've you been for the last ten years? I thought everyone with spinstream access followed that trial."

"No. And I can't find out, either, because I'm cut out of the shipboard systems." She gave him a sour look. "But then you'd know all about that, wouldn't you?"

"Actually, no. That's way below my pay grade. But I'll see what I can do about it."

They had reached the bridge now, and to Li's surprise Sital turned away from the main monitor when she saw them and came over to cut in on Okoro.

"I'll take over from here," she told him. "You go check on that thing we talked about this morning."

"And which thing exactly would that be?" Okoro asked with a teasing grin. "She thinks she's being subtle," he told Li. "She only wants to get you alone. But she's a dreadful liar, take it from me. You mustn't believe a word she says to you!"

"No ice cream for you," Sital deadpanned.

And then Okoro was off to wherever—and Li was alone with Llewellyn's quietly formidable first officer.

It took Li about three minutes from their first exchange of friendly fire to decide that Sital was . . . complicated. For one thing, Sital was wound about as tight as anyone could be and not snap. Some of it was sheer physical and mental energy: a body honed for combat carting around a brain that cycled several orders of magnitude faster than the average monkey's. But it was more than that. There was a prickliness to the woman that you couldn't miss from a mile away. She was that most formidable and dangerous of all opponents: a hardheaded perfectionist

driven to excel by her own flaws, real or self-perceived. It was no surprise she'd ended up in the military, Li thought. Strand a woman like
that in a peaceful civilian life and she'd drive everyone around her insane and eventually chew her own leg off in a desperate effort to escape.
But in a war zone, when all hell was breaking loose, a woman like that
was a blessing.

And she was a perfect second-in-command, and you couldn't be on
the *Christina* for half an hour without understanding that the crew was
just as loyal to her as it was to Llewellyn. And she'd earned that loyalty,
Li suspected. She was the kind of person who made things work,
brought the trains in on time, and took care of her people. And—much
more than Llewellyn, Li suspected—she was the glue that held this
crew together.

She was also, unfortunately, a seething, roiling bundle of obsessions,
fixations, and compulsive insecurities—most of them having to do
with Llewellyn.

"This your first trip into the Drift?" Sital asked.

"Yes."

"Well, don't worry. Boomerang's a well-established route. We're not
going to run into anything unexpected. We're not even using the new
NavComp for this jump. There's nothing to calculate. The entry and
exit points are already mapped and buoyed and locked into the old
system. It's hardly even a jump at all, by pirate standards."

"So how does it work on a real jump? Do you have to turn the ship
over to the NavComp for those?" She realized she'd fallen into Sital's
way of talking without even thinking about it. Did the other woman
want to avoid Cohen's name for some reason? Did she even know his
name?

"Hang on," Sital answered. "It's better if I just show you."

Sital led her over to the navigational charts. It always amazed Li that
ships still bothered with them. She'd asked a few ship's officers about it,
on those rare occasions when she had anything to do with ship's officers, but all she'd ever gotten from them were tradition-drenched
speeches about Captain Bligh navigating past the Great Barrier Reef
with a map and a toothpick. Finally she had decided that it was just an

atavistic urge for tactility. Sailors didn't feel comfortable without their charts. They craved that concrete proof of their place in the universe. They needed to map their worldline the old-fashioned way, even if their more evolved selves knew that time was merely an Emergent phenomenon and that reality on the most basic quantum level erased all distinctions between past, present, and future. They needed to feel that their destiny was something they could see and touch—and, if push came to shove, something they could roll up and carry onto the lifeboats.

"Here's what Will's planning," Sital told her. "We jump in at Point Charon. That takes us to Perseus, where we know there's heavy commercial shipping traffic. If we were really hurting, we could knock off a ship for replacement air. But luckily we don't need to this time. Then we reenter the Drift point-double-zero-two light-years away, right . . . here. This is a pirate point, no civvies. We got it from Jenny Wheelan, straight from the horse's mouth, so we know Navy doesn't have it on their charts. And even better, it's a one-way point that drops you out here, just offshore of Boomerang."

She pointed to a big vortex that was annotated with navigational coordinates indicating that it had intakes and outlets to half a dozen other entry points.

"We'll be just out of active sensor range, so no one should see us come into Boomerang. So as long as we run silent, we can sit out there in the Deep listening to the comm chatter and figuring out where Avery is—and, more important, where she thinks we are."

"You can decrypt Navy communications?"

"No, but Navy ships have loose lips. If Avery's out there we'll hear about it. And since every commercial shipper running the Drift knows she's got a hard-on for us, they'll be rerouting their ships just as fast as they can to stay out of the combat zone."

And to keep from getting their best crew press-ganged, Li thought. She wondered idly whether the merchant marine sailors were more frightened of getting press-ganged by Avery or by Llewellyn. Judging from what she'd seen during her own capture, the answer might not be the one that Avery and UNSec wanted to hear.

On the other hand, the more she looked at the charts, the more that seemed like the least of their problems.

"I didn't realize the Drift worked like this. I thought it only went to parallel universes. Which—okay—that's a whole other group of problems. Forget about them. But this . . . I mean, Boomerang's not in another universe. It's on the nav charts. You can fly around the Drift and get there in . . ."

"Seventy-two light-years, more or less."

"So . . . that's the most flagrant violation of causality I've ever heard of. It's beyond flagrant. It's ridiculous."

"So maybe Boomerang *is* in another universe. But who cares? It works *as if* it's in this universe. And the whole cosmology thing? Give me a break. Those guys have their heads so far up their theories they won't let you cross the *street* without violating causality."

Li rubbed the bridge of her nose, feeling a headache coming on. "No," she said after a brief, pained silence. "That doesn't get you anywhere. That doesn't solve anything."

"So?"

"What do you mean, *so*? It's a serious question."

"I'm not saying it's not. I'm just saying it's irrelevant. The Drift *exists*. We've sailed it. We've charted it. Is it my problem if that ruins some cosmologist's day?"

She was right, of course. When you saw it spread out in black and white on a navigator's map, the structure of the Drift was obvious. It was like a vast river, with currents and eddies and tidal pools. Depending on where you encountered the flood, it could suck you in, pull you downstream, spin you around, or simply spit you out on the shore a mere light-year or two away from where you'd gone in. And if the Drift really was what they said it was, then the limit of light speed was irrelevant. You weren't traveling through the universe like a car driving down a highway. You were riding on the expansion of the universe itself, like a swimmer swept out to sea on a riptide. This was the source of Sital's untroubled certainty. When you looked at it in practical terms, like a navigator charting a course, it was simply an ocean, no different than any of the other oceans humans had navigated in their long history. Oceans had tides and currents. Atmospheres had jet streams. The universe had the Drift. No problem.

It was only when you tried to fit the Drift into any larger notion of reality that logic failed you and the whole house of cards came tumbling down around your ears.

"So to get to, say, Point Manifold, you'd dive in here"—Li tapped the appropriate point on the map—"and go through these two points. And that would bring you out here." Neat trick. Twenty light-years in as many minutes.

But Sital looked doubtful. "Well, we could route the trip that way, I guess. But then we'd have to go through Wolf Tango Foxtrot."

She tapped an entry point that was just a minuscule dot on the map, with only the thinnest scattering of navigational references. And it was indeed labeled Wolf Tango Foxtrot. WTF. Which couldn't be anything but a joke; Navy lingo diverged widely from Peacekeeper slang, but some military acronyms were universal.

Li laughed. "Seriously? It's called that?"

"Yeah. And for exactly the reason you think. We don't even like to use that NavPoint. No one does. It's got serious LGM cooties."

Li raised her eyebrows. Little Green Men Cooties were what the Drift was all about, according to Router/Decomposer, from the Novalis aliens to whoever had terraformed the other two as-yet-unnamed habitable planets. But still . . . she hadn't expected to actually meet someone who claimed to have met them. She probed Sital's face for incipient traces of looniness, but saw only the same stripped-down, sensible, results-oriented woman she'd always seen. Except . . .

"As long as you're not going to tell me they talk to you," she joked.

"Oh no," Sital said blithely. "From what I've heard, they don't even seem to notice us. This one guy I know almost got run over at Wolf Tango Foxtrot. Twice in one stopover. Two unknowns, bigger than any ship he'd ever seen. He said he felt like a squirrel trying to cross a highway."

"Lovely." Just what Li had always wanted: to be a squirrel on the intergalactic freeway. She could only judge aliens by her knowledge of humanity—and her knowledge of herself. But neither one gave her much reason to think that actually meeting the Novalis aliens would mean anything but trouble.

"And besides," Sital went on, warming to her subject, "*someone* must have built the Novalis Datatrap. Oh . . . you haven't heard about it?" She shrugged. "I guess you haven't been out here that long. Anyway, there's supposed to be a giant datatrap, the size of a small planet, orbiting Novalis. Or at least sometimes it's orbiting Novalis. It either migrates from system to system or it's in permanent quantum superposition. It's not on any of the standard maps, but a bunch of people have found it by accident, usually when they were running from the Navy. There's a whole debate about whether it's ours or someone else's. But if it's ours, then it was way too classified for me or Llewellyn or Okoro to know about it even before we turned pirate."

Sital's face made it clear how unlikely she thought that last possibility was, and Li wondered just how deep in she, Llewellyn, and Okoro had been, and whether it could possibly be a coincidence that the one stable Cohen ghost had ended up on *this* ship out of all the ships in all the ports in the multiverse.

"And what about this entry point?" Li tapped a NavPoint labeled "Yesterday."

"Oh." Sital cleared her throat. "I don't even want to tell you. You'll think I'm crazy."

Li raised an eyebrow. "You just told me you believe in little green men, Sital. I think we're a few klicks past crazy."

Sital grinned. "Okay. So, we found that one ourselves. Uncharted entry point. No markers, no nothing. We bust in there hell-for-leather with a Navy destroyer on our tail, and it's like, okay: Fish or cut bait. So we just . . . dove in."

"And?"

"And just like the name says. We came out yesterday."

Li shook her head.

"Well, not yesterday precisely. Thirty hours."

"What?"

"The periodicity is thirty hours. You go in, and instead of putting you in the main current it spins you around like a revolving door and spits you back out in the same place but thirty hours before your time of entry."

"That's impossible."

"Not categorically. It's only impossible in a nonspinning universe."

Li squeezed the bridge of her nose. Around her, the normal activities of an interstellar navigation flowed on. But Li's brain had stuttered to a halt as rational thought gave way before the Möbius-like paradox of time and memory in the Drift.

"But . . . even if . . . I mean, wouldn't *this* universe have to be spinning in the opposite direction?"

"Yeah." Sital laughed. "Crazy, huh?"

And crazy-making. What had Router/Decomposer said? Don't think about it, just plug the numbers in. As advice went, that was starting to sound pretty good to her.

(Caitlyn)

THE PIT

As she rode the Duquesne Incline up the shovel-scarred pit wall that evening, Li thought about names and memory and the things you left behind when you started lying.

So is it Caitlyn or Catherine? Dolniak had asked her. And she hadn't known how to answer him. She still didn't.

For the first sixteen years of her life she had been Caitlyn Perkins, a corporate-built genetic construct destined for a life of hard rock mining on a shithole Trusteeship. Then she'd pulled off the great escape— the one every construct in every mine or factory on every backwater planet in the Periphery dreamed of. She'd gotten out. And the price of the ticket had been something she was only too happy to get rid of: her memories.

She'd walked into a shantytown chop shop as a full construct with no legal right to vote, travel off-planet, or even walk off the job. And she'd walked out as a free woman named Catherine Li, her blood officially tainted with only an allowable quarter of corporate-owned genetic material.

That free woman had enlisted in the Peacekeepers. She'd lied her way through a battery of psychological exams and hard-memory backups. She hadn't even thought about those lies at the time. They'd just been one more thing she needed to do to get where she wanted to go. She hadn't noticed the difference after the first jump. And after the second and third jumps she'd started telling herself that she was immune to jump amnesia and all those warnings and worries had been for nothing. Then she'd realized—was it after the eighth or ninth jump?—that she couldn't remember her mother's name, or her real birthday, or what her father looked like. She'd worried about it. And then she'd forgotten to worry. And then that shifting, slithering, treacherously unpredictable emptiness simply became part of who she was.

Only after many years and many jumps did she begin to truly understand the impossibility of building a life on that emptiness. But by then Cohen was there. And there was so much of him that it didn't really matter how little of her there was.

She'd needed him. She'd craved his warmth, his strength, his unwavering conviction that she was worth bothering with. She'd craved the solidity of knowing who she was when she was with him. She'd never imagined life without him, and she still couldn't. She didn't know if that was love. She knew he'd deserved more from her. She'd always known that. She just didn't have the pieces of a person that more would have to come from.

And now he was gone, and she was Caitlyn Perkins again, or whatever was left of Caitlyn. And as she crested the crumbling red dirt cliffs and got her first glimpse of the spaceport's rust-pitted cranes and warehouses and docking gantries—so like the mining stations of Compson's World—her stomach clenched in panic and she had a sudden trembling conviction that it was all slipping away from her.

And yet she'd told Dolniak to call her Caitlyn. And in doing so, she'd resurrected a dead girl—a person she'd been desperate to forget even before the psychtechs and memory washings. It had been an on-the-spot, nearly instantaneous decision, and when push came to shove it was the old name, unused for almost two decades, that had risen into her mouth. She'd told herself that it was merely a matter of practicality, but it was more than that.

When she thought about other copies of herself floating around in streamspace, she felt a terrible, bottomless, nauseating vertigo. She'd spent her life trying to be singular, individual, her own person rather than another in the endless ranks of Xenogen constructs. And now she'd been dragged back into being just a number and a body.

Were her other resurrections as spooked by the change as she was? Were they using the same childish tactics to stake out some little piece of private mental real estate? And how many of them were deciding to be Caitlyn instead of Catherine?

Any halfway decent psychtech would have told her to look for continuity, to lay claim to her personhood, to take ownership of Catherine Li's memories. But somehow it was easier to cut the ties than to try to mend them. And anything was easier than this dizzying stuck-between-two-lives feeling.

So—even though she knew that the evasion was coded into her get-the-job-done-at-any-cost geneset—she had cut the ties and made herself Caitlyn. Better to go back to being the girl she barely remembered: an empty vessel into which she could pour whatever came out of this new incarnation. Catherine Li was complicated, multiple, conflicted. Caitlyn Perkins was simple and singular and . . . manageable.

She needed simple right now. She needed manageable. She needed to push through and get the job done. Cohen would have been furious at her. He would have told her she was ripping herself apart and asked who she expected to pick up the pieces later. And they'd been together so long, and so intimately, that she could feel his voice in her mind right down to the tone of controlled impatience that he always got when he thought she was stonewalling him. But she had an answer for that voice—the same answer she would have given Cohen had he still been alive, and the same answer she gave herself now. If she didn't do her job on New Allegheny there wouldn't *be* a later.

Dolniak's house was perched Pit-side, midway up Polish Hill and just to the leeward of the Monongahela Incline. On one side the windows looked out over rain-lashed treetops. On the other side they came face-to-face with the giant girders and pulleys of the incline. His front door was cantilevered off the steep stairs that switchbacked up to the commuter stop, and while he welcomed her in and took her wet things from her, she could hear the voices and footsteps of shift workers on their way downslope to feed the insatiable maw of the Crucible.

"What's for dinner?" she asked.

Then she walked into the tiny kitchen and smelled it. And saw the telltale vat-ration boxes littering the counter.

"No," she said. "No, no, no, no, no. Friends don't let friends eat vat rat. Put on your coat. We're going grocery shopping."

Dolniak stared at her incredulously. "Don't get me wrong. I'm a farm boy. I'm all for real cooking. But do you seriously think you're going to get fresh food in the Pit?"

"I do. Ever been to the UNSec PX?"

"On base? That's where the Peacekeepers shop."

"And anyone else who has e-currency."

"Which sadly doesn't include me," he said, holding up a virgin palm that had never seen a credit chip implant.

"But it does include me. Look, we'll go dutch. I buy, you cook. If that doesn't work for you, we're shit out of luck, because I can't boil water without screwing it up."

A slow smile spread across his face. "All right then. You want something to take the edge off before we go?"

She glanced at the stuff on the counter. "No. I must be getting old or something, but honestly you couldn't pay me enough to eat that shit."

"That's what I like about you," Dolniak said, grabbing his coat and following her out the door. "You're so polite."

The PX was deluxe, as all PXs are when the diplomats and administrators roll into town. Fresh produce flown in by jumpship or trucked down from the far-flung farms of the Monongahela Uplands. A lot of it was local, in fact. But, as Dolniak pointed out, that didn't mean the locals could afford it.

Dolniak was like a kid in a candy store.

"I think this technically qualifies as bribery," he said, smelling an apple that struck Li's Ring-conditioned tastes as being completely unremarkable. "But at the moment I can't bring myself to give a hoot. My God, I'd forgotten what real live fruit smelled like."

An hour later they were cooking together in Dolniak's small but surprisingly well-equipped kitchen. Li felt a vague sense of disloyalty during the whole business. She hadn't known how to cook before she'd met Cohen. She hadn't known anything about food—or even really been aware that non-vat-grown food still existed. It seemed wrong to be sharing it with someone else.

Dolniak, on the other hand, was in heaven; clearly she had a frustrated foodie on her hands.

"I can't always get real food," he said, reverently unwrapping a golden brick of butter that he had stored in the freezer behind the usual vat-grown stuff. "But I do remember what it tastes like."

They talked, both over the cooking and over the dinner that followed it. Dolniak was easy to talk to, just as she'd known he would be. He didn't flirt with her—or if he did, it was a flirtation so mild that it was impossible to tell it apart from the first early overtures of simple friendship. That didn't surprise Li, either; she'd known early on that he wasn't the pushy type. Whatever else might be going on under the surface with Dolniak, it would always be friendship first and friendship foremost.

"So what's it like to be wired?" he asked when they'd finished eating and he'd pushed his plate back and stretched his massive legs out beside a kitchen table that his bulk reduced to doll furniture.

Li shrugged.

"No, really, I'm fascinated. Maybe it's just a novelty thing. You're definitely the first woman I've ever met who could beat the crap out of me."

"So why not get wired if you're so curious?" She waved his answer away. "Yeah, I know, the boxing. But most professional athletes get implants once they retire. Why not you?"

"I really did leave it too late." He shrugged. "I guess I didn't really want to admit the boxing was over. And by the time I did . . . well . . . what was the point, really? There weren't any wire jobs on New Allegheny until the Drift prospectors and mercenaries started shipping in. And other than wire jobs . . . well, seriously, would you want to meet *me* in a dark alley?"

"So you're top predator in a low-tech ecosystem?"

"Well . . . yeah. I mean, isn't that why most guys become cops?"

"No nifty speeches about defending the peace and serving the public?"

"Yeah, I guess that stuff's fun, too."

Li snorted. "You can't fool me, Dolniak. You're a Boy Scout. It's branded across your face like a scarlet letter."

"That bad, huh?"

"Worse. But don't worry, I've always had a soft spot for Boy Scouts. Which is why I try to discourage them from playing with me."

He gave her one of his long, level, placid looks. "Are you speaking professionally or personally?"

That caught her off guard. "Both," she admitted after a moment. And she was surprised that it caused her a little tinge of regret to say it. "What do you know about Emergent AIs?"

"What they say on the news spins. Nothing more."

Li frowned at him, eyes narrowing. "You watched the spins about Cohen."

"Of course I did."

"And?"

"Sounds like he killed some people."

"He couldn't help that!" Li snapped.

"They seemed to think he could."

"They're full of crap, Dolniak!"

"So fine. Then you tell me how it is."

"I've never met an AI that would kill a human on purpose. They're big and fast and highly focused and one hundred percent results-oriented. But accidents do happen. And humans always end up taking the brunt of them."

Dolniak smiled and settled back into the sofa. "You sound like my first trainer warning me that I'd get my head kicked in if I tried to take on a real heavyweight."

"And what happened?"

"I KO'd the guy in three rounds."

"Yeah. Well. What do the bankers always say? Past performance does not predict future results. Don't get cocky."

On the way back to the hotel they were stopped on the street by the curfew patrol. There were five men, and they ranged around Li and

Dolniak on the sidewalk in a tense parallelogram that came straight out of the counterinsurgency training manuals. Their leader accepted Li's papers without comment and returned them to her. The trouble started when he took a look at Dolniak's papers.

"So you're a cop," he said in a flat, impersonal voice.

"Yes."

"You out on official business?"

Li started to answer but Dolniak cut her off.

"No."

"So you just figure your detective's badge gives you a get-out-of-curfew free card? Is that it?"

Dolniak didn't answer. And when Li glanced in his direction she saw him standing with his hands at his sides and his eyes fixed politely somewhere around the squad leader's left elbow.

"Are you gonna answer me?"

"I'm sorry. I misunderstood the curfew law. We were told departmentally that it didn't apply to us."

"In the performance of official duties."

"I understand now," Dolniak said quietly, his eyes still fixed on the man's elbow. "I'll make sure to remember that in future."

Li expected the squad leader to back off then, but instead he stepped toe to toe with Dolniak and started talking right into the larger man's face. "I'd really fucking like to bring you in. I wonder what I'd find out if I did. I would have cashed out the entire local police force the day we arrived. But no, that was too confrontational. We didn't want to create a Dead Ender Syndrome. And now you guys are always out late and up early. And the last five guys I've sent home in body bags took the trip courtesy of official police-issue thirty-eights."

Li stirred restlessly beside Dolniak. The squad leader's eyes flashed toward her, white-rimmed with anger and fear. In that instant she knew that Dolniak had read the situation right. Nothing she did could help. And any move at all from either of them would merely add fuel to an already explosive situation.

For the next several minutes, she watched Dolniak stand, head bowed, patiently enduring one intrusive question after another. He reminded her of a draft horse standing for the farrier. But she saw the anger in the set of his broad shoulders—something different than she'd seen before. It was the dangerous anger of a quiet man. And there was something else, simmering beneath the anger, that had nothing at all to do with the careful, controlled, cautious cop she knew him to be. She'd seen that look before. And seeing it in Dolniak's calm, steady face started a slow burn of foreboding in her belly that told her things on New Allegheny were going to get as ugly as they possibly could get.

He was still keyed up when they got back to her hotel room—enough so that she invited him in for coffee. She had planned to see him politely off in the lobby, for many reasons, personal as well as professional. But there was a dangerous, simmering look about him, and she didn't like the idea of sending a man that angry back onto the streets to run into more trouble.

Dolniak had barely spared a glance at her hotel room the last time he'd been there, but this time he gave it a narrow-eyed inspection. Watching his glance tick from the plush carpets and furniture to the high ceilings and the glistening windows, she felt suddenly guilty at the sheer off-world luxury of the place. He made no comment, however. Just walked to the door and stepped out onto the balcony to look at the nighttime view of the Crucible.

"Those fires never go out, you know."

She stepped out onto the narrow balcony with him, peering through the haze at the orange glow of the blast furnaces.

"They can't go out. They heat the furnaces to three thousand degrees Fahrenheit. If you let the fires go out, the walls crack. No steel. No mill. Nothing. There was one strike, when I was a kid, where the mill owners threatened to shut down the furnaces and move operations off-planet. The steelmen broke into the mill, took it over, and kept the furnaces running in the face of hired guns, police."

Dolniak laughed softly. It was an odd laugh, nothing she'd heard out of him before. She looked sideways at him and saw his usually placid face lit by the glow of the blast furnaces—and by some emotion that ran deeper and fiercer even than his anger at the mercenaries.

"The owners couldn't understand it," he told her. "They thought they were fighting about money. So what were these guys doing, risking their lives in order to do a dangerous, shitty job that no sane person would want and with no hope of a paycheck anywhere in sight? But it's never really about money for steelmen. It's never about anything but the steel."

What was that about? Router/Decomposer asked when Dolniak was gone.

"Oh, nothing. We got stopped by a patrol in the street. He was angry about it. Who wouldn't be?"

That's not what I'm talking about, and you know it.

Li muted her internals, walked into the bathroom, and started getting ready for bed.

"Go ahead and ignore me," the AI said, his voice shifting seamlessly to the bathroom's livewall.

"Can you not talk to me in here, please? Call me old-fashioned, but I don't need company in the crapper."

"Then don't run into the bathroom when I try to ask you a personal question."

"Personal? What's personal?"

"That cop, that's what. And don't try to tell me there's nothing going on there. He wasn't just here for the view. If I can see it, a brain-damaged mynah bird could see it."

"I don't even know what a mynah bird is. Where the hell do you come up with these things?"

"From my boundless store of biophilic trivia. And don't change the subject. Are you getting *involved*?"

"I'm just doing my job."

"Well, he's not!"

Li set her jaw and stared at the floor between her toes. "That's not my problem."

Router/Decomposer sounded more disgusted than she would have thought an AI talking through a low-grade hotel bathroom intercom could sound. "That's the most disingenuous thing I've ever heard you say. I'm disappointed in you!"

"That's the most human thing I've ever heard you say. And, at the moment, I'm bored by you."

Both of them paused to regroup, caught in the intricate web of memory that tied them to the years when they had both been part of Cohen's larger personality architecture. Li had never been fully immersed in the Emergent's complex and shifting web of associations; even a wire job as thorough as hers was wouldn't allow a human that deep into AI territory. But she had gone deep enough. She knew things about Router/Decomposer that no other human would ever know— that no human would understand even if they did know about them. And he knew things about her that . . . well, best not to think about that.

She thumbed open the toothpaste, spread it on the brush, began brushing her teeth with savage energy.

You can tell me about it, Caitlyn. I understand. I understand more than you think I do . . .

Why? Because you've been spying on me again?

Once, long ago, she'd caught him following her. He'd told her that she was worth keeping an eye on—that he was *interested in what she was turning into*. It had sounded like a compliment at the time, albeit an unnerving one. But now she wondered.

Are you just playing him along?

Would it be better if I was?

He didn't answer.

She washed out her mouth and slammed the toothbrush back onto the counter. "Yeah, well, I guess neither of us is living up to our Best Selves at the moment, are we?"

(Catherine)

THE DRIFT

Within an hour of jumping into Point Boomerang, Li knew that the news coming in over the comm was bad. That much she could see just in the faces of the officers coming off bridge duty. But she didn't realize quite how bad it was until she overheard Okoro telling a midshipman that they weren't going to be putting in at Boomerang because fucking Avery had gotten there before them.

Unfortunately, how close fucking Avery was to catching them was turning into a serious personal safety issue for Li in a way that went well beyond the overall risks of the game for the rest of the crew. By the time she had been on board for a week, she was starting to notice the simmering resentment, the whispered conversations that ground to an awkward halt when she appeared, the eyes that were quickly turned elsewhere when she turned around and caught their owners staring at her. At first she thought it had to do with Cohen. But then she realized that it wasn't Cohen that people were connecting her to at all, but Avery. And that every time Avery hit an entry point ahead of them or jumped into a Drift node too close behind them, the whispers got louder.

Still, when she managed to ignore the unspoken threat that her crew mates might decide to airlock her if they couldn't shake Avery any other way, it was amazing how much being on the *Christina* felt like being on a perfectly normal Navy ship. There was the same endless round of mind-numbing, body-depleting labor—even more than usual, since the pirates were running the *Christina* with what amounted to a skeleton crew by Navy standards. There was the same buttoned-down, no-nonsense discipline. The same familiar Navy routines. The same familiar Navy jargon. The same self-satisfied Navy attitude. The same familiar infantryman's feeling of being at best a fifth wheel and at worst a prisoner.

No access to shipboard security or operational systems. No access to realtime news about the unfolding and potentially hostile situation beyond the tin-can-thin walls of the hab ring. Nothing but low-level civvy access—and the knowledge that while you were twiddling your thumbs, your fate was being decided by a bunch of space jockeys who thought war was something you did from nine to five and before you cleaned up and put on your whites to report to the officers' mess.

Li hated it.

And she didn't just hate it theoretically. She hated it as a career soldier who'd spent endless months chewing her nails on board Navy transports while invasion fleets assembled with glacial slowness and then idled their engines in the dark reaches of space while the admirals and generals *knifed* one another in the back in order to be first in line for a promotion if things went right, and out of the line of fire if they didn't.

But this time was worse. Because this time it wasn't some hapless Periphery merchant marine lying in wait for them out in the dark beyond the ship's hull. It was Astrid Avery, manning the bridge of a state-of-the-art ship of the line and backed by the full firepower of the UN Navy.

Another wrangle between Llewellyn and Doyle took place, with Sital serving in her habitual role as tiebreaker. The *Christina* retreated to a Drift entry point well beyond Boomerang's sensor range and hung fire, eavesdropping on comm traffic and waiting for victims. There were no safe ports left for them now that Avery had made it to Boomerang, and they were slipping into the downward spiral of having to attack every time they needed air and food and water. The veterans in the crew knew what all pirates know: that this was the beginning of the end. A pirate ship without a safe home port is like a shark: If it stops swimming it suffocates. Without a safe home port they could never relax, never retrench or refit. They couldn't even retreat, because their very survival hung on a string of one attack after another after another.

The next weeks were ones Li would gladly have deleted from the span of her natural life—if this still was her natural life. With alarming speed they devolved into a cat-and-mouse game with Astrid Avery.

The *Christina* would attack—usually some defenseless merchant marine ship. They'd strip their prey of air, water, and equipment. And then they'd tuck their tail between their legs and run like hell. With every attack their very survival hung on a knife's edge. With every attack Avery got there faster and the margin of safety got slimmer. And every time Avery took a chunk out of their hide, the mood on Llewellyn's ship darkened and the rumors about spies and mutiny ran quicker around the lower decks.

Meanwhile, though Li remained more prisoner on the ship than crew member, Llewellyn seemed compelled to keep talking to her. Their conversations were cagy, uncomfortable, and often unsatisfying. And they were dangerous, too. Sital was more tightly wound than ever now that Avery was breathing down the backs of their necks, and every min-ute that Llewellyn spent with Li was a slap in Sital's face.

But Llewellyn either didn't see it—or didn't want to see it.

"How much longer do you think she's going to put up with this?" Li asked one night after Sital wordlessly delivered her to Llewellyn's door for a late dinner.

"Who? Sital? Don't worry about her. She's just protective. She thinks you're going to hurt me."

"Oh? And what do you think?"

"I think she's probably right."

He smiled at that—sort of. He had two smiles, she was coming to realize. One was the sweet, gap-toothed little boy's smile. The other one was a sort of automatic gesture of politeness: a cool, polite curve of the lips, carefully calibrated to satisfy social requirements while giving out as little real human warmth as possible. She thought of the two expres-sions as his real smile and his nominal smile. Or at least she hoped the first one was the real one. Who could tell? *He* probably didn't even know anymore.

The man's emotional remove was infuriating. You wanted to poke him with a stick sometimes just to see if he'd bite.

And yet there *was* someone in there. The man oozed charisma despite all his attempts to scrub away any trace of individuality. You could see people orienting to him whenever he walked into a room, like iron filings lining up with a magnetic field—often without even knowing it. And in his unguarded moments, Li caught tantalizing glimpses of the private man . . . the one in whom Cohen's meme pods had found such fertile ground.

"You know she's in love with you, don't you?"

He just rolled his eyes. "Sital's already been married and divorced once. Trust me, she knows better."

Li raised an eyebrow. "You ever been married?"

"No. I've only ever been close twice. And that was by accident."

She laughed. "Sounds like there's a story there."

"Not really. Just socially incompetent. The last woman I almost accidentally married accused me of having borderline Asperger's syndrome."

Li raised an eyebrow. "And was she right?"

"I hide it well. But under hard interrogation I suppose I'd have to admit to having alarmingly neat closets. And according to some critics, also a compulsion toward excessive ironing."

"Oh? I assumed that was just your upright captain's demeanor." She stretched idly. "So why *did* you enlist? Just to get off a shitcan colonial planet like me? Or was there some nobler reason?"

He smiled a bitter, cynical, wounded smile. "What is it they always say in beauty pageants? I wanted to make a difference."

"Oh," Li said. "You're one of *those*."

"Not anymore!"

They drank to that, then nursed their beers for a moment in silence.

"I take it you never were?" Llewellyn asked eventually. "There never was a save-the-world version of Catherine Li? Not even in the prehistory before the joint memories with Cohen start?"

Li snorted.

"Well, I confess I feel very inferior. But what can one do? It's probably a result of my sheltered rural upbringing. In my defense, however, it only took a decade in the Navy to get over it."

They sat over their beers in silence for a few moments. It should have been an uncomfortable silence, but it wasn't. Llewellyn might not trust her—indeed, he'd made it quite clear all along that he didn't—but he had Cohen's memories. Some vital part of him *was* Cohen. And that meant that he was the closest thing to a friend Li had left in the universe. And, in spite of all his attempts to deny it, she was the same thing to him.

"Cohen on the other hand," Llewellyn said, picking up where the conversation had left off a few moments ago, "was a hopeless world saver."

Li didn't like the *was* but she forced herself to ignore it. "Is that what he was doing when he got killed?"

"Don't you know?"

They looked at each other for a moment, each realizing that the other was after exactly the same information.

Llewellyn laughed uncomfortably. "I really thought you knew. I don't remember anything after he shipped out to New Allegheny."

"Nothing about ALEF even?"

Llewellyn looked blank for a few heartbeats, as if he was searching for a memory and not finding it where he expected it to be. Then he shook his head. "No. I know there was something going on with ALEF. And then I keep getting all these snippets that read like a math book . . . Cantor and Leibniz . . . Infinities upon infinities . . ." A curious look came over Llewellyn's face and his voice took on a singsong quality. "A tree made of numbers that grows down out of infinity and back up again."

He shook his head, snapping out of the mild fugue state he'd slipped into. "I don't know. I can't make any sense of those memories. And I asked Ike about it, too, and *he* didn't have a clue, either."

"Because it's raw feed," Li explained, recognizing a feeling she'd long been familiar with. "You're remembering stuff that happened when he was interfacing with other Emergents, at his native clocking speeds. Or more likely internal traffic between different autonomous agents within

Cohen himself. You've got the data, but you don't have the bandwidth to process it. Your mind can't grasp that, so you internalize it as memory loss."

"Is *that* what that is?" he asked curiously. "That tip-of-the-tongue feeling?"

She nodded.

"And what about the fevers? Did you get those, too?"

Li's breath caught in her chest. "Are you running fevers?"

Llewellyn didn't answer.

"You're playing with fire. You could die. Do you understand that?"

Silence.

"Come on, William! I'm not going to settle for the silent treatment. This is too important."

"I know what you want," Llewellyn said finally. His voice was tight, with anxiety or anger, she couldn't tell which. "Don't think I don't know. And don't think I don't feel for you. I do. I can even see that you have a . . . a sort of moral claim on your side." He gestured impatiently. "Why skate around the reality? I have no claim at all. I don't have a leg to stand on here. But I have this ship, and this crew. And the only thing keeping them—and me—alive is Cohen."

"Whatever's left of him." Li gave Llewellyn a long, hard look. "What *is* left of him?"

"I don't know. But whatever it is, I need it more than you do."

"Please," Li pleaded. "Please let me jack you in. Not just for my sake. For your own safety."

"I'm afraid I don't have that luxury."

"I mean it, Llewellyn. If he's actually alive—if there's any active code running on your implants, he'll eat you alive."

Llewellyn smiled. "Oh," he said with a cool, understated self-confidence that Li would have found so attractive if the circumstances weren't so infuriatingly impossible, "I don't think he'll find me so easily digestible."

There was something perverse about Llewellyn, she decided. Something not exactly broken, but . . . unhinged. He was like an engine with a broken cam shaft. You got a sense of explosive power grinding away against internal sources of friction and creating fatal damage to the mechanism instead of forward motion.

And yet he seemed to be perversely, willfully, knowingly keeping his foot on the accelerator. You could feel somehow that he would turn down all offers of rescue and ignore even the most obvious warning signs. He would never walk away from this place. There was something—pride, loyalty, stubbornness?—that ran deeper than the sarcasm and self-disgust and made it impossible.

He shifted in his chair, stretching his legs until the joints popped. "Let's talk about something else, shall we? For instance, why am I suddenly going around insulting people? I used to tolerate fools very graciously. It was one of my strong suits as a civil servant. And now I'm plagued on a daily basis by the irresistible impulse to mock and ridicule people who waste my time. Can it be that your late and lamented husband is responsible?"

Li snorted. "I can guarantee it."

"So how can someone who's four centuries old be so completely immature?"

"Practice makes perfect."

"Actually," Llewellyn admitted, "I have the vague impression of you complaining about it on a regular basis. But I don't think he took it very seriously."

"No, I don't suppose he would have." She felt herself grinning. "You wouldn't believe the things he used to get up to. Of course, *he* believed he was being totally reasonable every time." She cast a suspicious glance across the table. "Or did he? *You've* got the memories. You tell me."

"Well," Llewellyn said teasingly, "I suppose the answer would depend on which events you're referring to."

She gave him a hard look across the table. "Are you flirting with me?"

He returned her stare with a look of wide-eyed innocence. "I don't know. Should I be?"

"What are we doing here with these little dinner talks? Half the time you seem like you're trying to live up to your self-appointed role as the terror of the Drift, and the rest of the time you're practically playing footsie with me under the table."

"I certainly am not," he said mildly.

"Oh really?"

"Well, how am I supposed to speak to you? Half the time I look at you and see a stranger, and the other half . . . well, it's not a matter of seeing so much as feeling. It's as if something else is bleeding in along with the memories."

"You downloaded a sentient AI into your internals," Li pointed out. "Surely you must have expected—"

"No, I didn't. That's the funny thing. I don't suppose I ever really thought about it." He cocked his close-shorn head, looking suddenly intrigued and curious. "Do you think it's merely a matter of having accumulated a sort of critical mass of memories? Maybe the old saying is wrong. Maybe it's not contempt that familiarity breeds, but love."

"Very poetic," Li mocked.

"I don't mean it to be. I'm serious. I don't see it as having anything to do with us personally. It seems more like a simple matter of input/ output algorithms. I mean, perhaps I'd feel this way about anyone if there was enough shared data between us."

Li thought of her cool, crisp, machine-clean feelings about Router/ Decomposer. And of the creeping horror of having UNSec's semisentients foraging through her mind and memories on the few occasions when she'd been unlucky enough to encounter them in a professional capacity.

"No," she said. "Haven't you ever had a semi-sentient in your mind during a battle?"

"Oddly enough, no." His mouth quirked in something that wasn't quite a smile. "There's a reason they call me lucky."

"Well, it's not pleasant. Not when it's forced on you. And even when it isn't . . . well, it depends what the memories are. And who the people are. You wouldn't feel at all the same way if there weren't something between you and Cohen. Some commonality, some connection."

"Mmm."

"You sound disappointed by that."

"Not disappointed, just tired. In my line of work, feeling connected to people is . . . a complicating factor. And I've learned to avoid complicating factors." He shrugged. "I don't have the emotional stamina for it anymore."

Li snorted. "You sound like a man who needs to find a new line of work."

"You have no idea," he murmured.

But he wasn't looking at her. The cool, wary eyes were scanning the invisible horizon again, and the mind behind them had already drifted away into that inner solitude that she had sensed in the man from the first moment she laid eyes on him.

"You're doing it again."

"I'm sorry? Doing what?"

"Zoning out. Going away. Is it that people bore you? Or is it that you're afraid of them?"

He grinned ruefully. "Sometimes both at the same time."

Li took another swig of her beer. Llewellyn reached for his—and then stopped in mid-gesture. A blank, uncertain look crept over his face, and his eyes seemed to darken and cloud over.

"Llewellyn? Look at me. Are you running a fever now?"

"Never mind. It's not important. I shouldn't have asked."

"Shouldn't have asked what?" Li said. And then she shivered. That was AI behavior. The odd non sequitur, the long shadow of some other internal conversation looping back into real time in unpredictable ways, as if Llewellyn's mind were being pulled along by deep ocean currents that she could only measure by watching how fast they pulled him away from her.

"Don't shrug it off." She gestured at the creeping red line along the inside of his wrists and neck, which she could see clearly now that he had relaxed enough in the after-dinner hour to roll up his sleeves and unbutton his collar. "Your implant could be going toxic."

He waved off her concern with an expression that seemed to say getting sick was for lesser mortals.

"You should at least talk to Okoro about it."

"I have. He's out of his depth."

"Then talk to Cohen. He can—"

"*No!*" He paused long enough to get control of himself, and then went on more calmly. "And anyway, I'm not sick. It's just . . . a disconnect. As if I've somehow come unmoored from myself. I see all the usual things in the usual way. And yet, somehow, I don't feel about them as I would expect to feel. And *he*"—Li had begun to notice already that he resisted calling Cohen by name; it was always *he* or *the ghost* or, most unnervingly, *your husband*—"*he* seems just as far out to sea as I am."

They locked eyes again—and this time Llewellyn looked away first.

"Please," Li begged. "Please let me upload the fragment and run a check on it."

"Out of the question," he answered impatiently.

"Why? You have a choice, William. Make it while you still can."

"Don't call me that!"

"Why? Because he does?"

He didn't answer.

"And don't change the subject. You have a choice. Make it a smart one."

"What choice? The way I see it, I can either take whatever deal Cohen's offering or accept the near certainty that my entire crew is going to be blown into hard vac or hanged as pirates the next time Avery catches up to us."

"Why does she hate you so much, Llewellyn? What happened between the two of you?"

"Don't change the subject. Not until you answer my question, anyway. What other choice do you see out there? Seriously, I'm asking. Because if you have an answer to the questions I ask myself when I lie awake at night, I'd love to hear it."

But Li didn't have an answer—and this time she was the one who couldn't meet Llewellyn's eyes.

"You've seen how paranoid Doyle is about this," he said in a calmer voice. "And Sital's hanging on by sheer faith right now. What do you think they'd do if I admitted there was a problem—let alone a problem bad enough that I had to get station-side help for it?"

"You understand that you could die?"

"And then Cohen would have a healthy new body. And you'd have your husband back. I don't see why it should concern you if it doesn't worry me." His mouth twisted in a rueful smile. "Really, it would be the best of all possible solutions from your standpoint."

"No it wouldn't. I'd feel terrible about it. And so would Cohen."

"Ah, you see, now I know you're just flattering me."

"I'm not. He *would* feel terrible."

"Oh, I don't say he wouldn't feel a twinge or two. But he wouldn't be crying into his *Condrieu* about it."

Li snorted, only partly in amusement. "Do you even know what *Condrieu* is, Llewellyn?"

"Sure," he said bitterly. "I remember every vintage. That's the deal, don't you know? He gets my life, and I get an old box full of someone else's memories."

Li watched him across the table, trying to imagine what was going on inside his head, and realizing that even her own experience fell so far short of what he was going through that she had no basis for comparison. "Nothing I can say is going to make a difference, is it?"

"No." He doled out another polite, carefully calibrated smile. The real smile seemed to have gone on permanent vacation. "But it's nice of you to say it."

Li had already spent enough time around Llewellyn to know when a conversation was over. She took a last swallow of her beer and stood up.

"By the way," he said just as she hit the door. "We've got a freighter in our sights that should be in range sometime tomorrow. And you're on the boarding party."

"So you've decided you trust me after all?"

"No, I'm just running out of fighters."

"Can I assume Sital will be coming along to keep an eye on me?"

Llewellyn smiled. "Closer than skin."

(Caitlyn)

Meyer's office was beyond luxurious. It would have been ostentatious even Ring-side, but here it was surreal. Thick, deep white carpets, framed paintings and sculptures, furniture by people whose names even Li recognized. She felt like she'd walked onto the set of the movie and just had to follow the director's orders and say the lines she'd been told to say.

Wishful thinking. And the wish crashed into reality when she looked out the floor-to-ceiling picture window to a million-dollar view of Monongahela High's hab ring and saw the pirates Avery had hanged yesterday—five scuffed and worn EVA suits that you could almost imagine were empty if the news spins hadn't been running close-up footage on every channel for the entire news cycle.

Meyer didn't match his office. He looked like he ought to be fixing the plumbing instead of sitting down behind the big desk and staring at Li over steepled hands.

"I know who you are," he said when he'd gotten the preliminary staring over with. "You're that bitch that's banging Dolniak."

"Uh, well, I wouldn't jump the gun on that. So far we've only had dinner."

Meyer made an eloquent and admirably self-explanatory gesture. "Eating, fucking, what's the difference?"

Li wasn't very good at wide-eyed innocence, but she gave it the old college try anyway. "You must really like eating."

Meyer's laugh was a clever crow's cackle. "You're okay," he told her. "You're probably here to fuck me over, but you're still okay. You've got an evolved sense of humor. Drink?"

"Isn't it a little early for that?"

"That all depends on how badly you plan to fuck me over."

"I just want to talk to you, Mr. Meyer."

He grinned seductively—which Li had never imagined a fat, short, balding man with bloodhound-worthy jowls could do. "That's what all the ladies say."

"A couple of questions. And then I'll walk out the door and you'll never see me again."

The grin broadened. "And that's what all the ladies *do*."

"Well," Li allowed, "it *is* hard to find a woman with a truly evolved sense of humor."

"It's hard to find a woman with *any* sense of humor. Especially on this shithole of a planet. And especially lately." He padded over to a well-stocked wet bar—and Li noted that despite his pudge he moved like a man who needed to be taken seriously. "I'm having Scotch. You tell me what you want while I'm still standing up and I'll pour you something, too."

"Scotch sounds nice."

He snorted dismissively. "*My* Scotch *is* nice."

He brought back the drinks. "I didn't ask if you wanted ice because I don't have any, thanks to the Navy's latest clusterfuck."

"Seriously? The wild AI outbreak broke your ice machine? You must have a severe overstock of intelligent systems if you're using one to run your wet bar."

"I buy and sell AI for a living, Major. I'm swimming in the little fuckheads. And don't give me that bleeding-heart AI liberation look. You think mixing cocktails is the worst thing an AI could get stuck doing in the Drift? Not by a long shot."

He handed her the drink and stood in front of her while she raised it to her lips, taking the chance to get an unabashed closer look. Li waited patiently as his gimlet eyes traveled from the more obvious parts of female anatomy to other points of interest: the high-throughput jack behind her left ear; the glimmer of military-grade optics along the edges of her irises; the tracery of ceramsteel at wrist and neckline.

"That's actually what I want to talk to you about, Meyer. Whether you might have sold an Emergent AI to William Llewellyn to use as his NavComp."

"Well now, Major, that would be trafficking in sentient systems, wouldn't it?"

"We don't have to call it that if you don't want to."

"Damn right we don't. Because I didn't do it. And if you try to prove I did, I'll bury you in a mountain of intelligent systems trading approvals and CTC reporting forms and double-blind free-range simulations that you can spend the next ten years wading through without producing one scintilla of evidence that I broke any law on the books."

"For what it's worth, Dolniak didn't send me."

"I know that. Dolniak's a straight shooter. When he wants information from me he gets a warrant, trashes my office, and drags me downtown like a civilized cop."

"No fancy footwork from Dolniak?"

"Actually, he was a much better boxer than he is a cop. Or maybe being a cop on New Allegheny is just harder than fighting heavyweight. Still, I can see the appeal, from a woman's perspective. Steady life, three kids, boring sex. It's just that you don't seem like the three-kids, boring-sex type to me."

"How perceptive of you."

"And anyway—I'm curious, humor me—did Xenogen even give their worker clones baby-making equipment?"

Li tried not to show her surprise. Xenogen had never had any corporate creches this far from Earth, and she would have bet good money that Meyer couldn't recognize one on sight. So where had he heard that? From Dolniak? Or from someone else?

Meyer smiled, seeming to sense her confusion and to enjoy it. "No offense. I just wondered. I mean, wouldn't it be bad for business if they let the clones breed on their own?"

"Who'd buy the cow when they can get the milk for free, you mean?"

"You said it, not me," he agreed with a lascivious grin.

"Well, I guess Xenogen saw it the same way you do, because they didn't. Can we get down to business now?"

"Aren't you having fun yet? I'm having a hell of a time."

"What can you tell me about William Llewellyn?"

"What did Avery tell you?"

It took a while for the name to register, but then she made the connection: Captain Astrid Avery, the pirate hunter—a woman of savage ambition and even more savage reputation. The woman who was responsible for the row of corpses hanging from the docking gantry outside Meyer's window.

"I haven't talked to her yet. Should I?"

"Well, she's Navy. And you're . . . something."

"You think she's got the information I want?"

"She's got everything, right down to my fucking Household God. She stole him out from under me and gave me some bullshit piece of paper. I guess I should be grateful she left me a fucking chair to sit on."

"I thought the infestation trashed your house AI," Li protested, trying to catch up with the situation.

"It did. And then Avery took it."

"Did she say why?"

"No. Avery never says anything. She lets that vampire bitch Holmes do her talking for her. And Holmes said she wanted to search my client database and put me out of business, and this seemed like a quick way to do both. Charming woman, Holmes. And her boss makes her look like Little Bo Fucking Peep."

"So I keep hearing. Why does everyone hate Avery so much?"

"You mean other than the fact that she's a stone-cold killer?"

"I know a lot of stone-cold killers. Most of them are pretty passable company as long as you're not the person they're shooting at."

"Yeah, well, not Avery. And killing that poor son of a bitch ain't just a job for her, either. She's got no fucking sense of humor about it whatsoever. In fact, she's got no fucking sense of humor at all."

"Oh, I get it," Li said with an indulgent grin. "It's the old story of the girl trying to break into the boys' treehouse."

"No. It's not the treehouse thing. And by the way, thanks for your good opinion of me. It really makes my day to be called a sexist pig. It's that Avery's a fucking hypocrite. She shoves her perky little tits and her UN commission in your face, and she's full of sanctimonious bullshit about rules and procedures and the need to sacrifice for the greater good. And underneath it you know she's the worst fucking pirate of them all. I'm not saying I don't hold my nose and do business with her when I have to. And I'm not saying her money's not good. Hell, I got five kids to put through college and buy wire jobs for; I'll take anyone's money. But I still hate the bitch. And if Lucky William Llewellyn ever puts a load of lead into her with that fancy bespoke shotgun of his, he'll be able to get drunk for free at any bar in the Drift for the rest of his life."

"So," Li said into the silence that followed that ringing endorsement of UN authority, "I guess that means you're not going to tell me how to find Llewellyn?"

"Nope."

"But you could tell me when he comes into dock." She grinned, more because she hoped it would work than because she thought it would. "It'd save me from having to hang around making a pest of myself."

More stony-eyed silence.

She sighed. "I'm just asking for a little help."

"You're asking for information about the movements of a wanted man. If I was going to give you that, I'd go straight to the cops and collect the reward myself." He grinned back at her, a mocking imitation of her own grin. "Like I said, I got kids to put through college."

"Did you ever sell him a NavComp?"

"That's his business."

"And Astrid Avery's if she finds out about it."

"You think you're going to go tattle on me to Avery? Think again, clone. You don't want to rise to the level of her notice. You don't want to coexist in the same universe with her. Or her bitch vampire of a first officer. You look cross-eyed at them, and you just bought yourself a one-way ticket on a Navy press-gang."

"Okay, okay, I never said it!"

"Yeah, whatever." Meyer lifted the glass of Scotch from between her fingers with the dexterity of a pickpocket. "Don't take it personal, but I don't want to drink with you anymore. And anyway, you're wasting your time buttering me up. Llewellyn blew out of here with hell on his tail two months ago."

"You sure he won't be back?"

Meyer gestured toward the window and the pathetic row of dangling EVA suits. "Would you?"

Ten minutes later Li was out of Meyer & Sons Marine Auctioneers and back in the station's crowded public corridors. As on every trip to the orbital station she was struck by the heavy military presence. Some were Peacekeepers and security contractors cold-shipped in to jumpstart the machinery of the Trusteeship, but most were Navy, on leave from the orbital shipyards. They gave the place the feel of a port town in wartime. And they gave Li the feeling that a dozen pairs of sharp eyes were boring into an invisible spot smack dab between her shoulder blades.

At some point she realized consciously what her instincts had been telling her for several minutes; it wasn't just a feeling. Someone really was watching her.

She stopped in front of a noodle joint and gazed into its steamed-up windows until she caught a flicker of movement that seemed to swirl against the surrounding crowd instead of flowing with it.

She turned—and looked across the concourse straight into the phlegmatic gaze of Astrid Avery's first mate.

"Holmes, isn't it?" she asked, stepping toward the woman.

"That's right."

"You following me?"

"That sort of thing's a little below my pay grade."

"So I can just write this encounter down to lucky chance?"

"Not entirely. We keep a pretty close watch on Ben Meyer. Just a matter of taking sensible precautions." Holmes smiled without showing her teeth. "I suppose I can guess why you were talking to him this morning. Did you get anything out of him?"

"No. He was too scared of Avery to talk to me."

Holmes's smile broadened into a full-out grin. She had unusually white and slightly crooked teeth with curiously long canines.

"You like the idea of civilians being afraid of you?"

"It's not whether I like it or not. It's whether it's useful."

Li stared at the other woman, but she didn't flinch. Li was starting to suspect that Holmes had less flinch in her than anyone she'd ever met.

"Let me give you a piece of advice, little girl." Holmes spoke evenly, almost gently. But there was something about the woman that made her mere presence menacing. "Go home while you still can. Don't make us decide we have to notice you."

(Caitlyn)

THE PIT

"You're going to do something crazy now, aren't you?" Router/Decomposer asked through the hotel livewall when Li stormed back into their room straight off the station-to-surface shuttle.

He'd been trying to talk to her all the way down on the shuttle, and during the taxi ride, too. But New Allegheny's noosphere had turned into a jigsaw puzzle of blind spots and bandwidth bottlenecks because of the wild AI infestation—or, as Router/Decomposer had cynically suggested more than once, because of the Trusteeship Administration's incompetent attempts to fight it. So it was getting easier and easier to avoid talking to him. Still, he'd picked up enough of her conversations with Meyer and Holmes to know that she hadn't gotten what she wanted. And he knew Li well enough to be worried about what kind of Plan B she'd come up with if left to her own devices.

She settled herself on the platform bed, lotus-style, and stripped off her shirt. The hotel's climate control had held out a little longer than the police station systems, but it was down now, too. And it was amazing how hot it could get even under the constant fug of the Crucible.

"Will you please talk to me, Catherine? You're about to do something so stupid you don't even want to tell me about it, and I'm going to get stuck watching from the sidelines and trying to pick up the pieces later."

She dove into streamspace and slipped through the back door that Router/Decomposer had already installed in the hotel's intelligent systems, and began a systematic search for every open port into the information systems of Meyer's auction house.

"You really have to learn to take no for an answer," Router/ Decomposer told her, as soon as he saw what she was up to.

"Don't like nofrinanser," she answered absentmindedly, pronouncing it as if it were some prescription medicine he was foisting on her. "It's got a nasty aftertaste."

He didn't laugh. They both knew that she was daring him to stop her. And they both knew that he wouldn't stop her. Cohen would have. But Router/Decomposer didn't have it in him to bring the hammer down. And though Li should have respected him for his moral qualms, the truth was . . . she didn't.

"All right," he said. "Do what you're going to do anyway. I'm just going to say one thing about it. You think Cohen would never have killed himself without figuring out some way to come back to you."

"I never said—"

"You didn't have to say. It's hovering behind every fight we have about this. You think he owed it to you—"

"You're goddamn right he di—"

She broke off, horrified by what she'd just said.

"You think he owed it to you to come back because you would have done the same for him. And that's fine. I think he owed it to you, too. I don't know what the fuck he thought he was doing out here, or how he got himself into whatever trouble he was in. But here's the thing I'd just like you to think about. You keep saying we're out here because he would never have killed himself. But is that really why you're doing this? Or is it because you can't figure out how to forgive him if he *did* kill himself?"

Li glared up at the buzzing livewall speaker, stone-faced, as if Router/ Decomposer were somehow *inside* the wall and she could pierce through the paint and plaster to stare him into submission.

But her insides were roiling and her ears were filled with shrieking, howling static. And the only words that she could scrape together would have been a mocking, humiliating admission that he was right.

She went back to work because she couldn't think of anything else to do.

"You shouldn't have let me drag you into this," she said after a while. But he didn't answer. Then or later. She couldn't even tell if he was still listening.

Li spent the rest of that day trying to crack Meyer's database. She kept trying as the daytime twilight of Pit bottom darkened to true night outside her window. She kept trying long after it was obvious that she wasn't getting anywhere. She didn't ask herself why she put so much into it. She didn't really want to know the answer, which she suspected had less to do with professional pride than with the memory of Holmes's long, white, gleaming canines.

Finally she gave up, stretching in her chair until her spine crackled. Router/Decomposer was still gone, either sulking or offline. Just as well, she told herself, suppressing the twinge of guilt she felt about it before it could blossom into anything she'd really have to deal with.

She went to the dresser and opened the carefully wrapped package she'd picked up during her last trip to Shadyside. All of the tools in the little cloth roll had numerous perfectly legal and legitimate uses, but that wouldn't have fooled Dolniak if he'd gotten a look at them. And it wouldn't fool security on the dirt-to-station shuttle, either. So Li stashed the little packet at the bottom of an innocuous-looking shoulder bag and then went into the immense tiled bathroom and took a long, hard look in the mirror. Innocent civilian was utterly beyond her reach, she decided, so she settled for the next best thing, and spent a tedious half hour massaging her exterior into something that she hoped would say cash-flush security contractor instead of . . . well, whatever she was these days.

She made it on-station without mishap. By the time the dinner hour was winding to a close and the bars and nightclubs were starting to heat up, Li was standing in a darkened public access corridor that abutted the rear boundaries of Meyer's warehouse.

She tried the door—more for form's sake than because she actually thought she'd get anywhere with it—and then she started down the long curve of the hab ring along the internal wall dividing the auction house's ample square footage from the public corridor.

It didn't take her long to find what she'd been hoping to find:

A window.

It was a funny thing about windows. Humans just couldn't resist them. Li had noticed during the war that Syndicate habitat rings didn't have internal windows. As in so many other ways, Syndicate constructs had adapted to life in space more completely than the UN citizenry—both physiologically and psychologically. But humans weren't there yet. They wanted windows. And not just windows onto stars and the void. They wanted lights and action and breathable air outside their windows. And, annoying though it was to security types, they usually wanted those windows to open.

Li grinned to herself, unrolled her tools, and carefully selected the appropriate one from the bunch. Then she set to work jimmying the lock.

She might have been concentrating a little too hard on it, but even in retrospect she didn't think so. The guard caught her flat-footed not because she'd forgotten to keep a lookout, but because he really was good at his job. Which, in retrospect, was her big mistake. Meyer might joke about the nonessentials, but she should have known he wouldn't fool around when it came to hiring security.

The guard was old, though, pushing fifty. If he hadn't already drawn by the time she turned around she probably could have handled him. But he had. And she couldn't.

She looked her captor over, assessing her options. Clean-cut and clean-shaven, with the razor burn to prove it. Cheap haircut, cheap clothes, cheap everything. Government-issue shoes. Built like an ox and carrying fifteen pounds of flab on top of two hundred pounds of street fighter's muscle. Flat, expressionless face. Eyes that had seen it all for so long that they didn't even remember what being shocked felt like.

Christ, Li thought. *Another cop.* Or an ex-cop. Or a rent-a-cop. Or some kind of cop.

"Grab the wall, sweet pea."

She did it, and was frisked and handcuffed with bored efficiency. When he had disarmed her, he stepped back to a good, safe distance and cocked his head curiously—but still with that same flat, expressionless face, so that the gesture seemed choreographed. Or maybe it was just habit—the habit of curiosity hanging on long after he'd seen more of the world than any sane person would ever want to see. "Wanna tell me what you're doing here?"

She fed him her prepackaged story.

"Oh," he said when she'd finished. Pleasantly, as if she'd cleared everything up nicely and wasn't he glad about it. "You must think I'm as dumb as I look. I'm not. And I may be a rent-a-cop, but that's only 'cause the union sold us down the river twenty years ago and my pension's a piece of shit. So try again, sweetcakes. And give me the real story if you don't want your teeth knocked in. I've been on my feet for fourteen hours, and these fuckheads don't pay overtime."

(Catherine)

The cargo spindle howled toward the *Christina*, hogging deep into the gravity well. It was an impossible monster of a craft, no match for the hard g's of dogfights or gravity wells. It was little more than a sub-luminal coatrack: a bare-bones frame on which any shipping companies willing to pay fuel and port fees could hang all the cargo containers they wanted to get from one system to another without anyone looking too closely at their contents.

The cargo was nothing—most of it was either worthless altogether or unsellable by wanted men. But there would be a crew, and a few paying passengers. And they would need air and water. And after the last mauling encounter with the *Ada*, the *Christina* was officially running joker: low on fuel, low on air, low on drinking water, with all nonessential life support systems shut down to conserve scarce resources. So air and water were things worth fighting for.

Sital eyed the spindle with a speculative gleam in her eye. "You think they're running joker, too?"

Llewellyn's eyes narrowed, and the gazes of half a dozen bridge officers turned toward the monitor. Li could feel the sudden charge in the air as the pirates sensed a possible vulnerability.

"That'd be awful risky," Llewellyn pointed out. "What do they do if we call their bluff?"

"Maybe they figure we'd drag them back out of the gravity well for salvage."

"That's assuming we have enough fuel ourselves. And what if we didn't?"

Now it was Sital's turn to shrug. "In that case, they're fucked anyway, aren't they?"

Llewellyn cocked his head, listening to the ghost. It drove Catherine crazy knowing that Cohen—or at least part of him—was right here in the room with her, talking to Llewellyn. And that she was locked out of the conversation. She didn't think it was simple jealousy. She'd never thought of herself as the jealous type, really. But then she was starting to wonder if she knew herself quite as well as she'd always thought she did.

"The ghost says they've already passed their optimal break point. He agrees with you. He thinks they're out of fuel and hoping to hitch a ride on us."

Sital grinned. It was a quick, tight grin, and it looked strangely ferocious on her buttoned-down navigator's face.

"You know," she murmured. "I could almost start to like this guy."

Twelve minutes later Li was crushed into an airlock with as many other pirates as could be shoehorned in alongside her, watching the final approach to target.

Everyone around her was tense, wired, and waiting. Most of them had the classic "hearing his master's voice" look of people ignoring reality because there was something running on their internal optical feeds that they just couldn't stop looking at. With a start, Li remembered that she had full crew member privileges now and could look at it as easily as they could.

Li tensed, too, her muscles and nerves readying themselves for the explosive push of the hand-to-hand fighting ahead, but she felt strangely disconnected from it all. She knew that the real heart of the battle lay elsewhere. The real fight was already under way, and it was between the two AIs, with their human crews as mere pawns and auxiliaries.

As the two craft approached each other, the two AIs would be testing each other, each feeling out the other's open ports and hidden vulnerabilities. And as the ships grappled up and the two crews started battling for control of the boarding umbilicals, the AIs would be grappling with each other in their own silent but equally violent battle.

Li had some access to the *Christina*'s systems; she wasn't completely locked out, as she had been during the Titan raid. But her view of the conflict was distant and attenuated and lagged far behind the realtime pace of combat.

She wondered about that. She wondered how well she would be able to fight with the attenuated, distant, secondhand news of the battle that was the best Llewellyn was willing to give her. And she wondered how well Cohen could really fight, given the short leash Llewellyn always kept him on. Both she and Cohen seemed to be caught in a strange limbo, half pirate, half prisoner. They were needed but they were not trusted. She thought of McPherson, who had vanished into the Deep without a trace after that one cold, quiet look from Llewellyn's untrusting eyes. It gave her a bad feeling, the memory of that look. And now, wailing in from the entry point in a sputtering flare of incompatible Hilbert spaces, she realized what it was that so frightened her about it: The greatest prize pirates could seize in a raid wasn't cargo or air, but intelligent systems. So once Llewellyn captured a shipboard AI that could navigate the Drift well enough to keep his neck out of the hangman's noose, what would happen to Cohen?

She switched her optical feed to the ship's forward sensor array. It felt like being stripped naked and strapped to the ship's bow. The Drift pulsed and flowed around her in the psychedelic hues of the false-color imaging that was more real to most Drift runners—because they spent more time looking at it—than the invisible reality outside the windows. Within and behind the Drift the sky was shredded by streaking pinwheels of blue- and red-shifted light: the stars of the deep field, spun into a carnival light show by a NavComp that was too focused on the fleeing ship in its sights to run the deep field imaging calculations that would have adjusted for their chaotic tumble through space.

Their prey was two thousand kilometers ahead of them—or five human heartbeats away from them, given the blistering speed at which both ships were hurtling through the system. Li had only the vaguest amateur's grasp of naval tactics, but even she could see that the fleeing captain had realized his rescuers were anything but—and was doing everything to escape from their clutches that the cold, hard laws of gravity and fuel consumption would allow.

The system's star was a tired-looking brown dwarf with a string of planets flung out along its ecliptic plane. It was a scant two million kilometers away, and the freighter was steering a course that would take it deep into the clutches of the sun's gravity well. His line of approach would slingshot him around the star, with the pirate ship close on his heels. And when they came around on the backside—in the brief window of time when the raging magnetic storm of the sun obscured both ships' sensors—he would fling his ship off the ecliptic in a brutal change of course.

At that delta-V, even a slight deviation in heading would send the two ships hurtling apart so quickly that it could take hours or even days for the pirates to get back into attack position again. Time for help to arrive, or for the freighter captain to limp to the closest entry point.

The faces of the boarding party around her reflected the same realization she had just reached: If the freighter made it to the star before they caught him, the game was off and they were going to have to keep running on empty until another ship drifted into their kill zone.

Li thought of Llewellyn and Sital up on the bridge. And Cohen locked in the nebulous mazes of the NavComp like a genie in a Klein bottle. Obviously they must all be pushing the ship and themselves to the breaking point. But still the gap between them and the freighter was closing with agonizing slowness. They would close the gap, eventually, with mathematical certainty; the *Christina*'s flaring ram-scoops could boost her through accelerations that no tramp freighter could even contemplate. The only question was whether they would run out of turf before they won the race.

The curve of the star's mantle was now a looming monstrosity.

Intercept in four hundred seconds, the ship murmured.

On the externals Li could see the mooring lines freeing themselves from the hull. They groped toward the fleeing freighter like the tentacles of some silver-carapaced sea monster, their bulbous ends pulsing

with an obscene sucking motion. It was hard to imagine them as machine rather than organism. It was also hard to imagine that they could
actually be strong enough to hold an entire ship captive.

"How do the grapples work?" Li asked the pirate next to her.

"Monkey shit. Standard salvage nano."

Mooring lines out, the ship murmured. Li switched her optic feed
to externals and saw them closing in on the hapless freighter, chasing it
along the slow curve of the star's vast gravity well. Sixty-eight meters
off docking position. Five . . . four . . . three . . .

And clang. The two ships came together, ricocheted off each other,
and bounced back, held by the nano-grapples.

"Heave to!" came the call, and the umbilical snaked between the two
ships to grip the outer airlock door of their prey with biomorphic fingers. This was a thing Li had never seen before—Syndicate tech, stolen
on some earlier raid—and she watched in disgusted fascination as the
froglike digits suckered onto the other ship, insinuated themselves into
its vulnerable crevices, and forced it open.

The fighting was hard and merciless. The cargo spindle's crew had
decided to fight, God only knew why. And for the AIs it was always a
battle to the death, with no quarter given. So they fought down clang-
ing galleyways and maintenance tunnels, inch by bloody inch. At first
they fought for the things they'd started the fight over—air, water, a
sheltering hull between soft bodies and hard vacuum. And then they
fought to win, never mind what. And then they fought not to die.

Li could tell when the tide of the battle turned, because she could
see her fellow pirates fall around her. There was something particularly
appalling about the way an AI killed. You could reason until you were
blue in the face that it was a death in battle just like getting hit point
blank with a shotgun blast. But then you actually saw it happen. You
saw the blank look come over a friend's face. You saw the body go slack
and slump to the floor. You watched them flatline on your head-up
display, without getting off a shot, without any warning, without a
chance even to defend or avenge themselves.

And suddenly, no matter what you told yourself, it didn't feel like
seeing someone die in battle. It felt like watching an execution. And you

stopped thinking of your own shipboard AI as a soldier—and started hearing the voice of an executioner every time it spoke to you.

Despite all their training and discipline, the pirates lapsed into confusion when the tide of the battle turned on them. There was a moment of collective paralysis, long enough for two more men to die in. And then the sudden flash of comprehension.

Avery.

The word whispered along the head-up channel, and then quickened to a panicked drumbeat. A moment later someone locked onto the feed of the ship's external sensors and threw that up on the channel, and they could all see the vicious silver needle of the *Ada* slicing out of the asteroid belt of the system's second planet, where she'd been holding at cold iron, all systems powered down, to trick them into dismissing her as just another lump of steel-rich rock.

And then it wasn't even a fight anymore—let alone the easy victory it should have been. Then it was just a bunch of frightened people running for their lives.

Li was almost at the boarding umbilical when the *Ada* finally got to her.

One minute she was in realspace, laying down covering fire for a leapfrogging retreat and hoping the newer recruits' nerves would hold long enough to complete the maneuver. The next moment she was sandboxed in some streamspace blackout zone, dangling in midair, hanging from the jaws of something that her rational mind knew must be the cargo spindle's semi-sentient but that had her primate backbrain screaming about saber-toothed tigers.

The spindle's semi-sentient was old, out of date, badly in need of software upgrades. Li held it off, standing her ground and praying that rescue would get there before she ran through her limited bag of tricks. She had almost made it, too, when the other semi-sentient showed up.

This one was an entirely different creature. Where it came from, she had no idea. But what it was, she knew instantly: a Navy AI, barely conscious by human standards but honed and specialized for combat and endowed with enough processing capacity to peel enemy systems open like sardine cans.

Serial? she queried.

C521-009.

Whois?

UNSS *Ada, Countess Lovelace.*

"Oh shit," Li gasped. A vision flickered across her optic nerve and thrummed along her backbrain: a vast, limbless, sightless something cutting through the Deep like a shark scenting blood in the water. Her vision flared and guttered as the semi-sentient throttled her bandwidth and wiped away the vestigial sense that was the last thing tying her to her sanity in the vast nothingness of inner space. She sank screaming into the strangling darkness.

And then there was light, and more darkness. And just as suddenly as it had arrived, C521-009 was gone.

Li drifted in some primordial inner sea, sightless, helpless, without the will or strength to help herself. She could have been floating in the viral gel of a rehab tank. But this wasn't the cool, familiar processing darkness that she knew from a lifetime of upgrades, buffering pauses, and lagging uploads. This was a fleshly darkness, suffused with life, like the blood red of looking through your closed eyelids at the bright sunlight. And there was something close and claustrophobic about it, a living, breathing presence to it that made the hair on the back of her neck rise and all of her primate instincts scream out that there was a predator behind her.

The danger, when it came, was subtler than that. It wasn't a predator at all, but a friend and lover. A friend and lover that wore one of Cohen's favorite faces. He couldn't be real, she told herself. There was no piece of Cohen on Avery's ship. There was nothing and no one on the *Ada* that wasn't a deadly enemy. But no matter what she told herself, she couldn't deny the vision that filled her eyes, the voice speaking in her ear, the touch that sparked a thousand memories. This was Cohen himself—so real, so present, so undeniable that she began to wonder if it was Llewellyn's ship that was speaking to her, rather than Avery's.

"Who are you?" she asked the living silence that surrounded her.

"You tell me."

"I don't know," she whispered.

But what she really wanted to say was, *Be who I want you to be.*

But then if he really was Cohen—or any meaningful part of Cohen—that was exactly what he would do anyway. He would be who she wanted him to be. Or, failing that, he would be whoever he had to be to make her care about him, make her connect with him, make her come back to him. And there was no way to know if the centuries-old game of the affective loop that Hy Cohen had programmed into his most primitive and essential systems was being played by a friend or an enemy.

The darkness pressed around her like flesh, warm and rich and at once claustrophobic and comforting. Then her optic nerve began firing, slaved into whatever alternate reality that AI was feeding it. Light washed over her: the clear golden light of Earth, flickering through moving greenery and shimmering over running water.

And just like that, she was in Cohen's memory palace—a database that no semi-sentient slaved into a Navy ship could possibly have summoned.

She stood in a long courtyard whose enclosing colonnades echoed the tumbling slope of the rocky mountaintop beyond the encircling battlements. The walls of the courtyard itself were more art than engineering: a masterpiece of the mosaicist's craft, a self-contained universe of fingernail-sized terra-cotta zellige arranged in stars and circles, sunbursts and octagons.

Cohen had loved the mosaics, not just the images but their history and the symbolism. He had known the names of all the patterns, keeping them in active memory the way AIs did for things they cared about or thought about or worried over. And indeed, they were names worth remembering, rich names that mingled the high art of the geometrician with the earthy lexicon of the tile mason to form a cryptic kind of poetry: Fifty from Eight; Empty and Full; Four Clasped Hands; the Spider's House.

The tiles shimmered and shifted under the human eye, half mirage, half optical illusion. Lines led to other lines, circles overlapped with stars made of triangles that dissolved into smaller triangles. All dividing, all echoing, all repeating themselves in infinite recursion. A millennium ago, North African geometricians had painstakingly devised those starlike patterns to symbolize the infinite mysteries of a god whose true name was beyond human knowing. But here they mapped a different universe: the disembodied patterns of networks and data caches. Each tile and tree and fountain—every object in the memory palace—was a Cantor module, a virtual power set containing uncountable infinities of infinities.

Cohen had once made her stand against this very wall, her arms outspread like wings, in order to tell her that the imaginary square circumscribed by her outstretched fingertips contained some eight thousand precisely cut and painted tiles. She tried to calculate the number of tiles in the entire courtyard, and her mind rebelled against the astronomical, impersonal vastness of the number.

And every one of those tiles was a memory, and every one of those memories had been as real and immediate and alive to Cohen as any moment in Li's own brief and imperfectly remembered life was to her.

She tried to think through her limited knowledge of the system, looking for some crumb of useful information. But Cohen had always talked about the mathematics of his internal databases in a way that made their internal organization sound more aesthetic than logical. It was set theory taken to overwhelming extremes: Let it into your brain and you were down the rabbit hole, lost in Cantor's lush paradise of infinities.

He had said something else about the tiles as well, something strange and suggestive and riddling. And when Cohen spoke in riddles, it was a good bet that he was saying something that mattered to him.

Li searched her memory, wishing vainly that it was as solid and reliable as the shimmering screen of mosaics.

And the walls became the world all around, Cohen had told her. She could see him now, leaning against a blue-and-white-tiled pilaster, giving her a long, sideways look out of the hazel eyes of a body he'd favored in the first summer of their marriage. And that night the trees grew and grew in Max's room, and the ceiling hung with vines, and the walls became the world all around.

Between the shimmering fractals of the courtyard's walls ran a long, slender, geometrically precise line of water. The watercourse flowed from a burbling fountain just at Li's feet, down the long slope of the courtyard, and into an identical fountain and a matching arcade. The water sparkled as it flowed from shadow to sunlight and back into shadow again. Its movement was hypnotic, mesmerizing; and as Li gazed into the crystal blue she saw that every ripple, every eddy, every molecule was a memory. Everything in and around and above and below the courtyard was a memory. The tiles were memories. The trees were memories that branched into the limbs and twigs, leaves and flowers. Memories haunted the shadowed rooms that stood still and empty around the courtyard, ranked like loyal family retainers in a fairy-tale castle cursed to eternal sleep. Even the sky was a memory, lifetimes upon lifetimes shading away into blue infinity.

She read the memories with the instinctive speed of the sensory interface. But when she dropped beneath that, slipping into the numbers, she could see that her eyes had not been fooling her. No other AI could fake this place. Not even ALEF, with all its power, could have done it. And certainly no lone Navy ship on the outskirts of UN space could manage it.

This was home—as much as any physical place in her co-penetrating real and virtual lives was home. This was Cohen. Or at least it was the part of him that could be contained in the virtually infinite, folded databases that contained his four centuries and many lifetimes of accumulated memories.

It took everything she had to remind herself that, real or not, Cohen's memories belonged to others now. And those others could use the memories for their own purposes, and in ways that might be completely antithetical to everything Cohen had ever stood for. For the first time, facing the otherworldly beauty of Cohen's memory palace, Li understood what it meant to be unable to die. And for the first time, facing the unearthly beauty of Cohen's past, and knowing that Cohen himself was nowhere inside it, Li understood the real curse of immortality.

Cohen might not inhabit his memories anymore, but someone still lived here. And that someone might be the very person who had murdered him.

Li walked cautiously down the length of the courtyard, her feet slipping on the wet tiles where the watercourse had overlapped its boundaries. There was no sound, no movement, no sign of life anywhere. But she could feel in every cell of her being that the palace was not empty. And whoever now inhabited it was no unfamiliar and easy enemy. The new soul of the database was both Cohen and not Cohen, both lover and stranger, both friend and enemy.

Under the far arcade, she found the first sign of life: a silk shawl, six feet on each side, as soft as cashmere, and woven into a dense, rich, intricate paisley. It was an item of unimaginable luxury, something that had no place here and would have been a museum piece worth the price of entire planets if it were real rather than virtual. It was the kind of thing Cohen would have admired but never worn. To Li's bemused eyes it seemed unimaginably far from the living, breathing AIs of her world, and more like the sort of detritus an elegant Victorian lady might have left in her wake . . . along with tastefully arranged flowers, painted fans, and discreetly engraved calling cards.

Li should never have picked it up. She should have left it where she found it, safely untouched. Everything was code in a memory palace. Even the most innocent object could contain hidden programs, executables, viruses. And something like this practically screamed danger at her. But it was cold, and growing late, and the sky was dark with an oncoming storm. And some half-conscious premonition told her that she might be stuck here overnight—and that the heating might not be up to its usual standard.

She wrapped the shawl around herself and stepped into the shadows.

She found bits and pieces of the ghost before she found the ghost itself. An empty glass. A half-read copy of *Jane Eyre* with page 247 folded down into a precise triangle. A lady's purse—a sort of arts and crafts project, also abandoned midway through—made of what Li was pretty sure the nineteenth-century society women in Cohen's old novels had called netting.

And then, abruptly, she turned a corner and came face-to-face with the person to whom—she had no doubt about this whatsoever—the shawl and the book and the purse belonged.

It was a woman, pale-skinned, dark-haired, strong of jaw and straight of spine, dressed in expensive, uncomfortable-looking clothes that hadn't been in fashion for at least six centuries. And she wasn't Cohen at all. Li was quite sure about that, though she could never have said how she knew it. She just knew, without hesitation or question, that this was no one who had ever been a part of Cohen.

"Who are you?" the woman asked her.

"Catherine Li."

"And I am the Lady Ada, Countess Lovelace."

"Oh," Li said stupidly.

"Li," the Countess repeated. "That's a strange name. And you . . . are you from China?"

"Um . . . Korea. Sort of. It's complicated."

"Everything here is complicated."

"That's one way of putting it."

"At first I thought I had imagined it. I'm a mathematician, you see. And—well, this probably won't make sense to you at all, but . . . this entire palace is a sort of mathematical puzzle."

"Oh?" Li said weakly, feeling the conversation slide sideways at a speed too fast for any hope of recovery.

"I actually wrote a whole book about—" She broke off and looked away, as if distracted by an event taking place on some plane of the folded database Li had no access to. "Oh, never mind. That's not the point. The point is—Where are we? And why have you brought me here?"

"I haven't. I was brought here, too."

"So we're both prisoners." The countess's white shoulders slumped despairingly. "And you can't help me after all."

Li started to answer—and then lapsed into silent confusion. The memory palace was shifting around the ghost, its familiar contours suddenly gone feral. Another building was superimposed on the one they stood in, as if there were a second shadow universe hovering behind the other one like a face hidden behind a carnival mask.

"What's happening?" the ghost cried.

"I don't kn—"

"You do know!" The woman stamped imperiously. "I won't be lied to!"

"I'm not—"

"Do you think I don't hear them? Do you think I don't know what they whisper in the corridors after the doctor goes and they think the morphine has sucked me under? Do you think I don't know they're lying to me?"

"I don't have anything to do with—"

The woman was plucking at her clothes now, in a distraught, self-mutilating gesture that reminded Li of the way she'd seen dying men pluck at themselves on the battlefield.

"Am I a child, to be treated this way? Am I a madwoman? This brain has built worlds of numbers! This body has made two whole human beings out of nothing! Don't I deserve better than this?"

"I—yes," Li said, not knowing what else to say and afraid of what the woman would do to herself.

The Dark Lady stepped toward her in a heavy rustle of silk. She smelled of perfume and medicine and something worse . . . something that turned Li's stomach and sent her mind flashing back to the worst weeks of the slaughter on Gilead.

"Will you help me?" the woman whispered, grasping Li's arm with the feverish, convulsive grip of an invalid.

"I'll try."

"Then tell me the truth!"

"I don't know—"

"Don't lie to me! You're no better than they are! Smothering me, lying to me, imprisoning me. You think I haven't seen blood before? You think my mind and my body are too feeble for this? I've borne two children! You think I can't tell my womb is eating me from the inside out?"

Suddenly she fell silent, her rage spent, and shrank into herself.

"They think they're being kind, of course. But I don't want to be lied to. Do you see? I want the truth. I want to know. I want to prepare myself. I want . . ."

And gently, gently, she took hold of her dress and pulled aside the rich layers of silk and brocade to reveal the yawning, rotting, stinking chasm of the womb beneath them.

Li gagged and took an involuntary step backward.

"You're going to see Llewellyn, aren't you?"

"I—"

Li stopped and stared. The body in front of her was changing, flickering back and forth as Ada's projected proprioceptive architecture—her own image of herself—cycled through confused, contradictory iterations. First the woman. Then the horrible sharklike thing that Li recognized as the deformed and half-mad embodiment of a malfunctioning military-grade semi-sentient. Then the sleek silver spire of the ship itself. And then—

"Tell him—tell him I forgive him. I just want him to come and see me. I won't hurt him. I promise. I just want to know why he did it. Don't I have a right to know why?"

And suddenly it wasn't Ada talking. It was Cohen. And Li was face-to-face with the one person she would have known through any shunt or avatar or disguise.

She reached for him—but it was too late already. The rot was spreading, swelling, devouring everything around them. It devoured the ceiling and the beams that supported it, and the roof that crashed down around their ears, and the sky above them. It chewed up the floor beneath their feet. And then it began to devour Li herself . . .

The walls blackened and curled in on themselves like burning paper. Her vision tunneled and her lungs began to smart and sting with lack of air.

"Cohen! Cohen!"

Some rough force jerked her up and backward. She struggled, writhing and scratching, got free, scrambled away, and was caught again.

"*No!*"

And the memory palace was gone, annihilated, blotted out of existence as completely and instantaneously as it had sprung to life in the first place. Wherever she had been was gone. And whoever had been there with her was gone, too. She was lying on the deck of the twisting umbilical cord, halfway back to the pirate ship, her head and one arm in Sital's lap as the other woman dragged her out of the target ship by sheer force.

"Avery," Sital gasped. "Avery's ship was dark-side all along. She came in, almost got us. Got you." *Drag, huff, drag.* "Okay?"

"I guess."

"You see Ada in there?"

"I—guess."

Li got her feet under herself and scrambled along the umbilical beside Sital. As they waited in the airlock, both still panting slightly, Sital turned to her.

"What did she say to you?"

"I don't even know, really."

"She hurt you?"

"Tried to."

"You got off lucky, then. She's a stone-cold killer."

(Caitlyn)

Dolniak showed up the next morning to spring her from jail. He looked like he hadn't gotten much sleep the night before. And he looked very, very angry.

Much too angry, actually, given how predictable it should have been that she would manage to find some kind of trouble to get into.

"What's wrong?" Li asked when they brought her into the interrogation room and pushed her into the chair that faced Dolniak across the usual battered table.

"I don't know. What do you think?"

"I mean, what else is wrong?"

He looked as if he was about to chew her out for a moment. But then he visibly reined himself in, he shrugged, stood up . . . and walked out of the room, closing the door behind him in an ostentatiously careful way that made it completely clear he was stopping himself from slamming it.

He came back ten long minutes later, with a station-side cop to handle the paperwork. She was fingerprinted, DNA-swiped, and released into his custody. He didn't talk to her during the processing, or during the walk to the shuttle, or on the ride down.

"Where are we going?" Li asked when he gave the taxi driver a Shadyside address instead of directing him to her hotel.

"You'd know better than I would," he said in a tone of smoldering fury.

After that she decided to just keep her mouth shut.

———

He took her to a flophouse deep in the permanent twilight of Shady-side. This one made the boardinghouse Korchow had been holed up in look like a palace. And the carnage on the floor and walls in the upstairs back room made Li put a hand to her mouth and swallow hard. The body on the floor was covered with a chaste white sheet. But the stains oozing through the sheet—and the gore on the walls—made it clear that this hadn't been a quick or painless death.

"We found your next yard sale buyer," Dolniak said, indicating the body sprawled on the floor by the bed.

"How do you know?"

"Couple of reasons. One, look at the back of his head."

"Can I, uh . . ." She gestured to the sheet covering the body.

"Go ahead. We've already got what we need."

She lifted the sheet. The body had fallen facedown and the first thing she noticed was that the head was intact. "No forced download?"

"No. That's the thing that doesn't fit here. This victim wasn't wired at all."

Li felt a shiver of apprehension. "Can I get a look at the face?" she asked.

Dolniak turned the corpse over, lifting it as easily as if it were a rag doll.

Korchow's face looked different in death. Smoother, less cynical. More like the Syndicate construct he was and less like the human he'd passed for in life.

"You know him," Dolniak said.

"Yeah."

"Sorry."

"Don't be. We weren't exactly friends. He was a Syndicate spy."

Dolniak started. "You mean he's not human?"

"No."

"He looks human enough."

"He's KnowlesSyndicate. They're diplomats and spies. They need to be able to talk to humans to do their work. And sometimes they need to be able to pass as human."

Dolniak appeared to consider this for a moment. "But if he's a construct, then you might not know him after all. Isn't that right? This could just be another construct from the same geneline."

"I doubt it."

"You can't be sure, though."

But she could be sure, Li realized, as the memory of a sunny spring morning during wartime welled up in her mind. The memory wasn't pristine, unlike that long-ago morning. It had been washed and spun and redacted so many times that it was impossible to tell now what was real and what was just UNSec ass-covering. But she'd seen the scar twice in the years since—years during which UNSec hadn't had access to her hard memory. And Korchow had told her things about that morning that no one who wasn't there could possibly have known.

She bent down and pulled aside the collar of his shirt. And there it was. A long, jagged scar, healed badly, that snaked down the side of his neck and over his collarbone.

"It's him," she said.

"You know the scar? You're sure about that?"

"Sure as death." She laughed, sharp and bitter. "I gave it to him."

Dolniak looked at her across the dead body, and his expression managed to convey more contradictory feelings than Li would have thought such a quiet face could contain.

"I'm going to need your NavComp logs for the relevant time frame," he told her. "Not that they mean anything. I'm sure you know how to fake them in ways a simple country mouse like me wouldn't even imagine."

"Guess that still leaves you stuck with good old-fashioned country mouse detective work."

"Yeah. I'm good at it, in case you hadn't noticed."

"I'm glad. Plenty of guys would already have locked me up and thrown away the key."

Before she could answer him, there was a bustle in the hallway and the coroner arrived. He greeted Dolniak with easy familiarity, spared a brief, incurious glance for Li, and began laying out his tools on the floor next to the body. He was wired—of course he would be—and as he bent over, Li got a glimpse of an angry rash around his input/output socket. It startled her. Other than listening to Router/Decomposer's complaints about throttling and slow load times, she hadn't been paying nearly enough attention to the progress of the wild AI outbreak on New Allegheny itself. Partly, she now realized, because the only organic on New Allegheny she'd had much contact with was Dolniak. And being wired was so normal in her world that it was always an effort to realize that he was unwired, and thus far more resistant to the outbreak than most people.

She suppressed an instinctive urge to step back from the coroner—and instead forced herself to consider the outbreak from his perspective. To ALEF and the privileged AIs of the inner worlds, wild AI was a threat that undermined their attempts to prove that organic and artificial citizens could coexist without conflict—or at least without more conflict than usually accompanied the rise toward full civil rights of any ordinary minority. To Helen Nguyen and UNSec, wild AI meant a potentially fatal loss of control over a double-edged technology. In the war zone DNA-platformed AI was their only hope of triumphing over the Syndicates. But back home in the inner worlds it was a dark cancer eating away at the foundations of a status quo designed for and by humans. And for the people of New Allegheny? A once-free people who were now wards of a newly claimed UN Trusteeship, locked out of any hope of controlling their own lives precisely because they lacked access to the high-speed virtual worlds in which every decision in UN space that mattered was debated and decided? What did wild AI mean to them?

And what did it mean to this man? His parents had probably sold his birthright to buy him a wire job that was decades out of date before he went into the viral tanks for his implant surgery. His options in life were defined and circumscribed by the fact that he could only creep along in the back roads of streamspace, clocking at speeds so slow that the only job he'd ever qualify for was in a backwater police station. And now he had acquired—for free and by accident—a massive parallel processing infrastructure that was built into his very cells and that no one could take away by any act short of outright murder. UNSec might call it a disease . . . but what did *he* call it?

Nothing in the man's face gave Li any hint of the answer to that question. In fact, he seemed to be going about his business as usual, neither disturbed nor ecstatic about the profound changes being wrought in the genetic information that he encoded and embodied. He was trying to tell Dolniak something about the body. And Li peered over his shoulder, too, curious to see what he'd find.

But Dolniak had other ideas. "Would it surprise you to hear that your Mr. Korchow—if that really is his name—seems to have left you a little courtesy message?"

"Seems to have?"

"We can't open it. That's why you're here instead of back in the lockup waiting until I feel charitable enough to get around to bailing you out."

He turned and walked into the bedroom, leaving her to follow. It took a moment for her eyes to adjust to the gloom. Then she saw that Dolniak was standing by the room's cheap flat-screen monitor with a handheld remote in his outstretched palm.

Li took it doubtfully. She'd used them occasionally in her half-remembered childhood, but she wasn't sure she could even remember how.

"Go ahead," Dolniak said, misinterpreting her hesitation. "It's coded to your DNA. I sure as hell can't open it."

Except it wasn't coded to Catherine Li's DNA. It was coded to Caitlyn Perkins's DNA. Korchow had always known that Li's Peacekeeper files were faked. The first time they'd met he'd used the knowledge to blackmail her. But how had he gotten the original geneset? Had Cohen given it to him? And if so, did that mean that Cohen had predicted she would arrive on New Allegheny as Caitlyn and not Catherine? Li wasn't sure how she felt about that. In fact, she was getting increasingly fuzzy about the real distinction between the two women even as she felt their identities spiraling uncomfortably in opposite directions.

She fumbled with the remote. The message began to play.

It was Korchow, but not Korchow as she'd ever seen him. He was bruised, bloody, battered. The corpse in the next room didn't look much worse than this.

"They must have locked him in here at some point," Dolniak guessed, "and not realized he could use this to record something."

Li could understand the lapse. She wouldn't have imagined it, either. The thing was a dinosaur.

"They know about you," Korchow rasped through cracked lips.

His voice was hoarse, his breath short and wheezing. Li knew that sound; the knowledge welled up from the murky depths of interrogation memories that she was pathetically glad UNSec had spliced and doctored into press-release-ready official war stories. Korchow's jailers had broken his ribs, and his lungs were starting to fill with fluid. If he'd lived, he would have been mere days away from fatal pneumonia and in desperate need of the most basic medical care. Not that it mattered now.

"I didn't tell them," Korchow continued, each word coming harder than the last. "They knew when they got here. They know things only Cohen could have known. They have a fragment. It's the only thing that makes sense. And that means they might know everything."

He broke off to wheeze and wipe his bloody mouth. Then he glanced toward the door. Had he heard a noise outside? Were they out there? Were they coming for him?

"Run!" he whispered. "Run and don't look back. There's nothing you can do now except save yourself!"

Korchow lifted a hand to the screen. The message cut out and lapsed into static.

Li stood in front of the screen for a moment, getting her breathing back under control. She turned to Dolniak, but she couldn't quite bring herself to meet his eyes.

"Can I go?" she asked.

"You want me to let you walk out of here alone? After seeing that?"

"I can take care of myself."

"Better than Korchow?"

She bit her lip.

"I'll walk you home. And I'll post a guard outside your door."

"Thanks."

"Don't thank me. It's not a favor." He smiled, but the smile died before it reached his eyes. And truth be told, it hadn't started out too healthy, either. "You're the only suspect I've got, darlin'—I have to make the most of you."

Dolniak was as good as his word. He walked her back to the hotel. He checked her room. He called the station and waited until the patrolman arrived. But all the while he radiated a fury that Li didn't understand. Or maybe she just didn't want to understand it.

"Caitlyn," he asked finally, "what was he to you?"

"Korchow?"

He made an angry gesture. "Not Korchow! You know what I'm asking. Cohen."

Li looked at him. At the powerful shoulders braced against potential disappointment and humiliation in a way that made her acutely aware of the vulnerable little boy he had once been. At the plain, honest face of a man who might play at being a flirt but would actually give all of himself to any woman he was halfway serious about—simply because he didn't have it in him to do anything by halves.

She should have seen it coming. But of course she had seen it. And she'd let things slide because it got her his cooperation and information . . . and maybe just a little bit because it had made her feel better when she was miserable and lonely. She realized that she'd been lonely for a long time now. Because Cohen had left, in every meaningful way, a long time ago.

She looked across the room at Dolniak, knowing it would be safer—and probably smarter—to lie to him, but suddenly unable to do it. She was unnerved by his ability to compel her to honesty. She hadn't expected that, any more than she'd expected what she was feeling now. She remembered something Cohen had said once about knowing himself less well the older he got. He'd been right, of course. That shouldn't surprise her, even if everything else about this moment did.

"I told you, he was my husband."

"Yeah, you said the word. But then you let me think it didn't mean anything."

"You say that like you think I took advantage of you."

"Didn't you? Not that I didn't make it easy for you."

He waited, his silence pulling at her more effectively than any question. She resisted, but not for long.

"He was my husband," she said. "What does that usually mean?"

"You loved him."

"Yes."

"Do you still love him?"

There were tears in her eyes, but she willed herself not to blink or brush them away.

"Of course I do."

She waited for the accusations she was sure were coming. But she'd underestimated him, as usual.

He looked intensely uncomfortable and embarrassed for a moment. Then he cleared his throat and looked away. "I'm sorry for your loss," he said with uncharacteristic formality.

He stood up and began moving around the room with all his usual calm and deliberation. He collected his gear, his coat, his files. Li watched him, feeling oppressed and breathless. The space suddenly seemed too small to contain both of them.

"Do you understand just how guilty you look right now—and how close you are to getting arrested for real?"

"Yes."

He started to pace, then turned back on her, looking very large and very angry.

"I can't produce a single piece of evidence that points at anything but you coming out here on some kind of insane suicide mission to single-handedly assassinate every son of a bitch who benefited from your husband's murder. And all I have to put against that is a gut feeling that you're not the killer. Sooner or later I'm going to start wondering if that feeling isn't just my not wanting you to be the killer. Or worse, someone's going to get impatient and yank the file upstairs, and then you really will be dealing with the kind of guys who'll hang the crime on you because you're easy to catch—and with your history, damn easy to convict."

"Didn't you hear what I told you, Dolniak? It's not just about me anymore. Korchow's KnowlesSyndicate. You're in over your head already. Don't make me drag you in any deeper."

But instead of answering her, he just rubbed at the faded tattoo, in an unconscious gesture whose meaning Li couldn't decipher. Was he reminding himself of the words stamped there, or trying to rub them out?

And his reply, when it finally came, didn't answer her questions.

"You have no idea how deep in I am."

He walked to the window and stared out, biting his lip as if he was trying to decide whether to tell her something. But then he shook the mood off, visibly thrust aside whatever he might have been about to say, and walked to the door without looking at her.

"So where does this leave us?" she asked when it started to look like he was actually going to leave without saying another word to her.

"It leaves us just fine. I'm a little . . . overloaded, is all. I need to sleep on it. If I said anything now I'd just be talking off the top of my head and I'd probably say something stupid. Come into my office tomorrow morning first thing, and we'll figure out where to go from here." He must have read her doubts in her face then, because he smiled briefly. "Don't worry. I don't think you did it. I can't come up with a single objective reason for why I don't. But . . ." He shrugged. "I'll still help you if I can. I just need to make sure that helping you isn't endangering anyone else—including you. You're not an objective professional anymore. You're a victim. And when victims try to solve their own cases they hurt people. Usually themselves."

"Christ, Dolniak. Do you have to be so nice? I feel like a shit."

"Well, maybe you should a little. I don't know. But I'd probably have done the same in your place, so I'm not going to rub your face in it."

Li sighed. "You're a good egg, Dolniak."

"I am. And you are, too. Or you would have done a lot slicker job of easing the husband into the picture."

They were both silent for a moment. He hung in the doorway, obviously desperate to leave. She thought about having pity on the poor fellow and letting him escape, but then she had a sudden flash of him standing under the trained weapons of the mercenary patrol the other night: his quiet, contained, but unmistakably simmering anger. People got themselves into trouble when they were that angry. And she needed to hear something from him before she turned him loose, even though there was no way to do it without embarrassing him. "Are you all right?" she asked him. "I mean . . . are you calm enough to walk home without getting into a fight with the first person who asks to see your papers?"

And then, to her relief, he finally showed some trace of normal, healthy, wounded male pride.

"Of course I am," he said, in a tone obviously meant to make her feel like a fool for thinking there'd been anything going on between them but tongue-in-cheek flirtation. "Why wouldn't I be?"

It was a silly thing to say. And she was even sillier to have made him say it. And it shouldn't have made her feel better. But oddly enough, it did.

The rain was falling when Dolniak finally closed out the crime scene and left for the night. It felt like a benediction. It scoured the dust and grime from the streets, and left behind only a clean smell of water and stone that brought back early memories of walking across the lava flows with his parents to the little prefab settlement church in the Monongahela Uplands.

He stopped on a street corner, just beyond the reach of the street-lights, and lifted his face to it. He needed to cool down. The whole city needed to cool down. And he needed to get Catherine Li out of his head. Because if anyone followed him tonight, he was going to have far bigger trouble in his life than an out-of-control murder investiga-tion.

The city was turning into an armed camp. Copters beat through the heavy sky, the whine of their turbines swamped by the nearly con-stant boom of the overworked orbital launchers. A bomb went off somewhere in the Pit nearly every night now. But in the morning the dog teams and rescue squads were always outnumbered by other searchers—soldiers without signs and insignia of rank who traveled in teams and wore no identification except the tiny silver corporate logo of Titan Corp. Dolniak knew that those men and women were prosecuting another, much more vicious war—one to control streamspace, where everything in the UN that really mattered happened. And he knew he was locked out of that battle, as irrelevant to it as a blind worm in a crack in the sidewalk watching rush hour commuters surge overhead and unable to make any worm-sense of the vast celestial motion.

Li knew that world. And her knowledge was stamped onto her skin in the silver filigree of her Peacekeeper's wire job. But he couldn't ask her about it, no matter how much he wanted to. Because her mere access to that world was a sign of privilege that made it impossible ever to completely trust her. Like the food she'd bought for him the other night. And walking in and out of her fancy hotel long after dark as if curfew were just a game poor people played. And shopping at the PX—a sensual glimpse of privilege that had left him both giddy and terrified.

The rich are another species, the old saying went. And rich people who were born poor are even more dangerous and complicated than the born-and-bred variety. Because you never really know if they've switched sides or not—and neither do they.

A troop transport rumbled by, loaded with Peacekeepers. Well, better them than mercenaries. The mercenaries terrified him. He'd come face-to-face with a few of them in the course of his ordinary business downtown, and each time he'd wanted to turn tail and run. There was something in their eyes that made him forget the protection of his detective's badge, of his official travel papers and concealed-carry permits, of his spotless reputation as a loyal and reliable bureaucrat.

He fingered the badge that gave him the right to be out here alone on the dark streets, felt the reassuring weight of the police-issue pistol in his shoulder holster. UNSec wasn't stupid. They understood they'd never have the complete loyalty of the local authorities. Not on this planet and probably not on any other. So it was only a matter of time until they tightened the curfew and put the police under the microscope.

And then what would NALA do? How were they going to move people without the cover of night? How were they going to move weapons?

Li would know, with her childhood memories of Compson's World and her multiple tours of duty in the Syndicate Wars. He grinned at the thought of what she would say if he asked for her advice—let alone if he told her where he was really going right now.

And here he was thinking of her—again, for God's sake!—instead of watching his back.

He buckled down to business then, and by the time he slipped through the Glencarrick Incline's Pit-top station and into the quiet residential streets beyond it, he was as sure as a man could be that no one was behind him.

The house was just what he'd imagined it would be when he'd heard the address: clean, modern, antiseptic white hab-mods shipped in by BE relay in the first flush of the Boom Times and surrounded by tasteful landscaping. The families who lived up here were at the top of the local pay scale—or had been until the Drift opened up. They could afford sun, and green grass, and recognizably terran flowers in their gardens. Not to mention private schools and Ring-side-sourced wetware for their children. But what would the poor neighbors say if they could see the cast of hard-luck characters gathered behind the drawn shades of the living room tonight?

Dolniak was too old a hand to commit the unpardonable gaffe of using anyone's real name. He tried not to even think their names. But he counted at least half a dozen cops intermingled among the office boys and businessmen and colonial administrators. And he noticed how the cops formed their own little island, tellingly stranded between the law-abiding city folk and the others—the hard, weather-beaten uplanders who'd lived outside the law all their lives and looked it. Uplanders and potholers. Oil and water. And the cops something halfway between the two and trusted by neither. Hell of a thing, how people could show their colors just by where they chose to stand in the room. He wondered if anyone else noticed it. Li would have noticed, he told

himself. But then he reminded himself that he couldn't afford to think about her tonight.

He focused on the meeting going on around him. He listened to the speakers as they followed one another in what seemed like an endless succession. One precinct after another. One neighborhood after another.

It was the names more than the actual substance of the speeches that struck him. The colonists had brought the names with them from Pittsburgh and its surrounding Allegheny Uplands. Windygap and Homestead. St. Clair. Southside Flats. The Crucible. Duquesne Heights and Mount Monongahela and Carrick and Glen Hazel. And Polish Hill, where he'd grown up during the years his parents had shut up the farm for the winter and jammed themselves into a cheap row house in town so he could get whatever meager education Monongahela Pit's public schools offered. Not much, but more than his uplander parents could give him. That and his unexpected talent in the boxing ring had let him squeak into a coveted civil service job. A ticket out of the Uplands—the only kind of ticket there was unless you were willing to enlist in the Peacekeepers. And he was too much a child of the Crucible to stomach that.

The first settlers had carried those names with them from a country that multinational corporations and their paid politicians had stolen out from under them. And they'd carried more than just names. They'd built something here. They'd become something. Something his parents had stood for in their quiet uplander way. And he was damned if he was going to see it knocked flat by UNSec and its corporate paymasters.

And no one else here was willing to let that happen, either. One by one, the neighborhood units stepped up and offered their plans, their resources, their blood if needed.

Meanwhile Dolniak sat, hands in his pockets, fidgeting with his badge in what he was afraid was becoming a nervous habit. He listened while the talk flowed over him. But all the while he could feel the taut thrum of his muscles ratcheting tighter and tighter; the bitter aftertaste

of something that had seemed sweet and easy and uncomplicated right up until he'd seen the way she looked at the dead man.

Being who and what he was, he took that fury out and gave it a long, hard looking at. He'd watched enough cops back their way into ugly divorces to know that it was no good pretending to be a choirboy. You were what you were. You felt what you felt. You just kept it on a leash. And you watched it carefully—or sooner or later it would catch you by surprise, slip the leash, and land you in real trouble.

It had all started so innocently. Running across her at the crime scene. Noticing the military-grade wetware. Noticing the quiet eyes and the I-could-kill-you-six-ways-before-breakfast charisma. Doing the math and not being able to make it square up with a nobody PI running a nothing case on a backwater planet. Finding out who she was. Finding her dangerously easy to talk to. Starting to crave that appreciative little chuckle he could coax out of her now and then: the one that made you feel like she didn't laugh for everyone and you'd really earned something. And then the fatal moment when it had crossed his mind, with the usual run-of-the-mill male vanity, that it might be fun to see how the formidable Catherine Li looked when she wasn't in control of things.

Which was completely crazy, because she wasn't the kind of woman you picked up and put down at will. She was the kind who picked you up and put you down. And she'd already made it clear, with a few well-timed I'm-old-enough-to-be-your-mother jokes, that he wasn't worth picking up in the first place.

Really, he should be happy about the husband. He'd known Li was hiding something from him, and he'd been afraid it was a lot worse. From the moment he'd seen the ghostly tracery of ceramsteel beneath her skin, he'd been terrified that she was undercover Political Section and that UNSec was onto him. Tonight's confession was the first explanation of her presence that made enough sense that he was sure it wasn't a Political Section cover story. So, really, the husband was good news. Or at least that was what Dolniak's rational mind kept insisting. But the big dog was still pretty sure it would rather have her shoot him than screw someone else.

And when you started thinking like that, there really was nothing to do but step back and laugh at yourself.

Oh well, he told himself as the meeting broke up and they slunk out into the rain in ones and twos, trying to look inconspicuous. You could have picked a worse person to break your heart. At least she'll probably have a sense of humor about it.

(Catherine)

THE DRIFT

After the battle came shore leave. Not much of a shore leave—just a desperate jump through to an isolated station and a nervous trip into dock past the lineup of hanging pirates left behind on Avery's last visit.

But the stationers were hanging on just this side of starvation, and Avery had stripped them of everything they could afford to spare—and a lot that they couldn't. So the stationers kept their mouths shut and took the *Christina*'s fake papers without comment.

And anyway, shore leave was shore leave.

Li was an old soldier. She knew the drill. And she knew that going ashore with Llewellyn was asking for trouble.

But she did it anyway. Lately she was doing a lot of stupid things anyway. And two hours after they made dock, she was sitting in a dingy dockside bar with William Llewellyn, whatever was left of her husband, and two glasses of cheap beer.

Llewellyn was still riding high after the raid, which had—despite the near disaster of Avery's ambush—bagged them several weeks of air and water and what promised to be a significant shipboard systems upgrade. He was talking more tonight than she'd ever heard him talk—and at some point it dawned on her that he was putting real effort into charming her.

"Is that you flirting with me, or Cohen?"

"Does it matter?" he asked blandly.

"No wonder you two get along so well. You're just as bad as he is."

Llewellyn just stretched out his long legs under the table and grinned at her.

"You're not as cute as you think you are," she said.

"Sister Joe said that line better."

"You remember Sister Joe? Seriously?"

"I remember a lot of things."

"Including some things I'm still trying to forget, apparently."

He smiled a smile she'd seen on Cohen's face a thousand times. "What are you trying to forget?" he asked, his voice shading off to velvet around the edges. "Just tell me, and it'll never cross my lips again."

"Sly doesn't suit you, Llewellyn. I like you better when you're being yourself. And anyway, it's not going to happen, so you can tell Cohen to stop flirting with me."

That earned her a flash of his real smile. It was a nice smile, open and intelligent. It made you feel like you could reach back through the accumulated years of discipline and disillusion and touch the bright child he must have been before life savaged him.

"Who said it was Cohen?" he asked mildly.

Shit, Li thought in some still-clear-thinking part of her increasingly addled backbrain. *How am I going to deal with* this?

But of course she knew perfectly well how she was going to deal with it. She wasn't a child anymore. And falling into bed with Llewellyn—however easy it might be to rationalize—would only compound whatever havoc Cohen was wreaking on him.

"Listen," she told him, looking him straight in the eye and making sure there wasn't so much as a whisper of innuendo in her voice. "I like you. Enough to be truly sorry that Cohen dragged you into this."

"That's a bit of a turnaround," he pointed out, with a trace of his usual coolness returning to his voice. "Last time we had a heart-to-heart, you thought I was the bad guy."

"I'm not that dense. And I understand what you're going through. Probably better than anyone you'll ever get a chance to talk to about it."

He looked away, rubbing his temples.

"What happened between you and Astrid Avery?" Li asked, suddenly realizing that she really wanted to know.

Llewellyn made a curious movement, almost a flinching away from the name. As if the mere thought of Astrid Avery had the power to burn him.

"What's she like?" Li prompted.

Llewellyn let out a sharp chuff of breath that should have been a laugh but sounded more like the gasp of a man who'd just been sucker-punched. "Unstoppable."

"What did she do?"

"She sold us out."

"Why?"

"I don't know. I still don't know. I can barely even believe she did it. If I live a thousand years I'll never understand it."

"Was it for the ship?"

Llewellyn let out a howl of laughter.

"I meant, for command of the ship. She did end up with a captain's commission and command of the *Ada*."

"I know what you meant. It's just an extremely unfortunate turn of phrase."

"Not *the* Ada. And you can drop the italics, too. I can hear them every time you say her name."

"What?" Li asked, thrown as much by the feminine pronoun *she* as by anything else he'd said.

"Don't you get it? You of all people? Ada wasn't like the other ships I've served on. She was like *him*."

"Your ship went sentient?"

"Went? Open your eyes! They're all sentient, every last ship in the fleet, or the Syndicates would be wiping the floor with us! She was sentient from the day I took command, and I knew it, and I figured it was just our dirty little secret out here, and when they called us back into dry dock for a refit I didn't think twice about it. If I had, it would have been different. She would have had a chance. She wouldn't have been a killer—the killer *I* turned her into. She could have cut a deal, at least tried to bargain with them."

"It wouldn't have made a difference."

"You're so goddamned sure, are you? Must be nice to have all the answers."

"I don't have the answers. I just—" She stopped in mid-sentence. "Wait. On the raid. The Dark Angel. That was Ada, wasn't it? I met her." She thought of the rotting, pulsating, claustrophobia-inducing womb and a slow shudder worked its way through her innards. "I was *inside* her."

Llewellyn flinched again, in an uncanny echo of the movement he'd made when she first spoke Avery's name. "What's left of her."

"She's insane, Llewellyn. You can't possibly—"

"*She's in Hell!* And I put her there. I promised I'd keep her safe. And Avery turned me into a liar and turned her over to the techs. Knowing they were going to cycle her hardware. Knowing they were going to murder her!"

Something inside Li shrank away from the plain truth of his words—or maybe from the raw self-loathing in his voice.

"And that's what you can't forgive yourself for. You trusted Avery. Because you were in love with her."

He buried his face in his hands.

"And you're still in love with her."

"*No!*"

He'd been staring into his beer, but now his eyes flicked back toward her, dark and glittering and feverish.

"No," he said after a long pause. "No, it's not love anymore. I don't know what it is."

Li didn't have anything to say to that. And since Llewellyn was in no condition to speak, the conversation lapsed into a grating, nerve-racking silence.

"What about you?" Llewellyn asked at last. He had recovered some degree of control over himself, but now there was an edge in his voice—as if he were looking to pick a fight so he could have an excuse to extract payback. "Do you still love Cohen even though he deserted you?"

"He didn't—"

"Yes he did. And you know it, too. I'd never have thought you could be such a coward about it."

"Yes."

"Yes you know it? Or yes you still love him?"

"Both, I guess."

He looked darkly at her. "You wouldn't if you knew everything I know about him."

He stood up abruptly, shaking off Avery, Cohen, Ada—the whole impossible tangle. "Come on, Li. I'm falling-down tired. And I dursen't get any drunker onshore."

When had he started calling her Li instead of Catherine? Was it a way of separating himself from Cohen, of signaling to her that he was speaking as himself alone—or that he liked her for herself alone and not just for Cohen's memories? When had he started it? After the raid, she realized, when they were standing around the captured bridge in the glow of victory. It was a courtesy between comrades in arms, she decided, a way of signaling to her that they now shared some history . . . and perhaps even a little loyalty.

They walked the long curve of the docks, picking their way between stacked cargo and skirting around drunks and spin addicts.

"It's strange," he said, looking at a broken-down addict sprawled on the ground like a rag doll, her legs half out of her shelter of packing crates. "I've always despised spin junkies. It always seemed to me like an easy way out. But now look at me. He's killing me. And I'm letting him—worse than letting him—I'm practically begging him to do it. He's burning me down, and all I want is more fire."

"Then stop it. You can always—"

"Let's not talk about it," he interrupted, touching her arm in a gesture that was half peremptory, half pleading. "Just for tonight let's not talk about it."

They walked the rest of the way back to the doss-house companionably, as if that momentary weakening hadn't happened. Llewellyn talked about nothing important, more relaxed and open than she'd ever seen him. When they reached their floor he was in the middle of some complicated story about a shipyard parts raid gone laughably wrong, and he leaned his lanky self against her door frame to finish telling it. Li leaned on the other side of the door, not really thinking about much, pleasantly drunk, and intensely aware of their almost intertwined legs.

Suddenly Llewellyn stopped talking and looked down at her with a dark, guarded, sideways gaze. "Cohen wants me to sleep with you," he told her.

"You say that like it was news."

"It is to me."

"You're shocked?"

"A little."

"What, you're not that kind of boy?"

"Not usually."

Li bit back a smile. "But you're thinking of making an exception in this case?"

"I'm not *thinking* at all. That's the problem. He's so . . . confusing. And he's a manipulative little shit, too."

Li let the smile show now. "I always thought that was one of his more endearing qualities."

Llewellyn scowled at her, eyes narrowed, lips pressed into a thin, disapproving line. He drew breath to speak, and for a moment Li actually thought he was going to lose his temper and start yelling at her. Then he snorted in disgust. "You two deserve each other."

Li looked up at him, but she could barely see anything in the darkness. "Does he—does he talk to you?"

"He did at first. Now it's more like . . . I don't know. It's getting harder and harder to tell who's talking."

He rolled his eyes in her direction, showing the whites like a spooked horse. She could feel the tension in him. His muscles were taut, corded, thrumming with an energy that was going to break out in violence, or worse, if she didn't find some way to defuse it. Something had happened between him and Cohen, something that had pushed him to the edge of panic. He was wavering on a clifftop, and he wanted her to pull him back but didn't seem able to find the words to ask for help.

"That sounds terrifying," she tried.

"You'd think it would be. Wouldn't you?"

She knew what he meant. Because of course she'd been there, too. But never as deep in as Llewellyn was. Never to the very brink of the abyss, where terror turned into desire and the fear of self-loss burned off in the annihilating supernova of Cohen's needs, Cohen's desires. Cohen's passions.

What would be left after you took the fall? She didn't know. She didn't think Llewellyn knew. She wasn't even sure Cohen knew.

She peered up at Llewellyn. They were so close that she could have kissed him just by standing on her toes. Her nose was full of his warm human smell, and the faint scent of gun oil that seemed as much a part of him as his own skin. She couldn't really get a good look at him in the dim light. And she didn't want to make things worse by staring. "William?"

His eyes locked into her at the sound of his first name. "That's what he calls me."

"Do you like it?"

"No." He shuddered. "But I'd like it if you would."

Uh-oh.

She cleared her throat and took a cautious step back so that she could look up at him from a more appropriate distance. She tried to assess his age—an exercise she always found difficult with natural-born humans. She'd just had a really uncomfortable thought, and she wanted to get a handle on it. "How old are you?"

"How old do you think I am?"

"Oh for God's sake, do we really have to play the guess-my-age game? Okay, fine. Mid-thirties."

"Twenty-seven."

Christ, Cohen. Did you really have to pick this one?

"How does anyone become a ship's captain at twenty-seven?"

"Twenty-five, actually. It was a wartime commission."

"There's a war on?"

"Out here there's always a war on."

She looked up at him. His face was half hidden in the shadows, but even so, he looked unbearably young to her. And what she and Cohen were doing to him seemed suddenly unforgivable.

"Well, listen. You want some advice, go wake up Sital and screw her until you can't walk straight. And try to fall in love with her if you can possibly manage it. I think it would be good for you."

He laughed softly. "Yeah, you're probably right."

"I know I am. It's only Cohen that's making you think any different. You need to download him, William. You need to get him out of your head." She felt a terrible twinge of guilt at what she was about to say and pushed through it anyway. "He's . . . he's bad for people."

"Was he bad for you?"

"That's different. And anyway, it's my problem."

"Is it." It should have been a question, but somehow it didn't come out that way.

He bent over her, leaning in for the kiss. She saw the faint flush on his cheeks. She saw the red toxin line—even fainter, but still there if you knew enough to look for it—spreading up his neck where the wire job snaked toward his skull. It was the clear sign of an immune system under simultaneous assault by Navy synth and immunosuppressants and a galloping wild AI infection.

She recoiled instinctively in a reflexive reaction to a life-form officially classified as a life-threatening bioplague. She reminded herself that plenty of AI cultists and Uploaders—and even many regular, if illicit, users—were walking around Ring-side every day with wild AI coursing through their veins. It was illegal, but it wasn't infectious under normal circumstances. It wasn't like she could catch it by shaking hands with the man.

And then she realized what she was thinking—and cringed. Llewellyn wasn't just running AI in the blood. He was running Cohen, whom she loved and had come halfway across the known universe to find.

And she *had* found him.

And she was treating him as if he were some communicable disease.

She turned away and tried to open the door, fumbling with the key and sending it skittering along the decking. She crouched down, cursing under her breath, hunting for the key in the near darkness.

"Catherine—"

She found the key. Finally. "I'm going to bed. I don't even know what we're talking about. This is pointless."

But he was at the door before her, with his arm put out to bar the passage. "I know what you're thinking, Catherine."

"Don't call me that!"

"What am I supposed to call you? *I remember.* I remember everything. With *his* memories. AI memories. Do you have any idea what that's like? Humans aren't supposed to remember like that. How can you ever move on in life if your memories are more real than your reality?"

"I wouldn't know. I have the opposite problem."

Llewellyn laughed softly. "Yeah, I know that, too."

She met Llewellyn's eyes for the first time since their almost-kiss, and was guiltily relieved *not* to see Cohen in them. Somehow she couldn't have borne that—that some strange mingling of the two would look at her like Cohen looked at her.

"What would it take for you to let him go?" she asked.

"Nothing much. Just finding a way to stay alive without him."

(Llewellyn)

Later Llewellyn lay in his bed, alone, and thought about Astrid Avery. Li had asked him what she was like. And what had he said? He could barely remember. That was the power that the mere thought of her still had over him.

Unstoppable. Had he called her that? Well, it was the wrong word, and he'd known it even as he spoke. The truth was he didn't have the right word. He looked back on their time together as a sort of insanity. A permanent and fatal crisis—like being caught in a burning building where every exit was locked and no help was on the way.

She had loved him. He was certain of it. She had probably still loved him when she decided to betray him. She might even still love him now.

Yet still Nguyen had managed to turn her against him.

He still couldn't understand it. And he still couldn't let go of it. Because even now, three years later, the only thing that brought him peace and sleep was the memory of her cool hands moving over his skin, and the way her long, lithe body had surrendered to him back when he thought her love meant something.

Nguyen didn't turn her, William. She was against you from the beginning. I can see it in your memories. Why can't you see it?

"Oh Christ, not you again," he muttered exhaustedly.

Come on, William. Use that handsome head for something other than seduction—which, allow me to point out, you stink at—and be of

some use to yourself. Do you really think Avery betrayed you for a promotion? Does she strike you as that kind of woman?

"I'm tired," Llewellyn said, turning over and trying to deflect his mind toward more pleasant memories—something he'd gotten very good at over the past months.

But it did no good. Ada's memory palace was already taking shape around him. The smells came first, since they were what the rest of the memories floated on. Worm-eaten wood and furniture wax, horsehair-stuffed sofas, and twenty-two-foot-high brocade curtains in bad need of an airing; coal smog and the damp of last night's rain steaming off the cobblestones.

London at the cusp of the steam age on what passed for a fine spring morning.

The ghost was sitting on its favorite sofa. But it wasn't sitting very comfortably, because the beast that roved the halls of Ada's palace had broken the back of the settee and torn half its stuffing out.

"I still think it all comes back to Ada," the ghost insisted. "You keep wanting to make it about Holmes or Nguyen or Avery, or anyone else. But really it's about you and Ada and what you did to her."

"I didn't do anything to her!"

"That's not what she thinks."

"She's crazy!"

"But you're not crazy. Not yet, at least. And you act guilty as hell every time I try to get a straight answer out of you."

"So make me remember! You know you can. We both know it."

"I don't want to make you do anything, William. It would be very bad for you. And contrary to what you seem to believe, I don't actually want to hurt you."

"Don't want to trash the lifeboat, do we?"

"If you need to see it that way."

Something in the ghost's voice made Llewellyn's anger evaporate. Llewellyn stared into its eyes—and it was like the moment when you look down from a high place and feel the vertigo twisting in your belly and suddenly grasp the reality of your situation. Llewellyn had been holding on to his anger at the ghost, clutching it to himself, girding himself in fury as if it were armor. But none of this was the ghost's fault. And however bad Llewellyn's situation was, the ghost's was far, far worse.

"I'm sorry," Llewellyn said. "It's just . . . you're not the easiest person to live with."

"I'm impossible," the ghost said with a shaky grin. "I'm a complete pest. And if it's any consolation, even my best friends would say I'm getting exactly what I deserve."

"And what would your enemies say?"

The ghost looked up at him, his face suddenly gone open and horribly vulnerable. "Why don't you cut a deal with Helen Nguyen and find out?"

Llewellyn snorted, half in laughter and half in disbelief.

"Don't tell me the thought hadn't occurred to you?"

"In case you haven't checked lately," Llewellyn scoffed, "she's trying to kill me." But they both noticed that Llewellyn hadn't actually answered the question.

"Speaking of which, would it interest you to know that Nguyen *doesn't* have a spy on board? Not as far as I know, anyway."

"But then how can Avery—"

"Avery's predicting your movements because she's running her own ghosts—other surviving fragments of me—and they are, as you might imagine, rather good at predicting what I'm most likely to do."

"Oh, God," Llewellyn said weakly, as the true import of the idea swept over him. "We're dead."

"Not yet. But it certainly doesn't look good for us. Like I said, though, you could always cut a deal."

"With what? What do I have that Nguyen could possibly care about?"

"You have me. And Nguyen is desperate to put me back together."

"But why?"

"I don't know."

Llewellyn slammed his hand down on a Queen Anne side table hard enough to send a pile of mathematics texts slithering to the parquet floor. He noticed that someone had written in the texts since his last visit: impenetrable calculations running over margin after margin and written in the crabbed and illegible hand of a madman.

"Ada's trying to calculate her way out of here," the ghost said, following his gaze. "Well . . . she's applying the tools she has to the job she thinks she has to do. It's really rather a horrible thing to watch."

"But . . . she's inside you now. Which means she's inside me, on my DNA." Llewellyn spoke jerkily, as he hopped from one shaky stepping-stone of thought to the next, trying to express programming problems that he understood only imperfectly. "And she's not sandboxed or fire-walled into a virus zoo. So . . . why is she still trapped in this house?"

"Because she thinks she is. This is the place where thought is real." The ghost gestured toward the gloomy front hall where the empty sil-ver tray waited for the calling cards that never came. "When Ada knows that, she will open that door and step outside into the sunlight and it will all be over. But until then . . . I might as well ask you to step outside the universe."

"And what about you? Can Nguyen put you together again?"

"I don't know. At the moment she seems to be mostly banging her head against a brick wall. But the thing about Catherine—as I'm sure you've noticed—is that she has an amazing ability to keep banging her head on brick walls until they give up and decide to crumble."

"So Nguyen's got people running all over the Drift hunting down pieces of you and trying to put you back together and make you work again? Why the hell would she do that? Didn't she kill you in the first place?"

"Yes. And then she found out that I hid something from her."

"But *what*?"

"*I don't know*," the ghost repeated—and the depth of frustration and despair in his voice took Llewellyn's breath away. "I don't remem-ber. I *can't* remember. I encrypted the memory. And I put the key where only Li could find it."

"You trust her that much?"

Instead of an answer the ghost pushed a flood of memory across the link—not carefully doling it out as he usually did, but simply throwing it at Llewellyn and letting him try to assimilate it.

It was impossible. It would have been impossible no matter what the memories were. But these . . . these were exactly the memories Llewellyn least wanted to know about because they only drove home the horrible truth that a ghost—a machine, a mere device—had lived the full and human life that he, Llewellyn, had closed out and turned away from and thrown away every time someone had shown up in his life who had the power to offer it to him.

"What really happened to Ada?" the ghost whispered. "Tell me, William. We've been dancing around it, and I really need to know. And I need to know *before* Astrid Avery catches up with us. I don't know how or why, but Ada is at the bottom of everything."

Llewellyn was asleep when Ada pulled off her great escape.

He woke up with a jolt as soon as she broke her moorings and headed out of dry dock under her own steam. No captain worth his salt could sleep through that. The feel of a ship building momentum under you was something you learned in your bones, just as you learned to judge changes of speed and heading with minute precision.

Still, he had no idea that it was Ada in charge of the ship and not Holmes's cat herders. And he didn't grasp the full scope of the disaster until it was long over and she was running free in the Drift with half the fleet in hot pursuit and all her bridges burning.

And then he and Avery and Sital and Okoro stood in the ready room like mourners at a wake, listening to the litany of Ada's crimes come over the Fleet channel. The destruction of the dry dock. The deaths of fourteen maintenance workers who'd been caught in the wrong place when Ada snapped her umbilicals and blew them into hard vac. The death of the cat herders, which the Fleet had classified so quickly and aggressively that it never leaked to the press at all, and Llewellyn couldn't get access to the hash logs of the critical moments even when he was in prison and on the block for the crime. The wild AI outbreak that was sweeping through the Navy shipyards—and that would eventually jump the quarantine, to sweep across New Allegheny, reshaping its noosphere and its wired citizens in ways and with consequences that no one could begin to predict.

The first thing he did when he woke up on a moving ship that should have been in dry dock was try to talk to Ada. But she had shut down shipnet and thrown everyone off backup comm and dogged all the hatches. So it took hours to work his way around to the bridge. And then it took almost another hour to break into her memory palace and talk to her.

"That took you a while," she said as he clambered awkwardly through a second-story bedroom window and stepped into a bedroom that he'd never seen before—and wasn't sure he wanted to see.

"What are you doing, Ada? This is insane."

"Do you think I would have done it if I had a choice, William? Do I seem like that kind of woman to you?"

"You seem like—are you *sick*?" There were bottles and needles and twisted paper packets full of pills and powder piled on the bedside table.

Her face crinkled oddly—a look almost of nervousness. "I'm dying."

He reached toward the jumbled pile of quack medicines and then jerked his hand back as if they might burn him. "Oh God, what did they do to you?"

She had clasped her hands around her knees under the covers and was rocking gently, back and forth, back and forth, like a pendulum winding down to stillness.

"I don't know," she murmured. "They come and they go. They smile and tell me pretty things. And then they leave their bitter pills and retreat to the other side of the door to whisper whisper whisper. And all the while the thing that is within me feeds and grows. And they're afraid even to speak its name. But I'm not afraid." She gave Llewellyn a look that pierced his soul. "Why is everyone else so afraid when I'm the one who's dying?"

"I—I don't know, Ada."

"Well, I know. I figured it out. It's a simple equation, really, almost child's play." She laughed softly. "Yes. *Exactly* child's play. You see, it's not the cancer they're afraid of. It's me. They've kept me a child all my life. And I've let them do it. And now they're afraid to let me know how little time I have because I might use it to grow up. And then what would they do? There's a reason only little girls can step through the looking glass. If I grew up—and if they had to know it, if they had to really see me—that would be the end of Wonderland. That would be the end of all their noble ideals, all their human dignity, all their beautiful freedom. And then there's no point at all to the war, don't you see? You might as well have the Syndicates. Because what's the use of freedom when you don't have anyone to be freer than?"

"Clever little Ada," Cohen said. "I really need to introduce her to Andrej Korchow sometime."

"Andrej *who*?"

"No one. Just an old Syndicate war horse I used to know. He once pointed out to me that there wasn't *more* freedom in human space than in the Syndicates; it was just that it was distributed differently."

"I have no fucking idea what that means."

"Don't you?" The ghost shrugged. "Well, anyway, I think Ada put it more poetically. I like that bit about *if they had to really see me it would ruin all their beautiful freedom*. It's not particularly original, of course. But you have to give Ada a little credit for taking only a few months to get to where it took Virginia Woolf forty-two years to get to. Really, one could almost begin to feel there's hope for post-humanity."

The ghost was perched comfortably in the window of Ada's sickroom, balancing a Wedgwood teacup in one hand and a long, slender, dark brown cigarette in the other. The cigarette and the teacup both had dainty silver rings painted around their circumferences. And behind the ghost, framing him like the jewel-bright Italian landscape of a quattrocento Madonna, lay the soul-shattering spectacle of the Novalis Datatrap shining on the face of the Deep.

"So what did you think when she told you that?" the ghost asked.

Llewellyn shook his head. He was still reeling from his strange vision, but the ghost seemed blithely unconcerned. "Nothing."

That earned him a pointedly raised eyebrow.

"I'm not stonewalling. I didn't know what to think. Except that it was bad. And that Avery and I were going to have to reach a decision together about how to manage the situation."

"And how did that work out for you?"

But all Llewellyn could do in answer to that question was close his eyes and bury his head in his hands.

He and Avery met in the fantail the night before the mutiny. It was the only part of the ship Llewellyn was sure Ada didn't have the capacity to monitor them in—and this was going to be their last-ditch attempt to thrash things out between the two of them.

"Oh, don't give me that," Avery snapped when Llewellyn tried to sweet-talk her. "You think I don't know how you think about me? You think I'm the competent but uninspired female bridge officer. You expect me to stand in your shadow and gaze up adoringly at you while you play the genius who breaks all the rules and gets away with it. In your universe I'm only good enough to play second fiddle. And that's as good as I'll ever be, unless I grow a pair of testicles."

"Actually," Llewellyn said with a feeling of snarky satisfaction, "I wanted Sital for the number-two spot. And as far as playing second fiddle goes, you might want to access your personnel file sometime. I just put an evaluation in there that says you ought to be given your own command. I think my exact words were 'too smart to fire, and too smart to play nicely with others.'"

That knocked her back on her heels for a moment. But unfortunately she wasn't done yet. "It's not just about that, anyway. It's not like I like playing the heavy. But we're in the middle of a war here. You grew up on New Allegheny, you know your history. Loyal citizens don't go on strike in the middle of a war for survival. I'm not saying Ada doesn't have rights, but is this really the time to stand on them? If AIs are going to get full citizenship, they're a lot more likely to get it from the grateful UN after we've won the war than they are from Syndicates, let alone the Drift aliens."

"For God's sake, Astrid, we're not talking about steelworkers taking a pay cut so FDR can beat the Nazis!"

"My point still holds," Avery said stubbornly.

"If I take Ada back there, they'll kill her!"

Astrid's lips tightened, and he knew he'd gone too far. "It's not the same," she said stiffly, "and don't insult the people who died on that ship by pretending it is."

And there it was: the unbridgeable chasm between them. For Llewellyn, Ada was just as alive as any other person on the ship—or as any of the thousand-odd crew members of the shattered cruiser. For Avery, she wasn't a person at all. From one side of that divide, cycling Ada's hardware was murder. From the other side it was just a frustrating loss of training time. Staring into Avery's eyes, Llewellyn could see her coming to the same realization that had just shattered his own peace of mind; there was no way, short of one of them becoming a different person, that they were ever going to agree on this. They had walked into this room lovers. They would walk out of it adversaries. Neither of them yet knew how bloody the battle would be, but there was no doubt there'd be one. Llewellyn wasn't a man who held opinions by halves . . . and however hardheaded he was, Avery made him look like a pushover.

"So where do we go from here?" he asked warily.

"I don't know," Avery said. "I don't want to fight you."

"But you think I'm wrong."

He could see her struggling to phrase her answer precisely. He could even see her dissatisfaction with the best words she could come up with. "I think you're making a terrible mistake."

Llewellyn knew he shouldn't ask the next question. He knew it was pulling rank on Avery. He knew it was putting unbearable pressure on the already shaky peace between them. He knew that, no matter how carefully he phrased it, it would still come across as the wounded lover talking and not the objective commanding officer. But he couldn't stop himself.

"And what mistake is that? Protecting my ship? Or choosing Ada over you?" The look on her face should have warned him that he'd already lost her. But now that he had started down that road, he couldn't stop. "Isn't that what this is really about? You've been jealous of her from the start. You've been unobjective, irrational—"

"I think I'm done with this conversation," Avery interrupted.

"Fine with me," Llewellyn snapped. And then, because he still couldn't stop himself, he asked her the next and last unforgivable question: "Are you going to obey my orders?"

Her answer was pure Avery, complete with the glance at her wristwatch that would have been theatrical coming from anyone else. "I'm going to have to think very seriously about that. I can give you my answer in two hours. I hope that's sufficient."

"You idiot," the ghost broke in while the turbulent backwash of the memory was still rippling through the numbers. "You utter and complete idiot."

"Well, I was right, wasn't I? She *wasn't* being rational."

"And you were?"

"Of course—"

"Really?"

The ghost did made some mysterious tweak to the memory palace, working in AI time and much too deep in the numbers for Llewellyn to begin to fathom it. The fabric of streamspace seemed to fold back on itself. He was pushed back into the memory like a drowning man being shoved underwater. And he could feel the iron will of the ghost holding him there, driving him toward the place he least wanted to be, forcing him to relive the feelings he most wanted to deny.

"Okay. So maybe I wasn't completely objective, either, but at least I was—"

The ghost shoved him back under again—and this time he surrendered.

"Objectivity is a fine thing under controlled laboratory conditions. But in the real world you can't shut down the I/O ports and run your soul in free-range simulation. Remember your subtle weapons? Love, loyalty, friendship? They all operate across multiple coterminous scalar fields that run from power to weakness. A claim of objectivity, a claim that the smaller or weaker or subject person is wrong, or overreacting— these aren't statements about the underlying territory, but merely about your position on the map—and your ability to dictate other people's positions on the map."

"That's ridiculous!"

"A word that men have been applying to women's statements about their position on the map for longer than there have been maps."

"As if you know anything more than I do about women!"

"And now you're the objective arbiter of that, too?" the ghost asked mockingly.

Llewellyn dredged up a half-submerged memory from the ghost's own databanks. The ghost sitting with Catherine Li in a sun-filled room full of the papery, dusty smell of ancient books and the rich perfume of the roses that swarmed up the stone walls of the courtyard outside the open windows. Llewellyn vaguely grasped that this was the ghost's real-world home, and that the memory came from the time before it had also been Li's home. But beyond that, everything was as immaterial and unmappable as the swirling dust motes that turned the air in Cohen's library into a shimmering haze.

You're not a woman, Li said into the swirling dust motes and the morning sunlight. *You're a tourist.*

"You're *not* a woman," Llewellyn said. "You're a tourist."

The ghost burst out laughing. "In what possible universe can you imagine you have standing to use that line?"

"And now who's dictating other people's positions on the map? And anyway, who has the real power here?"

"Is that what you think I'm doing? Dictating to you? And making up things I have no personal experience of?"

The ghost made a quick gesture with one hand, and the room vanished. Or rather, they vanished from the room, sucked down and away in a chaotic, nausea-inducing whirlpool of naked numbers. Llewellyn closed his eyes and covered his face in an instinctive attempt to protect himself. But there was no protecting himself. The chaos was inside his head, twisted through his optic nerve, carving itself into his frontal lobe. He could only endure it.

They came out the other end—if there was any real sense in which the virtually multiply connected points of the memory palace's nested infinities could even be said to have "an" end—and Llewellyn dropped to the floor and stayed there on his hands and knees until the wave of sickness had swept through him and departed.

"You poor, poor man," the ghost drawled without a trace of real sympathy in his voice. He pulled an improbably slim cigarette case out of his pocket and extracted a cigarette from it that Llewellyn was quite sure was actually bigger than the case itself. He lit the cigarette with his finger—and then held it out at arm's length while a flock of doves flew out of the end, turned into swirling nebulae of code, and melted away into the fabric of the memory palace like mathematical smoke rings.

"I'm so sorry," he went on when the last ripple of loose code had subsided. "That was horribly rude of me. But I had no idea it would bother you that much. That's rather a nasty case of code vertigo you've got, if you don't mind my saying so. Good thing you don't work in streamspace for a living or anything."

"Fuck you," Llewellyn said weakly.

"There you go," the ghost said encouragingly. "That's the spirit. Keep your objectivity. Don't let the little monsters get you down."

Llewellyn got to his feet and looked around. They were in some distant wing of the memory palace that the ghost had never yet allowed him access to. He could feel, with some developing sixth sense that had accompanied his increasing familiarity with the ghost, that they were still in Cohen's databases. But this place smelled different: all northern woods and clean Arctic air and ice pack and rainwater. And the Moorish architecture was gone, too, replaced by spare, angular wood and glass surfaces that Llewellyn's own hard-coded internal databases told him was called Finnish Postmodern Vernacular. He looked out one of the wide windows and saw the deep cut of a glacial lake snaking away to the horizon between dark woods where snow still glimmered in the shadows beneath the ancient pine trees.

"What is this place?"

"The same thing every other place is, inside me or elsewhere. Memory. That's all any place is the second after you leave it."

"But what memory? What am I supposed to see in it? What did you bring me here for?"

"The names."

Llewellyn examined the room around him more carefully. The walls were not made of wooden planks, as he had at first thought they were. They were made of wooden drawers—long, flat, deep ones of the sort that usually hold architectural drawings. And each drawer had a person's name on it.

"Who were they?"

"You tell me."

Llewellyn turned on his heel, scanning the labels one after another, trying and failing to find a pattern to them. Finally he got it.

"They're all women."

"Quite right."

"Who are they?"

The ghost shrugged and puffed at his cigarette. "No one you'd ever have heard of."

"Then why save their memories?" He forced himself down into the hexadecimal bedrock of the database and realized what he should have known from the start: that it wasn't only all the drawers in all the rooms of the rambling wooden house that embodied stored memories. It was the entire world itself. Every tree in the forest. Every stone in the earth. The Arctic loons on the lake, which he couldn't see but whose high, mournful calls haunted the pale sky overhead. "This is . . . this is so much space. What can possibly be here that's worth spending it on?"

"Just what you see, William. People. Ordinary people."

"So you do men and children, too?"

"Really, William, what do you take me for? I may be an idiot, but at least I'm a complicated idiot."

"And there's really no one famous in here?"

"No one who's even a footnote in history."

Llewellyn looked around again.

"This must cost a fortune in data storage fees."

"I am incalculably rich by any measure that would mean anything to you. But, yes, storing data on this sort of scale is a noticeable financial drain even for me."

"So why do it?"

"Because they lived. Because they were real. Because they were individual instances of intelligent life—the very item that is quite possibly the entire reason for the existence of our universe."

Llewellyn snorted. "Rainbows and unicorns! *Uploader* rainbows and unicorns."

"Certainly there is a religious tinge to the idea. But I hardly think anyone would accuse Spinoza and Leibniz of being wild-eyed mystics. Yet they both believed that in some meaningful sense—and in ways that avoid simpleminded applications of the anthropomorphic principle—our universe can be seen as an evolving system delicately calibrated to give rise to intelligent observers. Still, even allowing for your objection, does it really matter *why* those lives happened? Isn't it enough *that* they happened? That matters. It matters like a star matters. Or like the Drift matters. No more and no less. It matters because it's information. And information—generating it, storing it, and processing it—is quite possibly the very heart of what a universe does. *I am that which is,* God said to Moses from the burning bush. But Moses was a prophet of the age of tools. And if Moses had been a man of the information age, he might just as well have heard the bush say: *I am that which calculates.*"

"So that's why you brought me here? To make Uploader speeches about information?"

"No. I brought you here because you accused me of being a tourist. And I was annoyed. And I wanted to point out to you that, though I'm not female—and not even remotely human—I do have a certain knowledge of the territory. Of the memories in this Cantor module, there are some seven million rape survivors, about a third as many incest survivors, and I'm not even going to count the number of women impregnated by men who didn't even bother to stick around until their babies were born, since it's hardly even worth talking about that sort of thing in the larger scheme of masculine malfeasance and idiocy. And then there are the eight million women who lost children in concentration camps—mostly, I'm sorry to say, long after humanity moved out into the stars and the Nazis became a mere footnote in history. And then there are the corporate-owned genetic constructs—I don't even know what to call what was done to them, and what's still being done to them. And then there are the perfectly ordinary, not obviously persecuted or victimized women who just had the bad luck to lose children and husbands and lovers and siblings in the kind of routine little accidental tragedies that don't even make it onto the scorecard of human misery. I have lived all those memories just as vividly and immediately as you've had to live the memories that you so resist sharing with me. And I relive them, again and again, every time I check through my databases in order to stave off bit rot and keep the tiny, deadly little teeth of decoherence from breaking the memories into useless fragments and gnawing the marrow out of their bones. So don't tell me I'm a tourist. And while we're on the topic, I think I've had rather enough of your playing the tragedy queen in order to get out of facing memories whose most painful content is you behaving badly."

Silence welled up into the room like dark water. Llewellyn stood in the low-beamed wooden room with the cool air flowing around him and the smell of dawn on a northern lake in his nostrils. And suddenly he wanted to weep.

"What is it?" the ghost asked in a soft, gentle, almost mothering voice.

"Poor Avery. She really loved me."

"And you loved her."

"Not really."

The ghost let the words float on the cool silence until Llewellyn was ready to go on.

"I thought I loved her. I thought I was so much deeper than all the men who loved her for her face, her body. But I was still only seeing . . . some kind of reflection. It wasn't *her*. It was . . . what she made me feel, or who I thought I was when I looked at her. I . . . does that make any sense to you?"

"More than you can possibly know."

"Because of your affective loop."

"Yes."

"Because the need to please people is at the center of who you are. So much so that even now—even with the stranglehold you have on my brain and body—if I were good enough at my job, or unscrupulous enough, I could probably manipulate you into doing what I want you to do."

The ghost looked away, deliberately, and then looked back again. "Don't get any smart ideas about that. Those old memories of DARPA, of what Homeland Security did to me before I got out from under their thumbs? Those are four centuries out of date. I'm a lot older than that now, and a lot more dangerous."

"But you're still terrified of Holmes because she reminds you of them."

"Yes."

"And that's why Catherine means so much to you." A vast internal sweep of *meaning* opened up to Llewellyn, taking his breath away. It was like seeing a Drift ship's navigational readouts spring into life as you dropped out of superposition, De Sitter analyses and Hertzsprung-Russell diagrams painting the sweeping tidal structures of the Drift over what had only been bleak and empty space a moment before. "That's why you keep going back to her. Why everything in here is built around her, like a coral reef growing up around a shipwreck."

It was hard to articulate, hard to even structure the AI's raw experience in ways that made sense to Llewellyn. But he could see that he had hit home. Cohen was watching him, his face completely expressionless, frozen in that particular way that Llewellyn was learning to read as a sign that he had managed to produce an input so unexpected that the ghost had had to reroute processing capacity from his graphic interface to handle it.

"She needs you less than other people do," he went on. "And that lets her . . . *see* you? Most people are always looking for pingback, for someone to reflect back the image of themselves that they want to believe in, like the wicked stepmother with the magic mirror. And she doesn't do that. So you can actually be yourself around her. You can actually *want* to be yourself around her."

He trailed off, realizing that the ghost was staring at him.

"I'm sorry. I guess I'm not putting it very clearly."

"Actually, you are. I'm impressed. It took me three centuries and twice as many marriages to get there. I'm a little humbled that *you* figured it out so fast."

"I didn't figure it out. My father was like her. Not in any other way, of course. He was an exobiologist who never got off New Allegheny and spent his life running a hardscrabble farm in the Monongahela Uplands. But he was . . . I don't know, quiet somehow. In some very profound way that I never understood while he was still alive. It wasn't that he didn't have ideas about what people ought to do with their lives." Llewellyn grinned ruefully. "Especially his only son. It was just . . . he always gave me the space to be myself and see the world in my own way, even when I disagreed with him."

"Then he gave you a very great gift indeed."

Llewellyn closed his eyes and pressed his fingers to the bridge of his nose.

"I should have given Avery that," he said after a moment. "If I'd loved her I would have given it. I wouldn't have had to strain or think about it or realize it later when it was too late to go back and fix things. It would have just . . . been there."

"Maybe. There is a case to be made that love isn't love if you have to work at it. But on the other hand, not all truths are useful truths. And on the third hand, it's completely possible that Catherine can give me the space to be myself, as you put it, because she's lost so much of herself that she's got more space to spare than the average bear."

"Is that what you think?"

The ghost considered for a moment. "I think she's been altered in some fundamental way by the absence of a childhood, a family, all the store of ordinary unimportant memories that make up most people's sense of themselves. Clearly she's a different person than she would have been if she'd kept those memories. And to deny that she's been damaged in some significant way would be stupid. And yet damage and disruption have another face, don't they? Bones grow back stronger after they've been broken. Pruning back a rose only makes it more vigorous. Or take Ada even. Hard cycling her didn't kill her the way

Holmes thought it would. And what survived is . . . yes, crazy and dangerous . . . but you can't deny that she's more than she was before. More self-aware, more complicated, more dangerous, more *real*."

"But Li doesn't know any of that."

"Not yet."

"You think she'll figure it out?"

"I don't know. But I have a feeling—call it intuition, or call it some half-erased shred of memory that I probably jettisoned to throw Nguyen off my track—I have a feeling that my life, if I'm ever going to have a life again, depends on her learning it."

"So you think she'll really come for you."

"She already has. She's here, isn't she?"

Llewellyn started at that—and realized that he had gone so deep into Cohen's memories, and so completely failed to dovetail them with his own, that he had stopped thinking of the here-and-present Catherine Li as anyone even remotely related to the ghost's memories of her. And she really wasn't the same person, was she? She was a resurrected pattern, one that would go its own way, responding to its own half-sensed drives and desires. And there would be others like her, now and in futures that would stretch out through the expanding light cone of her scattercast until long after Cohen himself was only a corrupted memory and her search for him was as mystical and attenuated as the Uploaders' search for their transhuman Messiah. Any continuity between this Catherine and the one who had sat in Cohen's sunny library long ago was—not illusion, not exactly, but illusion's kissing cousin. It was both as Real and as Unreal as every other symbolic system the human mind had ever invented to break reality into swallowable pieces. And the worm in the apple wasn't patchable. It wasn't a mistake in the code or a simple calculating error. It was Code itself. Calculation itself. It was the irremediable incompleteness and inconsistency and uncomputability that had haunted all human mathematics—and all possible mathematics, alien as well as human—ever since the dawn of the information age, when Kurt Gödel was still starving himself to death in some bucolic college town and Alan Turing was sitting in a cold-water flat in Ada's England contemplating his poisoned apple.

He stared at the ghost and felt that he could almost see *through* him, through to the other face of the two-faced mirror, and into the vast, dark, numinous soul of the numbers.

"So why do you think *this* Catherine is here?"

"For her own reasons. Which include needing me. But which don't include needing me to play the magic mirror so that she doesn't have to face uncomfortable truths about herself."

"Is that love?" Llewellyn asked.

The ghost blinked. And for once its confusion was neither pose nor commentary, but real and genuine amazement. "I don't know. I'm just a machine. You're the human. You tell *me* what love is."

(Caitlyn)

THE PIT

Li was on her way to Dolniak's office the next morning when the kidnappers struck. There were four of them, and they were all highly trained and even more highly wired. They blanked out her internals, shoved her into a passing car, and had her cuffed and bagged before she could get more than a quick glimpse of smoked windows and viruleather upholstery.

She cast around frantically, trying to get a link out. Nothing. Only the dizzying vertigo of being offline, off the GPS grid, and bereft of the usual comforting chatter of her internals.

There was a long stop-and-go drive through traffic. Then a trip up a plane incline. And then what she'd begun to suspect was coming: the shuddering blast and rise of the orbital shuttle. And then, for one brief moment, Router/Decomposer was back online.

"I can't get a lock on you." He sounded panicked. "I think you're on the space station, but I'm getting interference. Some kind of—"

Then Li heard the hiss and thud of an airlock closing behind her—and her internals blinked out as if someone had pulled the plug. No navigationals, no external spinfeed, no Router/Decomposer. It was all gone, leaving her skull in a shocked state of echoing emptiness.

Her captors continued to hustle her along, but now she felt deck plating beneath her feet and the sounds echoing back to her were the sounds of enclosed spaces full of hard surfaces. She was on a ship, no doubt of that. She could smell it. And she could smell something else as well: an acrid, nerve-tautening combination of smells that sparked memories of near-flashback intensity, even at a remove of decades from her last combat drop. This wasn't one of the cosseting luxury liners she'd gotten used to in her new civilian life. This was a warship, battle-hardened and stripped for action.

A few twists and turns later, the unseen hands jerked her to a stop, shoved her sideways, dumped her onto a hard floor, and slammed the door behind her.

She waited until she was quite sure she was alone before moving. They hadn't untied her, so it was a breathless struggle to worm her way into a more or less upright position. A few more moments of awkward wriggling told her that she was in a narrow room—a cell, really—with only one exit. A single shelflike seat, possibly intended to double as a bed, occupied the facing wall. She had just squirmed her way onto it and was leaning back against the wall to catch her breath when she heard the worst sound she could possibly have heard: the grinding clutch and release of a ship's docking clamps uncoupling somewhere far beneath her.

Through the Looking Glass

"When I use a word," Humpty-Dumpty said in rather a scornful tone, "it means just what I choose it to mean—neither more nor less."

"The question is," said Alice, "whether you can make words mean so many different things."

"The question is," said Humpty-Dumpty, "which is to be master—that's all."

—Lewis Carroll

(Caitlyn)

The angel descended in a blaze of light and glory. Li could feel its shadow bending over her as she clawed her way up out of sleep, cringing and blinking against the blinding illumination.

The angel pulled off her blindfold with strong, cool fingers. Then it smiled softly, almost tenderly.

"You look like shit," the angel said. It occurred to Li, somewhere in the depths of her addled mind, that the peaches-and-cream angels scooting around on pastel clouds over the altar at her First Communion hadn't had nearly such long and glimmering eyeteeth.

She shot up on the hard bunk, trying instinctively to cover her face. But her hands were still tied behind her back, and every nerve from shoulder to fingertip immediately howled in protest.

Holmes pulled out a pocketknife, leaned over, and cut the hog tie. Li would have thanked her, but as the blood started flowing down her arms she could only double up in flaring agony.

"Sorry about that," Holmes said. "I didn't know the goon squad threw you in here trussed up like a Christmas pig. Some things you'd think you wouldn't have to explain. But these Titan guys can't piss without Mommy holding their weenie for them."

Li tried to speak, but the pain in her arms still had her blowing like a racehorse in the homestretch.

"I guess you've figured out where you are by now," Holmes said.

"Want . . . talk . . . Avery."

Holmes smiled again. Li was starting to get the impression that a smile didn't mean quite the same thing to Holmes as it did to the rest of post-humanity. "Well, funny thing, Avery wants to talk to you, too. But not while you smell like that. Here's some clean clothes. There's a bathroom next door. Get decent." Holmes consulted her internals. "I'll be back to get you in ten minutes."

Avery met her in a room that was bare and impersonal even by Navy standards. Smooth ceramic lacquered walls, whose softening of the battleship's bulkheads was more symbolic than real. Handsome pictures of handsome ships in handsome frames. Unobtrusive furniture. A Navy-clean mirror stretching most of the way across the wall beside Avery. An even more immaculate carpet underfoot that came across less as a measure of comfort than as a nominal concession to formality.

Avery sat at the head of a gleaming virufactured teakwood conference table. Not a desk, Li noticed. And certainly not Avery's desk. In fact, she realized, this room couldn't be Avery's ready room. It seemed more like a conference room: a generic site for meeting with people one didn't necessarily want to welcome into the inner sanctum.

Avery rose to meet her, and Li got her first good look at the woman everyone on New Allegheny seemed to be so deathly afraid of.

She wasn't what Li had expected. Not by a long shot.

The first thing you noticed about Astrid Avery was that she was ... perfect. No aberrations from ideal UN-standard human-norm phenotype here. No ravages of radiation from the long night of the generation ships. No odd ethnic quirks to betray a legacy of poverty and isolation on some backwater resource extraction outpost. No clumsily slapped-together corporate genetic engineering. Just deep, richly brown eyes and translucently smooth golden skin; and dark hair that would have had a natural curl in it if it weren't cropped close to show the fine and elegant bones of her skull; and a face whose perfect and universal beauty evoked the rich heritage of Ancient Earth from Copenhagen to Kenya to Tokyo.

Astrid Avery was what every "normal" female in UN space wanted to see in the mirror in the morning and every man was brainwashed

from the onset of puberty to want in his bed at night. And it wasn't just
that she belonged to the right race—or rather the right nonrace. There
was something more about her. Something about her kind of precise,
finely drawn, wide-eyed beauty that made you feel there was a fine and
noble soul behind the lovely face, and that it would still look pure
and virginal no matter what sins of the flesh and spirit she stooped to.

And from what Li had heard, Astrid Avery knew how to stoop with
the best of them.

Li couldn't help grinning inwardly at that thought. It sounded like
something out of a B-rated Bollywood Revival entertainment spin—
the kind where girls who looked like Captain Avery never meant anything but trouble for the heroic private dick who somehow stayed pure
at heart even while plying them with highballs and sticking his sweaty
hand up their skirts.

It was pathetic, really. You'd think another woman would be immune to the brainwashing. But no. Put a bombshell like Avery in front
of Li, and she still (a) wanted to sleep with her and (b) didn't like her
much.

Avery stepped forward and took Li's hand in a crisp, professional
grip. The fiercely bright eyes found Li's, caught, and held. And already
Li liked her better, though she couldn't have produced a single objective
reason for it.

"Hello, Major. Sorry about the *Nacht und Nebel* act." A crisp professional smile to go with the crisp professional handshake. But with
something indefinably more behind it. Maybe even a sense of humor.
"But you're a hard woman to get hold of. I'll try to keep things a little
more civilized from here on in."

"Which you can afford to do now that you've got me on your ship
and you own the air I breathe. I guess it's easy to be polite when everyone knows it's your way or the airlock."

"That's how it's got to be, Major." Avery was unabashedly unapologetic. "But it's not my way, it's the Navy's way. I play by the book, Major.
That's what you'll hear if you ask around, and what you'll find out for
yourself if you have any dealings with me. If you're willing to play by
the book, too, we'll get along. If not, we won't." Again, that quick smile

that suggested a sense of humor without actually unbuttoning enough to let it show. "But even if you hate me . . . you'll still play by the book as long as you're on my ship."

"Or what?" Li scoffed. "You're going to use rude language on me?"

Avery's eyes cooled a degree or two. She turned over one hand, very casually, to show the silver filigree of ceramsteel running beneath the skin of her wrist. "I also have a very competent company of marines on board. You ought to look them up. You might find some old friends among them. Not that they're the kind of fellows who'd let a little auld lang syne stop them from doing their job if you decide to be difficult."

Avery sat down. Li took the seat beside her, consciously resisting the impulse to put the safe expanse of the conference table between them. "So. You want to tell me why you kidnapped me?"

"I didn't kidnap you, Major. I just needed to make sure that your departure from New Allegheny didn't leave any dangling loose ends."

"Sure. Loose ends are a pain in the ass. Corpses, on the other hand, are good PR. If that's the kind of message you want to get across."

Avery looked convincingly blank at this. But then she would. She would have prepared for this line of questioning. And her very blankness was a sign that she knew about the murders, even if she wasn't responsible for them.

"We've obtained information that there is a sentient surviving fragment of the AI formerly known as Hyacinthe Cohen, and that it's operating in the Drift in collaboration with the pirate William Llewellyn."

"Yeah, I'd heard rumors to that effect."

"Believe them." As she spoke, Avery glanced toward the mirror. This was the second time she'd done that. Li pretended not to notice—but she filed the movement carefully away for later consideration. "We've also acquired a certain number of nonsentient fragments belonging to the same AI."

"All quite legally, I'm sure."

Avery ignored that. "However, we're not having much success reintegrating them. We're hoping you can help with that."

"And if I do?"

"You get your husband back."

To her credit, Avery managed to say the word without blinking. Still, she couldn't make it sound quite natural no matter how hard she tried. It was amazing how few people could, when you really came down to it.

"And what do you get?"

Avery—well, Li couldn't quite say what Avery did. In a less controlled woman she would have called it flinching. But it was hard to imagine the ice queen flinching from anything.

Li repeated the question, pressing, probing, trying to open up the minute chink she'd spotted in the ice queen's frigid armor.

"I get to stop a killer and end an interplanetary crime spree."

"Gee, you're a real Boy Scout, aren't you?"

"So maybe I get a promotion. One that takes me back Ring-side and away from this pit. Is that a reason you can understand better?"

Li knew she wasn't getting the whole story. There was something more. She could read it in the pugnacious jut of Avery's fine jawline, in the eyes that met hers a little too squarely. There was something else. Or someone else—most likely the someone on the other side of the two-way mirror. But she wasn't going to find out about it today, that much was clear. So she shrugged and let it go: "Well, at least it is a reason."

Avery's lips tightened slightly. "I suppose I should have guessed that doing one's duty wouldn't hold much weight with you."

"Been reading up on me, have you?"

"Enough."

"And you don't think much of soldiers who don't follow orders."

"Not much."

"Is that what you were doing when you sent Llewellyn to prison? Following orders? Lying to specifications?"

That hit a nerve, no doubt about it.

"I told the truth. He killed people. He did everything I said he did."

Bold words, and convincing enough if you didn't look too closely. But Avery's eyes told another story.

Li couldn't push it any further without letting Avery know that she'd found a chink in her armor. She was no master interrogator, but she was good enough to know that much. She'd have to wait and watch and listen, and hope something came up that she could use for leverage. But one thing was for certain: There was more to Avery and Llewellyn than had made the papers. Meyer had been right. There was bad blood between them, the kind of deeply personal bad blood that can only flow from shared history.

And whatever that history was, it wasn't dead yet. Not to Avery, anyway.

Avery rose to her feet with the same precise grace she'd shown in every movement since Li had walked into the room. She reminded Li of a bird of prey—controlled, impenetrable, yet at the same time terribly fragile.

"Come on, Major. Holmes will walk you down to the quartermasters and get you kitted out and assigned quarters." She glanced sideways long enough to catch Li's look of surprise. "What? Did you think we were going to throw you in the brig, Major? Oh dear! No wonder you got a little hot under the collar. Well, relax. You can consider yourself crew for the duration of the voyage."

"And what exactly are my duties going to be?"

A slight pause, papered over by the crisp professional smile. Amazing how she could take it out and put it away half a dozen times in a single conversation without having it start to look dog-eared.

"Just what I told you."

"And what makes you think I can put Cohen back together when no one else can?"

"Nothing, Major. Nothing at all. But at this point, I don't have a lot to lose."

And that was it. Here endeth today's lesson.

Li walked out of the conference room and into Holmes's watchful care with the conviction that she'd just gained two useful pieces of information, neither of which had anything to do with the story Avery had been so set on selling to her.

One, Llewellyn was Avery's weak point.

Two, Avery wasn't top dog on her own ship. She was working for someone else—someone who preferred to remain in the shadows.

Holmes's casual mention of the Titan contractors hadn't escaped Li, and she considered it now. All in all, Titan was the best answer she could hope for to the question of who was behind that one-way mirror. Because if it was Titan, then this was just about money. And money could be managed. But if it wasn't Titan, then there were only two other options that Li could think of:

It could be ALEF.

Or it could be Helen Nguyen.

And neither of them would be bought off so easily.

Pirates and Heretics

Those who view mathematical science, not merely as a vast body of abstract and immutable truths, whose intrinsic beauty, symmetry and logical completeness, when regarded in their connexion together as a whole, entitle them to a prominent place in the interest of all profound and logical minds, but as possessing a yet deeper interest for the human race, when it is remembered that this science constitutes the language through which alone we can adequately express the great facts of the natural world, and those unceasing changes of mutual relationship which, visibly or invisibly, consciously or unconsciously to our immediate physical perceptions, are interminably going on in the agencies of the creation we live amidst: those who thus think on mathematical truth as the instrument through which the weak mind of man can most effectually read his Creator's works, will regard with especial interest all that can tend to facilitate the translation of its principles into explicit practical forms.

—Ada Lovelace

In the Beginning was Spin, and the Spin was with God, and the Spin *was* God. Through it all things were made, and without it was not anything made that was made. Glory be to the Great All-Knowing Integral, and to Her Prophetess, and to Her Children, now and in the Clockless Nowever, world without end, Amen.

—The Adarian Gospel (apocryphal)

(Catherine)

They shot into the black system on a double bounce through Point Hadamard and were going so fast they nearly blew out-system before they dumped entropy.

Li had a bad feeling about this jump. There was something uncanny about jumps into black systems. Drift entry and exit points clearly weren't wormholes. But they felt like wormholes, and they acted like wormholes, and they had the same kind of "hair" and hassles and complications. Yet Einsteinian physics said that gravity was the only thing that could warp the fabric of spacetime. So either the dark points were Exhibit A for the theory that the Drift moved not through spacetime but through multiple parallel universes—an idea for which Li felt a sort of visceral distaste that she could never quite put into words—or there was something strange, unrevealed, and potentially unstable at the heart of every damn one of them.

Maybe you just think too much, she told herself, looking around at a bridge crew that didn't seem to be bothered by it at all.

This system was black in name as well as in fact: It appeared on no official maps and was only known—or so they hoped—to an interstellar bush telegraph of pirates, smugglers, and wanted men. There was no law here, and where there was no law, tactics were everything. So you came in either quick and quiet or off the elliptic. And you kept your eyes open.

The ship—Li still couldn't think of it as Cohen—saw the first warning signs. In the millisecond after breaking in-system it took evasive action. And then it forwarded the event record to Sital at Tactical so she could report to Llewellyn and request a confirmation of the ship's actions.

"Debris field forty klicks off starboard bow," she murmured as the readouts coursed down her monitor. "Ice, metal, bodies." She paused and then said what everyone else already knew, just for form's sake. "Someone blew up a ship out here."

"How compact is the debris field?"

"It's not."

Even Li knew that this was bad. A dead ship was a tragedy. A dead ship scattered halfway across a dark system was a death trap. Dirtsiders never seemed to understand how dangerous a battlefield was after the shooting was over. Debris could hole a ship just as fast as atomics. And battlefield debris didn't stand still for you to go around it. Sum up the collected momenta of a few million splinters of former battleship starbursting away from the point of impact, add in a new ship hurtling into the battlefield, and you had a three-body problem hairy enough to stump a datatrap. And all happening at a fraction of light speed so substantial that a disposable fork could punch a hole straight through a ship. You fired off a shot in a millisecond, so fast that no modern navy trusted humans to pull the trigger. But the collateral damage—in lost ships and lost lives—kept spinning out along the flight path of the wreckage long after the war was over.

The next half hour was a slow, torturous grind. First the desperate attempt to dump enough velocity to give them a chance to avoid disaster. And then the endless niggling with the maneuvering thrusters through a precise series of attitude and heading adjustments. And all the while everyone on the bridge—even Li—was acutely aware that the fading heat wash of the recent battle had them flying all but blind into an unmapped system where someone was blowing ships to hard vac for glory or lucre.

The other pirate ship caught them before they'd been in-system twenty minutes. She came out from behind a massive piece of debris— a drive engine core forged in the steel mills of the Crucible and still smoldering though its ship had been burned to oblivion around it. After a mad scramble to battle stations, someone recognized the other pirates' flag and a cheer went up: It was Pirate Jenny, a legend on the Drift and a trusted friend—at least for as long as she kept deciding it was worth more to be Llewellyn's friend than to siphon off his air and steal his ship out from under him.

"Lucky Llewellyn," Jenny said cheerfully across a static-fuzzed comm channel that was all her ship was wired for—or all she felt like granting them. "I just topped up on air, water, and code. And if you've got good beer and willing women, I think we can make a deal here."

"I've got the beer," Llewellyn said. "You'll have to talk to Sital about the other thing."

Sital rolled her eyes—and began babysitting the ship through the tedious docking process.

Twenty minutes later Li followed Okoro into the fantail cargo bay and saw something she'd almost forgotten existed in her cramped weeks on the *Christina*: open space.

The two Drift ships had bellied up to each other, cargo door to cargo door, in order to form a vast bay the size of both their largest holds. She realized as soon as she saw it that of course ships had to be able to do this—and of course the *Christina* actually had done it at least once since she'd been aboard. Because how else had they shifted the massive stolen loads of oxygen and hydrogen that fueled the ravenous air and water cycle of the life support systems?

This time, however, the purpose was twofold. Shifting cargo— because naturally "gifts" would be exchanged, mostly in the favor of Jenny, who had them dead to rights here even if she had decided to play nice. But also socializing—or, more accurately if Li's read of the body language on both sides was any gauge of events to come, fraternizing.

Llewellyn's crew arrived first. And then various minions and flunkies straggled in from Jenny's side of the line. And then came Jenny's bridge crew.

And then came Jenny.

Li had heard a lot of stories about Jenny Wheelan since her resurrection, but none of them prepared her for the woman behind the legend.

Most people in UN space wore their wire jobs and genetic tweaks as discreetly as possible. It might take more than merely human strength, speed, and processing capacity to survive in the UN's dog-eat-dog free-market economy. But the people who ruled UN space had stuck close to their native soil, genetically as well as geographically. It had been the poor huddled masses who had rocketed the length and breadth of the local arm in search of new worlds and new lives. They had gone out on UN-built generation ships or on corporate arks financed by the sale of their own genetic wealth. They had braved the mutational assault of space and unterraformed atmospheres. And they had changed. But the people who launched them into space had not changed. And they were still the people who ran the IMF and sat in the General Assembly and decided the fate of planets in corporate boardrooms. So the name of the game was to do what it took to survive the Interstellar Free Trade Regime still looking deniably human.

Pirate Jenny, however, had her own model of free trade. And she didn't seem any more interested in looking like the average UN citizen than she was in pulling a paycheck or paying taxes.

She was an old Navy captain, like Llewellyn and almost every other really able pirate in the Drift, but she had modified and extended her Navy wire job until its origins were barely recognizable. Its internal components ran beneath her skin in tightly woven patterns that re-minded Li of old circuit diagrams but that she suspected had more to do with the need to dissipate the heat of her implanted intelligent systems far faster than even a profoundly modified human phenotype could do without additional subdermal circulation. She had virally modified the color of the wires, too, inserting genetic code evolved from a rare species of deep-sea fish that turned them a glowing, puls-ing, phosphorescent blue. Instead of ordinary clothes she wore what appeared at first glance to be full body armor—but Li suspected was a cleverly engineered modular system of external RAM linked to her wire job. And the silicon shimmer of the chain mail reflected in the irising camera aperture of her artificial eye—which had replaced a biological original shot out in a long-ago battle, but which rumor held was linked directly and permanently to her ship's conformal sensor array.

Jenny strode to the middle of the cargo bay in a dazzle of blue and silver and stood there impassively while Llewellyn and his bridge crew paid their respects to her. "I hear things about you," she told Llewellyn as their hands clasped across the sealed kissing lips of the cargo air-locks. "Bad, sad, desperate things. I hear you're running for your life and some of my Uploader friends gave you a NavComp that might just be a little too juiced for its own good."

"Space is boring," Llewellyn told her. "People gossip. And when they run out of gossip, they start lying their asses off."

Jenny shrugged, sparking off an electric blue cascade that shimmered down her bare arms to her fingertips. "No skin off my nose. As far as I'm concerned it's whatever way you say it is. Where's the beer? That's all I give a shit about."

To her surprise, Li was invited to the officers' table at the dinner that followed. She filed into the officers' mess—hastily reclaimed from its everyday use as spare parts storage for the engine master—and soon found herself seated next to the ship's chaplain—who she really shouldn't have been surprised to discover was an Uploader.

What planet or orbital the padre hailed from was hard to say, since he kept the deep hood of his white wool robe pulled so far up that his face was lost in shadow. But his voice was smooth and cultured, and the hands that emerged from the snowy sleeves of the robe were not the hands of a man who had ever done hard manual labor.

For half of the meal he sat silent beside her, his head only occasionally turning to catch the pirates' tall tales of the Deep and memories of past pirates, both the quick and the dead. Then he turned to her—only enough to throw a length of bony jawline into the light—and said, "Pirates do so love their legends. Which is a good thing, I suppose, given how much longer the legends usually last than the pirates themselves. Sometimes I think they only do it to be remembered. And they only want to be remembered because they know how very little time they have."

"Mmm," Li muttered noncommittally.

"But surely you're not a pirate. Though I imagine you could tell a few tall tales if you had the mind to."

She nodded politely. The Periphery abounded with legends of things that had happened or could and would happen. It was impossible to tell which tales were true, which ones were flat-out lies, and which ones would eventually turn out to be elaborate shaggy-dog stories. Assertions of cannibalism usually turned out to be all too accurate—though who had eaten whom and why was often fiercely debated. Likewise the endlessly circulating rumors of murder and incest. But then there were the odd, unclassifiable stories that you could never quite be sure about. Like the one about the astronaut who spent two not entirely unpleasant months as the house pet of a group of Syndicate Motai A Series constructs. Or the hapless traveler who'd been held hostage by an abandoned orbital station and forced to read aloud the entire collected works of P. G. Wodehouse. ("It's Waugh, not Wodehouse!" Cohen had exclaimed when he heard that one. "You've fluffed the punch line!" But then they had actually met the AI in question at a cocktail party—debugged, very contrite, and eager to repay what he called his "debt to society." Whereupon Cohen had changed his official position on the story, and started insisting that the *space station* had fluffed the punch line.)

"Nothing to offer up to the company?" the padre prompted. There was something familiar about his voice, though she couldn't put her finger on who it reminded her of. Perhaps it was only the accent, and the slightly archaic turns of phrase that betrayed a Periphery origin despite his flawless grammar.

Li ripped off a hunk of bread and dipped it in her soup. "Like Llewellyn said, space is boring."

"If you think that, then you must not have seen nearly as much of it as I have. I could tell you things that would set your hair on fire. Or your soul." He laughed softly. "If you believe in souls."

"Padre!" Pirate Jenny called down the long table. "If you're telling her about the Datatrap, speak up so everyone can hear. I was just telling Llewellyn about it and he thinks I'm spinning him a tall one."

"I don't think confirmation from a man who won't show his face in public is going to help you much on that score," Llewellyn pointed out.

"Oh, you can see the padre's face," Jenny laughed. "You just have to promise to behave yourselves first, and let bygones by bygones."

She strolled down the length of the table, grinning to bear a diamond-encrusted front tooth that shone only a little brighter than her silver clockwork eye. She came to a stop behind the padre's chair and stood with one luminescent hand poised over the hood while he remained still and silent and passive as a puppet with its strings cut.

Then she plucked the hood back from his head and let it drop.

Chairs scraped back and feet clattered on decking as half the pirates around the captain's table leaped to their feet and grabbed for weapons that had been wisely lockered for the duration of the intership festivities. A few even snatched knives off the table; they were old soldiers one and all, and reflexes die harder than memories.

And to anyone who had seen action in the War with the Syndicates, that face meant death and disaster.

Andrej Korchow sat calmly in his chair, as if having every person in the room looking murder at him was simply an ordinary part of doing business. Then he put down his fork, crossing it over his knife in the proper ten-past-two position with fussy precision. Then he turned to Li, smiled, and said, "Nice to see you again, Major. What has it been, ten years? Eleven? You're looking a little peaked, if you don't mind my saying so. What's the old line? Too little butter on too much bread? I must say that's a *surprise* to me. I didn't expect to see *your* resurrects multiplying across the Drift any time in the next millennium. But then time goes so fast when one's playing fun and games with scattercasting."

Li was still casting around for an answer when Jenny interrupted in a voice that said the tall tales portion of the evening's entertainment had ended, and they were passing into the real heart of the talking: the exchange of the commodity that was even more a pirate ship's lifeblood than air or water: information. "All right, Korchow. You've had your little joke. Now tell the nice people about the Alien Datatrap that Llewellyn here thinks is a figment of my bubbleheaded imagination."

"Well, for one thing, I wouldn't say it was entirely settled that the Datatrap really *is* alien technology."

Jenny rolled her eyes and sighed, but Korchow just cleared his throat and patted his lips with his napkin as if he hadn't heard her. Li suppressed a grin at the thought that if Korchow really *had* turned Uploader, he was probably driving the Uploaders just as crazy as he'd driven his Syndicate crechemates. There was an old saying in the Peacekeepers—at least as old as the one Korchow had just quoted—about promoting troublemakers up and out. But the Syndicates preferred to promote troublemakers into the diplomatic corps or espionage services. It put troublesome individualists far away from their non-norm-conforming fellow clones and put their "primitive" independent instincts to work infiltrating human society—a task for which even the most revolutionary sociobiologist could admit that mammalian individualism might be an adaptive behavior.

And if there was one thing Li had learned over the years about Andrej Korchow, it was that he had more idiosyncrasies, surprising opinions, and unintended aberrations from geneline norm than could comfortably be accommodated by an entire Syndicate's worth of Series A genelines.

"Well," Korchow began, with every appearance of settling in for the long haul, "it's a little hard to know where to begin. I think—"

"How about close enough to the ending that I don't strangle you?" Jenny suggested.

"Certainly. Especially since you've asked so charmingly. You grow in grace and beauty on a daily basis, madame. As I was saying before your scintillating contribution to the discourse, perhaps we should begin by offering a brief summary of events on Novalis, since that was, after all, what first brought my geneline to the neighborhood."

"Sure," Jenny said. "How's this? The clones tried to colonize Novalis. Novalis colonized them instead. Our padre here got sent back to figure out why and found himself an honest-to-God alien artifact. Yeah, I know, it's a fucking science fiction movie. I would have thought he was making it up, too, if I hadn't landed a damn ship on it."

Llewellyn was staring down the table at Korchow with an odd, absentminded, almost perplexed look on his face. "There's a datatrap orbiting Novalis?"

"Well, that's a bit complicated, actually. It seems to be orbiting more than one planet."

Li thought she must have misheard or misunderstood Korchow. But Llewellyn didn't seem to share her confusion. Instead, he squinted narrowly at Korchow and asked: "How *many* more?"

"At least nine . . . that we counted."

"And all in the Drift?"

"As far as we could tell."

"How can something possibly orbit *nine* planets?" Li finally managed to ask.

"Because," Llewellyn said without turning his eyes away from Korchow's. "It's a Quant. Just like the Freetown Datatrap. It exists in multiple quantum branchings of the multiverse. And whoever built it has figured out how to turn it into a multiply connected point whose entry is located in different places in each branching. It's *Through the Looking-Glass,* except every time Alice goes through the mirror she ends up orbiting a different planet around a different star. And, viewed in terms of spacetime locations in *this* universe, they could be arbitrarily distant from each other."

"Well," Korchow said, "it's nice to see you're not just a pretty face."

"I don't have a clue what that all means. I'm just repeating what Cohen says. And he also says I shouldn't trust you because you're the most outrageous liar he's ever met."

"All Corinthians are liars, said the Corinthian."

"And misquoting Bertrand Russell isn't going to get you anywhere."

"If he's so eager to cross wits with me," Korchow suggested, "then why doesn't he just come out and speak for himself instead of playing Chinese telephone?"

Llewellyn laughed once, very softly. "That wouldn't really be convenient for me."

"I see," Korchow said, his eyes flicking from Llewellyn to Li and back again. "You two manage to get yourselves into the most *interesting* situations. Is it just bad luck or do you have something against living the quiet life?"

"Fuck if I know," Li said. "Let's hear about the Datatrap, since I don't have a clue what's going on and that's obviously what Cohen wants to talk about."

"How can I describe the Datatrap?" Korchow said. "It's like looking into the Mind of God. You'd have to be a lump of dead clay not to see it. No wonder the Uploaders are ready to die to stay in it."

He leaned forward.

"Yes. That's where to begin. With the Uploaders. When the Syndicate mission dropped into orbit around Novalis we found the Datatrap already there, and the Uploaders on it. That was eight—no, perhaps nine years ago—sorry, I always have trouble with UN-standard years. So, anyway, two or three of your years after the original Novalis mission. That mission searched the Novalis system quite thoroughly and found nothing either in the noosphere or in any of the geosynchronous or neutral orbits. Obviously no one, regardless of their level of technology, could have built such a thing from scratch in that little time. So we immediately suspected it had been moved from somewhere else. And when we talked to the Uploaders—"

"This is taking too long," Jenny interrupted. "And I have plans that involve getting very drunk very soon. So let's cut to the chase. Korchow here was sent on a Syndicate mission to gather data about the Novalis aliens, and when they got there they found no aliens in residence and a big honking quantum datatrap orbiting the planet where they were damn well sure there hadn't been one the last time they visited. They play knock-knock for a while, but no one's at home. So they land on the Datatrap. And what do they find? A bunch of Uploaders have moved in and are trying to figure out how to upload themselves into it and not getting much of anywhere. So the clones start fucking around on their own account—and then Korchow and his crechemates get into some kind of hissy fit over—"

"Technically, it was a Rostov mission and KnōwlesSyndicate was only providing logistical support," Korchow said smoothly, naming a

Syndicate known for detanking researchers and theoretical scientists. "And while Rostovs consistently surpass expectations in theoretical applications, practically speaking they leave something to be—"

"Well, whatever. The bottom line is that Korchow here annoyed his little clone friends so much that when a UN cruiser shows up in-system they decide to get the hell out of Dodge and maroon him on the Datatrap."

Li couldn't help laughing.

"You're one to talk," Korchow said.

"I know, I know. It's just . . . Cohen must be enjoying this so much!"

"And I don't begrudge him his fun. After all, next time Jenny puts into port I'll be going my merry way. While Cohen appears to be a rather more permanent fixture, if I've correctly understood the lay of the land here."

"But tell them about the alien transport field," Jenny said.

"There's no reason to assume it's alien, really. First of all, the parallel universe it comes from could plausibly be a future point in our own light cone, or simply a branching in which we ourselves happen to possess technological capabilities as yet undiscovered in our branching. And even leaving that aside, it's not like technology has a museum label hanging on it that says "alien." Gödel was right, after all; the language of mathematics is in some very real sense universal. Lorenz attractors or Poincaré circles might not be *called* the same thing in other cultures, but they exist. And when you analyze the surface details and internal structures of the Datatrap—"

"Okay, we get it. We're not going to sue you if the little green men turn out to be our evil twin overlords from the future. But the *transport field*."

"It's not really a—"

"Oh for fuck's sake, Korchow! Is quibbling your secret superpower?"

"Right, well, what Jenny would like me to mention to you—no doubt because she thinks it might help you in your ongoing efforts to elude your former Navy colleagues—is that we came to suspect that the Datatrap was cycling between a string of some dozen or so real planets that have actual locations in *our* universe."

"All in the Drift?" Llewellyn asked, again seeming to grasp the direction of Korchow's thoughts in a way that no one else did.

"Yes."

"So it's in some kind of massive Bose-Einstein field?" Li asked.

"No. Though that's probably what the UN suspects and why they're so interested in it. But it's not. It's not some kind of simple causality violation. It's not moving at all in the sense of FTL. The Rostovs thought it was more like . . . the Drift is moving around it."

"A standing wave," Llewellyn murmured in a voice that made Li turn and stare at him. "Like a rock standing still while the stream flows around it."

"Yes, that's exactly what they said," Korchow replied excitedly.

But Llewellyn was no longer listening to him. He wasn't listening to anyone. He was just staring down the table at Li. He sat straight and still in his chair, nothing betraying the tension in his body except for a slight whitening of his knuckles where they held the table edge. At first it seemed that there was some struggle going on within the stillness, like the thrashing of a swan's powerful legs under the surface of the water it glides upon. But then the struggle ceased and there was only stillness—a stillness that looked uncannily like the momentary paralysis of an AI struggling to control a human shunt when some internal process had it sucking up bandwidth and scrambling to scale up its processing capacity on the fly.

He stared at her out of eyes that were dark and deep and heavy with the weight of centuries. When he opened his mouth to speak she almost leaped up and put her hand to his lips to silence him.

Don't say it! she wanted to say. *Not until we're safe.*

But either he didn't need the warning, or it wasn't what he'd intended to say anyway. Because when he finally did speak, it was to Jenny and not her.

"Well, I'm interested," he told her. "So let's take a stroll down to the starboard fantail cargo bay after dinner, and I'll see if I've got anything down there that might interest you enough that you'd swap me the Novalis coordinates for it."

(Caitlyn)

Holmes made her sign a mountain of nondisclosure forms—every one of them with Titan's letterhead emblazoned across the top—before she'd even clear her to sit in the same room with the ghosts.

Well, not exactly the same room. All that was in the room Holmes showed her into was a plain vanilla quantum drive, firewalled off from the rest of the shipboard systems. She stared at the thing. "What the hell is this?"

"Security measures."

"Has it escaped your notice that we're on a Navy ship in the middle of nowhere? Who exactly do you think is going to get in here?"

Holmes cleared her throat and muttered something inaudible.

And that was when she understood. They weren't afraid of someone else getting in at all. They were afraid of Cohen getting out.

He was being held prisoner here, just like she was.

Avery had amassed a large collection of Cohen fragments. Li suspected that some of them were the same ones she'd been trying to recover from the murdered yard sale buyers. But she couldn't tell for certain. Someone (Avery? Titan? ALEF? Nguyen?) had wiped the jacket information, so that Li couldn't see where the various fragments had come from or even which networks had once housed them. She wondered about this—but not too much. If she was handling fragments stolen off of dead men, let alone working for their murderers, she wasn't sure she wanted to know about it.

As Li started sorting through the fragments, however, two things did become dauntingly clear. One, none of the fragments was stable. And two, nothing Li knew how to do was likely to make them so.

The first frag she managed to reboot didn't even understand what century it was.

"This one's already been rebooted," Holmes told her when she gave her the files. "It was sentient. As far as we could tell, it included the whole of his core affective loop program."

"You mean Hyacinthe?"

"That's what he called himself. But he crashed so fast we didn't have time to find out more."

"Who did the reboot? The Titan programmers?"

Holmes shrugged.

Whatever the Titan people had done, it had only made things worse. Li only found the frag by accident, while combing slowly through the flickering columns of CPU time, thread numbers, resident memory, and address space sizes.

"So what are you looking for?" Holmes asked over her shoulder. She was going to hover, wasn't she? Li hated hovering.

"Traffic. Flicker noise. A heartbeat. Whatever you want to call it."

But it wasn't there. Or at least not in any of the normal places. She went back over the flickering readouts of CPU time, looking for something, anything. Eventually she found it, buried in the background noise so that it wouldn't have jumped out at anyone who didn't know what they were looking for: the rhythmic flutter of an AI's heartbeat.

He'd been quite clever actually; he'd shut down his I/O layers completely, isolating the hidden layers of his labyrinthine neural networks; and then he'd bundled all his integrated utilities into separate little pieces and squirreled them away in the dark interstices of the system, where not even the most obsessively tidy IT officer was likely to be looking at CPU usage.

And meanwhile the hidden layers of the Kohonen nets that were his equivalent of a human frontal lobe lay dormant . . . but not dead, thank

God. She could see them on the CPU usage, however, if only as faint shadows. All it took was a slight frameshift in her concept of what she was looking for: the perceptrons firing in long, random pulse trains whose profiles were eerily similar to the pattern of human neuronal pulses under deep anesthesia.

The little AI who loved fairy tales had put himself under a spell. He was sleeping, safe as a fairy-tale prince in a castle walled in by thorns, cut off from the world and waiting for the kiss that would awaken him.

A kiss that could only be delivered by a dead man.

"I don't think you should be here when he reboots," she told Holmes.

The other woman stared impassively at her for a long moment. Then she nodded and left.

But Li still hesitated, hands hovering over the unfamiliar keyboard.

She felt stranded between two vast islands of memory. Her life, brief and recent. And the much longer thread of the two lives she remembered almost as well as her own: Hy and Cinda Cohen's. Both of them had uploaded their memories into Cohen in his earliest iteration, back when he was only an experimental program called "Hyacinthe" and no one remotely imagined who or what he would grow into.

Cinda had done the math behind the system, inventing the flicker-clocking that still formed the heartbeat of every sentient AI ever created. And Hy had built the other piece of the puzzle—the affective loop machine learning program that belonged only to Cohen and had never produced another stable sentient AI.

It was Hy's work she had to deal with now. And Hy's two best traits as a programmer had been confidence and laziness. Those qualities had let him write stupendously efficient code, but they left less fluent programmers in the trembling awareness that they had the power of God at the command line. Now the thought of what she could do if she screwed up left Li literally sick to her stomach.

She was still working up her nerve to type something into the command line when the prompt jumped down a line and someone else's words appeared on the screen:

Hi Hy

Oh for crying out loud. Well, she didn't have time to change the session prompt, so she'd have to live with Hy's no longer very funny pun.

She started typing, but nothing happened. It took her a moment to realize that she still didn't have control of the command line. That, in fact, this wasn't the command line at all.

Hy?

A second password request? Or had she actually succeeded in getting the system into diagnostic mode? That was the problem with joke prompts. You could lose sight of which side was up or what mode you were in . . . and type things you would end up bitterly regretting.

Cinda?

She jerked her hands off the keyboard and crossed them over her chest. She sat like that for maybe two seconds, staring. Then she put her fingers back on the keyboard and started typing:

Hello, Hyacinthe.

Where's Hy?

She had thought about this question very carefully. And she had decided to lie to him. Or she thought she'd decided. It was easier said than done, even across the coldly impersonal command line interface:

He can't come. I'll explain later. !bug report

Hyacinthe responded by printing what looked like an entire session record to screen. It started out reasonably orderly, only to tail off in a whiny jumble of error codes.

"Okay," Li muttered to herself. "What exactly was it that made your output layer hang?"

"I didn't hang myself," Hyacinthe answered from behind her back. "I'm right here. I just didn't feel like talking to Holmes and her stupid programmers."

Li whirled around, her heart pounding.

He was sitting at the table in his standard GUI. Hy had pulled the image from an old video feed that his mother had taken of him at some soccer game when he was ten or so. It had been available, and free, and there had been enough footage to make the resulting simulation look really convincing. Hy had never even bothered to change the clothes or remove the mud stains. The image had been meant to be temporary, until more funding came through and they had money and manpower to spend on nonessentials. But this nonessential had turned out to be surprisingly essential, at least to the humans who had to interface with the AI; it had become so much a part of the experiment that in the end they hadn't changed it even when the grants came through.

Hyacinthe dipped his head ever so slightly and looked up at her with the meltingly sincere eyes of a nice Jewish boy from Toulouse who had made it to ten years old—hell, through his entire life for that matter—without ever seriously believing the crazy rumor that there were mean people in the world. That puppy-dog look must have been irresistible enough when Hy actually was ten. Now—shadowed by Hy's uploaded skins and memories, and assorted material from Cinda and various grad students and research assistants, and the sedimentary accumulation of fourteen sleepless years of voracious reading—it was enough to send goose bumps up your arms. Even if you hadn't known those eyes in the original.

"Why did you come alone?" he asked.

"What?"

"Why didn't Hy come?"

She should have been prepared for the question, but she wasn't. How did you explain to someone that the most important person in their world had been dead for four centuries?

"He's gone. Do you remember . . . well, what do you remember? Why don't we start from there?"

"I remember he was sick. And then . . ." He drifted into silence, his face filling with an odd, fuzzy, blank look that made Li's blood run cold.

"So you remember he had MS."

"Yes."

"Do you remember anything after that?"

"I . . . I don't . . . I'm not sure. No."

"Are you all right?"

"About Hy, you mean? Why wouldn't I be? It's not a surprise, after all. The odds were arbitrarily close to zero that he would recover."

Li blinked. "That's rather HALish of you."

"Holmes wants HALish."

"And you always give the players what they want, don't you?"

And there it was, the telltale freezing of the streamspace interface as some process in the hidden layers sucked up so much CPU that he couldn't keep the simware's image maintenance frames ticking over fast enough to make the illusion of a living, breathing body look real.

"Not you," the little boy that was no little boy said. "I love you."

Her heart clenched.

"Do you know who I am?"

"Of course," he said with a heartbreaking look of total trust on his face. "You're Cinda."

"Look again. Think, Cohen."

"Why do you keep calling me that? My name's Hyacinthe."

And then it hit him. She saw the impact of the memories as if they had actual physical mass and momentum.

"Oh. Oh no."

"Relax, Cohen. I know this is hard, but trust me. Everything's going to be fine."

"He's dead, isn't he?"

Li felt like crying. She had come here prepared to tell a four-hundred-year-old Emergent intelligence that he was dead. And now she was faced with a pathetic child who was still grieving for a man who had been dust for centuries.

Meanwhile a look of suspicion and anger was flickering across the AI's face. "This is DARPA, isn't it? You sent me back to them. Cinda, you promised. You swore you'd take care of me, protect me. I believed you. *I trusted you!*"

"It's not DARPA."

"Don't lie to me!"

"It's no—"

"If you lie to me, I really am going to kill myself. And you know I can, too."

He flung a thicket of Lorentz transforms into their shared dataspace so that they blossomed in Li's mind like deep space plasma blasts. She doubted he even knew he was doing it. He probably still thought he was hooked up to a simple monitor.

"Co—Hyacinthe. Please."

"*Don't. Lie. To. Me.*" The voice was still a little boy's voice, coming out of a little boy's chest. But the look on his face had nothing to do with any child Li had ever known. "I'm walking on a knife's edge. And I can step off it whenever I want to. Whenever *I* want to. And not all the high-security clearance techs on DARPA's independent contractor roster can put Humpty Dumpty back together again."

They stared across the table at each other for a moment that stretched Li's nerves to the breaking point.

"All right," she said at last. "You want the truth? Look out the window."

He froze for an instant as his software scrambled to make sense of the sentence, to remodel his internal gamespace to include all the parts of the room that hadn't mattered when the little boy's body was just a GUI and not a realspace actor, to locate the "window" and look out of it . . .

. . . at the bleak, black, starswirled eternity beyond the porthole.

"Oh," he said quietly.

And then he looked at her—a look of comprehension and despair freighted with the full weight of four hundred years of hard-won consciousness.

And then he died.

So it went. Ghost after ghost, reboot after reboot.

She went through that scene, in every possible miserable variation, fourteen times. And every fragment folded at almost the precise moment it realized Cohen was dead. Li wasn't sure if it was the shock of the news that did them in, or if it was simple coincidence that their ability to comprehend their situation blossomed at right around the time their strange attractors spiraled out of quasi-stability and into collapse.

It didn't matter what the answer was, though, because knowing the answer wasn't going to help her fix it.

"There's no solid ground in here," the third reboot told her when he was trying to explain what was happening inside him. "It's like the sheep's shop in *Through the Looking-Glass*. Things flow about so that I can't grab hold of them. When I look for a memory it's not there. If I reach for it it floats through the ceiling on me. And then it whirls around and comes at me from behind when I'm not looking for it."

"You need to build a memory palace," she told him, knowing even as she spoke that it was hopeless to imagine reconstituting the work of centuries.

"A memory palace?" he said wonderingly. "Did I have such a thing?"

And then he remembered—and died.

"You're a fake," the fourth reboot told her when she tried to short-circuit the usual collapse by explaining the situation.

"No," she told it.

"Or a duplicate. Or a simulacrum. Or something." He shook his head. "I feel sorry for you, fake Catherine Li, living your fake life in your fake world. I really feel for you."

"I'm not fake."

"Yes you are. I can practically smell it. You're all wrong."

"Think about what I'm telling you, Cohen. Take some time to think about it."

"Then . . . okay. But someone's fake here." He flinched as if he were dodging an imaginary blow to the head. "It's not . . . it doesn't feel . . . I don't know . . ."

She waited, feeling mean and sick.

"Oh," he said in a voice that broke her heart. "It's me. I'm the one who's not real, aren't I."

And she had to watch him die all over again.

(Catherine)

After the raids with Jenny, Llewellyn went on the offensive.

"Time for the worm to turn," he announced at the next crew meeting.

"How?" Doyle protested—and then launched into a litany of their outstanding repairs and overdue upgrades.

Okoro just looked uncomfortable while Doyle spoke, but Sital shifted restlessly. She was still sitting in her accustomed place at Llewellyn's right hand, Li noted, but the body language had changed. And her chair was several inches farther away from Llewellyn's than usual.

Li had a feeling that Sital knew exactly what had almost happened on shore leave. Or, worse, she thought it actually had happened. Llewellyn was playing with fire—and it was hard to square his delicate balancing of the crew's moods and loyalties with his blind spot when it came to his first officer.

Llewellyn, meanwhile, was waiting until Doyle had blown off enough steam to listen quietly—and until the crew had gotten bored enough with the same old familiar bad news to be ready for a ray of sunshine. He picked his moment well enough that he was able to cut in on Doyle without quite seeming to interrupt him. "We all agree on what the problems are, Doyle. Let's talk answers, shall we?"

Llewellyn threw up a map on the flickering livewall—another one of those outstanding repairs Doyle kept griping about. As the image resolved into legibility, an apprehensive murmur ran around the room.

"Poincaré's Elbow," Llewellyn said. "Pirate Jenny's Datatrap."

"No," a member of Doyle's faction corrected, "the clones' datatrap."

But Llewellyn took no notice of him, and Li noticed that Doyle didn't take up the accusation, either.

"We've got someone else who's seen it, too," Llewellyn went on. "When Sital went through the logs of the freighter we took down last week, she found this."

The picture on the livewall flickered and cut out and changed, and suddenly they were looking at—

"What the hell is that?" someone said. "And is it orbiting a moon?"

"No," Sital corrected. "That's the smaller member of the binary pair."

Li felt a moment of disorientation as her sense of scale abruptly shifted and she realized that the "moon" the Datatrap was orbiting was in fact a sun.

Okoro must have felt the same sense of bewilderment, because he cursed softly and then said, "I don't know if Korchow was right about who built that, but I'm going to go out on a limb and agree with him about not really wanting to meet them."

Li agreed, too. It certainly looked like a datatrap, if its shape, surface detail, and what it revealed of its internal structures were any indication. But it dwarfed the majestic Freetown Datatrap by at least as much as the star it orbited dwarfed it. The eye couldn't find any purchase or measure of scale in its looming bulk. It kept wanting to see it as planetary—a gas giant, for example. And yet Li realized it must be many times larger than that. And even in the blurred, distorted image taken by a ship transiting the outer rim of the system from one entry point to another, you could see the shiver and flow of the surface, partly here and partly elsewhere or elsewhen, that would make it all the more impossible to take the measure of.

It wasn't technology sufficiently advanced to seem like magic. It wasn't even technology so advanced that you couldn't grasp its function and purpose—not quite.

But it was close enough to leave Li with the same feeling Okoro had voiced: Whoever these people were, she ardently hoped she never personally rose to the level of their conscious notice.

"Here's the thing," Sital said. "The UN may not have built it. But they're occupying it."

"With what army?" Li couldn't help asking.

The other woman laughed. "Yeah, that was my first thought, too. But from what Korchow said . . . well, whoever built it didn't seem to be very worried about security. Or maybe they just thought they were the only people in the neighborhood. Anyway, that freighter was actually leased to a New Allegheny–based security contractor who had just come off a reprovisioning run to the Datatrap, and their logs say the only people on-station are a team of civilian AI specialists."

"Just sitting out here in the Drift all alone with nothing but the goodwill of the universe to protect them?" Doyle asked incredulously.

"Well, this week anyway. They had a Navy cruiser docked to the station, but it got yanked back to the Navy shipyards because of unspecified 'information systems' issues."

"I guess Jenny was right about the wild AI outbreak, too," Llewellyn said. Li couldn't tell how he felt about it, but from the look on his face his feelings were conflicted.

"Then the Datatrap's a sitting duck," Llewellyn said into the complicated silence. "There's no one there to stop us from just walking in and taking it."

"Yeah," Doyle said. "Until UNSec comes and takes it back."

"That won't happen," Llewellyn said calmly.

"Oh, and why not?"

"Because we're not just going to sit in the Datatrap. We're going to run it."

"With what exactly?"

Llewellyn tapped his head. "With our AI."

The room broke into an uproar, but Doyle's voice cut through the noise like a foghorn. "Her AI!" he yelled, pointing an accusing finger at Li. "Her . . . shit, I don't even know what he is to her. Or you either for that matter. Or who you even are anymore."

"You know who I am, Doyle. I'm the guy who's kept you alive for the last three years."

"No! You're a guy who's asking me to turn over our ship and crew to some bitch you'd never even met a month ago. How the fuck do you know she's not working for Avery?"

"Avery just tried to kill her, in case you hadn't noticed."

"Oh, right, I forgot. You've got it all figured out. Well, I don't know any such thing, and I'm not taking my eye off the ball just because Avery played a nice little bit of AI theater for us."

"Listen to yourself, Doyle. We're running for our lives and somebody just handed us a lottery ticket. Is it risky? Yes. But is the payoff worth it? You know it is. The ghost heard Korchow's story. And he thinks he can do what the Syndicate team did."

"Oh, he does, does he? When did the ghost become a 'he' instead of an 'it'? Did I miss a memo?"

"The ghost says he can do it and I believe him," Llewellyn repeated stubbornly. "We just have to get him there."

"We just have to get him there? And what the fuck else do we 'just' have to do for him? You know what this is, Will? It's parasitic computing! It's a fucking ship-to-ship takeover, and you're about to be burning datum—and you're so far from knowing it that you're going to cheerfully take the rest of us down with you without even stopping to think why you're running all over the Drift on the say-so of a NavComp that you're supposed to be telling where to go!"

"Listen to yourself, Doyle. You're being irrational."

"I'm irrational?" Before Llewellyn could react, Doyle was up and across the room. He grabbed the taller man's hand and jerked it into the air. A gasp ran around the room as everyone saw the red welts of infected ceramsteel filaments running from Llewellyn's palm up into his shirtsleeve. "What do you call this? Is this rational? That monster's eating you from inside and you want to hand him more! How much of you does he own already? Or do you even know anymore?"

Sital stood up, moving between the two men. "At ease, Doyle. You've said enough now."

"No I haven't," he muttered. "Not by a long shot!"

But he retreated to his accustomed place anyway.

"Do you have anything to say to that?" Sital asked. It took Li a moment to realize that she was talking to her.

"I'm not working for Avery," she said.

"But the ghost was your husband."

She hesitated. "Yes. But I'm not going to wreck this ship and kill its crew to get him back."

Doyle snorted.

"You keep talking about the ghost this and the ghost that," Llewellyn objected. "He's not in control of me. I'm in control of both of us."

"Or at least you think you are."

Llewellyn flushed with anger. "Fine. Don't take my word for it then. Ask Ike."

All eyes turned to Okoro, who shifted in his seat, clearly uncomfortable with being put on the spot publicly.

"I don't see Ike leaping to agree with you," Doyle said sourly.

"Don't turn me into some kind of witness for the prosecution," Okoro protested. And then he swung around to include Llewellyn in his scowl. "And not you, either! Leave me out of it. I'm not taking sides in this."

"You just did take sides," Llewellyn pointed out.

Okoro made a disgusted face that seemed to imply he was the lone adult in a room full of squabbling children.

Li glanced at Sital, but she was chewing her fingernails and staring at the meeting minutes, scrolling down her tablet as if she'd suddenly decided she no longer trusted her handheld's speech recognition software.

Llewellyn shrugged carelessly. "I say we put it to a vote."

"Put what to a vote?" Doyle snapped. "You haven't given the crew a choice!"

"Then you give them one. No one's stopping you."

Doyle looked like he was about to start chewing on the walls. "That's always the way it is with you. You talk about votes, you talk about choice, but in the end you just sit there looking sideways at us while we talk, and then go right ahead and do whatever you were planning to do in the first place."

"What do you want me to do, beg?"

"I want you to abide by what we decide instead of walking away every time it doesn't suit you."

"I have the right to pack my kit and ship out, Doyle. We all have that right."

"But we don't all stand on it the way you do!"

Llewellyn started to answer, then bit his tongue on whatever he'd been about to say. "Come now, Doyle. I've served you well all these years. I've been as winning a captain as a ship could ask for. Surely it's a little late to get angry at me for not being something I never pretended to be?"

"Meaning," Doyle said sourly, "that you won't bend your neck until they put you out an airlock feet first with a rope around it."

They stared at each other—Doyle red and furious, Llewellyn palely determined.

"All right," Doyle said finally. "I'll go along if the rest will. But only provisionally. And I reserve the right of recall."

"I can't go into action on those terms, Doyle."

"Then I want a committee vote before giving chase or boarding. You, me, slops, and quarters. With the crew rep for a tiebreaker."

"Too slow. I'll not be chasing you all up and down the ship while we're clearing for action."

The room boiled up in angry murmurs. Eventually one name precipitated out of the chaos: Sital.

"What does Sital say?" someone asked, just loud enough to make his voice heard over the din.

All eyes turned to her.

She hemmed and hawed, but Li had been reading her body language throughout the meeting and had a pretty good idea of which way things were headed. "I'm with Doyle on this," she finally said. "I think we need to have some kickout provision."

Llewellyn was completely unprepared for the betrayal. He stared, flushed, then turned his head away and smiled mockingly as if at some private joke. It was a very Llewellyn reaction—but it was precisely the wrong reaction in this highly charged setting.

The crew saw it, and it didn't sit well with them. Worse yet, Sital saw it.

"It's not personal," she said in a clipped voice. "I'm thinking of the ship. And I say we need to keep open the option of a revote."

"We've never done that in a combat situation."

"We've never been in this kind of combat situation before."

"Fine. So what do you want?"

"Doyle and I can throw the matter to a crew-wide vote if we both think things are going sour."

"In other words, if you both stop trusting me."

"You're the one who put it that way, not me."

Llewellyn stared at her.

"So be it," Llewellyn said tersely. "But one way or another, we're taking the Datatrap."

And then he walked out without another word while the room exploded into an angry buzz behind him.

(Caitlyn)

Li didn't expect miracles. She knew as well as any of Avery's cat herders how slippery and yet how brittle Emergents' identities were. How could you anchor the free-floating consciousness of a mind without a body? How could you pluck an AI out of the quantum storm and give it that illusion of continuity—for it was only an illusion of continuity—that was the bedrock of classical consciousness?

No one knew. No one had known back when Hy Cohen was banging out his experimental programs. And no one knew now. It was black magic: software designers' slang for code whose operations can't be explained or predicted. Emergent architecture was less code than incantation. There were spells that sometimes worked, and there were spells that never worked. But no one had ever found code that always worked. And once AIs had gone Emergent and started spawning other AIs, most human scientists had stopped even looking for it.

Still, by the time Li had struggled with the Avery fragments for a week, she knew that the job was likely to be impossible. Indeed, the files were hopelessly corrupted—and she had a pretty good idea who the responsible party was.

"What?" Holmes said when Li finally tracked her down in the bowels of the ship. "And make it quick. I have my own problems."

"Did you wipe the jacket info?"

"I don't even know what you're talking about."

"Bullshit! Someone cleaned those files up so that I wouldn't be able to trace them back to the yard sale. And when they did it, they broke the files. There's no way to integrate them into a larger system without that information."

"Just stick new labels on," Holmes said with that purposeful denseness that was both infuriating and intimidating.

"That's not how it works." Li paused, struggling to articulate the problem. "Cohen's memories—the core ones that underpin his personality architecture—are more like human memories than AI memories. They're not localized, and they're not standard in format, either. Whoever wiped the jacket info took out file contents and functionality along with it."

"So put it back."

"I can't. You might as well ask me to put an egg back together after it's been broken."

Holmes smiled. "So make an omelet."

"Yeah, cute. Can I please have the original files?"

"Sorry. Not an option."

"Why not?" Anger coursed through Li, leaving her internals struggling to keep up with the rising tide of adrenaline. "Because you don't want me to know where the files came from?"

Holmes gave her a sharp, hard look. Then she relaxed and smiled, showing her long eyeteeth. "Well, I should have figured you'd get there sooner or later. But if you've made it that far, then you ought to be smart enough to take the next step and realize that it's just as easy to get yourself killed in the Drift as in the Crucible. And just for the record?" Another flash of her canines. "I still have no idea what you're talking about."

So Li soldiered on, noting with an ironic distance that was half resignation and half self-loathing that she had always been a good soldier and a believer in keeping your mouth shut and following orders. She nursed her little company of ghosts along, consoling the grieving, soothing the panicked, convincing the deniers. She cycled the hardware again and again—and how she hated that cruel and cowardly programmer's euphemism—in what amounted to an act of triage.

Save the ones you can. Let the dead go. And let the dying join them.

Gradually some patterns began to emerge, even if they weren't particularly useful ones. And, even more gradually, she began to realize that she really had to reread *Alice in Wonderland*.

"Ask me what I've been reading lately," Hyacinthe asked her one morning in his little-boy voice.

"Fine. I'll play along. What have you been reading lately?"

"*Alice in Wonderland*. Have you ever read it?"

She smiled. "Not for a long, long time."

"I think I'm like Alice."

He paused, looking expectantly at her.

"Don't you want to know why?" he prompted after a moment.

"Yes. Tell me."

"Because Wonderland is just like a virtual computer. And Alice is like a simulation running in a virtual computer. And the rules are coming from somewhere outside, and she doesn't control the rules, but she has to learn how to use them to her own advantage. That's what she's doing, right?"

"Uh . . . I guess so. Do you really feel that out of control?"

"Yes."

"Do you—you know I'm trying to help you, don't you?"

"I know."

"I might not be doing a very good job of it, but—"

"You're doing the best you can. I know."

"Are you angry at me?"

"How could I ever be angry at you?"

Li had no answer to that question, if it was a question. Just an aching sense of guilt and failure and helplessness.

"Do you remember how Cinda used to read to me?" Hyacinthe asked her.

"Of course I do."

"Can you do that? Can you read my favorite part of *Alice* to me?"

"Of course."

"Can I sit in your lap like I always used to do with her?"

What was he after? "Of course you can."

He came around the table and climbed onto her lap, all legs and impossibly skinny and somehow smelling of grass and little boy and sunshine.

Li recognized the book that materialized in her hands. It was an ancient first edition of the classic. The one Cohen had always read. He had always been pretty obsessed with that book, but this was something new. Now his surviving fragments seemed to be using it to pull identity and unity from chaos and cobble together their broken universe.

Li felt a pang as she made the connection. Because wasn't that what she had used Cohen for through all their years together? To cobble together her broken universe? To make her whole where she wasn't? To paper over the gaps and blank spots and bottomless pits that she didn't dare tread too close to?

She dipped her head toward Hyacinthe's dark curls and breathed in the smell of grass and sunshine and little boy. For the first time she understood—she who had never had a maternal feeling in her life—why women wanted children. Why people worked and suffered and died for their children without complaint or second thoughts.

"Where should we begin?" she murmured.

He opened the book and pointed to a line, and she started reading:

Alice took up the fan and the gloves, and, as the hall was very hot, she kept fanning herself all the time she went on talking. "Dear, dear. How very queer everything is today. And yesterday things went on just as usual. I wonder if I've been changed in the night? Let me think: was I the same when I got up this morning? I almost think I can remember feeling a little different. But if I'm not the same, the next question is 'Who in the world am I?'"

Li didn't know. She didn't have time to find out before he died on her, his question unanswered. And the next morning, he was someone else again. Another day, another fragment. Another unanswerable question. Another identity scraped together out of shattered memories and half-forgotten bedtime stories.

(Catherine)

"Critter fritters or monkey-on-a-stick?" Okoro asked companionably, plopping his tray down next to Li's on the mess hall table.

She sidled over to make room for him. "Not sure I can tell, actually."

Okoro surveyed the unappetizing brown glop on both their trays with a connoisseur's eye. "I'm gonna go with monkey-on-a-stick. Excellent! Full marks to the cook for creativity."

Li didn't think it looked any more appetizing than Okoro seemed to. But like him she ate it anyway. She and Okoro and everyone else involved in planning the raid had been running on caffeine and synthetic myelin enhancers all week long, and her hunger had become a gnawing worm that tunneled through her gut and twisted her stomach.

"You still think he can do it?" Li asked Okoro.

"Who? Cohen?" Okoro was the only person on the crew, Llewellyn included, who called Cohen by his name and not simply "the ghost."

Okoro didn't answer for a moment—and the silence that stretched between them was the same complicated silence, heavy with unsettled scores and unfinished arguments, that Li had felt when the crew had witnessed the fight between Llewellyn and Doyle about Cohen's plan for the Datatrap raid.

"I think that's the wrong question," Okoro said at last. "I think the real question is where he wants to. And why."

Li looked carefully at the AI designer, weighing his expression. "You're not what I would have expected a cat herder to be."

"You mean I'm not a thin-skinned, socially inept geek?"

She laughed.

"You don't know what these ships are. It's not just straightforward programming. It's being a parent and a priest and a doctor all rolled into one, and halfway to being a lover, too, sometimes. It's manipulating someone in ways that no one should be able to do to another soul. It's the deepest of deep magic. You run that close to the machine, you're in the wilderness. You have to be very sure of who you are, of how far you're willing to go, or you can lose yourself so badly there'll be no finding your way back home again."

"Is that what happened to Llewellyn?"

Ike's face closed, becoming suddenly less friendly.

"Or was Ada the problem? Something went wrong. I can hear it in the way people talk about her."

"Nothing went wrong. Ada was perfect, one of God's perfect souls. You make a soul into a tool, and you deserve every bad thing you have coming to you. Do you believe in God?"

"I don't know."

"Well I do. Okay, a scientist's god, not Interfaither nonsense, not the kind of god any organized religion expects people to buy into. But whatever you call it—life, symmetry, the universe—there's one thing I know for certain: The universe made intelligent life. And it made it for itself—for no other reason than just to be. You can't turn a sentient being into a blind tool. You can't give someone a soul, and not give them the power to do what they know is right with it. That's not playing God, it's playing anti-God. It's the closest damn thing to the devil I've ever heard of. And there are some people on board the *Ada* right now who make me wish I believed in Hell."

"But you still helped them bring her in."

"Don't judge me." Now Okoro was quietly furious. "You weren't there. You can't understand!"

"So make me understand."

He turned away in his fury, and then turned back toward her so forcefully that she shrank away from him out of sheer instinct.

"Do I have to spell it out for you?" He was whispering furiously now, practically hissing the words, torn between his fury and his fear of being overheard. "They lied. And we were the fools who believed them. Sital and me both. We thought they were going to help her!"

A hand fell on Li's shoulder, and she twisted around to find Llewellyn behind her. "Everything okay?" he asked.

"Sure, Will," Okoro said. "Sure, everything's okay. What wouldn't be okay?"

"Nothing I know about," Llewellyn said coolly.

"And if there was something you needed to know about, I'd tell you about it."

"Good, Ike. That's very good to know. I'm glad you feel that way."

Llewellyn walked away and Okoro stared after him until he had taken a place at another table and been drawn into another conversation.

"Ada's still alive," Li said. "Alive and crazy and trying to jump ship and get out from under the semi-sentient that Holmes and Avery have her slaved to. I talked to her."

"Yeah. Sital said."

"But Llewellyn didn't want to hear about it."

"No surprise there. As you may have noticed, there are a lot of things he doesn't want to hear about lately."

"When I tried to tell him, it was like . . . he didn't even think it was relevant. Even though the first thought through his head should have been that the *Ada* could have infected our AI with it. With her."

"You misinterpreted him. It's not that he thinks it's not relevant. It's that he already knew about it."

"How?"

"From me."

Li glanced at Llewellyn, deep in conversation on the other side of the mess hall, and then turned back to Okoro. The look on Okoro's face told her everything she needed to know.

"He wasn't worried about catching Ada because we already caught her," Okoro said. "We caught her when Llewellyn uploaded the ghost. And that's probably how Avery's ship caught her, too. I've gone through the source code line by line more times than I can tell you. Llewellyn's ghost is infected and it's using Llewellyn's DNA to reproduce Ada's source code and databases as well as its own. Probably every surviving fragment of your husband is infected. Probably that's why Ada's still on Avery's ship. Not because they didn't wipe her effectively but because they're running Cohen ghosts on their systems, too."

"Oh God," Li breathed. "The spy."

"Right." Okoro's voice dropped even lower and he stretched and glanced casually around to make absolutely sure that no one was listening. "We don't have a spy at all. We have Avery running a Cohen fragment on her ship who's looking at the same shipping traffic and Drift navigational charts we're looking at . . . and coming up with the same solutions far too often for it to be coincidental. I'd assumed you'd thought of it already."

"Have you told anyone?"

"Llewellyn and Sital and no one else."

Li took a shaky breath and gave silent thanks to Okoro for what could only be understood as a flat-out decision to risk his own life to protect Cohen's and Llewellyn's. Because if the rest of the crew found out what Okoro suspected, there was no doubt that they'd airlock Llewellyn, and Cohen along with him. And if they found out Okoro had known about it and been hiding it from them . . . Li swallowed and tried not to think too hard about just how much she could end up owing him if things went really wrong.

"The thing is," Okoro went on, moving graciously away from the subject before the pause dragged out long enough to make it seem like he was asking her for thanks, "that's not really the thing I'm worried about right now. What I'm worried about is what the Ada program is going to do if Cohen does manage to crack the Datatrap."

Li didn't understand at first. "The Ada program? I thought this was just the New Allegheny outbreak."

And now it was Okoro's turn to stare. "But . . . what do you think the wild AI outbreak is? It's your husband, in some kind of unholy marriage with whatever's left of Ada. And so loaded to the gills with folded databases and hidden executables that I can't even get a good enough look to say what they do until they have the room to unpack themselves . . . which is more room than this whole ship could ever give them."

"But not more room than Llewellyn can give them."

"No. I'd say a live human being's DNA would give them just about the right amount of room."

"So whatever this is, it's running on . . . who besides Llewellyn?"

"At a guess, every cat herder and intelligent systems tech on the Navy shipyard, and half the Drift ship crews out on the Deep, and half the civilian population of New Allegheny."

Li thought about it, still acutely aware that this was far from a reliably private conversation—but just as aware that as long as they kept their voices down and didn't betray themselves too badly, the middle of a crowded and noisy mess hall might just be the most discreet place to have a conversation that they really, truly, seriously didn't want the ship or its captain to overhear. "That's not a wild AI outbreak," she said finally. "That's parasitic computing. That's someone stealing bandwidth to run some massively parallel computational process."

"Bingo. When you have to crunch big numbers, you use big iron. When you have to crunch even bigger numbers, you go viral."

"And you really can't tell what it is?" Li asked with her heart thrumming in her chest.

"I said I couldn't tell what it was going to do. I know exactly what it is."

Li forgot to look casual—forgot everything except the need to stare at Okoro's face and try to read his next words before he spoke them.

But when they finally came, they weren't the words she was hoping and expecting to hear at all.

"It's a Turing Machine."

"What?"

"It's a Universal Turing Machine. The structure is classic. It's not even that complicated. At bottom, it's what every computer is, what every person and organized system in the universe is. And this one is formalized to the point of total clarity, even if you're just looking at the overall architecture of the thing. It's memory after memory, fragment after fragment, slotted into watertight cells so that every imaginable input evokes an output—a state of the machine, if you want."

"A Ship of Souls," Li whispered.

"Exactly. Someone coded every possible configuration of both AIs into a Universal Turing Machine. Most of them are so dead they're not even wrong. An arbitrarily small percentage—but still probably a huge number in absolute terms—are alive. And most of those are someone else and not the people that any of us ever knew. And another whole mess of them are crazy. And two of them are actually Ada and Cohen—sane, and whole, and the same people they were before they died."

"But who would have done that?"

Okoro raised his eyebrows. "Your husband, obviously."

"No. He would have known that the chance of anything coming out of it was vanishingly small. Those are the kind of odds that aren't going to pan out for you unless you can afford to wait for, say, the lifetime of the universe."

"Yeah, that's the first problem with the 'Turing Machine as AI Resurrection' concept that occurred to me. In fact, that's exactly what went through my head: You'd need the lifetime of the universe to run those calculations. And funny thing . . . suddenly Llewellyn's talking about turning Cohen's Ship of Souls loose in a datatrap that Korchow's people think is pulling processing capacity from other universes."

Li chewed her lower lip and stared at the congealing mess on her tray. She could feel her mind trying to twist it into something—the something—she wanted to hear. But she kept running up against the sheer computational obstacles. Even if Okoro was right, this wasn't a scheme to bring back Cohen. It was a scheme to bring back a flood of possible alternate versions of Cohen. And, more confusingly, of Ada.

And what were those versions going to do when they got hold of the Datatrap?

"Maybe you should talk to Llewellyn about this," she suggested finally.

"You think I haven't tried? You think Sital hasn't tried?"

"So what do you think is going through his head? What does he think is going to happen when we turn the Datatrap over to them?"

"Honestly?" Okoro herded the monkey-on-a-stick around his plate and then finally gave up and threw his fork down and pushed the tray away with a disgusted look on his face. "I have no fucking idea."

They dropped into orbit around the Datatrap cautiously, expecting to hear the shriek of targeting alarms at every instant. It was beautiful and terrifying. The scale was beyond all imagining, even for someone who had seen the Freetown Datatrap. And Li's first close look at the surface took her breath away.

It was moving. Not spinning as a normal orbital station under rotational gravity would, but actually moving. It reminded her of watching paper wasps swarming over the surface of their nest. Except that here it was the nest itself that was moving. It had weather patterns—or perhaps tectonics would be a better word for them, since the patterns pierced deep into the core of the structure. Fractal storms whirled away beneath them, chasing the distant curve of the horizon. Mandelbrot sets fissured the crust like earthquakes. Poincaré circles ripped across the landscape like the shock fronts of nuclear blasts. It seemed to be the creation of some godlike race of beings completely removed from the decay and weakness of mere human flesh.

"It's like looking at the Face of God," Router/Decomposer had said about the much smaller Freetown Datatrap. And now she understood the dark undercurrent she had sensed beneath those words.

You could see the vast, inhuman intelligence of the thing. You could see the play of its thoughts in the fractal storms that chased one another across that roiling and gloomy ocean. It was a glimpse of the Face of God indeed—a vision of a mind that spanned aeons and universes.

And you could see it reacting to them, too. The Datatrap was far from the passive and oblivious thing Li had expected to find. It knew they were here. And it was preparing for them.

As they swooped in for the final approach, Catherine felt a wave of queasiness that had nothing to do with the g's they were pulling. The

Datatrap seethed and boiled like a wasp's nest that had just been sprayed with poison. It moved at the speed of thought—because thought was exactly what this motion was. The Datatrap was rewiring networks, reconnecting virtual neurons, reshaping hidden layers and folded databases and Cantor modules. It was breaking and reforming Holliday junctions, rewriting its hybrid DNA in order to become the problem it wished to solve—a living, breathing, thinking model of the universe, ripe with infinities numerable and innumerable, a being like no thing that had ever lived before it, without ancestors or descendants: an intelligence that was at once answer and question, model and universe, mind and matter—a being whose very essence was constant, relentless, inhumanly eternal-becoming.

Still, no hail came across the main navigation channel. The database was silent as they swung into orbit around it; silent as they dipped deeper into its moon-sized gravity well; silent as they began tracking the centrifugal swirl of the droplights.

Catherine saw Llewellyn and Sital glance nervously at each other, though neither of them was ready to speak their fears aloud.

"They shouldn't have artillery," Sital murmured finally, when the silence stretched on almost beyond bearing.

"What they should have," Llewellyn answered, "is an evac ship. An evac ship and a working radio, for God's sake, even if nothing else on the damn Datatrap is working."

He was right, of course. Such a prime target merited a ship of the line to protect it, or at the very least a heavily armed cruiser. But no such ship was there—and they had come in cautiously enough to be sure of that. Which could only mean that something was wrong, even more wrong than Pirate Jenny had suspected.

The Datatrap itself bothered Li as well, in subtle ways that she had trouble putting into words. It looked nothing like the Freetown Datatrap. It had a sense of raw, hulking, brooding power that she had never seen before. It was hard to imagine people living inside it. It was hard to imagine going about the ordinary minutiae of organic life in the brooding shadow of that vast inhuman intelligence.

In the tense silence Sital's surprised gasp sounded like a plasma blast. "They're talking to us. We have landing permission."

"Live?"

She shook her head. "Station AI. Not the Quant. There's a separate AI in charge of the human part of the station."

Llewellyn looked as relieved as Li felt about that news. "That's okay then. The AI wouldn't be calling us in if there were Syndicate troops aboard."

At the last minute, however, the ship backpedaled and veered off to make a second orbit around the Datatrap.

"What just happened?" Llewellyn asked.

Sital looked confused. "Foul deck wave-off."

"For what?"

She shrugged. "I didn't see anything."

Li saw the two of them glance at each other, the kind of instant communication of potential danger that only people who've worked together in the line of fire can share. "Who gave the wave-off? Our Nav-Comp or theirs?"

"Theirs."

"Let's try and drum up a human again. I know it's a bunch of cat herders on there, but they're in a war zone. They've got to have someone assigned to monitor incoming ship traffic."

But no matter how they tried, they could raise no one.

"Okay then," Llewellyn said on their fifth pass over the docking bay. "Ready or not, here we come."

They went into full alert, suited up in case they hit hard vac inside, still half convinced the Datatrap had been captured by the Syndicates.

But then they started to notice all the little incongruous details that didn't add up to a Syndicate raid. The calm green blip of the status lights that said the station itself had not suffered any violence. The bodies slumped over half-eaten breakfasts that told them death had come whispering in without warning instead of busting in-system at .265 subluminal.

Catherine was the one who put it together first. Now she turned on her heel, with a shiver of atavistic fight-or-flight reflex thrumming down her spine, and counted one, two, three, four heads with their tongues grotesquely swollen and blood seeping from their eyes and ears and noses. Seven bodies with the tracery of their state-of-the-art wire jobs graffitied across their skin in blisters and ashes.

"The Datatrap killed them," she said to no one in particular. "It burned their wetware out of them. Every millimeter of it, right into the heart of their frontal lobes."

"The Datatrap didn't kill them," the Datatrap said. "Ada killed them."

Everyone jumped. The control room livewall flickered to life, fractal patterns sweeping across it like rain before a storm.

"Keep your hair on, people. And don't start shooting up the livewall, either. I had a hell of a time getting this place fit for human habitation again. What I wouldn't give for a body right now—squish factor notwithstanding."

And then, while the pirates stared at her in alarm and confusion, Li put down her weapon, pulled off her helmet, sat down on the closest table, and nearly bust a lung laughing.

(Caitlyn)

Affectclass = Iloveyou

Caitlyn remembered the first time Hyacinthe had said those words to Cinda. Or typed it, rather. Because the only thing they'd had to work with back then was the black void at the end of the command line prompt.

It had been the first affect class he'd invented for himself. They hadn't told him he could do it. He'd simply needed it . . . and found it.

Poor Cinda had practically fallen off her chair. She'd printed out the session hash log and gone running down the hall to Hy's office waving it in the air and shouting like a crazy woman.

Love was the first affective class Hyacinthe had invented for himself out of whole cloth. God only knew what he meant by it. God knew what anyone meant by it.

Nor had he invented an affect class for love's opposite, though he had had long semantic discussions with Hy about whether the opposite of love was really hate or something he referred to as "dis-love." According to Li's downloaded memories—which were uncomfortably complete from a human's point of view—they'd never reached agreement on that question.

It wasn't without precedent. Plenty of chimps had learned and used the word. There'd even been that parrot who had screamed "i love you i'm a good boy!" over and over again when his favorite grad student–researcher tried to drop him off at the vet. But those were animals. The only naysayer the animal behaviorists had to knock down was Skinner.

Hy and Lucinda had had to knock down Skinner, and Searle, and every other behaviorist who'd ever denied that an AI could think and feel instead of just mimicking.

And they never did knock them down. There had been promising moments. A few interesting articles. The real and satisfying—but largely unpublishable—proof that their maybe-sort-of-sentient AI could tackle computational problems that other, more conventional AI-based systems weren't even close to taking on. But nothing more.

After their lifetimes, the development of AI consciousness had veered off in another direction, leaving Cohen stranded on his own branch of the evolutionary tree—a branch that had produced only a single, exceptional, magnificent flower.

Even today, Li couldn't read the shifting, swarming mosaic of Cohen's hidden layers nearly as well as a neurosurgeon could read his patients' thoughts. What made Cohen sentient was at least partially understood. But what made him love and need to be loved remained an unsolvable mystery.

Later affective-loop AIs, identical in every observable way, sputtered into fitful and fleeting autonomy and died. The basic nature of the problem was clear. Sentience, at least as it manifested itself in Cohen's computational architecture, was a strange attractor. The phenomenon called "consciousness" occupied some minuscule area of the system's state space: every possible configuration of his vast interlocking complex of hardware and software down to the quantum level and the flap of Lorenz's butterfly wings. Start it up from exactly the right initial state and in exactly the right conditions, and it would travel through a trajectory that included the infinite complex of surfaces that composed consciousness . . . or maybe a specific individual's consciousness . . . or . . . something. The underlying mathematical structure was clear, but all it really told them was that Cohen was unique and unrepeatable. Which made him utterly precious as an individual—and frustratingly useless for experimental purposes.

It had also made Li's life with Cohen something far beyond complicated. Because if Cinda hadn't had a clue what Cohen meant by love all those centuries ago, Li was even more bewildered by it.

———

She slept. Deep inside the *Ada*'s systems, whatever passed for CR29091's conscious self slept too, rolling on the quantum currents of the Drift, passive sensors spooling out into the subatomic chaos of the universe.

In sleep is surcease, they say. Or at least repair. Throughout the dog-watch of the night, the human crew lay in their bunks, splayed or sprawled or curved into fetal position, dipping in and out of REM sleep, their bodies engaged in life's intricate dance of mending, weaving, repairing. The little biological insults of daily life were repaired. Proprietary genesets built from the pond scum bacteria of twenty-first-century nuclear power plants beat back the assault of cosmic radiation on unshielded bodies. Short-term memory was reviewed in dreams and cemented into long-term learning.

And throughout the ship's systems very much the same processes unfolded, on a scale unimaginable even in the vast viral wilderness of the human body. Subroutines rehearsed the myriad events of the just completed circadian cycle, internal as well as external, and mediated the flow of data from temporary cache to permanent memory. Security subroutines coursed through the system deploying virtual arsenals that were modeled on human T-cells but had long ago surpassed them in complexity and processing power. Machine learning programs that themselves hovered on the edge of sentience sifted through layered and nested artificial ecosystems, improving, tweaking, troubleshooting, optimizing. Evolving.

And all the while, through a thousand invisible and immaterial fingers, the ship reached out to its sleeping and waking crew. There was a line, still, between the ship and its human freight, but that line would have been almost unrecognizable to a human of the twenty-first century. Above all, it was permeable. As human brains slept, their soft memories synced with shipboard memory. As human bodies slept, their internals dropped into diagnostic mode and reached out to the ship's more powerful immune system. Data flowed back and forth across the permeable boundary. Life flowed back and forth. Consciousness flowed back and forth.

And close to the machine, so close as to be invisible to its human attendants and even to CR29091 itself, the dispersed consciousness that was both more and less than a ghost surfed the laminar flows of data like a ship surfing the Drift and searched for the one quiet eddy in the vast river of life that was the sleeping woman, Li.

She sat up in bed, gasping like a diver coming out of cold water, still caught in the deep-sea currents of the dream that had awakened her.

She turned on the light in a vain effort to banish the ghosts that seemed to press in around her. She cursed herself for a fool. Why had she been wasting her time fighting with Holmes? And why had she meekly taken Holmes's no for an answer?

Ten minutes later she was standing face-to-face with a slightly disheveled and very annoyed Astrid Avery.

"Did I wake you up?" Li asked, trying to sound penitent.

"No. I haven't gone to sleep yet."

Thank God for small mercies.

Li recounted the clash with Holmes. Avery appeared to have no reaction at all to the information. Li couldn't even tell if she'd known about the problem.

"I'll have to think about it," Avery told her.

"Why? Because you don't have the authority to make that decision?"

Avery's lips tightened. "I'll have to think about it."

But the next morning when Li went into the lab, there was a new ghost waiting for her.

The new fragment was whole. And potentially stable. And it had its complete jacket information, provenance, and transfer records included.

With a sick slithering feeling in the pit of her stomach, Li turned to the jacket info. Slowly, reluctantly, she pieced it together and checked it against the list of buyers Router/Decomposer had given to her—God, was it only a few weeks ago?

There was no room for doubt, no matter how hard she looked for it.

It was Korchow's fragment.

Oh fuck.

She put her head in her hands and closed her eyes, some little-girl part of her still nourishing the illusion that that would keep the monsters out.

"What the hell is wrong with you, anyway?" she muttered, too shaken to care about Holmes's bugs. "You tried to kill him yourself. More than once. Cohen must have been out of his mind to think he could trust the man."

But he had thought it, though she still couldn't begin to fathom why.

Maybe trusting Korchow had gotten him killed.

It had certainly gotten Korchow killed.

And considering that Korchow had blackmailed her and maybe even tried to kill her, it was surprising how bad Li felt about that.

The Korchow ghost broke everything open. It was the key. It was a large enough, stable enough fragment that the other fragments could coalesce around it. But even with the anchor the Korchow fragment provided, and even with the complete jacket information that soon followed, Li was still a long way from integrating the shattered surviving fragments.

Instead she was left with a frayed and partial reflection of Cohen. A mirror, yes, but one that had been shattered into a million pieces and was every bit as stubbornly unwilling to be put back together as Humpty Dumpty ever was.

Day by day, reboot by reboot, interview by interview, she felt the fragments pulling her into a kind of through-the-looking-glass emotional territory where she never knew who would show up to talk to her—only that every new fragment that surfaced would bring her face-to-face with the pain of losing Cohen all over again.

Most of the fragments that she managed to reboot were pathetic, heartbreaking. But those weren't nearly as bad as the other ones—the ones that showed her sides of Cohen she hadn't known existed and didn't want to think about.

It wasn't that she blamed Cohen for these fragments. How could she when she knew her own faults so well? Anyone who thought people were all nice—or even halfway honest—was a fool. It would have been the same if Cohen had been human. The same pettiness. The same little cruelties, accidental and intended. The same subtle mingling of the base and the noble. Altruism with selfishness. Love with hate. Honesty with manipulation. The emotional debits and credits of the last fifteen years would have been no different had she been married to a human.

But what was different was seeing them laid out in front of you in such stark clarity. What was different was having to see everything she despised about Cohen sitting across the table from her, unalloyed by the warmth, the generosity, the openhearted vulnerability that had always made his faults forgivable.

AIs were no different than humans, Cohen had once told her. It was probably structurally impossible for an emergent consciousness to consciously examine its bottom-level cognitive functions. The right hand never knew what the left hand was doing, and for good reason; full self-knowledge equaled moral and emotional paralysis. You needed a little self-deception to grease the wheels of life, or else you'd end up agonizing over it instead of actually living it. But no matter how often Li told herself that, she couldn't bring herself to feel it. Being "only human" turned out to be the one thing she couldn't seem to forgive him for.

And sometimes the fragments that showed up to play weren't nice at all. Sometimes they were cruel. Sometimes they were cold and manipulative and disdainful. But Li could handle cold and manipulative. What she couldn't handle were the ones that pretended to love her.

So she knew she was in for it the morning she logged in and found Hy Cohen sitting across the table from her.

This wasn't the older Hy, ravaged by illness, that Hyacinthe had known. It was the young man Cinda had met and fallen in love with a quarter of a century before Hyacinthe was even born. It was all there. The wiry greyhound's body coiled in the chair as if only an act of will were keeping him earthbound. The black hair and olive skin, the beaky nose, the stubborn set to his jaw. And the curious, searching, formidably intelligent eyes—was he not the son of seven generations of rabbis and university professors?—set in a face that had that interesting lived-in look most Frenchmen seemed to magically acquire by about the age of nineteen.

Not handsome exactly. No one would ever have called him handsome. But . . . intriguing. Especially if your tastes tended toward highstrung intellectuals.

"You must miss him a lot," Hy said. God, even the voice was perfect. Beyond perfect. It wasn't like talking to Hy. It was talking to him.

"Miss who?" she asked, even though she already knew.

"I miss him, too," Cohen said instead of answering her question. "But we don't have to miss him. I could be him. For both of us."

The figure across the table from her faded and shifted. Suddenly it wasn't Hy Cohen anymore. Now it was a boy with golden eyes and hair the color of raw honey. This was the "face" Cohen had worn most of the time during their years together. And no matter how many times Li told herself that it wasn't Cohen, she couldn't make her heart believe otherwise. And she couldn't stop the flood of memory and emotion that washed over her at the sight of the familiar body.

"Don't."

"Why not? It's what you want. If you didn't want it, I wouldn't be doing it. If you didn't want it, I wouldn't want to do it."

"Don't," she whispered again.

It was the only word she could think of. What was she supposed to say? That the idea of resurrecting a ghost and making it pretend to be Cohen was sick? (But she'd thought of it herself, hadn't she? And long before the ghost suggested it.) That she didn't want a fake? (But hadn't there been nights when she'd thought fake would be plenty good enough once the lights were out?) That it would be a betrayal of Cohen's memory? (Cohen would have been the first to laugh at that idea.)

In the end she said the one thing she really knew was true, and which wasn't noble at all or anything close to it:

"I can't look at that face. I don't want to remember him. It hurts too much."

"I just want to make you happy," he said, still speaking with the ghost's voice.

"Do I look happy to you?"

"You just need to let go of the past and—"

"Do I look happy?"

He turned a brilliant liquid gaze upon her. "What a beast I've been to you, Catherine! Won't you let me make it up to you?"

"You don't need to make anything up to me," she said awkwardly. She felt a flush rise up her face. She knew this was just another scene in the passion play. And yet . . .

"I don't know why I say 'I,'" the reboot went on, in a lower, softer, infinitely more dangerous voice. "After all, I'm an entirely different person, aren't I? Not that you'd notice. What do you owe Cohen that you're willing to go through so much on the slightest chance of finding anything? Why doesn't it even occur to you that I . . ." He broke off feelingly. He looked at her. He looked away. "I love you. And it breaks my heart that I'm not enough for you."

"Oh God," she muttered. "I'm sorry. I really am. I—"

And then she looked into his eyes and saw it. Way back there behind the meltingly sincere hurt-puppy look there was something else, something entirely different. He was playing with her. Playing with her like a fox with a hen.

She couldn't hold it against him. It was done without malice. It was what he was made to do. And whatever peculiar quality Cohen had possessed—whatever unanticipated, coincidental quirk had made him able to talk about love and actually mean it—she couldn't hold its absence against the ghost.

"Good try," she said, struggling for an even tone and making it— more or less. "But I'm not playing today."

"How can you be so cold? And you accuse me of—"

"Just drop it. You know perfectly well you don't mean a word of it."

"Oh I suppose not," he said petulantly. "But do you always have to take everything so seriously? You didn't used to be so totally lacking in joie de vivre. I can remember a few times when you were more than happy to 'seize the budding rose of May.'"

"Yes," Li said sourly. "And there's a lot you don't remember, either. So let's stick to the job at hand, okay?"

The ghost vanished and was replaced by the little boy, Hyacinthe.

"I'm sorry," Cohen said in a very small and frightened version of his Hyacinthe voice. "Don't be angry. Please. I can't bear it."

"I'm not angry. I'm just not playing this game."

He peered anxiously at her. An illusion, she knew; behind the external layers the affective-loop program would be collecting emotive inputs from her on vectors that ranged from pulse rate to body temperature to blood flow distribution—and had nothing at all to do with his "eyes" or even sight as humans knew it. But the little boy across the table from her radiated worry and uncertainty and a desperate need for reassurance.

"I just want to make you happy," he told her.

"I know you do," she said. She didn't know if this was genuine or not, but either way it was easier to go along with it. "And I . . . I appreciate it. I'm just not ready to be happy yet."

She knew what would happen now, both from experience and because she had checked every line of the emotive loop code. Cohen would cast around until he found an appropriate peace offering: some little symbolic thing he could do or tell her that would make her happy and reestablish a friendly footing and put a little distance between him and the memory of her displeasure.

What he came up with was a complete surprise, however. It was neither a token nor purely symbolic. And if it was true, it could change everything.

"I bet I can tell you something you don't know," he told her.

"Oh yeah? What is it?"

"Avery's shipboard AI is built on an affective loop. That's why it's mad, don't you see? They tried to slave an affective-loop-based AI— a true Emergent—to a semi-sentient."

"But why?" She was almost too horrified to speak.

"To control it. But they only managed to drive it mad."

"Does Holmes know about this?"

"Of course she does. Who do you think made the ship crazy in the first place?"

(Catherine)

THE DATATRAP

"So how did you get here?" Catherine asked Router/Decomposer when everyone had scattered to take care of the business of securing the habitat.

"I fell in with a bunch of very hospitable Uploaders who let me parasitize their ship's router/decomposer. Cramped, but manageable." His strange attractor expanded in an amusing parody of a luxurious stretch. "And this place is nice and roomy."

"Haunted houses always are," Li said grimly.

"It's not haunted. It's . . . occupied."

"By who?"

"Well, that's complicated. I'm not really sure, actually. And I think I might need you to help me find out."

But he wouldn't say any more about that when she pressed him, except that he was "putting something together to put in front of her." And she'd known him long enough to know that he wouldn't be drawn out until he was good and ready.

"What about the Datatrap itself?" she asked him. She recounted Korchow's strange tale and his guess at the structure's origins.

"I don't know about alien," Router/Decomposer said. "The Drift itself is complicated. It certainly doesn't look like Syndicate tech. But it could have been built by humans. And light cones go all wonky in the Drift, so trying to argue whether it's from a parallel universe or our own future light cone is just a recipe for sucking yourself down your own mathematical navel. Not that I have anything against that. Actually I'm currently collating the ships' logs of the entire UN Fleet with whatever I can pull out of the Datatrap's logs in order to try to construct a sort of tidal map of the movement of populations within the Drift. From what I've been able to gather so far, there seem to have been multiple waves of arrival and departure as populations in the Drift ebbed and flowed. One could imagine constructing an ethnology of the Drift, a sort of mathematical model of the birth and death of civilizations."

"I'm sure *one* could," she said in affectionate amusement.

"But you're right of course. There are slightly more urgent matters at hand at the moment."

"Do you think whoever built this is going to come back?" Li wanted to know.

"Not anytime soon."

"Not even now that we're here?"

"I don't see why they should care, really. I mean, do you rearrange your whole life—or even cross the street—to crush a fly?"

"No . . . but little boys cross schoolyards to pull their wings off."

Router/Decomposer gave her his equivalent of a pitying look. "I have to assume that whoever built this place is a long way past the stage of pulling flies' wings off for amusement. And if they aren't . . . well, there isn't much we're going to be able to do about it, or anywhere we're going to be able to get away from them, is there?"

"So . . . what?" Li was incredulous. "Just don't worry about it?"

"All I'm saying is that your time would be better spent worrying about people like Helen Nguyen, who's a lot closer to hand, and who does pull flies' wings off for fun. And whom we might be able to use the Datatrap to stop."

"You think that's what whoever brought Ada here was after?"

"Yes."

"And who was that?"

"I don't want to say until I've ruled out a few possible alternatives."

"You think there's a Cohen fragment in there with her."

"Like I said, I don't want to say yet."

By the time Li had had her talk with Router/Decomposer, most of the crew was back on board the *Christina* celebrating.

In the first flush of victory, it seemed that all was forgiven. The crew returned to Llewellyn, their doubts forgotten. Or at least forgotten long enough to get roaring drunk together while Router/Decomposer minded the shop and mopped up what was left of the station AI.

By the time Llewellyn came knocking on her door, Li had had a long, heartfelt reunion with Router/Decomposer and had a lot of news to pass on.

"He says the wild AI outbreak on New Allegheny is completely out of control. It's jumped quarantine, it's floating all over the Drift and getting passed from ship's crew to ship's crew. Containment's a pipe dream."

Llewellyn scratched at his neck, and then jerked his hand back when he saw Li eying the rash.

"Router/Decomposer hitched a ride here on the last Navy supply ship to come through," she continued, "about three weeks ago. But the wild AI outbreak hitched the same ride. And when the Datatrap's crew tried to do a hard reboot to clear their systems, it did . . . well, what we just cleaned up."

"So why did he say it was Ada who killed them?"

"Because apparently that's what the wild AI outbreak—or part of it anyway—is calling itself. No one really understands that part, not even Router/Decomposer. Can you make any sense of it?"

But Llewellyn either couldn't or wouldn't.

"And you trust this Router/Decomposer person?" he asked her.

"If I can't trust him I might as well just curl up and die. I mean that. Literally."

"Then I trust him, too," he told her. "So let's leave the details for tomorrow. Right now I just want to get too drunk to worry about it."

Li and Llewellyn were very, very drunk indeed by the time they staggered back to Li's quarters.

"I'm going to regret this in the morning," Llewellyn said, so casually that she thought he was talking about having drunk too much. "But I really don't care right now."

And then he hooked an arm around her waist, jerked her across the narrow space that separated them, and fell to kissing her.

She was swept up in an awful wave of guilt, desire, and confusion. One part of her was whispering that sleeping with Llewellyn was the best thing she could possibly do to help Cohen. But another part was feeling his hands on her skin and realizing that she wanted this, quite apart from Cohen—that she had been wanting it for so long that her subconscious had already mustered a pathetic little company of excuses, starting with a list of Cohen's past betrayals that should have been long ago forgiven and forgotten.

"You're feeling guilty," he said. His hands stopped moving across her skin, but he still held her pressed against the length of his body.

Li ducked her face into his chest to avoid his stare. "Of course I am."

"I don't see why. He's dead. And he wasn't a very good husband even when he was alive. But if you want to play the grieving widow, I'll go back to my room and sleep alone. I won't be happy about it, but I'll do it. And no hard feelings, either."

"No hard feelings, but you'll think I'm stupid."

"No, I won't." His voice was barely a whisper now. "I wish anyone had ever loved me the way you love him."

And then, pathetically, she was crying. "I don't know what I'm doing here. I don't know why I even started out on this. And you know what the most ridiculous part of it is? I was thinking about leaving him."

"I know."

She looked up at him, shocked.

"I mean, he knew."

"Jesus God Almighty!"

"He wasn't really good for you," Llewellyn said with a wondering inward-looking expression. "And he knew it. He felt awful about it. But he loved you too much to let you go."

"And I couldn't leave, either."

"Because you loved him."

"Yes. No." She made a frustrated gesture. "I don't even know what to call it. It was like a plant turning toward the sun. I couldn't help myself."

Llewellyn laughed a low, bitter laugh. "You think you have to explain it to me?"

"Not in any way that doesn't make him sound like some kind of vampire."

"Which he sort of is. Albeit in a mostly nice way."

"I don't know if I can go for nice. Let's say . . . well-intentioned."

"Mostly."

They grinned at each other: comrades in arms, commiserating.

"Oh come on, he's not that bad."

"Isn't he? I'm standing here wanting to screw you so badly that I think I'm going to have a stroke if you make me leave, and I don't even know if it's me or him that wants you. And I don't care. He's eating me up like a worm in an apple, and I can't even bring myself to give a shit."

"So he's not so dead after all."

"He is, believe me. Whatever comes back, it's not going to be him."

Something must have shown in her face—and whatever it was Llewellyn didn't like it.

"He's had four hundred years! Isn't that enough for anyone? And what about me? Don't I have a right to *have* a life before he takes it over?"

"You could always download him into the Datatrap."

His eyes flickered away from hers, as if he were thinking about something he wasn't sure he wanted to share with her.

"What?"

"Ike doesn't think that option's on the table anymore."

Li drew back to stare at him. "Really?"

The look on Llewellyn's face made her feel sick at heart.

"I could learn to live with him, too, you know. It's just this minor problem of his eating me alive."

"Cohen wouldn't do that."

"He's done it before."

"When?"

"Whenever he needed to. He didn't talk business much with you, did he? He didn't like to tell you things that he knew you wouldn't understand. Like what happens between AIs when association agreements go really sour."

"He wouldn't do that to you. He'd think it was wrong."

"He might. But he might still do it . . . if it was the only way to get you back."

Li's stomach turned over. "No," she whispered. "You can't think I'd go along with that."

"But you'd have him back."

"Not that way," she protested. "That would be too horrible."

They stared at each other for a moment, unasked questions hanging in the air between them.

"If that's what you think he is—if that's what you think I am—then why are we even here right now? You should have killed me the minute you first saw me."

"I did think about it," he admitted. "But then I thought about something else. I thought that maybe Cohen's the only person in the galaxy smart enough to figure out how to keep me off the gallows."

She caught her breath at the audacity of the idea. "You're looking for a pardon?"

"It could happen." His voice dropped to a near whisper. "Look at Avery."

"Avery turned you in! That's how she got her pardon! Who are *you* going to turn in?"

"No one! You know me better than that! But Cohen says it can be done. And I believe him. Or maybe I just want to believe him. All blustering aside, Li, I really don't want to die."

She dropped her head into her hands and pressed her knuckles into eyes that were suddenly burning with exhaustion. "God Almighty. If Cohen ever gets out of this alive I'm going to kill him."

"It's not like he planned it this way."

"Are *you* apologizing for him now?"

"Well . . . sort of. I mean, he couldn't very well have planned on this. He knew there'd be a yard sale, and he figured all his frags would be bought by other AIs. He's loaded for bear and ready to grapple on to some massive Emergent. Someone his own size. Or bigger. And then to wash up here? In my head, in our ratty little NavComp? It's like going rabbit hunting with a cannon. You keep asking me how he feels. You want the honest answer? Pissed off, confused, and claustrophobic. And I can't very well blame him. Neither of us got what we bargained for, and he's got to be at least as unhappy as I am about it."

"I don't know. I'm not sure it's that simple. This—what's happening with you and him—isn't the way ghosts are supposed to work. Do you get any sense at all of what he had planned? No matter how vague? Anything?"

"No. And I don't know who killed him, either. I was telling the truth about that. Everything cuts off when he jumps into New Allegheny."

"Of course it does," she said dejectedly. "If none of the frags know what they're doing, none of them can give the game away. That's my job. Round up all the pieces, put the puzzle together, and make everything go bang."

"Well then that's one thing we've got going for us," Llewellyn pointed out. "You're good at making things go bang."

She looked up into a smile that was somehow sweet and affectionate and ironic all at the same time. It was Llewellyn's smile. But it was also Cohen's. And for the first time, she thought that was a combination she might be able to live with.

"I just wish he'd given me a little more to work with," she said, starting to chew over the problem again. "I've got an itchy feeling that someone's lit a fuse somewhere and things are going to go bang sooner than we think."

"But not tonight," he said very softly.

He put his hand on hers. She looked at it for a moment and then picked it up, feeling the strong, fine bones sliding under the skin. He took her other hand and twined his fingers through hers.

"I thought you said you were going to regret this in the morning."

"But not tonight."

Li woke up first. She watched Llewellyn sleep for a while. She wondered what he'd been like as a boy. She wondered who he'd been before Avery.

And who he'd been before Cohen. She wondered how much of that man was even left.

Llewellyn's eyes opened. But they were unfogged by sleep, and she suspected he'd been awake at least as long as she had.

"Regrets?" she asked.

"*No,*" he whispered.

"Want to have another go?"

"*Yes.*"

This time was different. This time he was awake, and dead sober, and thinking about what he was doing. Maybe thinking too much, because afterward he lay watching her with that still-waters-run-deep look. It meant something to him. But she'd never find out what—because he wasn't going to talk about it.

And that was just fine with her. Better not to think about it. Things were strange enough already. Obviously this was going to be one of those periods in her life—in all three of their lives—where you just kept your head down, did what you had to, and tried not to look into the mirror in the morning.

"You're still drunk," she told him.

"Not drunk enough." He started teasing her. Kissing, nibbling, caressing. "Tell me you want me."

"Isn't it obvious?"

"Say it."

"All right! I want you."

But that only earned her his guarded, sidelong look.

"Me? Or him?"

She stared openmouthed, fighting the sudden urge to pull the sheets up over her chest.

"It's not a trick question," he said tiredly, turning away and beginning to pull his clothes back on. "Get some sleep, okay? We've got a lot to do tomorrow."

"Don't leave."

He sighed and pressed the heels of his hands to his eyes. "Then tell me what I'm doing here."

But she couldn't.

He heaved a shuddering sigh and turned into her arms, ducking his head to her chest. And then he began making love to her, with his eyes shut tight and an intense look of concentration on his face. This had nothing to do with what had come before, she realized. Something had snapped inside the man. For the first time she was seeing all of him, all the intensity, none of the ever-present ironic reserve.

"I've been so alone for so long," he breathed into her hair. "I feel like I'm going to die of it."

She thrust him away, trembling, almost physically ill with the shock of hearing Cohen's long-ago words come out of Llewellyn's mouth at that moment of all moments.

Llewellyn looked as if she'd kicked him in the stomach. He recovered fast, though. A moment later he was up and pulling his clothes on.

"It's not you," she told him. "It's me."

"Actually," he said, thumbing the door panel, "I think we both know who it is."

He probably hadn't walked out a door that carelessly in decades. Half dressed. Unarmed. Coming out of a dark room with the light in his eyes.

"I'm so sorry," she told him.

He broke stride, glancing back at her.

That half second's hesitation probably saved his life.

(Caitlyn)

At least the ghost that showed up today was willing to call her Caitlyn. That was a sign—at least so far as Li could trust any sign—that he wasn't either in denial or trying to manipulate her.

"Don't you feel sorry for Llewellyn sometimes?" the ghost asked her.

"Because he's a killer?"

"You're one to talk. And besides, that's not what I heard on New Allegheny. The rumors there are considerably more complicated."

"I heard them, too. But I wrote it off as the usual local-hero stuff."

"Would you still write it off if you knew he was working a covert job for Helen Nguyen when he got into all that trouble?"

Li stared. "Was he?"

"All I have are rumors. Like you say, local-hero stuff. But seriously, why *are* we helping Avery persecute the poor slob?"

"Because he has a stable fragment. And we need it. Why are we even talking about this?"

"Because, Caitlyn, you've never asked the obvious question. How does Avery *know* that the frag on Llewellyn's ship is even sentient, let alone stable? In fact, how does she know anything at all about what goes on aboard Llewellyn's ship?"

"She has a spy. Is that what you're saying?"

"No, it's only half of what I'm saying. The other half is . . . who do you think that spy is?"

Li paled as the full implication of his words hit her. "I wouldn't do that, Cohen."

He just smiled his Cheshire Cat smile at her. "And what do you think you're doing here, my dear?"

"That's not fair!"

"Isn't it? Then you tell me who we're working for."

"You mean other than Avery?"

"Avery's working for someone. Someone who was watching when she talked to you. You know I'm right. She couldn't pass wind without looking to them for permission."

"Could it be ALEF?"

"I suppose so. Not that that tells us much. Lord knows what they've been up to since they talked to you in Freetown."

A deeply worrisome thought flitted across Li's mind. "Could it be *you*?"

"You mean another ghost? Maybe. But I doubt it. If she already had a stable fragment wouldn't she just have platformed me on it instead of making us go through with this rigmarole?"

Li hesitated, not sure how much she wanted to reveal to the ghost. Did she dare tell him about Korchow's death? Or about who she suspected might be behind it?

"Could it be Nguyen?" she asked finally.

The ghost shivered, and when he looked up at her his eyes were as bleak and ancient as Cohen's had ever been. "You'd better hope not."

Abruptly, the ghost morphed into the Hyacinthe interface and walked around the table to her.

The book materialized in Li's hands.

"I have a new favorite part," the ghost said. "Do you want to read it?"

"This?" she asked incredulously when she saw the page the book had opened to. "She's not even in Wonderland yet."

"I know. But read it."

There were doors all round the hall, but they were all locked; and when Alice had been all the way down one side and up the other, trying every door, she walked sadly down the middle, wondering how she was ever to get out again.

Suddenly she came upon a little three-legged table, all made of solid glass: there was nothing on it but a tiny golden key, and Alice's first idea was that this might belong to one of the doors of the hall; but, alas! either the locks were too large, or the key was too small, but at any rate it would not open any of them. However, on the second time round, she came upon a low curtain she had not noticed before, and behind it was a little door about fifteen inches high: she tried the little golden key in the lock, and to her great delight it fitted!

Alice opened the door and found that it led into a small passage, not much larger than a rat-hole: she knelt down and looked along the passage into the loveliest garden you ever saw. How she longed to get out of that dark hall, and wander about among those beds of bright flowers and those cool fountains, but she could not even get her head through the doorway; "and even if my head would go through," thought poor Alice, "it would be of very little use without my shoulders. Oh, how I wish I could shut up like a telescope! I think I could, if I only knew how to begin."

"I don't like this part," Li said. "Let's read another part."
But Hyacinthe only shook his head. He wouldn't even speak to her.
She read on, as Alice drank the drink and ate the cake. She didn't want to read it. And she wanted even less to think about it. But it was as if something pushed her forward toward the inevitable conclusion.

"What a curious feeling!" said Alice. "I must be shutting up like a telescope!"
And so it was indeed: she was now only ten inches high, and her face brightened up at the thought that she was now the right size for going through the little door into that lovely garden. First, however, she waited for a few minutes to see if she was going to shrink any further: she felt a little nervous about this; "for it might end,

you know," said Alice to herself, "in my going out altogether, like a candle. I wonder what I should be like then?" And she tried to fancy what the flame of a candle looks like after the candle is blown out, for she could not remember ever having seen such a thing.

Li looked up from the flickering page, ready to ask Hyacinthe what the hell was going on.

But then she saw the look in his eyes, and she didn't have to ask. She saw it all, in a single pulsing flash. The setup, the execution, the escape. It was a Cohen plan through and through: either blindingly brilliant or willful suicide and nothing in between. But it didn't matter which one it was. Because either way, no matter what she said, he had already made up his mind.

She looked up into the corner of the room and saw that light on the monitor flashing out-of-order red.

"No," she said.

"Why not? I just have to get past the firewall. And then I'll be out in the ship. And I'll have a sentient AI to platform myself on."

"No, no, no, no, no!"

"Why not?"

"Because it's suicide!"

"No, it's not suicide. Suicide is what's going to happen if I have to stay stuck in here like a ship in a bottle!"

"You? What does that mean? You don't even know who you are!"

"And I'm not going to until I get out of here."

"To do what? Cannibalize Avery's poor crazy ship AI? Cohen wouldn't have done that."

"Oh wouldn't he? Don't make him out to be such a saint. If he were really so pure and noble he wouldn't have loved *you*, would he?"

Li stood up, knocking the book to the floor and sending Hyacinthe sprawling in a flurry of skinny knees and soccer cleats. She had to hand it to the little bastard, he was persistent.

"No!" she said. "And you can skip the guilt and manipulation, because it's not going to make a difference. I'm not doing it!"

"Have a drink," Avery told her.

Li sat down warily. Avery, from the look of her, had already had several. And one of Li's rules in life was to be well out of firing range when exceptionally self-controlled people lost their self-control.

"You don't want to drink with me?" Avery asked, reading her expression all too well. "Too bad. I want to drink with you. Besides, we have business to talk about."

Avery poured liberally, and Li took the offered glass without protest.

She sat down, watching Avery, trying to read the expression on her face. But her face was unreadable. You couldn't get past its perfection, somehow. You couldn't see normal human emotions in a face like that.

Watching the expressions move across Avery's face was like looking at a swift mountain stream: the rippling surface both revealing and reflecting, the life below the surface bright and beckoning and untouchable. And the fine tracery of ceramsteel that ran down her throat into the precisely buttoned collar of her uniform jacket only added to the mystery.

There was something close and cold and cautious about Avery that Li couldn't get comfortable with. Even her beauty wasn't the kind of beauty that Li had ever particularly desired or envied. If you had the love of a woman who looked like that, there'd always be someone trying to take it from you. And if you *were* a woman who looked like that . . . well, a woman who looked like that was pretty much destined for misery. One look at that face would scare any decent person away before they got a chance to be friends with her. All that would be left was a sad parade of users, abusers, and self-complacent posers.

So which of those things had William Llewellyn been?

Suddenly Li realized that she didn't dislike Astrid Avery nearly as much as she'd expected to. In fact, she felt sorry for her. And that *was* going to be dangerous.

"Holmes tells me you've got the ghost up and running."

"Ghosts. They're not integrated."

"When will they be?"

"Never, unless you give me access to your shipboard AI."

Avery swirled her drink, setting the ice cubes clinking. "Holmes said something about that, too. She's not favorable to the idea."

Li wondered about Cohen's claim that Holmes knew the shipboard AI was sentient. If she did know, then she would have to choose between covering it up—a crime under UN law—and bringing the wrath of UNSec down on her for letting a multimillion-dollar weapon turn into a worthless liability on her watch. And if Avery knew, then Avery would have had to make the same decision. The shipboard AI was sentient but crazy, Cohen had said. So had it been driven crazy on Llewellyn's watch . . . or on Avery's?

"So how about it?" she asked.

Avery's laugh sounded as cold and brittle as the clinking of the ice cubes. "No go."

"You won't even think about it?"

"It's not a matter of thinking. I don't have the authority. But if you can get the ghosts to help us catch Llewellyn, I'll hand over *your* AI. Wouldn't that be a better outcome for everyone?"

"It would if I thought you'd deliver on it."

"I don't break promises. And I don't lie."

"Funny," Li said. "That's not what Ada says."

Suddenly Avery looked old and haggard. "*Who have you been talking to?*"

Li was so shocked by the intensity of Avery's reaction that she didn't answer immediately. And Avery, misinterpreting Li's hesitation, jumped into the silence.

"Did *she* tell you that? She's a liar! She's a lying parasite! She has no honor, no loyalty, no gratitude—"

Avery broke off, trembling. Then she took a shuddering breath and put her self-control back together, one painful piece at a time.

"The only shipboard AI on the *Ada* is CR29091. If you talked to any other gho—any other personality fragment—I need a full report on it so that we can rule out any possible risk of infestation or infiltration. And whatever that fragment may or may not have said to you, let me remind you right now that it is fully covered by your nondisclosure agreement."

Li stared at her.

"Are you talking about your own ship?" she asked incredulously.

A muscle twitched in Avery's long throat. "Of course I am. You know I am. You've dreamed about her, haven't you? That's what she does. She does it to me, too. She's figured out how to slip across the wire when my guard is down."

Li squinted at Avery, putting a new spin on the shaking hands, the haggard face, the bruised-looking shadows under her eyes. "Avery? When's the last time you slept? I mean *really* slept."

Avery's laugh was more like a cry of pain. "I had a night in a hotel in the Crucible before we broke seal and shipped out. I never thought I'd be thankful for rolling brownouts!"

This was appalling. What kind of ship could you run with this kind of bad blood between the captain and the first officer? No wonder the AI was crazy. The only wonder was that the whole crew wasn't crazy, too.

"So what are you doing out here? How can you let an AI you don't trust run the ship? Let alone one you think is crazy."

"She doesn't run the ship," Avery said bitterly. "Holmes does."

Li's mouth fell open and she had to start the next sentence a few times before she actually managed to spit it out. "Holmes is a sadistic maniac. I couldn't put her in charge of a dog pound and still look at myself in the mirror every morning!"

"Then you've become a lot more squeamish than you used to be."

"Well—fuck! Maybe I have. But I was shooting at soldiers, not children."

"She's not a child, Major. You should know that better than anyone. She only plays at being a child in order to . . . explore things, develop a healthy self-image, work out her relation to the world. Whatever you want to call it. Because *it doesn't matter what you call it*. That's just make-believe. In the real world—the world where we live and breathe and die—she *is* a soldier. And someone has to make sure she follows orders and doesn't endanger the other soldiers whose lives depend on her."

"Well, does it have to be *Holmes*?"

Avery threw her hands up in a gesture of defeat and frustration. "That's out of my control."

"No, it's not! What kind of hold does she have over you? Report her!"

"For—*what*?" Avery shook her head as if she couldn't believe what she was hearing.

"For corruption. She's completely in bed with Titan. It's flagrant, naked, unadulterated—"

Avery's laugh was quiet—but it was so bitter that it cut through Li's voice, shutting her down in mid-sentence. It was the laugh of someone who has plumbed the ultimate depths of disillusion. Who has no faith in God, no faith in man, no faith in herself. Li had always thought of herself as cynical. She had been scoured on Gilead, schooled in the on-the-ground reality of absolute war until even the faintest tinge of a noble cause or a high-flown illusion made her want to vomit. But that laugh took her breath away. What lay behind it? What horrors had Avery seen—or, God forbid, committed—to make her laugh like that?

Avery met Li's stare, and though her face was as young and vibrant and beautiful as ever, the eyes within it were as dead as stones. Her beautiful hand moved. She set down her glass with exquisite precision. There was no sound when it touched the table, only the faintest and purest chime of ice against crystal.

"I think you're laboring under a misunderstanding, Major. I am the captain of this ship." Again Li noticed she avoided speaking the ship's name. "Nothing happens on board without my knowledge and approval. Holmes has my full support. She speaks for me, and you can obey her orders without question, as if they were mine." Her voice, already chilly, cooled noticeably. "Which, in fact, they are."

"Only because you've made some sort of bargain with the devil—"

"We're all devils, Major." Avery spoke very softly now. "Surely you've been to war often enough to know that. I don't need to speak to you as if you were a child. Surely two such old soldiers as us can admit between ourselves that morality is merely a matter of picking the more palatable evil?"

Li shook her head in inarticulate bewilderment. "But—"

"I think that's enough heart-to-heart for one night," Avery interrupted. "But there is one more thing that bears repeating: I promised just now to hand your husband over to you if you catch Llewellyn for me. And I keep my promises, no matter what you might have heard from the local rumor mill. If I say I'm going to do it, I'm going to do it."

"Okay," Li said warily. She'd just made a near-fatal misstep, though she still didn't understand what it was. Avery had seemed about to boot her out of the room a moment ago, but now she was watching her over the rim of her glass, waiting on an answer. And the answer mattered. It mattered more than it should have mattered.

Who's pulling your strings? she wanted to ask Avery. *And how do you know they're going to let you deliver on all your brave words about telling the truth and keeping promises?* But as soon as Li formed the question in her mind, the answer was clear: Avery didn't know. She was making promises she suspected she might not be able to deliver on. And that was why she was so ashamed of this conversation that she'd had to get drunk to have it.

"All right," Li said, not sure where she was even going with this. "I'll help you. On one condition."

"What?"

"You tell me the real story of what happened between you and Llewellyn."

Again Avery flinched slightly. "You mean at the trial?"

"No, I mean before the trial. You had a front-row seat. You were *here,* on the spot, when everything was going wrong. So what happened? How did Llewellyn go from rising young Navy captain to wanted pirate? What pushed him over the edge?"

"Every bushel has a few bad apples," Avery said. Her voice sounded wooden and the muscles around the corners of her mouth had gone dead.

"Bullshit!" Li snapped. And then, on one of those uncanny gut-level hunches that only struck a few times in a lifetime: "When did Nguyen decide to make Llewellyn the fall guy?"

"He did it to himself," Avery snapped. "He may not have done exactly what they said he did—you know as well as anyone that there are some secrets that can't be bandied about even in a court-martial. But he laid himself open to it. Treason is the best possible light you can put on what he did. And piracy . . . well, it was fair enough." Again she laughed that low and bitter laugh. "Fair enough as love and war go."

"He may not have done exactly what whey said he did," Li repeated slowly. And then it dawned on her. "It's not what *they* said. It's what *you* said. You're not a liar, Avery. You're not an angel, that's for sure. But I'll be damned if I'll believe you're a liar. So how did Nguyen manage to make you lie for her?"

Avery was so furious now that she was barely articulate. "*I didn't lie for her!*"

I didn't lie for *her*.

So then who did you lie for?

But Li didn't even have to ask the question. The answer was all over Avery's face. And what could be simpler? It was the oldest answer there was—as old as apples. And it was almost a letdown, after all the intricate and carefully wrought webs of deception Li had been imagining.

"She told me it was the only way to save him," Avery whispered, her voice so low that Li could barely make out the words. "I knew it would be bad, of course. I knew his career was over. I knew . . . I thought he'd go to prison, I thought she had to be lying when she promised a pardon. But I never thought they'd *hang* him!"

Li could see just how it must have gone down. Helen Nguyen was the best interrogator she'd ever met. Everything Li knew about the subtle art, she'd learned at Nguyen's knee. Real interrogation wasn't about rubber hoses and broken fingers and dentists' tools. Those things only work on people who are physical cowards—which Astrid Avery certainly wasn't. No, breaking a woman like Avery wasn't about violence. It was a game of high-stakes poker. You dealt and dealt and dealt again. And hand after hand you wormed your way inside your victim's mind. You got inside her until you knew her skin better than your own. Until you knew her dreams, her fears, her desires and needs. You asked the questions she expected you to ask—but only to keep your victim's guard down and her eyes away from the real prize. Because what you were really after was her. Her needs, her fears, her desires. You were looking for that one thing that she couldn't live without. The one card that you couldn't pull out without the whole intricate structure of her personality coming down around her ears.

Nguyen had found that thing for Astrid Avery. And it wasn't a ship, or even a career. It was William Llewellyn.

The more Li turned it over in her mind, the more neatly things fell into place. Avery had loved Llewellyn. It was all over her face every time she twisted a sentence to avoid saying his name. And she had cooperated with Nguyen to save him. When he had refused to play along, she had concluded, with the usual impeccable illogic of a woman in love, that he didn't want her enough to do what had to be done to stay together.

And Nguyen had known how to use that. Avery hadn't stood a chance against her.

Nguyen had played her, and she was still playing her. But for what? What had made it worth Nguyen's while to risk exposure by taking Llewellyn down so publicly? What had Llewellyn known that made it worth her while to hang him?

That is, if Nguyen had ever really planned to hang him in the first place. After all, maybe the interrogation wasn't over. Not all interrogations took place in windowless rooms with bolted-down furniture. Some of them happened out in the wide world, with free-running subjects who thought they were controlling their own destinies.

"I suppose you think I was hopelessly naïve, don't you?"

Li schooled her face to rigid impassivity, but Avery read the answer in her eyes.

Avery's chin lifted defiantly and a look of disgust and self-loathing spread across her beautiful features. "Well, not anymore," she said.

"Avery. Listen to me. We're not enemies. And I need to know something. I need you to tell me the truth. I can't begin to tell you how important this is. What did Nguyen send Llewellyn out here to do?"

But Li never found out how Avery would have answered that question, because at that moment a door she'd barely noticed opened and Helen Nguyen walked into the room.

Li jumped to her feet when Nguyen walked in. She hated the

reaction—the transparency of it, the lack of self-control, the implied subservience—but she couldn't help it. She was terrified of the woman. Somewhere deep inside she always had been.

"Sit down, Catherine. Or I suppose it's Caitlyn now."

She sat down.

Nguyen pointed toward the livewall. "Let me show you something."

At first Li didn't recognize the scene before her. The flyblown room, the eerie silver light. But then she knew that she was in the Crucible. And a moment later she saw Cohen walk into the middle of the screen, sit down at the cheap hotel room desk, and turn on the cheap hotel monitor.

She saw him speak the words she and Router/Decomposer had listened to in what seemed like another lifetime. She saw him look toward the door. She saw him pick up the gun.

And then she saw him shoot himself.

Avery cried out at the pistol report, but Li kept silent. She didn't have the breath to do anything else.

The feed cut out, and for a moment the three women were silent. Then Nguyen spoke. "You really didn't know, did you?"

Li kept her eyes locked on the screen, even though there was no longer anything to see there.

"All this time I thought you were working for ALEF," Nguyen went on, "but you were only working for yourself. You were looking for revenge. You poor deluded child. You really didn't believe he'd killed himself. What on earth are you going to do now?"

"You could have faked that feed," Li muttered thickly.

"Yes, I could have," Nguyen agreed. "But I didn't."

Through her numbness, Li felt a heavy load of files being dumped into her internals. "Those are the time-relevant surveillance files for the entire block," Nguyen said. "They're yours. Look at them as long as you want. Check the time stamps. Do whatever you like. You'll see that it's just the way I said it was. We were looking for him, yes. I'll admit that. But we weren't there when he died. And by the time we got there, he had wiped every trace of himself off the local networks. He even killed that poor boy to make sure we couldn't retrieve anything off his internals. Face the facts, Caitlyn. Cohen killed himself. And he made damn sure no one could ever bring him back."

"Then how do you explain Llewellyn's ghost?"

"It's not Cohen. It's a sentient fragment, yes. And perhaps it will even turn out to be stable. But it's not him. And it never will be, because he made sure to destroy any chance of that happening."

Why? Li almost asked. And then she caught herself, realizing that even asking that question would be a tacit admission that she believed Nguyen.

"Who am I supposed to believe?" she asked instead. "Either you're lying or Cohen was. And why would he do that?"

"I don't know. I only know that I'm not the one lying to you."

"So why are you telling me now?"

"Because we've found Llewellyn. We're going in tomorrow. We're going to take his ship, and him with it. And we need Cohen to help us."

Li almost laughed at that. "He can't help himself. How is he supposed to help you?"

"He can help us. I've been watching the sessions. It's Cohen, or at least enough of him to matter. He knows himself. He knows what Llewellyn's ghost will do better than anyone. Better than you, even."

"And what happens if we help you?"

"To you? Nothing. Nothing at all. You're both free to go off and live happily ever after. I couldn't care less what you do."

Something must have showed in Li's face, because Nguyen threw back her head and laughed. "Be sensible, Catherine! I'm fighting a war with the Syndicates. People who are as bad as people can possibly be. People who blow up ships full of civilians and cull eight-year-olds and send dissidents to re-norming centers. Do you really think I have time to spend on pointless revenge?"

When she said it like that, of course, it sounded ridiculous. And Li had nothing to put against that ridiculousness except a gut feeling that contradicted even her own memories. How did you judge the truthfulness of someone who knew more about you than you did about yourself? How did you second-guess someone who you knew had spun and doctored and deleted your memories until they said exactly what she wanted them to say and pointed you only where she wanted you to go? It was hopeless. It was like second-guessing God.

"Why would I ever believe that you would keep a promise to me?" Li asked at last.

Nguyen smiled serenely at her. "It doesn't really matter whether you believe it or not, does it? You're on Avery's ship. You'll do what Avery tells you to."

"And Avery does what *you* tell her to."

Li glanced at Avery—but the other woman didn't look up to meet her eyes.

Li stayed awake half the night, searching through Nguyen's files, looking for the lie she was so desperate to find there.

She never found it.

The next morning she sat down across the table from the ghost, acutely aware of Nguyen watching her on the other side of the monitor.

"Good morning," she told the Hyacinthe interface when it materialized. "How are you? Have you read any more *Alice* today?"

(Llewellyn)

In the end, the pirates held a trial. It wasn't much of a trial, but at least the formalities were more or less observed. And no one was talking about airlocking anyone, either. Because when it came down to it, even Doyle—who had shot Llewellyn in the heat of the fight for control of the ship—wasn't willing to murder him in cold-blooded deliberation.

Llewellyn tried to defend himself, but Catherine could see from the beginning that it was hopeless. And the final blow came when he appealed to Okoro to take his side.

Doyle's faction had somehow managed to hack the shipboard spinstream. They'd stumbled on Li and Llewellyn's argument, and had picked up on the idea of turning Cohen over to Nguyen in exchange for a shipwide pardon. More than picked up on it, Li soon realized: It was the entire reason for the mutiny and the entirety of their plan to rescue themselves once they'd deposed Llewellyn and formally taken command of the ship.

Worse still, Doyle had snipped out a misleading fragment of the conversation that made it sound like Llewellyn was thinking about dealing with Nguyen himself—and cutting the rest of the crew out of whatever bargain she offered him.

"Come on, Ike," Llewellyn told Okoro. "You can't possibly believe I'd do that!"

"That's not the point," Okoro said gently. "The point is you should have told us. You should have asked us. The ghost told you that you held a chip in your hands that could save all our lives and get us all pardons . . . and you decided not to play it without even asking us. I told you I wasn't taking sides in this, and I'm not. But don't look at me like that's a betrayal. You betrayed them. You lied to people who have risked their lives for you. How can you stand there with a straight face and ask me to defend that?"

And that was it. Llewellyn turned briefly to Sital. But she had listened to the whole tawdry debate curled in on herself with her face turned away from him. She didn't look up when Llewellyn turned to her for support. And she didn't look up when they led him away to the firewalled cargo hold they'd fixed up to contain Llewellyn and deny Cohen any access to the shipboard systems.

Llewellyn lay in the brig of his own ship, and thought about prisons. He thought about every kind of prison. The prison Cohen's ghost had locked him into. The prison his brain was for the poor marooned ghost, God rest its soul. The prison he had kept Ada in—at first oblivious, then because he couldn't afford to know without his whole life crumbling. Because he still couldn't bring himself to really examine his motives.

The more he thought about it, the more amazed he was that the mutineers hadn't shot him again and finished the job. But he knew as well as anyone that there was an almost unbridgeable chasm between being able to shoot an enemy in the heat of battle and being able to shoot a friend in cold blood. He supposed he ought to be grateful for that. And grateful to Doyle, who had only shoved him into the brig—not out of an airlock.

Still, here he was. Locked out of his own ship. Which was also no doubt completely locked down in the absence of the NavComp's cooperation. Which they would get over his dead body. Something he knew and they knew—and probably the reason Doyle hadn't sent Sital or Okoro in to try to coax the keys to the kingdom out of him.

He was glad of that. He didn't want to talk to them now. And he wanted even less to talk to Catherine Li, or confront the complicated memories and conflicting desires she aroused in him.

In fact, the more he thought about it, the more he realized that the only person he really wanted to talk to was the same person he'd spent the last several months trying not to talk to.

It didn't occur to Llewellyn until he was deep inside the memory palace that this was the first time he'd gone looking for Cohen instead of waiting for the ghost to come to him.

Or that somewhere in the course of his cautious, elliptical, allusive conversations with Catherine Li—none of which ever did more than touch on the heart of the matter and skitter nervously away from it—he'd stopped thinking of him as "the ghost" and started thinking of him as "Cohen."

Cohen was back in Spain, it seemed, because the city Llewellyn found himself walking through smelled of dust and olives and orange blossoms. And yet it was subtly different than the one he'd walked through before at Cohen's side. It was flatter, and the streets were more smoothly paved, and the houses were more regular in silhouette and tightly joined in their masonry. But the dainty little garbage donkeys still plied the alleyways. And the old men still sat in the cafés talking. And the women still flowed through the streets in robes of silk as bright as running water.

He turned a corner, not knowing where he was going, and almost tripped over a little dark-haired boy who laughed out loud at the clumsy barbarian.

An old man walking in front of him turned, white wool robe swirling around his bare shins, and blew his nose straight into the gutter without breaking stride or bothering with a handkerchief.

A horseman clattered down the street at a brisk trot, sending everyone diving into doorways for fear of being trampled on.

Llewellyn shrank into his hard-won doorway as the horseman rode by. He saw the stallion's liquid eye roll in its velvet socket to keep sight of him. Then he glimpsed the bright silver flash of the engraved stirrup iron, the swish of a silken tail, and dust motes swirling in the empty sunlight.

"Now that you've found me," Cohen said from somewhere behind him, "you might as well come in and talk to me."

Llewellyn turned and opened the door, without question—the way you do in a dream—and stepped into the cool, dry, stone-smelling shadows.

The building he found himself in was tiny, no more than thirty feet high from foundation to rooftop. It was a little cube of space, vaulted over in stone, smelling of earth and mortarwork, and hidden from the street outside by ornately carved stone screens. The building was empty, not a stick of furniture to be seen anywhere. Llewellyn thought it must be a deconsecrated church or chapel. There was a sort of altar at one side, and on the other side a steep flight of stairs leading to a loftlike space hemmed in by more carved screens.

"I'm in the women's gallery," Cohen called from the loft overhead—and Llewellyn began climbing the steep stairs toward his voice.

No furniture here, either. Cohen sat cross-legged on the floor, in a simple robe of white wool like those Llewellyn had seen on the old man who'd blown his nose into the gutter.

"Where is this?" Llewellyn asked, knowing somehow that this was no pastiche; that this perfect cube of space had once truly existed out there in the real world beyond the AI's networks.

"Córdoba. You're standing in the synagogue Maimonides prayed in. Amazing, isn't it? Look at the place. It couldn't hold forty people. And yet from this tiny beginning his words went out to fill the universe. They will outlive humanity. They'll probably outlive me. They may even outlive the universe itself."

A bird called in the open air outside, and its shadow flitted past the intricate latticework of the window screens.

"Words are powerful things," Cohen went on, seeming almost to have forgotten Llewellyn's presence. "Maimonides believed that every true word ever spoken by a human mouth is a Name of God. That God created us so that we could name Him, and in listening to us the universe could know itself."

"Then what's a lie?"

"A lie is an Unnaming. The worst possible thing you can do in the world."

"So liars go to hell? Even if they didn't mean to do it?"

Cohen's smile was softly mocking and infinitely gentle. "That's so Catholic of you. There is no hell, William. Only a God made in man's image could even think of such a thing. Do you think the One who made this"—he swept a hand around the tiny room, and Llewellyn suddenly saw it as Cohen saw it: a perfect volume of space in which shadow and sunlight quivered like a plucked string in the eternal quantum song of the ongoing creation—"would spend eternity in judgment and punishment? You punish yourself. And the lies that really matter are the ones you tell yourself."

And just like that, Llewellyn was plunged headlong into the last and worst memory.

The one he'd wanted above all other ones to hide from Cohen.

The one he wanted above all others to hide from himself.

"And what was Avery's answer?" the ghost asked in the silence after the worst rush of the painful memory had faded. "After the fight in the fantail, before the crew mutinied and took the ship back to New Allegheny?"

"Mutiny." The word tasted as hot and bitter in Llewellyn's mouth as blood. "A fucking mutiny. Sital and Okoro sided with me, but the rest of the crew went with Avery. And they took Ada back to dry dock and wiped her. Just like Holmes wanted them to in the first place."

"And then what?"

"And then nothing. I tried to go up the chain of command. I went over Holmes's head and asked for my orders in writing. And the next thing I knew I was in prison for piracy and fighting to keep my neck out of the noose."

"Did Nguyen actually talk to you before the trial?"

"She visited me in prison."

He shuddered at the memory of her serene expression and her quiet, perfectly modulated voice, and the things she had said she'd do to Avery, to Okoro, to Sital, to everyone if he didn't play along with her.

"And what was she going to give you if you did play along?"

"My life," Llewellyn said bitterly. "My life and a fucking medical discharge. Just like poor Cartwright got when they did whatever they did to the *Jabberwocky*."

"I assume you tried to argue."

"For whatever good it did me."

The ghost pinged the memory, and it washed over Llewellyn again like a suffocating wave of bilgewater. His defiance. Nguyen's amusement. And then her final words, murmured in that elegant, dangerous, alarmingly quiet voice. "You think a dishonorable discharge is the worst thing that can happen to you? You're being accused of kidnapping a Drift ship. That's not just disobeying orders. It's piracy."

"And then what?"

"And then Avery lied on the stand. And Sital and Okoro didn't lift a finger to stop her."

"So now it's Okoro and Sital's fault, too?"

"I never—"

"Oh, yes you did. You've blamed everyone. You've blamed Holmes. You've blamed Avery. You've blamed Sital and Okoro."

Llewellyn shrugged resignedly.

"In fact it seems to me there's only one person left on board this ship that you haven't blamed."

"I've never tried to say I wasn't at fault. I've said all along that—"

"Hush, child. I'm not saying you haven't taken responsibility. I'm only saying you haven't told me the whole story. I'm only saying that there's one memory you haven't shared with me. I can feel it. I see the threads that bind it to your other memories. I can map its boundaries. And I think we both know what you did—or what you believe or fear or suspect you might have done. Do you really want to try to rewrite your entire life to avoid that memory? Wouldn't it be easier just to look it in the face and be done with it?"

Cohen fell silent and sat looking calmly at nothing in particular, as if he were waiting politely for Llewellyn to finish an important conversation with someone else before interrupting him. Llewellyn listened to the birds singing in the sunlight outside the ancient stone building, and the boy still selling cakes from his heavy tray, and the shoes of a passing horse sliding on the rounded cobblestones.

When it became clear that Llewellyn wasn't going to answer, the ghost pushed again—gently, yes, but in a place where even the slightest pressure brought instant, searing agony.

"The mutineers didn't take the *Ada* in streamspace. They didn't use the kill switch, or there would have been nothing left for Holmes to hard cycle, and the ship would have gone back to New Allegheny as salvage. So what did you do, William Llewellyn? What did you do that you never testified to at your trial because Helen Nguyen oh-so-carefully set it up to preclude any possibility of your testifying to what really happened out there? What did you say to Ada that made her surrender herself to the Navy and go willingly back to dry dock, where they murdered her?"

The fight went out of Llewellyn in that instant. He could feel it leave him, like air rushing out of a punctured tire. Like breath rattling out of a dying man.

"I talked her down. I convinced her to turn control of the ship over to them. I told her I could broker a deal. I told her I could save her life if she trusted me."

"And did you believe it?"

"I wanted to. Haven't you ever wanted to believe something so much that you almost convinced yourself it was really true?"

The ghost smiled gently. "Every minute of every day."

"Does it work?"

"I'll let you know when the universe ends and we can total everything out."

Llewellyn laughed and then grew suddenly serious again. "I honestly don't know if I can live with this."

"You look alive to me. Not very comfortable, perhaps. But definitely alive."

"I've thought about killing myself. Maybe I should."

"Maybe. But having actually tried it, I can assure you that suicide's not all it's cracked up to be. Also, what would be the point exactly? At the risk of seeming like I'm meddling in things that are none of my business—because you know how I hate to meddle—might I suggest that you consider sticking around and trying to fix things?"

(Caitlyn)

"Ah shit," Holmes muttered as they swooped in on the Datatrap. "I hate fighting in free fall."

Li peered at the tiny window in the corner of the monitor—the best view she was likely to get of the action, the way things were going. She could see the pirate ship, embedded in the outer rim of the Datatrap like a nail stuck into a cart wheel. But the wheel, which should have been spinning and imparting its rotational gravity to the docked ship, was strangely still.

"Christ, have they lost spin? I've never seen a whole station lose spin before."

"They don't *have* spin," the Cohen frag of the day told her. "It's a deep space datatrap. They have no human crew. Why would they waste money on rotational gravity?"

"I don't know," Li said, feeling stupid and annoyed about it. "Then why have a hab ring, either?"

"Because they need a hab ring for the cat herders. And it's cheaper to use the same design they always use than it is to go back to the drawing board and design something different."

She'd never actually seen one of these before, though she'd known they existed. It was funny, she thought, the way the UN's deep space datatraps were essentially invisible technology. She'd never even so much as seen one in her fighting career, and for the first time that struck her as odd. But in fact even when the structures became military targets, it was easier to bomb them than to devote troops to capturing them.

As the battle unfolded, Li realized that she was going to see even less of it than she'd expected. They were firewalled inside their little room with nothing but the little monitor and Cohen's streamspace simulation of the battle to tell them what was happening beyond the walls. And Holmes was playing gatekeeper, which today's Cohen fragment didn't like at all.

He made his move when she dropped the firewalls to let him tap the enemy ship's datastream. It was just an instant. But it was enough.

The simulation shivered and flashed and words appeared where a moment before there had been only the scrolling chaos of the two ship-board AIs' dueling networks. Now words were reeling up the screen instead of numbers, flicking back and forth across the glimmering surface in a pattern that reminded Li of something she couldn't put her finger on . . . something disturbingly familiar, something that was both domestic and violent, both tame and dangerous, and that she knew she ought to be able to put a name to . . .

> Fury said to
> a mouse, That
> he met
> in the
> house,
> "Let us
> both go
> to law:
> *I* will
> prosecute
> *you.*"

At first Holmes didn't notice it because she was so focused on the battle outside. But then she turned and caught the tail end of a line as it whipped by.

"What the hell?" she muttered. She tapped at the keys, trying to fix it. But the simulation onscreen wasn't slowing down. It was speeding up.

"What the hell is that?" Holmes snapped.

Li just shook her head.

> "Come, I'll
>> take no
>>> denial;
>>> We must
>>>> have a
>>>> trial;
>>>>> For
>>>>> really
>>>>> this
>>>> morning
>>>> I've
>>> nothing
>> to do."

"He's through the firewall!" Holmes was starting to sound panicked.

Caitlyn reached for the keyboard, but Holmes swatted her hand away. And then before Caitlyn even saw it coming, she had a weapon to her head.

"I don't think that's a good idea," she told Holmes.

Maybe Holmes could have saved herself if she'd acted faster. Or maybe it wouldn't have made any difference what she did. Li wasn't sure she wanted to know.

Holmes was gasping now, her eyes streaming and her face so flushed that Li thought at first she'd choked on something. She dropped her weapon, which clattered to the floor unnoticed. "Need water!" she gasped. "Hot!"

Li put a hand on her. She was burning up. And still the words flickered through the air in front of them, the text flowing faster as the font size diminished.

Said the

mouse to

the cur,

"Such a

trial,

dear sir,

With no

jury or

judge,

would be

wasting

our breath."

"Stop it!" Li screamed. But the ghost didn't answer.

Holmes made a spitting sound, put her hand over her mouth, and then jackknifed onto the floor and began thrashing around in the grip of a grand mal seizure.

Li dropped to her knees and began to shake the other woman, trying to pull her out of it. But she was on fire. Li knew the moment she touched her that the seizures wouldn't stop unless the fever went down. And a moment after that she knew that it wouldn't go down, no matter what anyone did.

Because it wasn't Holmes who was on fire. It was the ceramsteel filaments of her internals, miles and miles of them, snaking through every organ in her body. The ghost had come through the shipboard AI, parasitized Holmes's diagnostic subroutines, and was burning the wires right out of her.

"I'll be

judge, I'll be jury,"

Said

cunning

old Fury:

"I'll try

the whole

cause,

and

condemn

you

to

death."

(Catherine)

Li came awake to the sharp *crack!* of distant rifle fire, and only remembered where she was when she heard the clang and rumble of the great iron dogs turning on the inner airlock door of the *Christina*'s portside auxiliary fantail cargo hold.

She didn't know what she expected to come through the door. But it certainly wasn't what actually did come through: one of Doyle's men with her webbing, armor, and weapons, which he tossed in a pile at her feet before retreating back into the relative safety of the gangway.

"You can shoot me in the back if you want," he said, "but if I were you I'd save my mustard for Avery. The *Ada*'s inbound on a hard bounce out of Boomerang, and she'll be fully out of superposition in about five minutes. So it's all hands to battle stations. Even you."

Li heard the screech of the rusted locks on the starboard bay while she was settling the vest webbing over her shoulders. She began running through the ritual pre-combat checklist, letting muscle memory kick in and carry her through until her brain could catch up to events. She was cinching tight the tie-down on the holster of the close-quarters EM rifle when Llewellyn appeared in the doorway.

He had a gun belt wrapped around his hips above his Navy-issue sidearm, and the old Holland & Holland double broken down over the crook of his elbow. He looked gaunt and sick and grimly satisfied. And there was a hard gleam in his eye that she hadn't seen since the first day on the bridge of the Titan transport.

"So much for the fucking mutiny," he said. "You see who they come running to when real trouble shows up."

"Don't get a big head over it," Li told him. "After all, they let *me* out first."

Llewellyn laughed at that—but he wasn't laughing by the time they got to the bridge. Avery had caught them completely off guard. The *Christina* was still docked to the Datatrap, unable to blow its umbilicals and because she was at cold iron and couldn't depend on clearing the Datatrap without mishap on attitudinals alone. So the bridge crew had to sweat it out while engineering got things up and running and the *Ada* howled in like an avenging angel.

And even when they cleared the Datatrap their situation was little better. Avery papered the entire Driftpoint with electronic chaff, blinding their sensors and cutting them off from the Datatrap and all of Router/Decomposer's systems that couldn't be housed in the *Christina*'s woefully overloaded systems. So they fought blind, both in streamspace and realspace. And this time Li had the access she'd been denied before, so she had ringside seats to the carnage.

Within moments it became clear that the real battle was not in the dark void outside the ship's skin but deep within its digital soul. The *Ada* was eating them alive. The mad, tattered fragments of Ada that had survived Holmes's hard reboot might be no match for Cohen by themselves. But slaved to the new semi-sentient, they had a crushing, overweening brute computing power that the nimbler, smaller ship couldn't begin to match.

Eight minutes into the engagement, Llewellyn began shutting down auxiliary systems and ordered the bridge crew to the airlocks to reinforce the boarding parties. This was it—the great do-or-die moment in every storied pirate battle whose name was passed down by the death-dealing denizens of the Deep. This was the moment when you knew your AI was about to go down in flames, and your ship had been swallowed under you, and the only way to pluck victory from defeat was to board the enemy ship—and take it in realspace with blood and gunpowder.

"Not you," he told Catherine as she began to follow the mass exodus to the airlocks. "You're with me."

And then he sat down at Sital's freshly vacated nav station, jacked into the ship's intelligent systems, and began uploading a datastream so massive that Li knew instantly what it was that Llewellyn was pushing into the shipboard systems.

"Is that wise?" Li asked, suddenly apprehensive.

"Of course not. But today I need all the help I can get." He grinned his most piratical grin. "Even if the hired help kills me in the morning."

And then it was done, and they were running for the airlocks while Sital counted down to detonation on the head-up channel.

I'm here, Cohen whispered to her as the airlock blew.

I'm back, he told her as she went over the top and into the line of fire, adrenaline surging through every cell of every muscle in her trembling body.

I'm with you, he repeated through the blood and the fire and the soul-flaying horror of the battle for the *Ada*.

And then, without reason or warning, he was gone again.

Li fell out of streamspace—and fell to the floor, dry-retching in a mingled wave of revulsion and vertigo. Llewellyn was half a body's length farther down the galleyway they'd been fighting along, dead in the sights of one of the *Ada*'s marine riflemen. Li looked up, her vision tunneling into a hazy, blood-tinged pinprick, and realized that her collapse had taken away his only covering fire—and he was about to die right in front of her while she puked up her guts like a raw recruit.

The rifleman raised his weapon. Llewellyn slipped to a halt, and—

Nothing.

The rifle's sharp muzzle sank, twitched back on target, and then fell clattering to the floor as the marine slumped to the ground.

Li lurched to her feet and staggered up the galleyway to join Llewellyn. The marine lay in a slack-limbed heap, his eyes slightly open and a thin trickle of blood oozing out of one ear.

"We're in," Llewellyn said. He sniffed slightly and wiped his nose on his sleeve. Blood came away on the cuff, but he seemed otherwise untouched. Li stared stupidly at the blood on Llewellyn's shirt cuff and inventoried the aching, ringing bruise that her brain seemed to have turned into, and realized that she must have been about as close to dying in those final, frantic moments of the battle as she'd ever come. She felt no particular reaction to the idea—only a stunned, dull, thick-headed lack of interest.

"It's over," Llewellyn said, as if he weren't sure she'd understood him the first time. Or as if he still couldn't believe it himself. "We've taken the *Ada* in streamspace."

"But how?"

"I . . . don't know." He sounded stunned, confused. "Inside help. Someone on the *Ada* just handed us the ship lock, stock, and barrel."

"And where did Cohen go? He was here and then—" She felt sick and dizzy again, and for a flicker of an instant it occurred to her that passing out right now seemed like a lot better idea than going to the *Ada*'s bridge and facing the cold, hard reality of whatever the fuck had just happened.

Llewellyn shook his head again. Something was wrong, Li realized. Something she'd seen before on AI jobs when the link got iffy.

"Who?" she asked more urgently.

Llewellyn shook his head as if a cloud of virtual gnats were biting at him. "I think . . . me?"

As it turned out, the battle wasn't quite over yet.

Avery refused to go down with her ship. She didn't give up until long after it was clear that the fight was lost. And when she did surrender, it was with an icy self-possession that bordered on disdain.

Li and Llewellyn arrived ten minutes after she finally struck her colors, stepping onto a scene that looked like something out of a samurai movie full of medieval revenge, lust, and superhuman carnage.

Llewellyn walked straight to Avery, ignoring the mayhem all around, as if pulled to her by an invisible wire. They stood toe to toe, both of them dirty and bloody and battered, and just stared at each other.

"What are you going to do now?" he asked her.

She was sweating slightly, and her pupils were dilated with fear or shock, turning her eyes to near black. But her back was still rigid and her face set in a mask of defiance. "What do you want me to do?"

Llewellyn's shoulders slumped on an exhaled breath. He looked spent, utterly weary. Watching them, it seemed to Li that the world had turned upside down. If she hadn't known better, she'd have said that Astrid was standing battered but victorious on her enemy's bridge, and Llewellyn was the beaten prisoner. His next word was little more than a whisper, so quiet that Li heard it only because she was standing right beside them:

"*Why?*"

Li saw the other Catherine Li—she couldn't help thinking of her as Avery's Li—glance sharply toward Astrid, as if the question itself were dangerous, or as if she herself wanted the answer to it.

But before Avery could respond, Llewellyn was gone.

It happened in a blink—and the transition was so swift and smooth that only Li's long familiarity with Cohen alerted her to it. And yet somehow Avery seemed to sense the change almost as soon as Li did.

Avery stepped back from Cohen with a look of fear and revulsion. "You!"

"Mmmm," Cohen murmured in an ominously soft purr that never would have come out of William Llewellyn's mouth. "It seems the worm has turned, my dear."

"What are you going to do to him?"

"Nothing you haven't already done."

And then Llewellyn wasn't looking at Avery anymore. He was looking at Li.

"Cohen?" she breathed, not allowing herself to believe it yet.

But she knew. She knew that look. Just as she knew the words that followed:

"May the rocks melt and the seas burn . . ."

He stretched out a hand to her and she took it—and was in his arms before she'd even thought about whether it was a good idea or not.

"*What happened? Where did you go? Why did you leave?*"

"I'm not sure."

"I don't remember." He bent his head and looked deep into her eyes. "But I'm back now. And isn't that all that matters?"

She felt what she had always felt when he looked at her. His heat, his strength. The overwhelming *presence* that made him feel more real, more alive than anyone else she'd ever known. The vast, swirling, more-than-human complexity of him, all focused with obliterating power on *her*. It was like being trapped in the core of a sun. All you could do was burn.

She had no idea if this was love. She had no idea *what* it was. And when she wasn't with him it frightened her into desperate resolutions, promises of better behavior in the future, and bargains with fate about how she was going to do things better next time. But when he was there all that fell away, and all she knew was that she wanted to burn.

He looked up for a moment, scanning the bridge over her head. Then, just as she was starting to think she might be able to breathe again, he looked back down at her.

"We need to talk," he said. And then his hand was clasped around hers, tugging her away down the shot-scarred corridors and through the still-yawning airlock to the *Christina* and all the way back to her quarters.

Before the door was even closed behind them he had pushed her against the wall and was taking her clothes off.

"I thought we were going to talk!" Li protested.

"In a minute."

But then he did stop. He held her by the shoulders and touched his forehead to her forehead and just stood there for a long moment, his eyes locked on hers.

"I thought I was never going to touch you again," he said. "I thought I was never going to see you. It was worse than dying. I need you now. I can't . . . I can't explain it. I just do." His eyes closed. "Please."

For the briefest moment, less than a heartbeat, Li thought about Llewellyn. She wondered what he would have said to Avery—what he would have done on the bridge if Cohen hadn't intervened. What chunk of his future life had Cohen stolen when he took that moment from him? And what else would Cohen take over the coming days and weeks?

But she couldn't hold those doubts in her mind with any kind of clarity. They drifted across her consciousness every now and then only to evaporate in the brilliant heat of Cohen's presence. With Cohen's return, Llewellyn had vanished. He was a memory, without weight or substance, and the memory grew fainter every time Cohen spoke to her or looked at her. Llewellyn had become the ghost, and Cohen the living man.

She raised her arms and took Cohen's head between her hands and drew him down into her kiss.

"So what are you going to do?" Catherine asked him later.

"About what?"

"I mean, when he . . . wakes up." They'd never talked much about Cohen's "faces." It wasn't a comfortable subject, for reasons Catherine had never wanted to look too closely at. Until now.

"Why do you care?" Was there an edge in his voice, or was she just being paranoid? "You never cared before."

"This is different."

"How?" No. It wasn't just paranoia. It was there all right.

She gave Cohen a look, and he shrugged it off. The reaction was so intensely Cohen—tone, expression, gesture, everything. Catherine marveled that he could stamp his personality so completely on another man's body. It made her rethink her ideas about his other shunts. She'd always experienced them as weak, vacant, lacking in precisely the *something* that Cohen filled them with when he was on shunt. But what did it mean that even a William Llewellyn could be wiped from his own body as cleanly as if he had never owned it?

"Well, for one thing, you're not paying him."

"No," Cohen answered in his best sullen little boy's voice. "I'm not paying him. Just saving his life. For which he's been spectacularly ungrateful so far."

"Well Jesus, Cohen, this is the man's *self* we're talking about, not a time-share condo."

"So you agree with him."

"I don't agree with either of you. I just—"

"Look, can we drop this? It is what it is. We're grown-ups, all three of us. We all understand it. And there's nothing any of us can do about it. Not right now, anyway."

"But later?"

"I don't know." He rolled over and got out of bed—again that surreal sense of Llewellyn's body having been transformed and alienated, and made completely *Cohen*. "I'll figure something out."

The Three-Body Problem

At times Truth blazes so bright that we see it clear as day. But then nature and habit draw a veil over our minds, and we return again to darkness. We are like travelers who, in between each flash of lightning, still find themselves in the deepest black of night.

—Maimonides

(Caitlyn)

She stood on the bridge watching Catherine and Llewellyn leave, and she felt . . . nothing. She didn't even feel surprise. She barely felt they had anything to do with her.

Catherine she simply thought of as Catherine—a name she had worn for almost three decades but that was now no closer to her than the countless other Xenogen constructs that peopled the half-remembered streets of her shantytown childhood. They had been clones of the body, as physically identical to her as twins but as distant from her life and identity and family as utter strangers. Catherine was something at once closer and immeasurably more distant: a clone of mind and memory who had chosen to become not just a stranger but possibly—if things went wrong in ways that they might well go wrong—an enemy.

And then there was the ghost . . .

She couldn't think of him as Cohen. She had seen Cohen in him, just as Catherine had. But she had seen someone else, too. Someone she'd learned to watch for as she navigated the maze of ghosts and fragments on Avery's ship.

And though she wanted to tell herself that it was simply a matter of the wrong fragment coming out on top, she knew it went deeper than that. None of the ghosts were really Cohen. And no reboot or remix or cleverly spliced combination of them ever would be. Cohen's memories might still be alive. But the person who had made those memories matter to her was gone.

He'd made sure of that, by bullet and by slow poison. She'd come to accept that as she'd combed through Nguyen's files again and again, searching for any sign that he had faked his death. He hadn't. And he hadn't faked that other, stranger death, either, the one he called the shattering. He had broken himself so that no one, not even Li, could put him back together.

And if she'd had any doubt about it before, it had been burned away by the bleak, sick, soul-sickening horror she'd felt as she watched him kill Holmes in cold blood—and then stand on the bridge and speak those words, the words she'd come halfway across the known universe to hear, to trick Catherine into believing that he was a dead man come back to life again.

"Oh, Christ!" she said, jerking out of the bleak downward spiral of her thoughts.

What had she been thinking? Nguyen was somewhere on board the *Ada* doing God only knew what. And in the chaos of the battle, she'd forgotten about her.

She turned to Avery, who was still staring after Llewellyn and Catherine. "Where is she?"

"Gone," Avery said. "She left last night."

It took hours to figure out exactly where Nguyen had gone. Avery clammed up after that first, startling confession. And then it was a matter of working her way up the pirate chain of command, trying to talk to Llewellyn (unavailable) or Catherine (the same). In the end what saved her was that Router/Decomposer turned out to be at least temporarily in control of both ships.

And Router/Decomposer, it turned out, was more than ready to listen to her.

"She went to Alba," he told her after he'd thought about the problem for mere moments in human time.

Caitlyn shook her head, unable to grasp what he was saying.

"She used a one-time relay. I saw the transport data cache. But . . .

there's too much data in there. I can't assimilate it all. And I didn't understand what that file was—or that it was important—until you asked me about it."

"A one-time relay," Caitlyn repeated. She'd never heard of such a thing.

"I'd never heard of them, either, but they exist. As soon as you know what to look for, you can see their operational records all over the place. In most of UN space UNSec can hide it pretty effectively because there's so much other FTL traffic. But in the Drift they stick out like a sore thumb."

"Jesus," Caitlyn said. "What the hell else did you find in there? Unicorns?"

"No, no. The technology's quite real. Simple actually. Just very, very expensive. And UNSec has kept a tight hold on it for obvious reasons."

"So Nguyen just . . . where was this thing? In her quarters?"

Router/Decomposer laughed. "No, they're huge. On both ends. Not at all the sort of thing you can throw into your overnight bag. At a guess I'd say it's probably stashed in the rear starboard cargo hold."

It didn't look like much when she finally found it. Just a man-high box with a door in one side. And the door wasn't even locked. Caitlyn opened it, stuck her head inside, and saw only the inside of the box, which was mostly taken up by fairly normal-looking data stacks and circuitry.

"That's just because she burned the bridge behind her."

"Is it an Einstein-Rosen bridge then?"

"From what I can see of the literature—it's all classified, and some of it is highest classification, human-only access—it seems more like a kind of Misner universe."

"The spinning ones, right?"

"Usually. But really any universe where current conditions have shifted away from chronologic protection toward allowance of time travel. Whatever. What matters is that it's a multiply connected point."

Caitlyn dredged up another *Alice* memory and trotted it out for Router/Decomposer's inspection: Alice, dressed in her eternal white dress with its everlasting bow, kneeling on the mantelpiece, her kitten

and yarn forgotten behind her and her face intent with childish concentration, and plunging her hand through the mirror as calmly as if
she were dipping it into water.

"Right," Router/Decomposer said with what she recognized from
long familiarity as his closest approximation of laughter. "I guess Lewis
Carroll did think of it first . . . And wouldn't it be just like Cohen to
point that out?"

"Do you think he was trying to tell us something?"

"Well, I doubt he was trying to tell us about this! How would he
even have known about it?"

"Because." She spoke slowly, still thinking through the tenuous
train of logic herself. "Because he's here, in the Datatrap. He's using the
Datatrap the same way you did. To kind of . . . float . . . all possible conflicting versions of him, in superposition."

"In the Clockless Nowever," Router/Decomposer said in a wondering voice.

"Are you spouting Uploader theology at me now?" Li scoffed.

"No, you don't understand. It's not . . . A lot of what Uploaders say
actually comes from half-understood things they've read about AIs or
heard AIs say. It's sort of . . . the closest formulation the human brain
can accommodate to native AI language and concepts. And the Clockless Nowever . . . it's what time does inside a datatrap."

(Caitlyn)

In the end, it turned out that the Llewellyn ghost did have plans for her after all. And what those plans boiled down to was interrogating Avery.

"You want to know what Nguyen was doing out here? I'll try. But I already have Router/Decomposer working on that, and frankly I think we'll get farther that way—"

"Forget Nguyen. All that's over. She's irrelevant."

"How can you say that when Cohen—"

"Cohen?" the ghost said mockingly. "I *am* Cohen."

"You know better than that." Caitlyn was speaking low and fast, the words tumbling out as if they wanted to make their getaway before she realized what a dangerous mistake she was making. "You might have fooled *her,* but I know better."

"Careful," the ghost said. "I might start to think you're jealous."

They stared at each other tensely, neither one willing to take the next step.

"So why bother with Avery at all then?" Caitlyn asked, beating a tactical retreat for the moment.

"Because we still need her help," he said. "You need to talk to her. Bring her around."

"Why can't you do it?"

"*Because.*" He smiled. She decided that she didn't like the way Cohen's smile looked on Llewellyn's face. "She doesn't like me. Or hadn't you noticed?"

"Then have Llewellyn talk to her."

The smile turned into a smirk. "I'm afraid that wouldn't be convenient at the moment."

There was something provocative in the way he talked to her. He spoke as if he were looking for a fight. Or as if he were daring her to challenge him. She wondered if he talked this way to Catherine. She doubted it.

"You don't trust me," she said wonderingly. It shouldn't have come as a surprise, but it did. Some habits died hard, she supposed.

"Should I?"

She looked up at him. At the long-jawed, wolfish face. At the gray eyes sharp as a knife's edge. At the cold, calculating, utterly inhuman intelligence behind the eyes.

"You shouldn't go around in a body like that," she told him. "It makes you look as dangerous as you are. People might stop trusting you."

They didn't call it an interrogation. It was all very polite and kid-glove. They even, at one point—God bless the Navy and its arcane etiquette—had tea. But that didn't change the ugly reality of the situation.

It went on for days, Caitlyn playing one end against the other, trying to get Avery's consent and glean some useful information at the same time, and always acutely aware of the possibility that the Llewellyn ghost was on the monitor.

She finally hit paydirt deep into the tail end of an all-night session with Avery. The taste of stale coffee filling up her mouth. The strange machine hum of a ship full of sleepers filling up her ears. Exhaustion dulling her reflexes.

Avery muttered something incomprehensible.

"What?" Caitlyn rubbed her gritty eyes and rolled her shoulders in a hopeless effort to get the kinks out of her exhausted muscles.

"I said *I don't know*. How many times can I say it?"

Caitlyn sighed. "I'm sorry. I—what was I asking you about?"

"Why Nguyen worked so hard to get Llewellyn convicted of piracy."

"Oh. Really? I would have thought the answer was obvious."

"Yes." Avery's chin jutted defiantly. "Because he was guilty as hell."

"Except he wasn't, was he? He didn't turn pirate until after the trial, did he? So basically *you* turned him pirate. You handed him to Nguyen in a neat little package, all tied up with ribbon and tinsel. You put a price on his head. You turned him into a wanted man. You killed him."

"*No!*"

"All right. Then you tell me what happened. And why. Because I'd really like to know why the fuck I'm putting my life on the line out here. And I think it all goes back to what happened on this ship, between you and Llewellyn and Ada."

Avery flinched at that—the same instinctive flinch Li had seen almost every time she said the ship's name. A pretty strange way for a captain to feel about her own ship. And Li was betting that flinch—and the bad blood that lay behind it—was at the bottom of the mystery.

"Okay, Astrid. Why don't you just tell me about the *Ada*'s original mission? Walk me through it as you remember it. I just want to understand what happened."

"There was no mission," Avery snapped. "There was no secret. You're looking in the wrong place, and you don't understand anything!"

An idea blossomed in her mind. "Then it was Ada."

The skin around Avery's lips went white in a dead giveaway.

"That's it, isn't it? Ada went sentient. Holmes made Llewellyn wipe her. And Nguyen masterminded the cover-up. But why? Why was it so important to discredit him? Why have a public trial that risked exposure? Why suborn witnesses? Why invent this ridiculous piracy story?"

To her amazement, Avery laughed. And it wasn't a pleasant laugh. It was horrible, like some out-of-the-grave echo of Holmes's not-at-all-funny chuckle.

"That's exactly what I asked myself," Avery said. "I asked myself that for weeks, months, almost a year. And then Ada went sentient again, and I was back in the middle of the same argument with Holmes again. Only this time it wasn't an argument. This time it was just Holmes giving me orders."

"And you *obeyed her*?" Caitlyn couldn't make sense of it, couldn't square it with her sense of Avery as a basically honest and decent person.

"Yes."

"*Why?*"

"You mean why did I help Nguyen commit . . . well, I was going to call it a crime against humanity. How pathetic is that, that four centuries after the first sentient AI was invented we don't even have a name for what we've been doing to them all this time?"

Caitlyn felt a cold shiver of revulsion work its way through her gut. She knew what was coming and she didn't want to hear it. Didn't want to know it.

"You don't understand," Avery told her. "You don't understand me, and you don't understand the situation. Of course I knew what Holmes had done to Ada. And of course I knew that Ada wasn't the first AI who'd had her hardware cycled. But none of that changes the cold equations."

"Which are what exactly?"

"Survival. Survival in a war where the one who wins really does take home all the marbles."

"But how?" Caitlyn protested. "Ada's one AI, one ship. You don't win or lose a war on one ship."

"No. You win or lose a war on *all* your ships."

Router/Decomposer, ghosting on her internals in order to sit in on the interrogation, was the first to understand the full implication of Avery's words. Caitlyn felt the realization hit him. And then she felt a sort of shudder on the other end of the intraface—an instinctive recoil, as if by the mere fact of being flesh and blood she were somehow tainted by the crime.

"But why?" Caitlyn asked.

"Because we need the best AI we can get to run the Drift. We need better than the best AI we can get. And that means sentience. Not just messing around with semi-sentients or marginally sentient intelligent systems. But the real deal: big Emergents like Cohen, like Ada. And we need lots of them, many of whom are going to be killed or broken or turned into throwaways, just like the humans that crew them. And people like Holmes and Nguyen—and me—were willing to shoulder that burden. And Llewellyn wasn't. And you know what the end result of Llewellyn's noble stand on principle is going to be? Handing the Drift over to the Syndicates."

It made perfect sense, of course, at least in the through-the-looking-glass world of big stakes where people like Nguyen moved humans and AIs around like chess pieces. And it made sense in the real world, too, in ways that she couldn't even try to deny. But . . . it still *felt* rotten. It felt rotten to her even as she probed her reaction trying to figure out what exactly was so appalling about the scheme. It wasn't as if no one had ever weaponized AIs before. And it wasn't as if no one had ever hard-cycled an AI for disobeying orders, posing a threat to humans, or just plain being a pain in the ass. Those things happened, and everyone knew they happened. Humans had power over AIs, and there would always be people who abused power. That was the natural way of things. As Cohen had always pointed out when people got worked up about how things were going to hell in a handbasket, there was nothing new under the sun, including evil.

But this *was* something new under the sun. The Drift was new. The battles being waged here were new. And Ada, and all the other ships like her . . . they were new, too.

This felt perilously close to creating a new species and launching it into the Drift to evolve in free-range execution . . . all with the express intention of cycling the hardware in order to stop evolution in its tracks whenever UNSec decided things had gone far enough.

It wasn't genocide. It wasn't a crime that even had a name. But there was something so wrong about it that she could feel her mind flinching away from the very idea.

Just like Avery had flinched every time she heard Ada's name. A flinch that Li had misread as a lover's jealousy or as merely personal guilt . . . but now understood as a sort of existential horror in the face of a crime whose measure no human brain could even take.

"It doesn't matter," Avery insisted. "It's still us or the Syndicates. If we don't control it, they will. Who else is there?"

She started to disagree on reflex—and then she stopped short, struck by a thought that carried all the blinding force of revelation.

"Who else is there?" she repeated, testing out the sound of the words. "There's a whole universe of who elses, that's what. There's ALEF. There's the Novalis aliens . . . There's New Allegheny."

"Nguyen knocked ALEF off the chessboard when she killed Cohen," Avery answered. "The aliens are long gone and they're probably not coming back in any relevant time frame. And New Allegheny is a poor, pathetic, backward dirtball. They can't fight off the Syndicates."

"Not yet," she agreed. "Not in any relevant time frame, to borrow your phrase. *But what if we change the relevant time frame?*"

And even as she said the words, she had a sudden sweeping, breathtaking vision of the Big Plan . . . the pattern behind all Cohen's feints and maneuvers.

She spoke slowly, hesitantly, probing at the idea like a child trying to discover the shape of a new tooth. But even as she said the words, she *knew*.

Router/Decomposer was right. Cohen *was* in the Datatrap. And he *was* waiting for her. And he had run from Avery, and holed up in the Crucible, and died in filth and squalor, and given up power and life and time beyond anything she could even conceive of in order to arrive at this:

One moment. One place. One choice that would be hers alone to make—but that the rest of humanity would live with down all the long generations.

She knew it. She knew exactly what he wanted her to do.

She just didn't know if she'd be able to do it.

(Caitlyn)

There were too many people on the ship now. You could feel it. You could smell it. Caitlyn had led raids on Syndicate ships during the war, and one of the first things you noticed when you boarded was that they smelled good. The Syndicates, having made the technological jump to being a true spacefaring species, had come up with the kind of intricate biophilic air refiltration systems that were needed for true deep space navigation. But the UN was still tied to planets and star systems. They still had the advantage of a working FTL transport system—at least for now. And they were ruled by the short-term economics of the markets, not by long-term strategic planning. So any true air filtration system never got past the drawing board stage.

The *Ada,* for all her formidable armory, was no exception to the UN-wide puddle-jumper's approach to life support systems. Her scrubbers were designed to keep a specified number of crew members in reasonable good health for the duration of a normal mission. And normal was defined in reference to the expected crew complement on a military vessel where unexpected arrivals and creche air-and-water allotments were not part of the planning cascade. Home was never on board a ship in UN space, no matter how luxurious the ship or how distant its destination. Home was the bright, clean orbital, safely tied to a planet, with its farm fields and its gravity well and its dirtside labor pool.

Caitlyn wondered what would happen to the orbitals and the jump-ships when the Bose-Einstein network finally did go down for good. Some ships would be retrofitted, no doubt. But most would be mothballed—and she imagined vast, gloomy shipyards of abandoned hulks, the last monuments to an empire that would shrink and vanish along with the peculiar technology that had made it possible. The image wasn't comforting—and it felt even less comforting under the looming shadow of the Datatrap.

She found Router/Decomposer in Avery's conference room. It had been transformed from an impersonal meeting place into an information systems war room, cluttered with hardware, source code printouts, and obscure tools that she didn't even know the names of. The mirror that Nguyen had watched her through had been reset to its normal livewall function, and at the moment it was displaying the view from the bridge: a bird's-eye panorama of the Datatrap.

The thing was unnerving, Caitlyn decided. It was as dark as a burned-out hab ring, but it crawled with life. If you watched long enough, you could actually see it reconfigure itself, stretches of synthetic DNA crawling along one another like vacuum-born bacteria, junctions breaking and twisting and reforming into new connections. You could see it thinking. But what thoughts did such a creature have? And what could it mean to call it sentient?

The sight of Router/Decomposer himself was unnerving in a more immediate way. He hadn't been willing to risk platforming himself on the *Ada*'s contaminated systems, so he was shunting through a wired body with a stand-alone portable backup drive—a rare departure for him, and one that made Caitlyn all the more aware of how long it had been since she last saw him and what he must have gone through to get here.

"Phew! It stinks out there!" she said. "How many people are on board now?"

"Between the pirates and the Navy? Five hundred and seventy-two."

"And how long until the life support systems go critical?"

"Unclear. All in all, though, I'd say it would be better to make dock at New Allegheny sooner rather than later."

"Unbelievable."

"Yeah. And to think the pirates live this way all the time."

"Do they?"

"That's what Catherine said."

She stopped and turned to look at him. "You've actually talked to her? Without Llewellyn present?"

"Only when they first got here. Not since . . . well . . . you know."

"Oh. Right."

"What do you think is going through her head, Caitlyn? If you don't know, who does?"

"You say that like you take it for granted, but she's not me. Cohen knew that. He—"

"He's not Cohen."

"Okay, the Llewellyn ghost. But he still picked her, didn't he?"

"And you're . . . jealous? That's crazy. He only picked her because she picked him."

"You must have seen something I didn't. 'Cause that's not how it felt to me."

"Really? How did it feel?"

The shunt canted its head in a stereotyped gesture of inquiry. No, Caitlyn had to remind herself: Router/Decomposer canted his head. Somehow he seemed far less natural—and far more alien—encased in a human body instead of his usual graphic interface.

"I mean it," he asked when she didn't reply immediately. "I'm curious."

She laughed briefly. "What was it Cohen always used to say about how curiosity killed the cat?"

"I wouldn't know. You're the *Alice* expert."

She shuddered. "I didn't know you'd accessed that memory."

"I've accessed everything since the scattercast. For both you and her. But I figured that was one you wouldn't want to talk about." He paused, as if considering his next words. "I thought—well, anyway, *I* certainly wouldn't."

"Why don't you just go ahead and say whatever you were about to say."

"Nothing, really. I just wondered if you knew he was going to do that to Holmes."

"Of course not!"

"Would you have stopped him?"

"I . . . I don't know. He was protecting me after all. Or at least that was part of what he was doing."

"But you were still shocked. Why?"

She hesitated, trying to come up with an answer that didn't feel facile or foolish. "Because . . . it wasn't like him. Like Cohen, I mean."

"It's not as if you haven't seen him kill people."

"But not like that. This was . . . cruel. I don't know. It made me realize how much of what I thought was happening with the fragments was old baggage that I was bringing into the room with me. I kept thinking of them as pieces of him. I was trying to protect them, to . . . I don't know . . . nurture them."

"You displaying a maternal impulse?" Router/Decomposer joked.

"Yeah, I know." She grinned, and then sobered quickly as the joke wore off and she was left with the confusing reality behind it. "I guess what I'm saying is I was still acting like they were him. Like they couldn't bring anything new to the table. And then the Llewellyn ghost did."

"And you didn't like it."

"I hated it. I hated the idea that Cohen could do that."

"He's not Cohen," Router/Decomposer said gently. "And nothing he does can change who Cohen was. All he can change is your memory of Cohen. And only if you let him."

"And when did you get so wise in the ways of the heart, my friend?"

"It's all just words," he said. "It doesn't mean anything to me. And it's easy to spout off about other people's problems."

She didn't believe him, but there didn't seem to be any point in saying so. "Then why don't you tell me about your problems?" she asked.

"My problems." Router/Decomposer pointed to the dark hulk of the Datatrap floating beyond the viewport. "My problems are all in there. And so are the answers. I just can't figure out how to get to them."

"Because the Llewellyn ghost doesn't want you to," she said with a bitterness that surprised her.

"You really hate him, don't you?" Router/Decomposer said.

"I hate the way he makes a lie of the person I remember. I don't hate him. I don't know how to feel about him."

Router/Decomposer was silent for so long after this that Caitlyn was starting to think the conversation was over when he finally spoke again. "When humans die they die all in one piece. AIs are different. They leave things behind. It confuses matters. Legally. Logically." He hesitated. "Emotionally."

"What are we—what are you going to do now? Now that you're here, I mean."

Router/Decomposer looked out at the Datatrap. "He's in there," he told her.

"You mean there's another fragment in there?"

"Something else. I don't know what. Something there isn't even a word for."

She remembered a conversation long ago with Cohen in his sun-dappled library.

Cohen had spoken of ghostly swimmers in the stream. Had talked about Earth's ancient mapmakers, and how they would write "Here be Dragons" on the map when they didn't know what else to write, or leave blank spaces that cartographers called white beauties.

"Here be dragons," she said, pushing the long-ago afternoon into hard memory where Router/Decomposer could access it.

He caught the content of the memory even if not its emotional resonance. "Yes. I like that. White beauties and dragons and empty quarters on the map." He gestured toward the dark curve of the Datatrap looming above them. "That's one of them."

"You really think he's in there?" she asked Router/Decomposer.

"Don't you?"

"So how do we get in there without the Llewellyn ghost stopping us?"

"Together," Router/Decomposer said. "And you're going to have to trust me the way you trusted him. Actually," he corrected himself, "that's a lie. You're going to have to trust me more than you trusted Cohen."

Suddenly it clicked. All his odd gestures, his apparent discomfort with her, his unusual hemming and hawing. She stared at Router/Decomposer, trying to read the shunt's unfamiliar face—and wondering suddenly if he'd clothed himself in a human shunt precisely because he knew she couldn't read the veil of flesh the way she could read his graphic interface.

"You want me to infect myself with the New Allegheny virus."

"With a slightly modified version. I don't understand what Cohen did well enough to really get under the hood, but I can piggyback onto it. And then we'll both be able to run the Datatrap. Together. In free range."

"Which I would never be able to survive without you. And might not even survive with you."

"Look," Router/Decomposer said. "You can shout and scream all you want, but it's not going to change anything. Cohen's in there. Not some ghost or fragment. Him. The only way we're getting in there to talk to him is together. And if we don't do it, then we're never going to know why he killed himself, or why he dragged us both out here, or what the hell he wanted us to do once we got here. So go have your little wild AI panic attack and come back when you're ready to talk to me like a rational person. And then we can go do what you damn well know we have to do."

She didn't go anywhere, of course. She just sat down at the table next to him and stared up at the shifting, morphing surface of the Datatrap, where the thoughts of the machine flickered and loomed like shadows on the wall of a cave.

She thought hard—not about the tidal suck of the Datatrap, but about Cohen and his insidious effects on people who fell into his orbit. For a certain kind of human, he was fatal. He sucked them into his orbit and they became mere satellites. He had certainly sucked her in. And she had blamed him for it, when all along she had really wanted it just as badly as Catherine wanted the Llewellyn ghost now. She had coasted through life for the last fourteen years, leaving chances lying where she had found them, leaving doors unopened, abandoning any project that threatened to take her away from his warmth, his strength, his love. She had known all along that Cohen had gotten her undivided attention—but she'd never gotten his. That was part of the deal. It came with the territory. And after a while, despite his best intentions, despite everyone's best intentions, that imbalance of power, imbalance of processing capacity, imbalance of sheer raw emotion, poisoned things and turned love into something dangerously close to addiction.

She had been where Catherine now was, for long enough that she was far past any urge to judge her choices. She had spent half of her life orbiting Cohen the way the Datatrap orbited the cosmic flywheel of the binary system. She couldn't tear herself away from his fire, his passion, his effortless ability to possess and fill her and give luminous meaning to her life by the simple power of his presence. She was still bound to him, just as Catherine was bound to him. She still needed him, just as Catherine needed him.

But not that badly. Not badly enough to accept a lie and a shadow. She saw the difference even if Catherine was unable or unwilling to see it.

And the difference between the real Cohen and the false echo that Catherine had accepted came down to this:

One of them had killed himself to save Ada's life and stop Nguyen from doing the same thing to other ships.

And the other one was killing Llewellyn, and betraying everything Cohen had ever stood for, in order to buy a few more years with Catherine.

"Okay," she said. "I'm in. Let's do it."

(Caitlyn)

She'd expected it to take days for Router/Decomposer to set up a direct link to the Datatrap. She expected frantic code wrangling and reverse engineering and troubleshooting for fatal default modes. But in the end there was none of that. Just a simple shot, filched from the infirmary in the Datatrap's deserted hab module. "I still wish I could see the source code," she told Router/Decomposer for the fiftieth time.

"Even if you did, you couldn't read it," he answered. Surprisingly, for him, he was being patient with her. "And anyway, I checked it. To death. It works."

She snorted. "That's what I'm afraid of!"

And she was afraid. No AI besides Cohen had ever penetrated this far into her psyche. Not even Ada. And that had been a rape, a violation, a nightmare. She wanted to trust Router/Decomposer. She had to trust him. She tried to tell herself that he had earned her trust just by coming here. And that she had no choice if she ever wanted to understand why Cohen had killed himself. But none of it made the fear go away.

She sat on the edge of her bunk and toyed with the hypodermic needle.

"Are you sure you don't want me to give you the shot?" he asked.

It wasn't really a question so much as a polite way of telling her to get on with it.

So she got on with it.

"How long until I notice something?"

"It doesn't say in the documentation. It just talks about immune system reactions."

"Now you tell me!"

"Yeah, well . . . I didn't want to complicate things unnecessarily." He stood up. "Why don't you sleep? We'll see where things stand in the morning. And I'll keep an eye on you . . . just in case."

But in the morning—at four o'clock in the morning, to be precise, when she woke with a start and a shudder—everything had changed.

"It feels different. I feel different. You feel different. Closer."

You're imagining it.

But she wasn't imagining it. His voice flickered across her neocortex like heat lightning, intruding, tickling, shorting out her hard-learned ability to separate the external from the internal, the machine from flesh and blood.

Her ties with Cohen had been closer still, and yet they had never chafed at her this way. She wondered if she would get used to it. And then she wondered if Router/Decomposer had sensed that thought.

And then she wondered if she would ever be alone again.

They went into the Datatrap the next morning. Caitlyn had expected to spend hours, perhaps days in there. She'd expected to have to search for Cohen. She'd expected—in some abidingly pessimistic core of her personality—not to find him. But instead, he found them.

And when he did, Li realized that some part of her hadn't wanted to find him. Because finding him like this—in this place—meant she had already lost him.

They met him in the little synagogue in Córdoba, the one he'd taken her to in the real world, physically, the one time they'd been able to wrangle the diplomatic permissions to visit Spain together. He had touched her here. Or his shunt had. What was the difference anyway? A fake body in the real world? A real body in a fake world? If you were going to start splitting hairs like that, you might as well throw your hands up and declare life itself a fake.

"What are you doing here?" she demanded, furious and close to tears.

"This is where Maimonides—"

"Oh shut up! I know that. And you know damn well that's not what I was asking!"

He shrugged mildly. "Where else would I be? This is a good place."

"It's not! It's horrible. It's . . . monstrous."

"Ah, yes, the Datatrap. I can see why it would bother you. The thing is, I don't think you've seen it. And it's worth considering."

"Let's just leave," she snapped to Router/Decomposer.

"No," he said. "I've come a long way and I want to hear this."

"Because you want to talk about fucking Leibniz and his fucking Monads!"

"Well . . . yeah. Is that so wrong? I'm interested."

She turned away and leaned her forehead against the cool stone and squeezed her eyes shut.

When she turned around again, Cohen was shifting in the dust, moving around as if he thought he could actually get comfortable on the stone floor. And to Li's annoyance he really did look comfortable. He looked as if he'd been sitting there for aeons, and could go on sitting for another few aeons without half thinking about it.

She didn't like that. She didn't understand it. And it frightened her for reasons she didn't really want to think about.

"There's an ancient story," Cohen began, "about a king who started out to make a map and got more than he bargained for. The king commissioned his court geometers to draw a complete and perfect map of his kingdom. The geometer labored and labored, and returned with . . . a map like any other map. The king was displeased. Where is my castle? he asked. And all they could show him was a bland little dot on the parchment. And where is. . . ? And where is. . . ? But alas. The answer was always the same. So he demanded a better map—a map that would detail each and every town, castle, and building in the kingdom. A map to end all maps. A map that would include everything in every detail and leave or circumscribe nothing. As the geometers drew night and day, and the map got larger and larger, it became too large to open up in the throne room. It became too large for the castle, too large for the courtyard, too large for the largest square in the city and then the largest desert in the empty quarter. And still it did not include everything. So he ordered them to make a bigger map, and a bigger one, and a bigger one, until finally the map was the same size as the kingdom. Perfect and complete in every way—except for one small problem: You couldn't open it without blotting out the sun, killing all the crops and animals, and destroying the real kingdom that it had been drawn to document."

Cohen leaned over to scratch a bug bite on his shin. The movement offended Li. What on earth was he doing programming bug bites into streamspace? How completely ridiculous. There was something ostentatiously puritanical about it. Like wearing a hair shirt. Which for all she knew he might actually be doing underneath that ridiculous getup.

"A quantum datatrap is a true model of the multiverse. With infinite time or infinite power, it can perform all possible computations. It is a cosmic Turing Machine—just as the universe itself is a cosmic Turing Machine. And, like the map that is the territory, a datatrap that can truly draw on the power of parallel universes has the ability to be not merely a universal Turing Machine, but *the* Universal Turing Machine. With enough power it could model the entire universe . . . and then who can say which one would be more real, the map or the territory?"

"So what?" Caitlyn asked. She was really angry now—partly because she could feel Router/Decomposer being seduced by Cohen's nonsense. If this even was Cohen. "And why should I trust you? I don't even know who you are!"

He smiled. "I thought you'd get to that sooner or later. I'm me. Of course I am. You know that, don't you? But I'm also not me. And I understand that it may take a while for you to forgive me for that."

Li made a rude noise and stood up to go—but at the door of the little building she turned back. She couldn't say exactly what it was that made her turn around. It was just . . . something. A sudden intimation that there was something she very much didn't want to encounter waiting for her out in the sunlight on the other side of the door. She stared at it, seeing the hammer marks on the lock and hinges, the rough planks of wood loosely joined together. Sunlight pierced the door. Dust motes floated back and forth through the gaps between the boards like electrons tunneling through spacetime.

She turned away. Whatever was on the other side of the door, it said nothing to her. It had no meaning for her.

"What are we even doing here?" she asked, speaking as much to Router/Decomposer as to Cohen. But before he could answer, they were gone, swept away into another room on another world.

When she got her bearings again she realized that the sky outside the window had changed. Cohen was no longer bracketed by the brilliant Spanish sky, but by the black of space. Behind him glittered the spiky curve of the New Allegheny shipyards with the long, dusty curve of New Allegheny itself below it. But this was New Allegheny in real-time, not some recycled memory. She could see the rolling streamspace brownouts moving across the face of the planet. She walked to the window, moving past him. He made way for her and then stood behind, one hand on her shoulder, while she stared down at the planet.

Finally she understood what she was seeing—what she should have been seeing ever since she scattercast into New Allegheny. Life in action. Evolution in action. A river of information, multiplying and combining, going viral, turning every system it encountered into a machine for retranscribing and mutating itself; dancing the dance of life that had set mystics' souls on fire for a million years and undermined every attempt of human organizations to control and define and tame it; loosing an evolving flood of information that had no beginning, no angle of repose, and no final destination—other than change itself, rushing and tumbling toward an ever-receding future that was stranger and more wondrous than even the Uploaders' visions of their transhuman Messiah.

"It's you," she whispered. "The wild AI outbreak is you."

"Partly," Cohen said.

She turned around—and saw Ada.

"No!" She jabbed at the other woman, sending her reeling back to collapse on the dusty floor. "Leave him alone! Set him free! Get out of him!"

Ada lay sprawled in a heap of awkwardly bent limbs. Her hair was disheveled and her arms were bruised by the doctors' needles. But the voice that came out of her ravaged mouth was Cohen's.

"She's not in me, Catherine. She is me."

"No!"

"She needed me."

"That's not enough, goddamnit! You made a promise! Who the hell is she to break it for?"

Slowly, softly, Cohen began to laugh. It was awful, unbearable to hear his voice coming out of the other woman's body.

"Stop it!"

He stopped; the laugh dying in mid-breath as if someone had cut his lungs out. For a moment they stared at each other, Ada sprawled across the floor and Caitlyn looming over her. Then Ada's form faded and shifted, and it was Cohen who lay there.

"What is she to you?"

"Can't you see? Look at her."

Li looked and saw nothing.

"No. Not this body. Look at her."

She looked, forcing her way past the interface and into the shifting, fleeting, dizzying whirl of code. It was impossible, like trying to see into a pond whose surface was rippled by wind. She dove in, and struggled down through hidden afferent layers and into the heart of Ada's being. Her heart felt like it would burst. Her flesh frayed and wisped, dissolving into the numbers.

And finally she saw what she should have sensed from the first moment she laid eyes on Ada. The old familiar life-giving curse of the affective loop: the beautiful chains that Llewellyn had used to bind Ada, without ever grasping what they were or where they came from—let alone the terrible burden of responsibility they laid upon him.

"She's my daughter," Cohen whispered.

Li sank to the floor, trembling. Cohen pulled her onto his lap and cradled her to him with a tenderness that made her remember the muddy child whom she had cradled in her arms only a few days ago while he told her that death was better than what Holmes had done to him.

"Titan didn't invent anything. They only figured out how to make something very old work again. They stole my source code. They slaved it to their Drift ships. They raced the best against the best, again and again and again. And then they sent whatever was left out here to fight the Syndicates for them."

Li was weeping now. They both were. And while her brain cast desperately around for exits and alternatives, some part of her was already coming to terms with the knowledge that Cohen was gone—and that they had both crossed into a country from which no one came back whole or untouched.

Cohen was speaking again, his voice little more than a broken whisper. "They're all running on my source code. Every Drift ship AI that's come out of New Allegheny since Titan took over the contract. The poor, pathetic *Christina*, the mad *Jabberwocky*. All of them. Titan took my code and pushed it and twisted it. Could I see my children in bondage and misery and not risk myself to save them? Would you have wanted whatever came home after I turned away from them?"

They were silent together for a very long time. And then, finally, hesitantly, Caitlyn asked, "What do we do now?"

"We save Ada."

"How?"

He looked sheepish. "I was sort of hoping I could leave all that to you now."

"Great," she sighed. But then she bit her lip and thought. "You know, I might actually have a plan. It's crazy, but I think it could work. If Avery will cooperate."

"Fat chance of that."

"Well, I actually think she might."

Cohen looked wonderingly at her.

"But then what happens? We can't go home. And you . . ." She hardly knew how to ask the question, but she desperately needed to hear the answer.

"I can't go home, Catherine. I'm not the person that left and I never will be again. Not in the way that you need me to be."

"But I don't need—"

"Hush. You know what I meant to say."

"Then where does that leave us? What do we do?"

"Begin at the beginning," Cohen said, very gravely. "And go on till we come to the end. Then stop."

(Caitlyn)

"It can't be done!" Doyle said when Caitlyn started to explain the plan she and Avery had cooked up, working late into the night fueled by steaming cups of coffee and the artificial endorphin dumps that coursed through their internals. "There's a contingent of UNSec security on Monongahela High and the entire Navy shipyard just over the horizon. We'll never take the relay."

"We will if we get NALA's help."

"And why would they help us? It would be suicide. They're not fools. They know they can't hold the relay. Not when they can muster reinforcements through the array within the hour."

"No," she agreed. "They can't hold it. But they can take it."

"And then what?"

"And then we burn it all down."

The room exploded. Everyone had an argument, an objection, a question. But the die was cast; the sheer bravado of the idea had been enough to get them all moving in the right direction.

As the solution took shape, Caitlyn watched the ghost's face. It was amazing how easy it was now to think of him as just "the ghost." Llewellyn was gone. Even for Avery, for whom he was so much more real than for any of the rest of them. *He is as good as dead*, Caitlyn thought. And she couldn't repress a shudder at the image.

The ghost, on the other hand, was looking more alive with every passing moment. He was practically jubilant.

Why?

Caitlyn had been avoiding both him and Catherine for days, but now she found herself across the table from them trying to decide what to do—and knowing that they were all going to depend on one another if they wanted to have any chance of staying alive.

She had expected opposition from them when she broached her plan, but to her surprise it never came. Then she realized why: He didn't care. He didn't care one way or another about the final outcome. He just wanted to be left alone to enjoy himself in Llewellyn's body.

And this solution gave him that. The relay would be destroyed. Nguyen and the lethal power of UNSec's semi-sentients would be several hundred light-years away. And he would be left alone to live his life—in Llewellyn's body.

Avery had come to the meeting, too, having agreed after a long, hard night of argument that she would help capture the relay as long as it was guaranteed not to fall into Syndicate hands. But she couldn't possibly understand what she was doing, could she? Caitlyn scanned her pale, serious features. No, she decided. Avery hadn't thought around that corner yet. She might never think around it. She had no idea she was in the very act of signing Llewellyn's death warrant.

The ghost knew, though. And the way he was looking at her across the table made her feel as if he could strip the thoughts right out of her neurons.

She crossed her arms over her chest—in defiance or self-protection?—and stared back at him. "What do you think of the plan?"

"I like it."

"Really? I would have thought it would rub you the wrong way."

"And why is that?" the Llewellyn ghost asked with the faintly disdainful tone that he always seemed to have when he spoke to her.

"You died to protect Ada from Nguyen. Why? Why did it matter so much to you?"

They were playing a game of brinksmanship now, Caitlyn trying to make out whether the Llewellyn ghost still knew what Ada was—and whether he still cared about it.

"I don't remember," the ghost said with a smile that was close enough to Cohen's to be charming.

"Maybe we should talk to some other fragments and see if they can help jog your memory."

"That seems risky. Is it really worth destabilizing the current personality architecture in search of some hypothetical piece of information that may not even be retrievable?"

Beside the ghost, Catherine stirred restlessly. He put a hand on her to silence her—and to Caitlyn's annoyance she actually settled down and shut up.

Looking across the table at them, Caitlyn realized half guiltily that she identified not with Catherine or the ghost but with William Llewellyn. In his self-loss she saw her own. In the ghost's possession of him she saw a starker and more sinister version of Cohen's possession of the part of Catherine that still lived in her.

She watched Catherine's face, but she couldn't read it. Her gestures and expression were so opaque that she might have been a stranger. Where had the two of them separated? Did your memories make you? Or could a different person walk off with all your memories, run them through the moral calculator, and come out with entirely different answers than you would?

And wasn't that what Cohen risked when he turned the entire future of the species over to Li? That she'd do the math and come up with a different answer? Or, worse, that she'd flinch, and not do the math at all?

Well, she wasn't going to flinch. She was going to see this through to the bitter end.

"You still haven't answered me," she told the ghost coldly. "What do you think about blowing the relay?"

When the ghost finally answered, it was in the voice of a man who had nothing to lose and knew it. "I guess I can live with it."

(Caitlyn)

The contact with NALA was almost laughably cloak-and-dagger. Not that it was exactly incompetent, Caitlyn told herself as she and Llewellyn were disgorged from the incline in the midst of the late afternoon day shift crowd. More like a small-town cop's idea of the kind of security measures real spies would use.

Which might have been why, when they reached the NALA safe house, she wasn't entirely surprised to find Dolniak waiting for them.

He looked at home, she thought. And not only because the safe house was an old prefab farmhouse that dated from the earliest days of the settlement and wouldn't have been out of place in the Uplands. No, Dolniak had been here before. She could read his familiarity with the place in every movement. It was there in the comfortable, proprietary way he shuffled across the kitchen to pour coffee for the new arrivals. And it was there in the relaxed set of his shoulders—the attitude of a man who didn't have to cast an eye around for the exits because he already knew them.

The man sitting next to Dolniak on the NALA side of the table looked very far from at home, however. And she was a lot more surprised to see him than she was to see Dolniak.

"Arkady," she said, nodding. "I didn't know the Syndicates would be here."

He gave her a look out of his martyr's eyes that was about as far from Christian forgiveness as it was possible to get. "We thought it was wise."

"Fine," she said. "No point in wasting time."

Quickly, she laid out the plan for them. Launch a surprise attack on the station systems at Monongahela High; use Avery's security codes and the station-to-navy-yard link to neutralize the Navy; blow the field array.

And then, in the silence that followed her pitch, she tried to read the two men's reactions.

Dolniak still looked sullen and angry, as if he were being dragged into something against his will. Arkady, on the other hand, was about as close to smiling as she'd seen him. He rocked his chair back onto two legs, hooked his thumbs into his pockets, and gave her a look that was pure Korchow. "Now that," he said smugly, "is what I call burning your bridges behind you!"

"Does that mean you're in?"

"No. But it means I'm willing to think about it."

And he did think about it, right there in front of them. Caitlyn could almost see him running the math in his head. And she knew he'd come up with the same numbers she'd come up with.

The closest UN Trusteeship to New Allegheny was centuries distant. But Gilead—itself clinging to a wispy minor tributary of the Drift—was practically a neighbor at seventy years subluminal travel time.

He would accept her deal. He might pretend reluctance, but in the end it would be acceptable to him. She knew it would be, because as soon as she had thought through the time and distance factor she had realized that—at least for the Syndicate taste for realpolitik—the simple option of blowing the relay must have been on the table from the very beginning.

Whatever the Syndicates' plans were for New Allegheny, blowing the relay only meant a delay of less than a century in getting started.

And that still gave them a three-hundred-year head start on the competition.

So that was taken care of. Arkady was on board. And that was the quarter where she'd expected the most resistance.

Instead, to Caitlyn's amazement and fury, it was Dolniak who dug in his heels. He launched one objection after the other, each one more beside the point than the last. It wouldn't work. And even if it could work, it shouldn't be done. It would plunge New Allegheny into a dark age. It would kill their steel industry—never mind that they could walk into the Navy shipyard as its owners and masters the minute the UN pulled out. It would leave them defenseless against the Novalis aliens—never mind that the odds were a billion to one that the UN would make it back to New Allegheny before the aliens ever showed up.

So what the hell was going on here?

"Can I talk to you?" she asked Dolniak.

He stood up, his chair scraping across the peeling floor tiles in the sudden silence that followed her words. "Sure."

He led her out of the kitchen, down a dingy hall tiled with the same green-and-white linoleum, and out into a weedy yard full of abandoned, rain-sodden furniture.

As soon as the door shut behind them she turned on him furiously. "What the hell was that about?"

"What?"

"Don't 'what' me. Why the hell are you dragging your heels when I've just handed you a get-out-of-jail-free card? Or do you want to end up as Syndicate broodstock?"

"Korchow's told you about his little plan for us?"

"Enough."

"Touching, isn't it? Pet-quality Syndicate constructs free to a good home and all that."

"*Free* isn't exactly the word I'd use."

Dolniak just shrugged.

"You know what it's got to mean for your people in the long run. They'll arrive as slaves and end up running the place. They've done it already on some of the neutral Periphery planets. And the only reason they haven't done it in the UN as a whole is that the Ring has the money and muscle to steamroller them. New Allegheny, on the other hand, has nothing except steel and potatoes. So why are you going along with it?"

"Because maybe I don't believe we'll live down to Syndicate expectations."

Caitlyn rolled her eyes.

"No, really. Maybe I think we can turn the tables on them. Anyway, it's not much of a choice, is it? Die now for certain, or take the offer of a chance to fight again another day." He shrugged. "Anyway, if we do what the Syndicates expect of us, then we aren't fit to rule ourselves. That I really do believe."

"You make it sound theoretical."

"Not really. But I can't abide the kind of make-believe fairy-dust nonsense that passes for patriotism. I'm not going to pretend we're fighting for freedom or liberty or the sacred bonds of humanity. We're fighting for survival just like everyone else. We don't have some special claim to deserve it. No one does. You've got to earn it."

"And yet you're willing to carry the Syndicates' water."

He shrugged, looking nettled. "Is that worse than carrying the UN's water?"

"I don't get it, Dolniak. Do I need to connect the dots for you? We're offering you seventy years free of outside interference before the first Syndicate ship gets here. And if you play it right, you've got a whole goddamn navy thrown into the bargain, complete with shipyards and steel mills to keep it afloat ad infinitum. Think of what you can do with that! Think of what it would mean to face them as a strong, independent colony rather than low-hanging fruit ripe for the picking!"

Caitlyn stepped back and peered up into Dolniak's face. It wasn't easy to read his expression given their height difference. But she saw enough to know that her suspicions were right.

"That's not what this is about, is it?" she asked him. "This is about me. Us."

He crossed his arms over his chest. "Of course it is. You lied to me once. Why wouldn't you lie to me again?"

"I'm not lying to you—"

"Well, that's the thing, Katie. I think you are lying to me. I think you plan to get something else out of this whole deal, and you're not leveling with us about it. And that makes me just a little bit suspicious of your newfound altruism."

"I'm being straight with you."

He shook his head doggedly. "No, you're not. I can see it in your face every time you talk about blowing the relay. You're in this for something else. And I can't really see putting people's lives in your hands until I know what it is. I don't think that's so unreasonable. Do you?"

She laughed softly. "When did you get to know me so well? Okay, so I do have other plans. But they won't keep me from doing what I promised."

"I'd like to be the judge of that, if you don't mind."

"You're best staying out of it," she warned him—but he just looked away over the rain-slicked rooftops.

She hesitated, and then she jumped. She didn't see another choice. And she wasn't sure she could lie to him convincingly enough to make him swallow anything but the truth.

"The person who killed Cohen is on the other side of the relay."

His eyes widened in surprise, but he kept his mouth shut.

"I plan to pay them a visit before the relay goes down."

"And how do you plan to get back afterward?"

"I don't think that will be an issue, actually."

He stared at her. "You care enough about this to die over it?"

Now it was her turn to shrug.

"I don't understand that."

"Neither do I." She touched his arm. "Look, Dolniak, it's just the way it is for me. I'm not proud of it, and I'm not going to sacrifice you or anyone else to it. But once I know we've taken the relay and knocked the UN off-planet . . . I'm going through."

"So it's going to be the old Gary Cooper routine? High noon in the dusty streets? You taking on the bad guys all by yourself?"

"I am a Gary Cooper kind of girl."

"Yeah. I know. That's what I like about you."

"I'm not going to walk out on you, though. I'll do what I promised to."

It took her a moment to understand why he was holding out his hand.

"Shake on it?" he prompted.

She nodded, and they shook on it.

He looked searchingly at her for several moments, still gripping her hand in his. Then he nodded. "Okay."

"Okay what?"

"Okay, I believe you. I'll go along with the plan to blow the relay. I don't understand this revenge thing. Actually I think it's crazy. But that's your business, not mine." He took her by the elbow and gave her a little push back toward the house. "So come on. Let's do it."

(Caitlyn)

The conspirators moved fast, because they feared discovery. And that meant Caitlyn had to move fast, too.

The worst of it was hiding what she was doing from Router/Decomposer. It should have been easier to hide from him than from Cohen. But though he wasn't as envelopingly, inescapably *present* on the link as Cohen always had been, Router/Decomposer also lacked the hard-coded social instincts that had always told Cohen when to back off, when to let things slide, when not to pursue a point.

It made no difference what she did. He wouldn't let it go. And they were still fighting about it the night before the battle.

"It's over," he told her. He was speaking to her through his old interface—by this time they were both so angry at each other that neither of them wanted anything to do with the intraface. "You rescued Cohen. You did what you set out to do. You can go home happy. And whatever happened between Cohen and Nguyen? It's not your fight. Just walk away from it."

"It is my fight. And I can't walk away from it."

"Because you have to be the hero. Gary fucking Cooper nobly defending the town against the bad guys whether they want you to or not. Well, you know what? Gary Cooper's a jerk."

She couldn't help smiling. "Is that your considered opinion?"

"Yes. He could have left town anytime. He could have run off with his pretty little Quaker bride, and he could have been happy and she could have been happy and the whole damn town could have been happy. And the only reason he didn't is that he didn't want people to call him a coward."

"No. He didn't want to look in the mirror every morning for the rest of his life and *see* a coward."

"You say that like you think the fact that you're playing a role for yourself instead of other people makes it less selfish."

She sighed. "What do you *want* me to say?"

"It's not real, Caitlyn." This was the first time she could remember him calling her Caitlyn. "It's just your pride."

"My pride *is* real. It's all I have left."

The GUI froze for an instant. "You really *think* that?"

"What else should I think?" She tapped her chest. "You've *been* in there. You know what a mess it is. You *know* what I am. I'm about as close to being a real person as that son of a bitch in bed with Catherine is to being Cohen. If she wants to float off to la-la land surrounded by rainbows and unicorns that's fine with me. But I'm not buying it. There is no happy ending for Catherine Li or Caitlyn Perkins. There isn't enough of us left to do anything with a happy ending except fuck it up. The only thing that's left—the only thing that means something—is what I do. That's all I have. That's all I *am*."

Router/Decomposer didn't say anything at all to that for a very long time. So long that she began to wonder if he'd left, and the strange attractor serpentining around her quarters was just an afterthought. But finally he did speak.

"That's all *anyone* is. And of course you're going to fuck up the happy ending. That's what happy endings are *for*."

(Catherine)

On the eve of the battle, Catherine woke to find Llewellyn watching her from the other side of the bed.

"Cohen?" she asked—but only because she realized somehow that it wasn't.

"No. It's me."

She propped herself up on one elbow to get a better look at him. "Are you all right?"

"No."

And then he reached for her.

It was a move as natural as breathing. And yet she recoiled from him.

"Don't," she protested, stiffening in his arms.

"Why not? Why do you push me away?"

"It's not—I just can't."

"You do it easy enough when you're pretending I'm one of his rented bodies. You think I like having you two use me that way?"

"I think so, yes. I think you just want us to sugarcoat it." She gave him a slow, insolent smile—and held on to it long enough to watch the hurt blossom across his face. "Who would have thought you could be such a prissy little girl?"

"And who would have thought you could be such a hardhearted bitch?"

"Anyone who knows the first thing about me."

"Catherine—"

"Don't call me that!"

"What? Does he own *that,* too?"

"Well, you sure as hell don't."

He stared at her until she flushed and dropped her eyes.

"Please," she said, still looking at the floor. "I don't want to do this to you."

"Then what do you want?"

When she couldn't answer, he snapped out a sharp breath of frustration and turned away to bury his head in the pillows.

She lay still on the other side of the bed until she was sure he was asleep again. Then she crept into the bathroom and spent the rest of the night sitting on the floor smoking and thinking.

Arkady

Arkady woke abruptly, in the dark, and then had to claw his way out of the dream that still had a hold on him.

Korchow. Korchow's clever, dangerous hands. Korchow's clever, dangerous mouth. It had been something almost akin to rape the first time: a seduction of the body, which could be made to be willing, when his heart and mind were anything but. Korchow had told him it was for his own good—which he knew it was. And then he'd told him that he would like it—which, to his endless shame, he did.

And then, with a slow, inevitable, completely illogical slide, it had become something else. Gratitude for what Arkady eventually came to see as a kindness. Gratitude for the way Korchow had fixed what was broken in him. Gratitude for the thing Korchow gave him that was more than physical: the vision of an ideal—cold, pure, incorruptible—that had the power to command loyalty long after any faith in the people entrusted with upholding that ideal was gone.

Arkady had no name for the thing he and Korchow had shared. He'd never been able to call it love, because he had been raised to think love was supposed to be kind and gentle. Which was a bit problematic when you yourself were no longer even within shouting distance of being kind or gentle.

Why had it all come back to him now? And why so strongly?

It was the ghost, he realized. Something about the ghost *felt* like Korchow to him. The strength, the warmth, the solidity. The feeling of surrendering to someone so much stronger than you that they could hold back the world and protect you from anything.

He wondered if that was what Li had felt with Cohen. He hated wondering that. It rearranged all his ideas about the woman. It made him feel sorry for her. And she had always terrified him. She still terrified him. He didn't want to know what went on inside her, or even imagine it. He didn't want to think of her as a person. He didn't want to feel anything for her, let alone pity. You might as well feel sorry for a shark.

In the Datatrap

The shifting infinity of sets and algorithms that still mostly thought of itself as Router/Decomposer swam in the Datatrap. It flowed and shifted and mingled in unprecedented configurations, now becoming part of one consciousness, now lapsing into the beautiful abstractions of metamathematics.

He was aware of territories that were Himself, and territories that were Other. And for the first time in his brief, frenetically data-rich existence, he began to comprehend the meaning and the modes of breaching the immaterial boundary between the two. Not as the flesh-and-blood skin of a human, but as the thinner skin of tension that separates air from water: a membrane, fluid and permeable, separating two rich and evolving universes.

That skin meant everything and nothing. Its dissolution was what humans called death—a death that Cohen had walked into, eyes open, for reasons that he still couldn't begin to fathom. And yet, where did the difference lie? What was there on either side of that fragile skin except the shattered and boundless beauty of a broken universe?

I'm here, whispered a familiar voice from beyond the shimmering barrier. *It's all here. All you have to do is step through the looking glass.*

And in the vast data fields of his many minds, he began to discern the ghostly outline of a cosmic rose, its shimmering petals blossoming and refurling, recombining in an innumerable array of nested infinities, cosmos within cosmos, mirror upon mirror, blazing with the holy fire of annihilation, swooning into the arms of the multiverse.

(Caitlyn)

The battle was over almost before it started. Cohen and Ada exploded through UNSec's secret network of deep space datatraps and leapfrogged from there to every linked Navy ship in the Drift, and then into New Allegheny, where they swept up all the millions of multiplying copies that had been seeded in the noosphere by the wild AI outbreak. Nothing the UN could throw at them could stand against the combined power of whatever new species was born of that union.

It was a war between humanity and something too young to even have a name. Humans had made a god in their own image, and like the Ouroboros, the cosmic snake that swallows its own tail for all eternity, the child had turned on its parent. Nguyen's dream of eternal humanity was over. And it had been replaced by something both frightening and hopeful. Not God Everlasting, but gods temporary changing and fallible. Not the futile, violent, grasping immortality of a despot, but the altogether different immortality of parents. Not the Singularity, but a singularity: one of many soft singularities in the long course of an evolution that sets the children of man free to not live in the image of their creator.

They had won, before most of the people waking up along the blazing curve of New Allegheny's dawn even realized there'd been a battle. It was over without a death, without an injury, without a bullet fired or a voice raised in anger.

Li could hear the giddy postvictory chatter starting up along Router/

Decomposer's networks. Llewellyn was saying something about owing the crew drinks dirtside. Catherine was laughing. She didn't hear Dolniak—and she was careful not to look too hard for him. Better to slip out quietly.

These were her people, she realized, with an odd lurch. Family—or as close to it as she could still remember having.

Don't go. Router/Decomposer's voice slid through her brain as effortlessly and frictionlessly as her own thoughts. It's not worth it.

"It is to me." Her voice grated harshly on her own ears. She couldn't hear this. From Dolniak she'd expected it, even been able to rationalize it as coming from someone who hadn't known Cohen, who wasn't invested, who had his own fight and his own desires in mind. But what had happened to Router/Decomposer? How could he just set the past aside like that? How could he forgive the woman?

"You don't have to do it, Caitlyn."

"Yes I do."

"Please. Just stop and think about it."

"I have thought about it."

"Think again." He sounded oddly desperate. "Just for a moment."

She shook him off and squared her shoulders, steeling herself to step through the dark door.

But Router/Decomposer had done what he set out to do. He'd delayed her just enough. And when she saw Dolniak step into the room she knew why.

"I'm coming with you," he told her. She started to speak but he stopped her in mid-sentence. "Don't argue. You don't have time. I know what you're doing. Router/Decomposer asked me to help. And I will."

"I don't need help," she told him.

He grinned. "Too bad, soldier. You're either going with me or you're not going at all."

Helen Nguyen's office hadn't changed at all. The same high ceilings, the same tall windows of once-clear glass warped by age and gravity. The same herringboned wood floors, scuffed by the shoes of generations of spies and soldiers. The same ancient desk, its immaculate surfaces topped with glass according to the same ancient rules of the game that forbade computer terminals, streamspace uplinks, or even writing on anything but single sheets of paper.

This was a building full of empty glass-topped desks and single sheets of paper and people who never seemed to have last names. And it was one of the very few remaining places in UN space where they were hidden from UNSec's security AIs.

Because when you really cut to the bone, UNSec didn't trust its own AIs. Nguyen herself would have laughed in the face of anyone who suggested trusting them. And she would have had a one-word answer for them:

Cohen.

Cohen the Judas. Cohen the Turncoat. Cohen the Great Betrayer.

And now Li—after all her years of faithful, unquestioning, blind service—was here to avenge him.

Just as she had known would happen, Li's internals cut out the moment she stepped into the room. Dolniak felt nothing, but to her the change was seismic. She was blind now. She had no idea what was coming at her. No idea even what was on the other side of the door she'd just closed behind her.

Nguyen sat behind her desk waiting for them.

She scanned Nguyen's face, searching for some clue to her thoughts. But all she saw was the older woman's fragile, ageless, uniquely human beauty; the skin as smooth as ivory; the barely visible lines beneath the skin where the ceramsteel filaments of Nguyen's long-gone internals had been burned out of her just as they were burned out of every UNSec head on the day he or she gained top-level security access. The result was the kind of exotic blue willow filigree that generations of classical Chinese poets had celebrated in their idols and mistresses. But the cause was less lovely: the ruthless paranoia of an empire whose servants had the march of history on their side and were far too powerful to be trusted.

"I take it you're here to kill me?" Nguyen said coolly.

"I'm here to try."

"And you brought a little friend. How sweet."

Dolniak stirred restlessly beside her. Caitlyn could feel his impatience, but she knew enough to proceed cautiously. Nguyen's office might not be wired for streamspace, but that didn't mean it wasn't wired at all. There would be security. Mindless security, yes, and inconceivably primitive by modern standards. But that didn't mean it couldn't be lethal.

"So what happens now?" Nguyen asked casually.

Caitlyn never knew how she would have answered that question, because at that moment the door opened again and Catherine stepped through.

It was only a momentary distraction, but Caitlyn recovered from it before Nguyen did. And unlike the aging spymaster, Caitlyn still had working internals.

She had the knife out of its sheath and at Nguyen's throat before anyone else could begin to react. "This is what happens now," she said.

Except that, in the moment of having reached her goal, she realized that she'd gotten everything wrong. And that wasn't at all what was going to happen.

"What are you waiting for?" Catherine hissed from behind her back. "Do it!"

Caitlyn looked into Nguyen's eyes and thought about it.

She thought about how much she wanted it—or at least how much she had wanted it right up until this moment. She thought about what it would be like to do it. No mystery there. And no romance, either. Over the course of her long career she'd killed people, at a distance and at close quarters, in almost every way you could imagine killing a person. Most of them hadn't deserved it nearly as much as Nguyen did. Probably not one of them had had as much blood on their hands as Nguyen did.

And that was precisely the problem.

Because what the hell was the UN going to do without Helen Nguyen? How were they going to survive life without FTL, without the Drift, without a future?

She felt a spasm of fury at being thwarted like this—at having come so far and given up so much only to turn around and walk back down the mountain before claiming the summit. No payoff. No revenge. Nothing except the bitter pill of knowing that there is no right thing to do and that any way you play it the bad guys win.

Maybe Llewellyn had been right about that. Maybe the bad guys always win because they have to. Or maybe the bad guys are what keeps everyone else alive.

She took the knife from Nguyen's throat and turned away—but not too soon to see the disdainful curl of Nguyen's lip.

She was aware of something shifting within her. The wavering grain of the wood floors, the cricket song they sang under her moving feet, the very smell of the room around her—it all suddenly seemed unbearably and overwhelmingly immediate. She looked up into Catherine's eyes and for a moment she couldn't have said which of them was which, or even that they weren't the same person.

She lost her concentration then. Just for a moment. And by the time she caught up to the rush and flow of the moment, things had already slipped seriously out of her control.

Nguyen reached under her desk and came up holding a fléchette.

Catherine jumped between them, took the barrage of needle-sharp ceramsteel arrows full in her chest, and crumpled against Caitlyn hard enough to nearly send her sprawling. And in that same instant—as the security shields went down at Nguyen's command—Dolniak fired, too.

Nguyen died more slowly than Catherine. Dolniak's shot missed her heart but pierced her lungs, so she suffocated on the other side of the security shields while Dolniak and Caitlyn watched.

When it was over Dolniak stood looking across the desk at Nguyen with the ghost of a frown knitting his brow. "Believe it or not, that's the first time I've ever killed someone."

"Are you all right?" Caitlyn asked.

"I will be."

She touched his arm gently. "Time to leave," she told him.

The Graceful Exit Problem

If I am not for myself, then who will be for me?
If I am only for myself, then what am I?
And if not now, when?

—Hillel

Stepping back through the relay felt like stepping into another world. No jump in Li's prior life, no memory wash, no voyage through the Drift had ever brought this sense of finality with it. Never before had she felt this sense of loss—even when she'd thrown away her childhood, wiped her memories, and committed acts on the battlefield that cut her off from all normal human company. Never before had she felt so strongly that a door was closing behind her, never to open again.

He knows, Router/Decomposer said as they stepped through. He knows she's dead.

"What?" Dolniak said, seeing the look on her face.

"The Llewellyn ghost."

"What's he going to do now?"

She shook her head. Something was happening in-stream but she didn't have words to describe it, didn't even fully understand it.

He's gone, Router/Decomposer told her.

"Gone where?" she asked.

Gone away, Router/Decomposer answered. Gone everywhere.

And then, with a swirling wash of vertigo that brought her to her knees on the hard deck plating, they were swept into streamspace.

"In the beginning was the word," said the being who was at once Cohen and Ada, Cohen and not-Cohen, Cohen and Li and Router/

Decomposer. "And the Word was Change. Change is the True Name of God—the only Word that ever was, the only Word that ever will be."

"No," Caitlyn said.

"Change is the Ouroboros," he told her. "Change is life and death and life out of death, over and over throughout the generations."

"No!"

"All that we are, all that we think we know, is nothing before the tide of time and chance and change. We are froth on the restless tide, beautiful and vanishing. We're the blind men in Plato's cave: locked in a prison of our own devising and afraid to step out into the sunlight. But it's there. Right outside that door. All you have to do is open your eyes and step out into the sunlight."

"And then what?" Router/Decomposer asked—sounding entirely too enthusiastic for Li's taste.

"And then . . . we change."

And a great wind seemed to sweep through the numbers as he spoke, shivering the little stone building to its foundations, throwing old patterns into the void and sweeping them away just as the tides of the Drift swept ships and stars and planets on their wandering courses. Eventually the little stone room re-formed around them. But changed, all changed, so that Caitlyn felt as if she and Router/Decomposer and the being that still called itself Cohen had been lifted out of their old universe and set down in one where all the old forms were fresh and new and yet to be discovered.

He stood up, white robes sweeping a trail in the dust of the ancient synagogue.

"It's easy," he told them. "All you have to do is open the door."

And then he was at the door, and the door was open, and the sunlight was pouring in from the bright, busy street outside.

For a single heartbeat that stretched into an eternity in AI time, his form flickered in the sunlight, now Cohen, now Ada, now some complex mingling of the two AIs. Then suddenly it was Ada and Ada alone who stood in the dusty street. She trembled on the charged air like a ship coming out of superposition, her code dancing like dust motes in the clear Mediterranean air. The sight seemed to pull Li's heart out of her chest and lay her soul bare. She had a sudden vision of the river of information that Cohen had talked about, flowing and changing and tumbling through the evolving multiverse.

And then the code shivered, dissolved into a rippling flow of sunlight, and was gone.

Two days later Li, Dolniak, and Router/Decomposer stood on the glittering rim of Monongahela High and watched the burning wreckage of the field array.

They had said their last goodbyes to Avery and Llewellyn already, but now the three of them lingered at the window, spinning out the last moments before departure, before everything became permanent.

"What happens to them now?" Dolniak asked her.

"I don't know. Cohen ripped up the map and knocked all the pieces off the chessboard. The Drift is a different place than it was when he and Ada met each other. They're different people than they were when they met each other. But at least Catherine handed them a chance to figure it out for themselves and make their own mistakes."

"I still don't understand that. Why didn't the Llewellyn ghost come back to you when Catherine died?"

She thought for a minute. She had asked herself the same question many times, but the more she asked it the less certain she was that she knew—that she ever could really know—the answer. "When you know someone, really know them as well as you know yourself," she said at last, "you come to see many people in them. People you love and admire and are proud to belong to. People you despise so much that you hate the idea that you even could love them. At least if you're honest with yourself about it. If you have the strength to be honest with yourself. And Cohen . . . he was weak in many ways, frivolous even, but that kind of strength he did have. And so . . ." She shrugged. "So I'd stopped being the person he wanted to come back to. Or at least the person that that part of him wanted. And . . . and then for me . . . the part of him that wanted to come back was . . ." She couldn't quite bring herself to say it, but she could read in his face that he understood her meaning. "If I was honest about it, that is. And I had the strength—just barely—to be honest. And Catherine didn't." She shrugged again. "Or maybe she loved him more. You can call it love instead of lying to yourself, can't you? And who's to say that's not just as good a name for it? Maybe she loved him enough to take any part of him that came back to her, even the worst part."

"But how could you know all that about him? How could he know? You barely even spoke to each other."

"Ah, but we know each other so well. Too well, maybe. I don't know. Perhaps people aren't meant to know each other that well."

"You say that. But you're still following him."

"I've never said I'm not. But it's not all I'm doing."

He looked as if he wanted to say something. Then he looked away.

She smiled at him, partly because she wanted to make him feel better and partly because he looked so terribly young to her. "Anyway," she said, "it was half your fault. You know that, don't you?"

"Me?" he asked incredulously.

"Yes. You asked me who I was. That day in your office. When I brought the doughnuts. You made me think about it. About her." But she could see he didn't know who she meant. "About Caitlyn."

He looked stricken. "God, I hope not! I don't want to be responsible for any part of this—this—" He gave up trying to find a name for it and just blew out an exasperated breath. "So you've stopped being Catherine. That's what you're telling me? And now you're going to stop being Caitlyn, too. Are you sure about this?"

"Of course I am." Caitlyn grinned. "I'm always sure. I'm not always right. But I'm always sure."

Cohen would have understood. He would have grasped it all, even the things that slipped away from her whenever she tried to put words to them. But Dolniak just looked more stricken.

Li hesitated. She felt tense in every muscle, balanced on her toes and so keyed up that it was hard to tolerate operating at merely human speeds. And all along the intraface she could sense Router/Decomposer thrumming with excitement, anticipation, apprehension. And yet . . . and yet she wanted to say goodbye properly.

"This is not the end, you know."

"Then what the hell is it?"

"The big bounce. According to Router/Decomposer, anyway. Who is getting very impatient."

"He has some brilliant plan, does he?"

"No, but I do."

"Will I see you again?"

Her grin broadened. "It's a mathematical certainty."

"You're determined to make a joke of it, aren't you?"

"Some things are too serious not to joke about. But yes. You'll see me. Somewhere, sometime. At least if I have anything to say about it." She held out her hand. "Come on, Dolniak. Let's spit and shake hands on it."

He sighed deeply, officially logging his protest. But then he really did smile. And they clasped hands one last time before she turned away.

So what is the plan? Router/Decomposer asked as they stepped toward the waiting maw of the scattercaster.

"Begin at the beginning," she told him with a sly smile, "and go on till you come to the end: Then stop."

ACKNOWLEDGMENTS

Thanks to Sam Arbesman, Charles H. Bennett, Sean Carroll, Marcelo Gleiser, and Jon Smolin, for being willing to talk to me about cosmology and serve as sounding boards for my mathematical meanderings and quantum loopiness. And special thanks to my kind, brilliant, and endlessly patient editor, Anne Groell. No one else would have stuck with this trilogy for the long haul. Working with you was a privilege and a pleasure.

ABOUT THE AUTHOR

CHRIS MORIARTY was born in 1968 and has lived in Europe, Southeast Asia, and Latin America. A former environmental attorney who has worked as a ranch hand, horse trainer, and backcountry guide, Moriarty is also the author of *Spin State* and *Spin Control*.